World One of THE GATEV[illegible] SERIES

THE TEMPLE OF THE SKY

CLOSE THE WORLD. ENTER THE NEXT

GLEN JOHNSON

PublishAmerica
Baltimore

First printing

At the specific preference of the author, PublishAmerica allowed this work to remain exactly as the author intended, verbatim, without editorial input.

ISBN: 1-4137-7586-1
PUBLISHED BY PUBLISHAMERICA, LLLP
www.publishamerica.com
Baltimore

Printed in the United States of America

This book is lovingly dedicated to the memory of my Grandmother

Edith Mary Leek
1912 to 1985

Forever in my heart and thoughts

To earthling man his way does not belong.
It does not belong to man who is
walking even to direct his step.

- JEREMIAH 10:23

Acknowledgements

Being a writer is seldom a solitary quest; so with that in mind I would like to thank some people, firstly my family: **Gary T. Johnson** (for giving me my first laptop that started my writing career), and **Pauline & Clive Milner**, for their unwavering support. And to a long list of friends: **Richard Plaine** who read through the raw manuscript and helped with the editing. To **Veronica Cecilia Turvein Molina** the best Argentine chief in Mexico City, whose friendship helped me through a difficult time. And a special thank you to **Susanna Molina**, for being there when I needed someone to talk too. And to **Gabriel Chanfreau** who brought a small piece of sanity to my life each day. And this wouldn't be complete without saying thanks to **Jet Stokes**, **Jamie Kerr**, **Peter Butler**, **Anthony Pike** and **Jimmy Carter**. And as always, any mistakes are of my own making.

1
The Beginning of the End

The darkness was doing nothing to improve Takahashi Morio's sullen mood; he could barely see his dirty callused hand held up in front of his face, because the low-lying cloud was blocking out the little amount of light that the waxy moon was giving off.

His dark Asian eyes roamed back and forth, calculating the best route to head off in; it was a little more difficult to see the towering columns of smoke when darkness closed in.

But the lack of illumination didn't concern Takahashi, if anything he preferred the darkness, the comfort and false sense of protection and security that it gave. It was reassuring to him. He didn't want anyone to see what he was doing anyway. Not that there would be anyone this far out. But you could never be too careful, not in this place. If he had learned one thing with his time spent here, it was never to take anything for granted, never to relax, and never let down your vigilance. Not that this place ever gave you the chance to. But for now it was quiet, far too quiet.

He moved fast, swiftly, running at full pelt through the tangled thick undergrowth. Braches whipped and slashed at him; long thin cuts crisscrossed his dirty face and bare tanned arms. Brambles pulled and ripped at his clothing. His feet stumbled on roots and stones that were hidden deep on the moldy leaf covered ground.

He gave a half crazed laugh, because his first name Morio meant *Forest Boy* in Japanese. "How fitting," he jeered as another sharp branch grazed his forehead.

Takahashi ran like a man possessed. As he ran he mumbled over and over a Japanese song he had learnt as a small child; it was sung by the *Gods of Good Fortune* as they sailed in their fine boat – *The Ship of Riches*: "*It is a long night. The gods of luck sleep. They all open their eyes. They ride in a boat on the waves. The sound is pleasing."*

"Please," he whispered. "*Kaze-No-Kami*, Great God of the Wind, let your wind be at my back." He had seen many unexplainable things in his time here, and he reasoned if these things can happen, then the ancient Gods could really exist; because in this world a living Man God ruled, he had witnessed his awesome, dark powers firsthand.

Takahashi knew what he had to do; knew that it had to be done. He had gone over it in his mind, over and over like a twisted mantra that he had heard the orange robed monks mumble as they slowly use to walk the dusty street with their begging almsbowls. This was the only way he knew how to stop it, stop it from happening again to someone else; someone who wouldn't be as strong as he was, someone who wouldn't live as long as him. Not that you could call this living, this wasn't a life; life had meaning. In his distorted memory he knew he once had a purpose, but that had been long washed away by the fear of this place. It was that distant corroded memory that he know held onto.

Takahashi fingers were numb, but it wasn't from the cold, because it wasn't cold. The low-lying cloud was holding all the heat in, making it stuffy, clammy. It was because of the task that lay ahead that made him numb. The size of the task he was undertaking. He knew the risks, knew he wouldn't be around to see the sun rise in the morning. *Amaterasu*; the Sun Goddess, would not look upon his face again. Not that you could see the sun here, there was always a thick blanket of clouds over the sky. It was never completely light, never completely dark. It was like a kind of dull colorless light, as if the light had to pass through a dirty cloth. But tonight was different as if it knew what he was about to do, and was teasing him to try.

"*Emma-O*, God of Death, Judge of the Dead and Lord of the Afterlife, please judge me well." He had never used so many deities' names in such a short space of time; he was afraid of forgetting and offending any of his peoples Gods – just incase.

Takahashi could see it in front of him now, in the clearing.

Once again he looked heavenwards and said a silent request to *Tsuki-Yumi*, the God of the Moon, so he could light the way.

It was an awe inspiring sight, one born of nightmares. A towering mound of earth had been raised, with a huge wrought iron bowl wedged on top; this had an orangey-gray substance pouring from its circumference that mingled with the ever shifting sky. The gateway itself was a smooth pewter surface that was surrounded with carved images; two fear inspiring guardians, also fashioned from blacken metal, which encompassed the gateway, the two dragons' heads almost touching with a strange golden emblem wedge between them: their tall skeletal bodies creating the gateways arch.

"*Uwibami*," he uttered in reverent awe. *Uwibami* was the name of the legendary dragon that would snatch men from their horse and devour them.

All about, in the clearing that led to the woods, lay broken bones and scattered skulls; offerings once made to the gateway, a testament to the cruelty and barbarity that the gateway inspires. Long bending poles are dotted about here and there holding colorful banners and strange flags, twisting and flapping in the seemingly stagnant air. Also towering standing stones make a circle around the gateway, mere feet away from the woods, these having strange cipher and symbols etched on them. They stand like huge protective sentinels; akin to the style and shape of Stonehenge; not that Takahashi had even been to Stonehenge, but he had seen pictures.

The area gave off a strange unnatural light. A light that seemed to seep out of the very ground itself, a light that mocked *Tsuki-Yumi*. The Gateway glowed with confidence, and if it didn't sound too strange he would swear it was watching him, waiting for him. He half expected the dragons' metal heads to turn to look in his direction.

He knew even with the task ahead he could do it if he had hope. But then this place always had hope; it put it there before you, just before it snatched it away; along with you life.

Takahashi took a quick look behind him but saw nothing, but then again you never did, not before it was to late. Slowly he made his way towards it. He tried not to make any noise. He'd learned how to tread silently when he first arrived in this place. If you made a noise - any noise - it would be your last. He had been lucky the first time he had only attracted a small predator. It took him many days to heal and in all that time he had been vulnerable, an easy target. He had learned his lesson then, and he didn't want to repeat that same painful mistake now.

Crawling at a snails pace, he made his way to the edge of the clearing and stopped still - dead still. He used one of the tall standing stone to conceal his body.

Fearing that even the sound of his breath would give him away, he held it. The sound of his heart beating was deafening in his ears, he would swear they could hear it. He had to calm down, take control. He knew if he panicked he would die. Logic saved him; he knew that if they had seen him they would have been making their way towards him by now.

Takahashi also knew the Evil One had called them to protect it. He had brought them from somewhere else to stand guard. They stood almost as tall as him. But they were built for speed. They had powerful legs, with which they could run faster than him. You could only hope they would tire before you. They could run fast but only for a short burst. Their arms were longer than seemed practical, but they could drop down and run on all fours. The main thing that drew your attention was the tail; long and sleek - powerful. They could break a man's back in one vicious sweep. If that didn't work then the barbed claw on the end would. They never kill outright; they feed on your fear, your pain and your tears. They would let you heal yourself and then they would come back to where you lay and start over again. They don't kill for food -not many things in this place do - but they do it for pleasure and simply because they can.

The strange creatures brought to mind the name *Gaki*, the Japanese Demon God of Death.

The mist rolled over their sleek reptilian bodies, taught skin, clawed hands. They looked around the clearing with their small but sharp eyes; with a strange orange glow that seemed to make your legs want to give out from under your own weight. It was rare to see so many in one place. They had their own family groups, which hunted together, but never in this number, because even these creatures are in the food chain here. Another strange thing was they were all male. Normally any two would fight among themselves. But here coming in from the forest directly ahead was maybe eight or nine, possibly more still hidden behind the trees thick foliage directly opposite.

They carried weapons in their hands. Some had the long spears that they could throw with uncanny precision. Never a death throw, always hitting their victims in the calf on the back of the legs making them fall, so they could slowly finish them off. Others carried weapons of their choice. They used the skin of other animals to cover themselves. In the scheme of things in this place they were above average intelligence. But he doesn't want them to cleaver, he needs to control them, use them like he uses everything else.

That's why he hates our kind, can't stand us being here. We think for ourselves and that is one thing he will not allow, cannot allow. Because in the moment things start thinking for themselves he loses all control over them. If only he would let us leave, stop others from coming through. But no they still come, will always come not knowing what awaits them. Not being able to stop themselves: coming in search of something. For everyone it's something different. Takahashi can't remember his reasons many don't, after they have been here for sometime. That's if they live that long.

That's why he's trying to stop this evil. Stop it before more arrive. It's been many weeks now since the last came through, which is longer than normal. That's why he is here now to see, to try and change the course of things. Not that many haven't tried before him, many have. None have returned; their bones crunch under his tattered boots. If he doesn't succeed then at least it will be over for him. It's those he leaves behind that he feels sorry for.

Movement to Takahashi's left catches his attention. Maybe it was the wind? Maybe it was just a small foraging animal? Then another movement. Was it simply a banner flapping, catching his eyes attention? He then realizes that they weren't hiding in the trees behind the others, but rather they were circling around to where he was, using the stones and the gateway to block themselves from view. It's too late for him now. In one swift movement he's knocked hard to the ground. There's a flash of tearing skin, a spray of warm crimson blood, a cracking of bones and ripping of sinew. For Takahashi Morio it will soon be all over, after they've had their fun. With his last breath he begged *Emma-O*, Judge of the Dead and Lord of the Afterlife to judge him well. It was now time to find out if the Gods really did exist.

The others like him stay well in the background. He was the one who wanted to try. It had been his idea. Wasn't it? They had been asked to secretly follow him, to return his body.

Now quietly they start to move back in to the cover of the darkness. They try to get as far away from this place as possible. Not just because of the fear it leaks, but because they could hear Takahashi's blood curdling screams. Even though it was getting weak it would go on for sometime, until he could scream no more - run out of Gods names to holler. Then they would let him heal and start over again. If he was lucky they would bore of their game and kill him quickly. That's if he is lucky.

The Dark Lord of his world had known he was coming, he always knows when they are about to try; always offering them hope. This one had failed, they always do. He enjoys seeing them try, letting them get so far, and then taking that hope away. Fear; fear is what makes him so powerful.

But evil knows there's one thing it has no control over, and that is love. Yes they banded together but that was out of need. The more of you there are the less chance it would be you who was next; they are like a large shoal of fish. There is no love between them here. They are afraid to love because the moment you start loving someone, something, is the moment that it gets taken away from you. Love was just another word. What's in a word? They have many words here. Like friend, friend is used in the same context as the word death - it came as a friend because it gave you release.

But he knew that the one thing he could not fight against, the one thing that he had no control over was about to enter through the Gateway – enter his world.

2
The Brothers

"Come on, no look, put your foot on my hands that's what there for," Garry Wolff said as he was crouched over, with his hands knotted together so they would be strong enough to take his younger brothers weight. "No your left foot, look I'll go over and pull you up."

"I said I can do it; it's just you're not holding still," came his brother Glyn's, slightly miffed remark.

"Look we haven't got all night you know," Garry said while straightening up, unknotting his hands. He removed his rolly from his mouth and blew a plume of blue smoke in to the cold night air.

"I could have got it that time." This time he carried a little more irritation in his voice. "Look we're making enough noise to wake the dead," Glyn announced if anything to himself, because his brother was walking away in the other direction around the base of the wall, he could hear his trainers squelching on the boggy ground. Glyn waved the foul smelling Golden Virginia smoke away from his face.

"Now where are you going?"

But Garry couldn't hear him; he was well out of earshot, because Glyn was only just able to hear himself.

"*Nob-jockey*."

Garry had always done this; he never listened to his younger brother's advice. There wasn't much of an age gap between them, just over ten months: they joked that when Glyn went in it was still warm. And if it weren't for the fact that they looked slightly alike you would never believe they were brothers. *Like chalk and cheese*, some would say. It was more like, *cheese and as thick as a brick*, if you asked Glyn.

They were both slightly stocky for their age, with their height struggling to reach just over five foot five; this gave them the appearance of being slightly tubby. Both having mousy brown hair, and round porkpie faces. But they were far from unfit, just big boned, as Glyn would say. Or, *built like a Shit-Brick-House*, as Garry put it. They looked like they should be on a rugby team; and Garry's broken nose added to the effect - a gift from his younger brother.

Garry didn't help matters by wearing a cream tee-shirt, a beige hoody and thick denim jacket. It made him look even rounder. Glyn on the other hand never seemed to feel the cold. He had a simple black tee-shirt with a thin black ribbed cardigan over the top.

Walking around the base of the wall Glyn wasn't paying attention and walked straight into his brother's back. He was to busy trying not to get any more mud on his blue slip-on Adidas trainers and plain jeans.

"Shit, you could have given me some warning here," which came out rather muffled, because he was rubbing his nose with his hand. He gave his brother one of his stares that was kind of wasted, because his brother wasn't even facing him, and his glasses were probably steamed up by now anyway, from all the mist that seemed to be hanging in the air. And if it didn't sound too strange, he would swear the mist was hanging onto their clothes, following them around.

Garry was listening intently to any sound that might be coming from the direction of the house, just over the wall not far from where they now stood. He snuffed out his rolly on the brick wall, leaving a black score. And before that one even fell to the ground he was reaching for his dented tin to roll another.

The house was not huge, but still large by normal standards. The same family had been living in it for as long as anyone could remember. Well that was up until several weeks ago, when they all seemed to have just disappeared. Some say they were in over their heads, buying up all the land around them. This wasn't overly expensive, or good for much of anything. It was just barren hilly land, with rocks sticking out everywhere. Even the farmers around weren't interested in letting their sheep feed on the grass. Not that there was much grass around here. Nothing seemed to want to grow close to the structure. What did grow near it seemed to have a tired sort of look about it; contaminated even.

They had put up fences everywhere. The place seemed like a large maze. Anyone would've had trouble trying to get their car up to the house, what with all the sticking out rocks, the boggy ground and all the fences. But then not many people use to try. The owners had no form of transportation, so they had no need of easy access. If anything it looked like they were trying to keep something in, just as much as trying to keep everyone else out.

There were a few people whom some would say, had the honor of getting over their doorstep: the Doctor, who was sometimes called out and the school overseer, who had to go twice a year to check on the four children, who were taught at home by their mother. But even these only saw the rear of the house. Going in through the back door and into a small hallway and then into one small room. The room they were always taken to. Never taken around the house, never shown any of the things in it. They were there for a reason, never offered anything to drink. Sometimes not even offered a seat in which to sit, but were left standing. They did what they had to and would then be promptly asked to leave; a firm arm steering them towards the exit.

People who came up this way would sometimes hear the children in one of the fields around the house playing. But they never heard any laughter. There was never any joy in their voices and the strange songs they sang, seemingly in a different language. You can understand why there were people passing around rumors, people that were whispering, gossiping.

There were always children and adults going missing around this area. But then people always disappear. Going off somewhere different, trying to leave problems behind, and trying to make new lives for themselves, going off into the big enticing cities to make their fortunes. Some return, others are never heard from again. They just disappeared, vanished without a so-called trace.

The Stevenson's, as they were called seemed different; they wanted to lock themselves away in their own prison as it were, never leaving. They grew their own food, had their own water supply from the warren of caves and caverns that wormed there way all around this area. They had no reason to disappear or rather they had no need to, they were as some said, *already lost to themselves*.

Glyn poked Garry in the base of his spine, trying to get some sort of response out of him, even if it was a smack across the head. Anything was better than just standing here in the cold eerie silence.

The moon was almost full and sometimes it could be seen through the low-lying clouds. It was going to start to rain soon he could feel it, the light breeze that was stirring just before a downpour was making a shiver run down his spine. The fact that he couldn't hear any other noises around him, not even the call of an owl or a small rodent, nothing. Not even bats doing their somersaults and other aerial acrobatic movements in the air around them. All was still.

"Ah you idiot! What you go and do that for?"

"Sorry, didn't see you there," came Glyn's reply.

"What do you mean you didn't see me, you just walked straight into the back of me? Retard," he said rubbing the base of his spine with the back of his hand, sprinkling cigarette embers everywhere.

"Look I said I'm sorry," Glyn answered staring up at the darkened sky.

"No you didn't."

"Well, I just did, so get over it," he said taking a step backwards just incase his brother had the idea of hitting him back.

"A hundred thousand swimming sperm and you were the strongest?" Glyn whispered to his brother's back. "I swear I'm adopted," sarcasm was Glyn's forte. And it bugged him that he was walking behind his brother so he had to breathe in all his secondhand smoke; a smell he couldn't stomach.

"So what are we up to, out here in the middle of the night?" he asked, scratching his neck just so he had something to do with his cold hands, before hitching them back over the straps of his threadbare rucksack.

"Just curious that's all. People are saying all sort's of things about this place."

"What do you mean, people are talking?" Now Glyn was nervous.

"Like there's a lot of stuff in there left behind. If you know what I mean?" Garry said, winking at his brother. Which looked freaky, because he had to look over his shoulder to do so, and the moon was behind him, which highlighted the pupils of his eyes and made them seem like there was a flicker of light coming from inside his skull? His brother would say that that was *all* that was in there.

Smoke lazily curled up Garry's face, pouring out his nostrils like a bull's in cold weather.

The night was getting along and Glyn had to be up for work in just over nine hours. So he was hoping that his brother would get fed up and would want to start getting back soon. Not that he was looking forward to getting back to the Esso Service Station, with all the condescending looks from people who thought they were better than him, because he was serving them petrol.

"Over there. Is that a break in the wall?" He was pointing over to his left. His voice made Glyn jump, he had been daydreaming. It was late and he was overtired and when he got tired he started to drift off into his own little world. All he wanted to do was get back to their old battered and scratched faded green Ford Escort and head back home. He wasn't looking forward to the walk back, because of all the stones and stupid fences that they had to climb over. The car had to be left over by the road, which was a good ten minutes walk or rather climb away.

"I hope you're not expecting me to carry anything back with me, not over this sort of terrain. Not that there would be much left in there. I heard there was all kinds of people up here taking all their furniture and such."

"That's true, but it's a big house and there's the basement and all those caves under it. They're bound to have missed something, don't you think?" His last remark was emphasized by the shrug of his shoulders as if to say, *well you never know.*

"Hey don't you go thinking I'm about to start crawling around in any shitty caves. These are new jeans you know? I didn't work eight hours just to buy these and then mess them up.

"I just want to have a look around in the house that's why I'm here. I just want to see if what the people say is true. You know about all the strange pictures and the weird writing on some of the walls and stuff!"

"They are just nuts; mad. That's why they locked themselves up in there, all that writing just proves what everyone's always said; psychos."

"No their not mad, mad is what they call you when you're poor, eccentric is what they were because they had money, and lots of it."

"So are we going to get this over with or not? I'm cold, tired and my feet are killing me." Glyn was stamping his feet as if to emphasize the fact that he could hardly feel them. But as always Garry wasn't paying him the slightest bit of attention, he had already set off in the direction of the hole in the wall.

"Fine... I wasn't talking to you anyway," he said in a whisper, which was strange because there wasn't another living soul around for kilometres? But for some reason it seemed right, or rather appropriate to talk in low reverent tones, because the house gave off a strange air about it, made you want to respect it. And if it didn't sound too strange he would swear the empty windows were looking out over the landscape inspecting it; watching it - watching them!

As they climbed over the rubble and an assortment of junk that seemed to have been piled up in the gap through the wall, they had to keep the flash lamp pointed down towards the ground continually; in fear they would trip and impale themselves on one of the many metal objects that were forced into the hole that stuck out in all directions.

"Maybe we should have gone over the wall, there's less chance of impaling ourselves." And as by emphasizing the fact Garry pushed another pole to the side so he could crawl over. It wasn't until they were so far through the hole they realized just how thick the wall was. It must have been a good four even five feet thick.

"Wow, they could keep an army out with this sort of wall."

"Or an army in. What the hell would someone need a wall this thick around here for? It's not as if there's going to be a revolt anytime soon. The length some people will go to keep them Jehovah's Witnesses out is truly impressive." They were both laughing hard. Garry's laugh turned into a smokers fit. He flicked his cigarette butt at the wall.

It took them a moment to realize they had come to a stop in front of a stagnant stretch of water.

"You've got to be kidding me. No way is that a motte," Glyn said poking it with a piece of pipe he had taken out of the assortment of metal crammed in the hole. Now as they shined the torch around, they soon realized it was an old pond that had been made in the corner of the garden to go up to the wall. It had the same look of the garden about it. All boggy and over run, the pond hadn't been cleaned for what could have been years, even decades by the look of it.

"You would think that with the amount of time they spent in and around their house they would have kept it clean and tidy." As Glyn said this, he was picking up what looked like an old tire with the end of the pole out of the pond, or rather stagnant bog, which seemed to describe it better.

Luckily for them the wall had fallen in on itself and had made a kind of walkway over the rancid smelling water. There was only a short jump at the end, to get to the relatively dry ground on the other side. The large wall made the garden seem even darker than the area around. There were a few trees that had grown close to the house, they were big and impressively old but looked slightly deformed. Also if it didn't sound strange, the house seemed to look older the closer you got to it.

It didn't really have any design to it. It was just big, square and well, there really. There was no other way of describing it. It didn't look Georgian or Elizabethan or even gothic. The only way you could describe it was to say that someone made it that hadn't actually seen a house before in their life, but had been told what one should look like. The walls looked very solid, to solid for the purpose of just a run-of-the-mill house. The windows compared to the size of the house were very small, too small really to let any decent light in. But they were just the right size to look out of, to keep watch on the land that was all around it. It looked like a children's deformed drawing. You half expected a stick family stood besides it, with large white fluffy clouds floating above and a wobbly fence around it.

The other strange thing they noticed as they slowly made their way around the building was that they were walking over jutted out bits of rock, as if there had been a huge explosion underground and it had forced all the rocks to jut out everywhere. Huge slabs of stone sometimes the size of a family car were lying on their sides, as if picked up and let fall to where they would finally come to rest. For who knows how long?

What did make them wonder was that if all these stones were everywhere like this, then the amount of effort it must have taken to clear the area - so that they could build the house here - seemed too much? The only other answer they could think of was that all these stones were forced up after the house was built: but for the house to still be standing and in one piece seemed even more unbelievable. And what would cause such a cataclysmic seismic disturbance?

They made their way around what they would have called the front of the house. But because all the windows were so small and doted around all over the place with no sort of order, they could only presume it was the front. That was until they got around the corner and then they saw it.

It was huge. The front door must have taken up a good quarter of the front of the house. The size of it was immense compared to the rest of the building and completely out of character to everything they had seen so far. It looked even more solid than the walls themselves. The doors looked old, very old; it was made out of very dark wood, almost black. In this light it looked almost like a dark hole cut in to the front of the building.

"What the fucks that? You're not going to tell me that is the front door. I'd hate to see the size of the cat that comes out that cat flap," Garry said pointing to what seemed like a smaller door inlaid inside the bigger one. When they got closer and shined the torch at the door, the first thing they noticed was that the door seemed to absorb most of the light being shined onto it. And when they ran their hands over it, it had a strange kind of texture. On closer examination they could see it was thousands of what could only be described as letters, only it was too small to read and was carved on the complete surface of the door. Well for what they could see anyway because the door was way too tall for them to see if it had writing on the top in this light.

"Look this is getting way to weird. I say we go now, this place gives me the creeps," Glyn said taking a step back.

"You know all those people are suppose to be coming back here tomorrow with all those Cambridge snobs, to look the whole place over, because of all this shit," Garry said hitting the door with the butt of the torch, but the sound was completely absorbed by the door as if it hadn't even been hit at all. He examined the door while pushing his glasses up the bridge of his nose.

"They say that all this stuff may be worth a lot of money." He clicked his tongue a few times on the roof of his mouth, as he decided on what else to say.

"Faye's brother, you know old Hopalong, well he use to study all sorts of dip shit stuff up at the college before he had to come home to look after his mum. You know after her stroke. Well he say's in all the time he was up there studying ancient history he never saw anything like this. He's the one who's getting all them geek type people down here tomorrow," Garry said running his hand over the strange texture once again.

"Well, if it's so important why haven't they got anyone up here now looking after the place?" Glyn asked with a smug smile.

"Because legally the property still belongs to the Stevenson's, even though they just up and disappeared. The only reason Faye's brother was up here was because he now works for the bailiffs to makes ends meet, what with looking after his mum and all."

"But they have only been gone for a couple of weeks; I thought you had to go months without paying to get them to turn up?" Glyn asked, he twirled his eyebrow piercing absentmindedly.

"You do. They haven't been paying for stuff for months apparently. It's only when the bailiff's turned up for the third time, and broke in to take possession, that they noticed no one was here," Garry said giving the door a push, just to test it, even though he knew it wouldn't of been left open. Not that he would be able to move it even if it was.

"They had to get in through the back door after seeing this," he said waving his hand at the door. "They knew it would take a bulldozer to get through it." Garry eyed the door up and down as if he could work out how to get in.

"So how come if the Stevenson's still own this place the geeks are coming over to look around?" Glyn asked, taking a few steps backwards with his arms out wide to try and gauge the width of the door.

"You know you could get a double Decker bus through this thing if you wanted." Garry either didn't hear his brothers' comment, or as normal ignored him.

Garry continued as if his brother hadn't spoken: "Well apparently the National Trust has something to do with it, they got to hear about this place and they pulled a few strings. They have a lot more power than some people think; a couple of the people who are coming down here tomorrow are working for them." After giving his local gossip talk, Garry started walking off around towards the back of the house.

"So you're saying that the National Trust is the ones who are pulling all the strings on this one?" Glyn asked as he started to follow his brother.

"The government can step in and do what they like, to anyone at anytime. After hearing about this place it was passed on to one of their off branch sections," Garry said, as he climbed over a large rock which was more or less resting propped up against the dark wall; scuffing his brown leather trainers in the process.

"They say there could be more to this place then some think, like it has some sort of religious meaning or some crap like that. The Stevenson's also had no other living relatives other than those who lived in this house; problem is they couldn't be sure how many of them there were living up here apparently. Then because no other relatives are around to claim the property, it now belongs to the Government." Garry once again shrugged.

"Surely it takes longer than a few weeks before they can just come and claim this place? I thought people had to have been gone for seven years before they are claimed as dead?" Glyn was now sliding down the other side of the rock that his brother had just climbed over. His bag caught, and for a moment his feet dangled just inches from the ground, before it unlatched and he hit the ground with a jolt.

"Well I don't know about all that I'm no lawyer. All I have heard is the National Trust is coming to claim this place tomorrow, because they say important items may be lost if they have to wait any longer," Garry said while adjusting the bag on his own back.

"There has to be more to it than that surely? I've never heard of the National Trust doing anything like this before," Glyn said as he got his own torch out from his rucksack, because his brother kept flashing the thing around everywhere, up and down the walls trying to look through the small windows, when Glyn would rather be able to see where he was going.

"Who knows what they really want to do and to be honest I don't really give a monkey shit, because I don't plan to be around when they get here," Garry announced, as he brought the flashlight to a halt on the back door.

"That's strange old Hopalong said they had to smash the back door in because no one would answer. It was their third call without anyone responding so they could legally gain access," Garry stated, while rubbing his hand over the door, which he noticed had the same sort of writing on it as the front door, but in some way it seemed different but he couldn't explain why. His silver rings clipped the surface, making a knocking sound. The one difference he could see though was what looked like slightly lighter coloured wooden lines all over the door, going more or less from the middle out, as if it was a pane of glass and someone had smacked it with an object and had fractured it, then been painstakingly glued back together again. But that sounded ridiculous, so he didn't bother telling his brother. Instead he was trying to work out how to get in through the door because there was no way either of them could fit through one of the windows. Even a small child would've had difficulty.

They wandered around the other side of the house just to see if there was a bigger window. But there wasn't and soon they were back in front of the rear door. That's when Glyn first noticed. "There's no handle? Nothing!" He was right there was no form of handle or any push plate, nada. There was just a solid looking door.

"You know I don't think I saw a handle of any sort on the front door either," Glyn said as he started to rub his hand over the surface of the wood. Then that's when it happened? No noise nothing, not even a squeak from the hinges, it just silently glided open.

Both looked up expecting someone to be standing at the doorway. Maybe the Trust did have someone keeping an eye on the place. But no one came out. No voice raised in anger demanding to know what they were doing here. In a sense they probably would of preferred someone standing blocking the doorway, rather than the silence that seemed to flow from the house.

They got up slowly helping each other. They had jumped back with such alarm at the door opening that they had fallen on the floor in a heap.

Rubbing dirt off the seat of his pants Glyn was the first to gain his power of speech. "That almost gave me a heart attack. I think I need to change my underwear." He would have kicked the door as to stress his point, but he was reluctant to touch the thing, he could have sworn the surface rippled under his hand just before it opened. But with the shock of the last few minutes he wasn't sure himself now, so he said nothing to his brother.

"I tell you I'm thirty-one going on a hundred and one after that," Garry said with one hand on the wall and the other one resting on is chest, over his heart. "And don't worry; I think your nut catchers will be fine. Oh, and if you ever make me jump like that again, I swear I will break every bone in your damn body. And pull that eyebrow piercing out like a grenade clip." Garry always resorted to macho talk when he was scared and tried to cover over his feelings. This had always gotten him in trouble. If there was a problem he was more likely to lash out than talk it through.

"Me? It wasn't me, the door just opened," but Glyn's voice was sort of lost because he had his head in the doorway, and the hall seemed to suck the sound right out of his mouth before it had even left his lips.

"What did you say?" Now Garry had gained his composure he was standing directly behind his brother.

"We're not going to be those sort of people who walk into impending danger with nothing more than a torch are we?" Glyn commented, looking over his shoulder at his brother, who at this point was leaning on Glyn and looking over his shoulder down the hallway.

"You might only have a torch but I go nowhere without my trusty friend," Garry said, while holding up an eight-inch blade, which he had pulled out from inside his jacket. He licked his finger and ran it along the length of the blade.

"What did you go and bring that for?" Glyn asked eyeing the blade as the moonlight sparkled off the tip. Glyn was just happy that his brother hadn't brought more of his collection of knives. Most normal people started to collect interesting things when they were about to reach thirty-something. But Garry seemed obsessed with anything sharp. Oh well, Glyn thought, he could have brought one of his Lord of the Rings memorabilia weapons. They looked impressive, but couldn't cut shit.

"I only brought it to help pry any stubborn little artefacts that might be left hanging around." He turned the blade around in his hand and looked at it as if he never seen it before. "I tell you I'm glad I did because this is starting to get weird." He now had another skinny cigarette hanging from his lips, squeezed together at one end because he had run out of filters.

They started to make their way down the hallway, which was very short and only had two doors coming off of it. They first went into the small room that had a carpeted floor, which didn't quite reach all the way to the walls, but stopped just short. There was just two chairs, high back wooden ones, which had no real design to them whatsoever, they were well, just chairs, four legs a place to park your bum and a flat area in which to lean back on. They looked crude and home made. The only other thing in the small room was the table that didn't look any better than the seating. No wonder the bailiffs hadn't taken them. There was nothing else in the room; there weren't any pictures on any of the walls, not even wallpaper. Just bare walls void of anything, painted a plain dirty white colour. Even the light bulb that hung from the ceiling didn't have any lampshade on it. From the look of it, it could have been a prison cell; all it needed was a small metal cot in one of the corners and a rusty bucket to piss in.

"Wow, what a bunch of party animals. I tell you, if the rest of the house is like this we might as well save ourselves the time and trouble and leave now," Garry said kicking the chair over. He was rewarded by it falling apart. He flicked ash on the floor.

Looking around the small room Glyn asked, "What on earth did the bailiffs find worth taking around here?"

"They didn't, after they supposedly broke the back door in and looked inside this room, they left," Garry replied.

"What do you mean just left?" Glyn was now looking straight at his brother.

"They couldn't get through the other door, the one leading to the rest of the house," Garry said as he tried to stick the point of the knife in the wall, and was disappointed to find he couldn't even make a mark on it. This seemed strange, because on closer inspection the walls seem to have faded symbols etched over some of its surface.

"So even though they found a way through the back door they couldn't get through this one?" Glyn asked. They had both left the small room and were now standing in front of the only door left in the hallway. The torch's light once again seemed to be swallowed by the doors surface.

"So what you're saying is that the bailiffs came to the house to take possession of their belongings. No one was home, so they broke in, supposedly through the back door.

"Then after looking around that small room and finding nothing of interest, they then tried to get into the rest of the house through this door," Glyn said shining his torch on the door once again. "And they couldn't get through, but because of the strange writing on the door, which would probably look more impressive during the daylight. And on account of these doors and the strange look to the house in general, the Government is going to step in to take control of the place, under the pretence of being interested in it because of some National Trust charter or whatever they like to call it. And all this because Faye's brother Hopalong just happened to phone a couple of his old friends up at the college, who just happened to have connections," Glyn said once again looking straight at his brother.

"Yep that's about the lot I would say. All that happened this morning, the cavalry are coming first thing tomorrow. That's why we're here now, to have a look around before they start charging to get in." Garry seemed to think this was funny and chuckled to himself. "So they don't know what's on the other side of this door, so they won't miss anything, if you get what I'm saying?" Garry said winking at Glyn, which was wasted because Glyn was looking intently at the door surface.

"The only problem is how do we get through it? Because unlike the prison cell here," Garry said, pointing to the small room they had just left, which had a normal looking door, with a normal looking handle on it. "But this one," he stated pointing at the strange door again. "Is like the other doors and it doesn't have a handle."

"I don't think it's going to be too much of a problem," Glyn said as he lifted his hand and placed it on the door, the door like the other one silently swung open.

"How the hell did you?" Garry started to ask, but the words died on his lips at the sight of what lay in the room before them.

3
No Loose Ends

Adam Peterson; or better known to his friends as Hopalong; sat at the computer table with his back to his bedroom door, which was shut to keep his sister Faye from just walking in, and interrupting him while he studied.

He didn't mind having to come home to look after his mother, after she had had the stroke. After all she was his mum and she had looked after him for the last twenty-two years, even after he had left home, and was living in the college dorms. His mother would come up to see how he was. Bringing him his favorite snacks and nibbles, because now he was a fulltime student his grant didn't cover such pleasures as descent food.

They had always been close, him and his mum, more so after his dad had died unexpectedly at work, while trying to move some heavy machinery without the proper equipment, it had falling backwards and killed him instantly. And having to work through all the legal jargon after, where the company wouldn't pay any compensation because his death was a result of him not following company regulations by not using the proper lifting apparatus.

That was all in the past now because he had other problems and responsibilities. He was still able, with special permission, because of his home situation, to carry on with his course, which was in ancient Egyptology. He just loved everything to do with the past but his one passion was Egypt, the Pharaohs the ancient way of life. He still hoped to pass the course with flying colours because he was still in the top of his year, even though he was doing his work only in the evenings then e-mailing it off to the college.

But to look after his mother and sister he had to get a job. The only one being available at this time paying the sort of money he needed to look after his family, and pay for the monthly repayments on his computer, that he needed in order to still do his college course, was being a bailiff for the local county courts. It was a thankless job, which no one else wanted because of what was involved. But the money was good and that, as far as Adam was concerned was the main reason he stuck to it.

Until today when he stumbled on probably one of the most important finds of the decade. He still couldn't fully grasp what he had seen, but from the first sight of the front door to the house he had known that what lay in front of him was important. He couldn't understand how the other two groups of bailiffs hadn't noticed the way the house looked, when they called two times previous?

He had stood there just staring at it not quite comprehending the significance, and the changes it will make in his life. The door was old, that he could tell straight away any fool could, but the writing on it was strange.

One of the courses he had to take in order to do Egyptology was ancient writings, which covers more-or-less all forms of writing from ancient Mongolian, Hebrew, Greek, Babylonian and Oriental just to name a few. Not to completely learn the language, because to learn one would take years on it's own, but to see the difference in their variables, the way in which the different forms of writing seemed similar yet completely different. The way they had changed down through the eons, and how some had completely been forgotten.

He could not recognize the form of writing in front of him. It didn't even look similar to anything he had seen before. Why was it so small, almost illegible? Why was this form of writing on a door, hung on hinges on a house on the outskirts of a small town, on the southwest coastline of Devon in England? This being just the entrance, then what would be on the inside of this house? What treasures lay ahead of him just beyond this strange door?

Just then he had heard the crash, he had completely forgotten the reason he was here and the two people he had come with, Jamie Claymore and Rich Hampton were nowhere in sight. They were his two fellow workers that he had just climbed over this terrain with, in order to get to this house. He had found them around the back of the building, with a small battering ram in their hands and the remains of a door, all in pieces around their feet. With Jamie twiddling his ear piercing as if it would stimulate his brain and help evaluate the situation. Rich was hunched over rolling a fag.

The door they had just smashed in, as far as Adam could see was also covered in the small writing. He couldn't believe that they had just smashed it up. It had then taken him a good twenty minutes to convince them to leave the house and not to carry out the warrant. He didn't want them to trample around inside and possibly damage something else. He had to promise them all sorts of things in order to make them leave with him. He said he would come up with some sort of excuse for not carrying out the warrant, he promised everything would work out okay. They had no idea what they had stumbled across, and the thought of getting the rest of the afternoon off had won them over.

The first thing he did when he got home, was e-mail the college to let them know what he had found, he had even drawn a few pictures, and had included them in with his report, and a map to show the houses location. It was answered quicker than normal, and they said they would be there first thing in the morning, to pick him up, so he could take them straight out to the site in question.

He had gotten off the computer to the college just over four hours ago, and was now finishing off his normal days college work. Hopefully something big was going to come of this. He could just see himself on the front cover of the local newspaper, or even the national papers or even a few magazines. The only thing he wishes he hadn't done was tell his sister. But he was so excited when he got home; he just had to tell her and his mother. His mum couldn't speak anymore and they weren't even sure she could even comprehend conversation, but he knew she could understand what he was saying; he could see it in her glassy eyes.

There was a clamor downstairs.

If that cat had knocked the plant over again there was going to be trouble. He didn't like the thing, the only reason he kept it was because it would sit on his mother's lap for hours. It had never sat with anyone before; it was not a person cat, always hissing at you if you put your hand out and so on. But since his mothers' stroke, the cat seemed to realize something was wrong, only sitting with his mother never anyone else, as if it was comforting her.

There was a draft blowing from behind him. If his sister was sneaking in to his room again there was going to be big trouble. He spun the chair around and was about to shout at her, when he saw the person just standing there, he was trying to sneak up from behind, and it was only the draft from the door that had given him away.

The stranger was dressed completely in black, from the black mask that allowed only his piercing green eyes to be seen, down to his black soft-soled shoes that were made for stealth. What looked like cheese wire was stretched from one gloved hand to the other, but now he knew that approach wasn't going to work, he was silently slipping it back into one of the folds of his black garments and was now banishing a long strangely curved dagger.

It was all over within a heartbeat.

Hopalong now lay on the floor with darkness swallowing over his vision. He didn't feel any pain; he hadn't really had time to. In all this, his only thoughts were for his mother, and who would now look after her and his sister. He lay on the cold wooden floor with a small pool of sticky red liquid blossoming around him like some exotic flower. Then came the coldness, the feeling of complete rest, then the darkness... Then eternal sleep.

But he didn't have to worry about his mother or his sister anymore, no one would. They had succumbed to the same fate as him. There was to be no clues, nothing. The house was to be raised to the ground and the two next to it, a freak gas explosion, a leak they would come to say. The bodies were burned, well beyond recognition; the only way to identify them was through their dental records. It was a shame about the other five people who happened to be unlucky enough to be in the houses next door, but it was to not look too obvious.

There was another tragic accident on the other side of town, Jamie Claymore and Rich Hampton plus nine others from their group of seventeen mates, were out celebrating a friends stag night when they died. Mowed down by a lorry when it veered out of control, then jackknifed into the White Hart pub, they had all only moments before walk in to. It would eventually be put down to the driver having a heart attack behind the wheel. Even though the family, plus his doctor said he had never had any previous heart problems before.

Family said: "It wouldn't bring back the people who had died."

But then others would simply say: "You can't leave loose ends."

4
The Trust

The secret Trust organization had assembled a group of six – six of the very best.

Firstly the leader Jethro E. Stokes, he was forty-three, tall and lanky, but with well defined muscles, crafted from a lifetime of military training and hardships. He has short cropped dark brown hair, mainly because it would never go were he wanted it too, with piercing celery-green eyes like coke-bottle glass. He was known as Jet to his friends and family. But these weren't family here; this was business, work, his life. He was the leader of this small group, their coded handle of Wedge Group, mainly because of their uncanny ability to be able to get themselves into any location required during their training missions. Here he was known simply as the Captain.

Next it was Thomas Gonzalez Barbosa, twenty-four and of average height and build, but with a tinted brown skin, brown eyes and obsidian black hair as if a relative of distant past had come from Latin America - he was in fact second generation Mexican American, as his name implied; even though he didn't know any Spanish apart from a little high school Spanish. Known to everyone as Flatfoot, even though he was the explosive expert, he had a tendency to be loud on his feet in times when silence was called for. But he was the best in the business at what he does, that's why he was also part of the team.

There was also Jonathan Gonzalez Barbosa, Flatfoot's brother, some years older he was twenty-eight and was the map and surveillance expert. His code or nick name was Brains, not because of Intelligence but because he looked like the puppet Brains from the children's television program *The Thunderbirds*.

David Crispin was the fourth in the team and the oldest. He was forty-six and a little short and stubby, even after all his training. His head was clean shaven and his eyes were almond colored. He is the teams' computer expert. If there was a computer ever built then he could get into it. Hopper was his nickname because he was a bit unstable at times – adrenaline causing him to take needless and reckless risks, but his head was always screwed on in times of need. He was covered from head to toe in tattoos that would make a hardened hells angel jealous; sometimes they call him a mini Vin Diesel.

Then there was Doctor Danny. Michaels or Doc as he was called. He was the team medic, the serious one of the group. His uniform was always immaculate over his muscular frame, even when on training missions. His sandy blonde hair always brushed and creamed impeccably to one side. At Twenty-five he wasn't the youngest but the fact he was a Special Forces field medic at that age shows why he was part of the team, even with his quirky cleanliness. He looked like a poster perfect image for the army.

Sarah Jenkins was the psychologist, because you never know when a good shrink would come in handy, not just with the team, but it was also important to be able to understand the actions and thoughts of your enemy. At twenty-two she was already well documented within the military circles for some of her accomplishments in new research areas. Nicknamed Babe because of being the youngest in the group, but also partly because of her striking figure and long blonde tied back hair and iceberg blue colored eyes; and busty cleavage, they all joked that no one wore a military uniform better than her.

All had their basic military training, also the advanced Special Forces training. All were well versed in arm-to-arm combat, weapons training. Have plenty of hands on experience. That was up until eight months ago when they were all pulled out of their regular position and put together as a new group. They had to go through, and over a lot of their old training. They were all now the best they could physically be in their particular fields. Now all worked perfectly together as a group, and had learned to like and more importantly – trust one another.

Each had been hand picked because of their particular backgrounds.

The Captain had returned off of an eight months leave, after a boating accident where he and his wife and two children were caught in a freak storm between the Gulf of Mexico and The Caribbean Sea. All had ended up in the water, even though they all had their life jackets on, only he survived because of his stamina. He was still clutching to the body of his youngest daughter when they found him. She had drowned. But the bodies of his wife and oldest daughter were never recovered. This was his first assignment since the accident. He was eager to throw himself completely into his work; it was his way of coping with what had happened.

Flatfoot and Brains were both orphaned at an early age, after their mother had died in a tragic fire at their home. They bounced around different boarding schools and homes until they were old enough to get into the army, where they both then proceeded to excel in their different talents.

Hopper was an only child of a single mother, who was shunned by her family for not having an abortion. So he grew up not having, or knowing any of his relatives. Then his mother got into drugs, to as she put it, "Cope with her life." He found her overdosed when he was nineteen. Then within a couple months he was in the army following a course in computers. His talent for computers and cryptographic programming soon became apparent, when he broke the National Security Agencies standard key encryption superalgorithm program, when he hacked into their main database to see if his application had been accepted. Instead of prosecuting someone that could bypass all their security that had been written by the world's best programmers, they offered him a job. Before long he was transferred to the Trust.

Doc had a similar story to the others. His parents had died in a car crash after they left a Christmas party. They had taken a short cut on the way home. His father didn't really know the road, plus with alcohol in his blood, he overturned the car in a marshy ditch. Doc was the only one left conscious; he didn't have the knowledge needed to save them. Sitting at their funeral days later, he swore he would learn medicine to help others. But his parents hadn't had much money; there wasn't anything left after the cost of the funerals to put him through medical school. So he joined the army to become a military Doctor, they trained you and it cost you nothing. But the most important thing was he got to save others.

Babe was different, she had family, but she just chose to break away from them. She wanted to, and had learned psychology. She had an honors degree, but being young and female, all the different partnerships rejected her. Partly because her father was rich and powerful and had his hand in getting her shunned. They had already chosen a husband for her, and had her whole life mapped out before she was even seventeen. She chose to go her own way, leave her family and do what she wanted to do. The only place her father had no hold was in the army, so that's where she went. She learned new tactics; within a couple of years she was well ahead in her group, writing new thesis papers on the effects of War Syndrome. That's why she was here now, as part of this grouping, part of this team.

That's why these were all chosen, why they were here now, they had no loved ones to miss them when they didn't come back.

They had all been assembled in a room, in the main part of the building, that was located over seven hundred and forty-two feet below ground level. Its location was in the Nevada desert just a 144 kilometres from Las Vegas - America's playground. To all those in the room it was called Base Bravo, a 9.66 by 16.09 kilometer area. To all those outside the walls - in the paranoid world - it had many different names, it was referred to as Dreamland, Watertown, Area S4, or Groom lake Military Base, or best known for its alien conspiracies as Area 51.

They had been brought together for their first debriefing as a new group. There was a sort of nervousness in the room. They had been in this building now for just over eight months, not allowed outside their training rooms or to intermingle with any other people in the building, not allowed to talk to any of the other groups. They had been sort of shuffled away in their own part of the building, and now they were just looking forward to getting out.

They were told that a transmission had been intercepted over the Internet, all the right words and descriptions were used to describe what they had been looking for, for some time now. Below the floor they were on, sat two thousand and sixty-four Gibson Super Computers, each one capable of running a small city on its own, together they were linked through the phone lines and internet superhighways picking up key words and phrases, analyzing all the conversations going on not just in America but in all countries capable of fiber optics and any form of telecommunication.

They were told that it had been found. That they were going to be sent there as soon as the debriefing had finished. The information having now been intercepted, down loaded, then wiped off the Internet - and considering that the Internet was created in the late 1960s as a project of the U.S. Department of Defense: because the military needed a reliable communication network that would continue to function even if parts of it were out of order, a thing that usually happens during wartime – then this was easily accomplished by the Trusts Hackers, considering they had Slipjacks backdoors in all aspects of the World Wide Web.

All those that had found the Gateway - including all those that knew about it - had been taken care of by a small Special Forces group stationed in England. The finder sent the message to a small college. No one, not even those sent to eliminate the finders knew why. They just followed their orders. Only a few choice people - including those in the room - knew about its existence

Once they were told what they were expected to do, they quietly filed out of the room. None spoke to each other. They didn't even look at one another. They were to deep in their own thoughts, and what they were about to under take. The enormousness of the task that lay ahead of them, and the fact that there were only six of them to do it, no backup, no rescue team, just them - along with a planeload of equipment.

Within an hour they were loaded on to the Sikorsy S-65 helicopter, and shuttled across to the bases airfield; which was the longest airstrip in the world, almost 8.05 kilometers long. They were then loaded onto a prototype aircraft. They looked back towards the place that had been called home to them for the last eight months.

They were now bound for England, a small southwesterly corner known as Devon, to a section called Dartmoor, where a house was situated. A house they were about to get very familiar with. A house that held many secrets and nightmares.

5
The Walls Have Eyes

Glyn and Garry both stood motionless outside the doorway looking in. "You've got to be kidding me," Glyn said. Neither of them had attempted to move through the door. But both just stood there looking in, holding on firmly to the doors wide frame.

Garry's roly lay on the floor, having tumbled from his lips without him even noticing.

The room they were now looking in to was immense. In must have taken up the whole inside of the house, and if it didn't sound impossible they would swear it was larger than the house itself.

The room was completely made up of the same rocks that jutted up everywhere outside. The walls weren't one complete lump of rock, rather thousands of small over-laying slabs of granite type stone. The rocks were jutting out in all different directions crisscrossing over each other, all around the room, making a more-or-less circular area. The roof looked like that of a cavern, with large stalactites hanging down, but unlike the rest of the room these were giving off a soft orange glow, which even though it wasn't that strong, still illuminated the whole chamber.

This wasn't what they were expecting, so they didn't quite know how to react, they just stood there with their mouths hanging open looking in. They could see what they could only guess was the area where the front door should have been. But from inside the room looking across you couldn't see the door, just a hole in the side of the wall, where the rocks gave way to what in all sense 'n' purposes was a tunnel leading off in to the distance. From where they were they couldn't see the tunnels end because of it twisting slightly to the right.

Glyn took a step into the room, and was instantly pulled back by his cardigan by Garry.

"Let go, what are you doing?" Glyn asked, pulling his brothers hand off his shoulder.

"No, what do you think you're doing?" came Garry's response.

"You can't go in there this is all wrong, can't you feel it?" Garry asked looking over Glyn's shoulder into the room where his brother now stood.

"It's only a cave of some sort. It could possibly be an ancient meeting place or spiritual ground of some type, which has been forgotten. That's what those people who were living here did they looked after it. And over there," Glyn pointed to the tunnel, "leads off to where they had their living quarters and such like." He shrugged his shoulders.

"But that's where the door should be, the whole place is wrong, all laid out wrong, it's just too weird, let's leave it to the Trust, they will be here tomorrow. They will probably give it a look over and we're set to hear about it in the paper or something," Garry said taking a step away from the door.

"Look things always seem bad at night, but we can't come back tomorrow in the daylight because the Trust will probably have the whole place locked down. Then they won't open it up to the public for months, and then we have to pay to look around. They're bound to put ropes and barriers up to stop you from getting to close to the walls and that, but we could look around now and climb on what we like. Come on where's your sense of adventure, it was your idea in the first place to come here remember?" Glyn said, as he started to make his way across the room, which sloped downwards as you walked towards its center.

Garry started to follow his brother more slowly, looking up at the walls as he did. They seemed to be moving. In the sense that as he moved towards the heart of the room it became like an optical illusion, where the entire chambers walls became perfectly smooth when you were standing in the exact center. All the stones were cut and positioned in what at first looked jumbled and erratic, were in fact positioned in the exact right place, so they all lined up together the closer you got to the hub of the room, to the point where the walls looked perfectly smooth almost like a dull green bottle colored glass.

Garry was looking at the walls, he didn't see his brother who was looking down, and he walked straight into him.

Garry didn't even notice hitting him. "Have you seen what happens to the walls as you get closer to the middle?" Garry asked while still looking out towards the walls. Even his craving for nicotine was momentarily forgotten.

"Never mind the walls look at the floor," Glyn whispered while still looking down.

As Garry now looked down he noticed the writing, which from his central position in the middle of the room, he could see the writing under his feet start to circle out in a continuous sweeping circle, out towards the walls in a fan shape with seven different branching arms coming off of the middle, then when they hit the walls they ran straight up.

"Wow this place is something else," Garry stated, whistling through his gapped teeth, and pushing his glasses back up on to the bridge of his broken nose.

"The writing must be written on all different parts of the stones, so when they're all in position the writing goes straight up," Glyn said, as he too noticed that the walls were all now smooth.

"But I didn't see the writing on the floor as we walked in?" Garry stated.

"That's because all the writing is carved out of the rock at an angle, so when we're standing in the middle the light from the ceiling catches the impressions on the floor, then we can see it," was Glyn's guess.

But Garry wasn't listening he was looking up.

Then following his brother's gaze he also looked up. Glyn saw why his brother was ignoring him.

Just like the walls, the ceiling from the side looked jagged and in disarray, but from beneath the ceiling was a circular spiral going away from them up into the far distance. Spiraling slowly in a lazy circle skywards was what looked like an orangey gray thick fog, which was tapering off the top of the seven pillars of writing, which were running up the walls.

"Jesus H. Christ, now that is impressive," Glyn whispered, straining his neck looking upwards.

"Impressive. What do you mean impressive? That's one word I wouldn't use," Garry said.

"So what word would you use?" Glyn asked still staring up towards the large swirling mass that was being drawn away from them up into the distance.

"Try; let's get the hell out of here. This isn't right, none of it is. I don't want to be here anymore," Garry muttered, now peering around the large room again. "Have you noticed there are no windows on the inside? Where have the windows gone?" Glyn was now looking straight at his brother.

"Come on there is an answer for everything, all you have to do is look close enough and everything becomes clear in the end," Glyn said now walking towards the wall. But as he got closer to it he realized that he could see straight through it, not completely transparent, but enough so that when you were standing close enough you could swear you could see what was on the other side. "I think that's your answer to there being no windows," Glyn said pointing his finger towards the glassy wall closest to himself.

"What do you -" Garry was cut short because he could now see what his brother was looking at. "SHIT, now that is impressive," Garry shouted, forgetting his fear for a moment. He was now completely taken in by the sight that lay before his eyes.

"How is that possible?" came Garry's voice, now uttered in a weak whisper.

"I don't know. But there's loads of things in this world man can't explain," Glyn answered peering once again around the room. "Like the pyramids of ancient Egypt, where there so perfectly in-line with the stars that even some of the equipment today wouldn't have been able to do such a good job; the way the passages are in perfect alignment with different constellations. And the ancient Incas, some of their calendars were so exact they could predict weather conditions well in advance. How did they cut the stones to some of their walls, which were so perfectly aligned, and interlocking that they didn't need any sort of adhesive? Those walls are still standing after thousands of years, surviving adverse weather conditions and erosion, when some of our walls with all our so called superior technology, would be lucky to still be standing after just fifty years or so?"

"So you're saying just because we don't understand it, it doesn't mean it's not possible?" was Garry's response as he walked towards the wall with his hand outstretched as if about to touch it, then just before doing so he withdrew it.

"Well say two hundred years ago, you tell someone from that time that one day we would be able to walk on the surface of the moon. Even send probes to Mars that land. That we can get to America in just over four hours by using a large metal machine that resembled a bird in appearance. That a small screen, only a few inches thick, that hanging on the wall can show you live pictures from someone standing on another continent, or another planet. That you could pick up a piece of plastic, put it to your ear and you can talk to anyone anywhere in the world, and that a large majority of people carry a similar device in their pocket that can link them to almost anyone anywhere, and speak to them whenever they like -"

"Okay, I think I get the message."

"All I'm saying is that once those specialists from Hoperlong's college get here with their Trust friends, and they have a look around, they might be able to shed some light on it. Not that we'll be here to listen, but you know what I'm saying?" Glyn said, looking out through the wall to the outside world, were he could see the hazy moon peeking out from behind thick boiling clouds.

And then it hit him like a kick in the chest. First complete panic overtook his senses; logic couldn't answer the question his brain was now screaming.

"What the -" Glyn was turning around in circles franticly searching the entire wall with his panic widened eyes.

"What, what's wrong? Glyn... Glyn!" Garry grabbed his brother's shoulder and spun him round to face him. "What's your problem? You're freaking me out here bro." He was shaking his younger brother. Glyn was too rattled to even notice that the knife was inches from his face, while being shaken.

Then Glyn looked his brother in the eyes, while pointing to the wall behind them. "The door we just came through," Glyn's eyes were now franticly scanned all the walls, looking around at them all once again, just in case they had simply been playing a trick on him. "Well it's gone, it's not there anymore?"

6
Then There Was Three

The Gateway doesn't seem to radiate as much fear during the daylight; the dull daylight seems to dilute the uneasy feeling you get as you approach it. Even the towering stones and metallic dragons seemed to be sleeping. As the light rises it brings hope. You have survived another night, in this nightmare of a world.

As a group they waited several hours, making sure the Lank's had retreated, and that none were still scouting the area, because they knew humans seldom traveled alone.

Eventually they moved from their hiding place and go to retrieve the body of their companion. He was lucky they had grown tired of playing with him. His screaming had still lasted well in to the night. But now he had rest, he was no longer trapped here as they were. In a perverted kind of way they felt envious of him; he was now free, but they still had to live the nightmare.

The group looked a sorry excuse for a collection of human beings. Mismatched clothes, all ripped and torn. Hair all matted, covered in mud and red dust.

They picked up what was left of his body and put it on a make shift stretcher; made from tree branches lashed together with vines. Then they started to make their way back to camp. If it could be call that. It was small homes made from branches and mud, just enough to keep out the elements. But a camp it couldn't really be called. It held hundreds of others, all who had come through the Gateway and had survived making it to the hill; which it was situated on. It was the only safe place in this intelligent evil world where they could let their guard down and relax.

They had to walk for many hours over rough terrain, over rivers, through forest and across the expanse of barren land where nothing grows, not even weeds. They still stayed alert there were two to carry the stretcher, four to defend in case of attack. But nothing had as yet. But then it never did, it let you get so far, so you could just start to see the side of the hill where your homes were, where the protective wall that surrounded the village was, then you would start to lower your guard - then they would attack.

You were never sure what it would send against you? It could be one of many of its creations. It could be some of the Lank's as they called them, lizard type creatures that had killed their companion from the night before. Or a large Moregone that even though it was large, and slow, was still incredibly powerful. It could only be described as a larger version of a Lank, but fatter, much fatter, and almost three and a half times its height, standing at almost twenty foot tall and instead of having a whip like tail, this creature had a fat squat one with spikes running its entire length. But unlike the Lank this creature was almost dumb, living manly on reflexes and instinct. And it was very rarely seen this far from the forest.

Then that's why this place was so bad, it was so unpredictable.

They only had perhaps quarter of a mile to go before they reached the safety of their protective wall, when they were attacked.

The small group was making their way up the slope towards the low-lying bushes that cover about forty percent of the hill, when the creatures charged. First giving off their high pitched scream that seemed to run straight through you, and make your knees want to give out from beneath you. They always let you know they are coming; they feed off your fear as much as on your flesh. They were small, averaging just over three foot tall, made up manly of two powerful legs, a long neck and a tail for balance, having only short arms, with three clawed fingers on the end, but they rarely got to use their clawed hands because their most feared weapon was their saliva; as their head jerks backwards they could fire a ball of spit up to twenty yards, almost always hitting the victim in the eyes causing permanent damage, with excruciating pain. Then they would rush at you.

They never attacked in groups of less than thirty. Taking bites out of you as you stumbled around on the ground, tearing at the terrain with your bleeding hands trying to get a chance to pull yourself to your feet to carry on, as the pain in your eyes started to feel like they were about to burst out of your head.

It was all over in less than four minutes. They were now slowly bleeding to death with all the bites that had been inflicted. All the people in the village could do was watch and hear their screaming; many had to turn away and cover their ears. Few had the courage needed to help.

Only once had the gates been opened to send aid to ones being attacked outside, the others stood watching helplessly as these also were struck to the ground.

They had fought well, using what weapons they had. The creatures though were just to fast, and too many. Like all the others that had tried before them they had failed.

It still remains open.

Even now it still spewed forth the constant billowing tower of orangey-gray cloud, that could only be described as looking like smoke churning out of the top, slowly, lazily spiraling up into the sky above until it reached the cloud line where it mingles with the sky, causing the constant thick dull cloud layer that hangs over the complete atmosphere as far as the eye could see - stretching from horizon to expanding horizon.

From their location on top of the hill they could see four billowing clouds rising up into the atmosphere. All located in different parts of this cruel world. Some so far in the distance that they were nothing more than thin cords rising skywards, but you could tell they were the same as the one close to them.

That was until about eighteen months ago, (if that sort of time applied here) because one had stopped sending out its foul cloud. They could only guess and draw hope that one of the other; possibly many groups such as theirs had shut one down. That's what gave them hope, made them keep trying. Not the thought that there were more like them stuck in this cruel world. But the thought that there were more to help stop this evil, stop others from getting across and becoming prisoners such as they are.

That's what keeps them going, that's their hope, the hope that others wouldn't fall victim to the same fate as them - prisoners in this dying world; a world that needed to suck the life from another - their own world - in order to sustain itself.

7
The Second as the First

There still wasn't the normal chatter that came from the group. Rather just quiet contemplation. They still had to get their own heads around what they had just heard, before they could start to talk to one another about it. It wasn't everyday you were told there was another dimension running parallel to our own, another world! Now your job was to cross over to that world and shut the Gateway down. They only partly knew what was in store for them.

They were told there had been a message intercepted a description of the outside of the building. The fact it was a building didn't so much as give it away, rather the description of the door. The way the young man had described the writing. The way the building had been positioned; its location. They knew the sort of area and stone composition they needed to look for. But that still only narrowed it down to a couple of countries; a country was a big thing. They could have teams out for years in one country alone and could still miss it. That's why the computers were tapped into everything. Let someone else find them, let them do the hard work; all they had to do is wait and listen. Before long something would turn up. It's a human trait wanting to tell someone else about what you have found - wanting the glory, the acknowledgment from it. It had taken almost two years before they had heard word about the second one.

They already had control of the first. Found by a group of young potholers; spelunking, looking for the extreme cave, going all the way to Gombe Stream National Park, to a place called Kigoma, situated in Tanzania, which boarders the longest freshwater lake in the world – Lake Tanganyika, kept full by the river Ruizizi.

For over two weeks they had been making their way through the mountains of Tanzania, trying to find a deeper cave, a harder cave, to take them that much closer to the extreme.

That's when the perfect cave was found, between the City Kigoma and Ujiji, in the Kigoma regional district.

They traveled down almost four hundred feet below the lakes level. They had to be careful, the lake is the second deepest in the world, of 4,700 feet, and flooding was a genuine concern.

That's when they discovered it - a wooden door!

It was large and delicately inscribed, a door this far under the ground? Their first instinct was curiosity. The door had opened easily, to reveal a large circular space with writing on the level flooring. All the team stayed back, apart from one. His name was Jason Kelly, an I.T. specialist from Silicon Valley. He worked as an annalist for G. Tec, a new dot.com company. This was his first time in Africa; it seemed like a way to release the pressure building up, meeting all the deadlines. He had been potholing for years and when a group of his friends suggested it, he was the first to jump at the chance.

He had entered the cave through the door, while all the others hung back.

That was the last they had seen of him - as they put it almost a week later while in the American Embassy in Dar es Salaam almost 800 kilometers away, on the other side of the country. He had just disappeared in front of their eyes. One minute he was walking towards the center of the room the next he vanished? At first the embassy diplomats attributed it to them watching too many X-files and the 4400, being an elaborate plan for getting away with what was probably a drunken fight, where one of the group was struck and killed, and now they were trying to cover it up with an unrealistic fantasy.

But word soon got back to the American National Intelligence Agency. Before the day was out a team of eight specialists was sent over to check out their story. The rest as they say is history.

They found out the story was true. Telling the Tanzania Government it was murder, then sending the group of potholers home for trial. They were never seen or heard from again. They were put on an Alliance Air flight from Dar es Salaam, to Washington DC, on December 9th - Tanzania's Independence Day.

It was a tragic airplane crash where everyone - all four hundred and sixty-eight on board the Boeing 747 died. It was put down to the air company running unfit planes, and using to many second hand parts. A complicated three hundred page report was filed, vaguely mentioning something to do with corroded fuel lines beneath the luggage holding area. No one ever questioned the decision of the American Aviation Investigation Board, who was brought in because U.S citizens had died over international waters. Then again who could question them? And this was Africa after all. A plane crash was the least of their worries.

The whole area was then bought off the Tanzania Government for a small research base, studying the rock and mineral depositories in the area. The Kigoma representatives didn't care if it was used for a nuclear dumping ground for the amount of money the Americans paid for it.

First, five small farms were resettled, then they had the whole under ground cavern dug around, all the dirt and rocks removed and a large dome building built over the top, with outbuildings and labs set up around the outer ring, with a thick dam-like construction built to stop the water from Lake Tanganyika flooding it when the Ruizizi river brought its annual flood waters.

Over two hundred and eleven of the world's best scientists, geologists and nuclear sub-particle specialists, founded under the secrecy of a small American government offshoot known only as the Trust; a group run by the legendary – supposedly fabled - Majestic Twelve: the twelve most powerful individuals on the planet, whose influence controlled the armies, stock markets and governments of the world.

The six Trust military representatives now sat on the prototype Blackbird Phase II, where up to twenty people plus equipment could be taken almost anywhere around the globe in a matter of mere hours. Their destination, a small British military base, on Dartmoor, between Widencombe in the Moor and Manaton, where their transport had to be picked up.

They were then to go alone, just the six of them, to confirm the existence of the second Gateway. Then get word by decrypted satellite relay back to Bravo Base, where the Trust would then start the process of getting the ground around the house the property of the American Government. This isn't as difficult as it sounded. Different countries set up all sorts of research stations and military bases, of all kinds, all around the world. The country in question can do nothing but say yes. They never know when they would need the favor in return.

If it were another Gateway as they suspected, then after the message was sent they would then have to pass through the portal and close it down from the other side. As they already found out, it doesn't need the Gateway on the other side in order to keep it functioning. They didn't need the other side. All they needed was what the gate on this side produces.

8
The Calling

Garry turned to where his brother was looking. All he could see was walls. All around the smooth surface reflected the soft light. From where they where standing the only exit was the gaping hole in the other wall, opposite where they had initially entered.

"Maybe it's the way the walls are. The way the light reflects, and as we get closer we'll be able to see the door again," was all Garry could think to suggest, because of the complete look of utter desolation on his brothers face, even though he was starting to feel very uneasy himself.

"You could be right? That's it! The doors still there, it's just hidden from view." Glyn seemed to relax as he said this; he then started walking towards the wall where they had first emerged. But upon reaching the wall, moving away from the center of the room, it started to fragment again becoming less regular and uneven. The rocks were once again sticking out in all directions. But no door. Glyn started to move around the large room, maybe he was mistaken; maybe they had come in from this side, from over here rather than over there? But no matter which part of the wall he walked past they were all the same; all except for one part of the wall. This was the part he was now standing in front of, looking down the gaping tunnel.

His brother came to stand next to him.

Glyn hadn't moved from in front of the hole. Rather he just stood there staring down it.

"You know I think I can feel a soft breeze coming from it?" Glyn said, standing motionless, his hands flaccid by his sides.

"I wonder what's in the tunnel," Garry asked, as he now stood next to his brother, also staring down the large yawning hole.

Garry looked at Glyn sideways. "I can't feel anything." No he couldn't feel anything but he would swear he heard soft voices, whispering, echoing and being repeated over and over, with a touch of sadness and deep remorse in them.

"There's definitely a breeze. It feels quite warm." Glyn had taken on a look of absolute peace, as if his mind was somewhere else?

"You're not going weird on me or anything are you?" Garry asked, nudging his brother with his elbow. That seemed to bring his brother round.

"What... Did you say something?" Glyn had taken his eyes off the tunnel for the first time and was now looking at his brother.

"Thought I was losing you for a minute there," Garry said, smiling nervously, seeing the strange look on his brothers' face. Garry had seen this look many times, just before his brother became uncontrollably drunk; a moment before his face is a blank sheet as if preparing for the madness to come.

"Losing me? What do you mean losing me?" Glyn asked frowning.

"It doesn't matter. Look the only option we have is going down this thing," Garry said waving at the tunnel in front of them. "That seems the only way out."

"Or the only way in," whispered Glyn.

"What do you mean, or in?" Garry was now giving his brother one of his looks, which was wasted. Glyn was looking down the tunnel once again.

Did Glyn have a bottle of something on him? Garry wondered, and not for the first time tonight. Had he taken a gulp for courage back at the car, and now the whisky was taking its effect? Garry was a beer drinker, but beer had no effect of his brother, who called it vinegar. Spirits was his brother's preferred poison. But normally his breath stunk of the stuff, and apart from the normal gotten smell that emanated from his brothers mouth, tonight whisky wasn't part of it.

"I'm not to sure, I can't really say. But I feel like I belong somewhere down there, as if it's calling me." With that Glyn started to climb the couple steps into the mouth of the tunnel.

By the time Garry realized what he was doing, and started to climb after him, he was already a good distance down its length.

"Hey, wait up shit-breath, what are you trying to do, leave me behind?"

Glyn didn't respond. Rather he kept walking at the same automated pace.

Garry was about to grab his brother and spin him around to see what was going on. Then Garry noticed that the tunnel was getting lighter? "Hey is it me, or is it getting lighter in here?"

"I know," was all the answer his brother gave. He didn't stop walking or turn to address his brother but just kept going, until they walked around the corner and came to a dead end. All the walls of the tunnel were quite rugged with the same writing as on the floor in the main chamber, wrapping itself around the wall, over the ceiling and down across the floor then back up the wall. One continuous line swirling around and around down the tunnel, made up of millions of small, almost incoherent symbols all linked together.

The end wall was different, again perfectly smooth, almost like glass, not unlike the walls of the cavern they just left. But this wall didn't have any writing on it. It wasn't see-through but solid looking, and giving off the strange light that they had noticed. Garry stopped to look at this new development and wondered what they were going to do now? When he realized his brother hadn't stopped walking, but rather was heading directly towards the wall?

That's when it happened, before Garry could do anything about it, his brother walked right up to the wall, then straight through, as if it wasn't there. Then with nothing more than what could only be described as a ripple, Glyn simply disappeared?

9
Wheels Within Wheels

The Captain was now getting irate. "What do you mean you haven't had confirmation yet?" He was standing stock still, directly in front of the British army Lieutenant who had come out to meet them.

"Excuse me Sir, what type of aircraft was that?" The young officer asked as the phase II Blackbird hurtled down the runway; disappearing silently and gracefully into the night sky.

"Don't change the subject, Lieutenant; Lieutenant is it?" The Captain knew perfectly well that he was. He was the one now changing the subject, getting the Lieutenant away from questioning the transport they had arrived in.

"As I was saying, before you rudely interrupted me, what do you mean you have no confirmation of our inspection?" Carrying on before the young man could get his thoughts into gear. "That's not good enough Lieutenant..." The Captain paused, leaning forward waiting for the officer to give his name.

"Lieutenant Sir. Lieutenant Kerr Sir," the young officer said, coming to a ridged stance.

"I'm sorry Sir; nothing has come through explaining your visit. Sir." The young Lieutenant was now beginning to gain his composure. "If you would like to give me time to check the communications room, I'm sure the orders would be there waiting. Sir." He was about to turn around when.

"No time, no time." The Captain was now dressed in the uniform of a British Commander. All the others in his group were dressed as British army personal - done while on the plane trip over. They were now playing out a role of a British army inspection team.

"See what would be the point? We're supposed to surprise you, that's what we do." He had now given up his ridged stance; he now had his arm around the young Lieutenants Kerr's shoulder and was walking him towards the main control room.

"I can see you must be in charge at the moment. It's good that you ask all these questions and it will be going down in my report." They already knew that only the Lieutenant was going to be on duty at this time of night. The officer in overall charge would be tucked away in his nice warm bed by this hour. Their surveillance from the Special Forces clearance team - who got rid of all the loose ends in this area - informed them of these important facts.

"As I said it's just a routine base check, you wouldn't want to go dragging your supervising officer out of bed for something as insignificant as this would you?" The Captain came to a stop and looked the young office direct in the face, not moving a muscle. Until finally.

"Of course not Sir, I can deal with this," he answered giving his leg a nervous scratch. Only a few moments ago he had been sitting in his small office, watching porn on his portable DVD player. Going from watching a busty girl getting done from both ends, to having a male officer walk around with his arm across his shoulder was no comparison.

"Good. You're going to get a glowing report from me young man. The British army needs young officers like you, being able to take control of the situation such as this."

Then within a heart beat the Captain was giving orders to the men and woman he had brought with him. "Hopper, up into the main control room if you would be so kind. Flatfoot, make ready the gift. Brains, Doc and Babe get the transport sorted out, and get the area ready for departure."

The young Kerr seemed confused about what was going on, what with the commander using nicknames and the fact they needed transport?

"What.... What. Are you going somewhere? What are they doing over there?" The officer was starting to get confused about the whole situation.

Now they were in the hanger out of the way of the soldiers outside, three of the Captains team was going over the collection of military vehicles.

"Don't worry young man, all is under control. It will all be over before you know it," the Captain said walking the young officer over to, then through, one of the doors leading off into the main control room, which the Captain had memorized from the blue prints that had been given to him to study on the way over the North Atlantic ocean.

"What do you mean 'it will soon be over'?" Then the young man slumped to the floor. No noise, no mess, just a small powerful injection administered to the back of the neck.

The last thought of Lieutenant Kerr was - *someone was going to find out what he had been watching on his DVD player that still rested on his desk.*

It took less than twenty minutes to get the small base under their control. There were only eight guards on night duty. All were taken out within a matter of a few minutes, with a powerful projectile sleeping drug, the same that was given to the young Lieutenant. It also had an after effect of making the subject very groggy - like a very rough hangover, with them forgetting the last couple hour's worth of memory, but it would return gradually and they were planning on being long gone by then.

The sleeping quarters were flooded with another less potent sleeping drug, just to make sure none of them stirred. Hopper wiped all the reference to their aircraft landing of the main flightlog computers, as well as all their activity off the circuitry cameras. They had their videos overlapped to make it look like nothing out of the ordinary had happened. Also the vehicle register was changed so the transport of their choice no longer registered in the base files.

All this was necessary because of the time schedule. They needed to get to the site as quickly as possible. The Blackbird II was the only fast option available. The only problem with them being, that you can't parachute out of a plane moving that fast, and there was no guarantee that all the equipment would land in the same area. Besides the plane needed a longer runway, and a civilian runway was out of the question, bringing civilians into the equation made things more difficult and complicated. Plus, they needed a vehicle for this operation and one couldn't be fitted into the Blackbird, even the phase II had only so much space.

So their only other option was taking control of a small military base, which would have the equipment and landing strip they needed. This was one of two available at such short notice; they had picked the smaller of the two in the area. This one was slightly further away from the site than the other, but less of a risk in obtaining control over it.

The Captain looked around. "Good work men, all here and accounted for? All files are erased? All subjects are under control?" He looked down at his watch. "Just under twenty minutes, good work."

They were now in the all-terrain vehicle - along with an ample supply of fuel - on their way to the checkpoint, just over eighteen minutes away from their present location.

The truck was a new version of the classic 6x6 ten wheel drive 2.5 ton Cargo Truck, M35A. This one had a solid metal back covering, rather than the tarpaulin that joined into the front driver's position, making it open planed.

It was also fitted with a machine gun pedestal mounted from a roof hatch just behind the drivers section. This gave it a more M109 Shop/Command Van type appearance but with a lower integrated roof, with no windows. The Captain would have preferred the V-100 Commando Armored Car, which was parked next to it, but there simply wasn't room for all their equipment.

"Is the gift in position?" The Captain asked looking over to Flatfoot.

"Yes sir," Flatfoot said while looking down at his watch. "Should be starting anytime within the next ten or so minutes, Sir." He was referring to a small device, which had been left in the vehicle hanger next to the main control room.

"It won't go off before they start to wake. Will it?"

"No sir. Set to go off when they just start to stir, Captain."

"It should keep them busy for a while." They had left a small gadget that had started to release a powerful and untraceable chemical that can eat through almost all types of materials. It would start to mix with some of the barrels of fuel in the holding area, causing an almighty explosion, which would probably rip the roof of off the vehicle bay. Hiding any clues left behind to suggest anyone had been there. Later it would probably be put down to an electrical malfunction or storing chemicals in the wrong location.

Also it was a distraction to keep them from thinking about why they were all lying on the ground, just starting to come around from what seemed like a very deep sleep?

10
The Color Orange

Garry just stood there. His mind must be playing tricks on him because he would have sworn his brother just walked straight through the solid wall?

"Glyn.... Glyn." All he could do was shout. He wasn't sure what else he could do. He didn't want to take a step any closer to the wall than he had to. So he just stood there, staring at the smooth surface of the contoured rock. He needed a fag, but his fingers were trembling too much to try and roll one. He wished he had brought a pack of straights with him.

"Come on what you waiting for?" came a voice, he would swear originated from the other side of the barrier. Just then Glyn's face glided through, only his face nothing else. It looked like is had been sliced off and then hung there on its own. It was only the fact that it had an impatient look on it, and started talking again that Garry realized he wasn't going completely mad.

"Come on it's easy, it feels like diving into a pool of thick lukewarm water, a strange sensation but it doesn't hurt or anything." With that the face disappeared, leaving his brother in the tunnel, quiet and alone once again.

"Come on you won't believe what's on this side?" The voice sounded softer as if facing away in another direction.

Garry took a couple of steps closer until he was standing within arms length of the wall. He put his hand out as if to touch it. As his hand got closer he could feel a slight rise in the surface temperature. Then he put his hand through the wall as if it wasn't there. It felt strange, he could wiggle his fingers and his arm around, it felt just as Glyn had described it.

Until he tried to pull his arm out, he couldn't it was stuck fast. Even though he could move it from side to side, up and down, any way except out. He was starting to panic and was about to shout for his brother, when a hand appeared out of the wall, grabbed him by the arm and unceremoniously pulled him through.

Garry spat out a mouthful of dirt. "What the hell you go and do that for?" He asked grumpily, while slowly climbing to his feet, while brushing dirt off his faded jeans.

"Well it will be dark by the time you ambled through," came Glyn's voice off to one side.

"What do you mean, it will soon be dark? It's the middle of the night." He then realized it was light, not artificial light, but sunlight. Even though it was a sort of dull colorless light, it was still daylight.

Looking up he noticed they were outside, in what looked like a clearing with a line of trees possibly twenty or thirty foot away. Looking behind him for the first time was what could only be described as a wall, just a wall. It looked the same from this side as it did from the other, plain and smooth with a dull glassy look about it. But on this side it wasn't at the end of a tunnel. Rather it was on a large mound. The large mound being possibly thirty or forty foot high and from this side the wall looked almost twice the size as it did when they came through it.

Then he noticed the towering metal dragons forced into the ground and curved up around the arch of the gateway. Standing so close he could see the indents from the hammers that had molded the dull black metal into its fearsome shapes.

Looking straight up he could see the dull light reflecting off the strange symbol resting between the dragons' foreheads. Above them rested the edge of the vast black iron bowl.

Nothing grew on the mound. Come to think of it nothing grew around it until you got to the tree line, not even weeds, just dirty looking soil. But that wasn't the most alarming thing about it. Rather more disturbing was the spiraling mass of orangey gray cloud that was billowing out from the top of the bowl, lazily spiraling up into the sky. This seemed to then mingle with the layer that was hanging over all the sky already - this also was a dull orange color.

But most disquieting of all was the bones and skulls that randomly littered the ground around the mound. Possibly once piled into high stacks, now having been scattered; dragged around by scavenging animals.

"What? Where are we?" Garry asked, while staring at his brother, who was looking over too a large hill in the far distance, which had towering ominous dark mountains behind. "Glyn, ay ass-hole." His brother was still ignoring him. "Come on what's going on? This is defiantly freaking me out now," he said as he grabbed Glyn's arm and spun him around to get his full attention.

But as his brother turned he noticed something different about him. Everything was strange, his stance, the way he held himself. Most of all his eyes, they were now shining bright orange like beacon lights.

11
The Ripple

They waited almost two hours before they finally opened the large wooden gates, to send runners out to fetch the bodies. Now instead of one body they had four. Three unbelievably had survived the onslaught of the Spitters, as they were aptly named. They were brought into the safety of the village, surrounded by the protective wall. It would take many weeks for them to be healed. For they needed all their combined energy to keep the protective wall sustained throughout the day and especially the night.

They had let this place get the better of them only once. That was all it needed to teach them a hard lesson.

Once, when a hunting party was returning from the valley below, they got almost to the point the people this morning reached, when they had been attacked by a hunting party of Lanks, maybe eight or nine of them? It was hard to count their numbers because of the speed they can move over short distances, making them seem like a blur of leathery skin.

They attacked the group of four tired travelers, running swiftly over the distance from the woods, to the left of the village; quite a distance, but not so for the Lanks, they had reached the hunting party perhaps a hundred foot or so from the safety of the protective walls. Cries were being shouted throughout the village as to what to do? The order was given to drop the power being held over the wall and for everyone to use their individual powers to help the four now running towards them for their lives.

They started hurling spears, helped along by a burst of magic, pushing it that much faster and towards the creatures' pumping heart. Others used their power to churn up the ground, small stones and leaves, whatever was lying around, gouging chunks of the earth up and spraying it across the paths of the charging Lanks. Others – the more powerful - were literally picking up the Lanks with their minds and hurling the bodies at the ground with bone crushing force.

That when they realized what they had done. By taking the power in themselves they had left the walls unprotected. The rest of the Lanks were now surging into the village from the other side of the hill, jumping the wall from behind, while all the attention was being held by the fight out front. A group of around seventeen more Lanks were now over the back wall and attacking the women and children, as well as the men who hadn't got to the fray at the front yet.

It was all just an elaborate scam to get them to drop their defenses for just a moment. It had worked. Forty-one was left dead, sixteen badly injured; four seriously, three of them died that same night.

They had learned the hard way. Now no matter what happens on the other side of the fence they never let their guard down, never releasing the magic sustaining the fortification.

That's why they had left it so long before going out to retrieve the bodies, just in case there was more hiding away, ready to attack. Dead was dead, their companions were going nowhere. As callus as it sounded, they still had the living to worry about.

They had the three in the healing hut, ministering to them making them as comfy as possible, so they could heal themselves fully, or to die, whatever was their fate. Some friends and family would pray for them to live, others for them to give up the fight so they could have peaceful eternal rest. Fathers would have tears in their eyes because their son had passed away, and because they were still left behind.

That's when it was felt. A ripple surged through the ground, like the same sort of effect as someone throwing a large stone in to a pond. The ground moved under their feet, shifting, rising then falling again. They could actually see the ripple running along the straw covered floor, first a large ripple, then all the others after in slowing becoming smaller and smaller, making straw billow up into the air. It had the effect of making everything flat, for only a split second everything lost shape and texture; everything turned two dimensional, having no substance, until suddenly everything reverted back to the way it was before - as if nothing untoward had happened.

Coben Hathanen, the leader of the village, walked briskly from his small round hut. Like everyone else in the village he had felt the wave running through the ground. He was a tall man, in his early fifties, his skin as black as the night, so black it was almost blue like a raven's wing. He had arrived here many years ago, and was perhaps the most powerful among those in the village. But that's not why he was the leader; he was the leader because he was an intelligent man, and a compassionate man. A man who knew what lengths he had to go to in order to defend all those under his care. He never shrank back from that responsibility, whatever the cost.

Coben started to sing a Kwa chant under his breath: "*Who are we looking for. Who are we looking for? It's Equiano we're looking for. Has he gone to the stream? Let him come back. Has he gone to the farm? Let him return. It's Equiano we're looking for.*"

Raven, the young man besides him, had heard the song many times before. He knew Hathanen was African, had come through the very same Gateway he had. The song was about a young eleven year old, a son of a tribal chieftain, who had been kidnapped in 1755 and sold in to the slave trade along with ten to twelve million other Africans.

Raven also knew that Coben had been in a resistance group fighting the slave traders, after escaping from a Death March, which was a walk of over a thousand kilometers to the closest coastline, were they would then be hustled aboard ships like cattle, chained together; then sold in the New World to harvest crops.

After his escape Coben had then been a leading figure in the resistance in trying to destroy the coasts sixty slave trading posts. But upon hearing word that his family were hiding in a village that was about to be attacked he traveled to rescue them. It was a trap. Few survived, Coben being one of them. His family had been slaughtered like animals. He went in to hiding after becoming grief stricken. He found a deep cave in an area between the City of Kigoma and Ujiji, which were only mud villages when he knew them.

"Raven, did you see where that originated from?" Coben asked standing beside the young man, after climbing up the ladder to the rickety southern watchtower.

"Yes, it appeared to originate from the vicinity of the closest Gateway," Raven said pointing towards the nearest pillar of smoke that was rising up into the churning cloud covered sky.

"Just as I thought." Coben just stood there and looked out facing the desolate land. The entire village stood around the base of the wooden tower. Some were looking out over the landscape, others up at their leader. None were speaking; all remained silent letting their leader think.

Coben stood rigid, his fingers softly playing over a colorful carved jade stone amulet that he wore around his throat - the one he had taken from his wife's butchered body; the sort that the chieftain's wife wore. He tucked it back under his clothing. He had changed the threadbare string many times, because it was hundreds of years old.

"Raven, you and Lake go to the closest Gateway and see what is transpiring there." That was it. He started to climb down the ladder and to make his way back to his hut. No one questioned his orders. People started to go back to their own huts, others started to make ready the twos provisions.

Lake made her way to her own hut to get herself ready. Lake was twenty-six, with slim build, mouse colored hair, and just above average height. She could run at tremendous speed. Her ability or 'gift', as some called it, was being able to confuse the minds of others; if you weren't looking for her you wouldn't see her. She had been on many such missions, checking out different areas for Coben. Most of the time he gave no explanation for these trips, but all the trips became obvious once they got to the given location. Not once had they been sent out on a wild goose chase.

Raven was already at the meeting point when Lake arrived.

Raven at Twenty-three was also a great runner; his stamina was the same as Lake's, that's why they almost always got to go on scouting parties together; complementing each other. He was quite short, not as tall as Lake, but more muscular. His 'gift' was being able to make himself almost weightless; being able to jump great distances, flying across ravines. He could quickly disappear into the branches of a soaring tree within a couple of leaps.

There wasn't any great send off. Once they were both there, they picked up the small bags of provisions and slung them onto their backs. Both then looked at Coben who was standing off to one side. Coben gave the order for the gate to be opened. They both nodded towards him, and then they were gone, bounding through the gate, charging down the steep hillside. Within only moments they were out of sight of the watchman on the tower. The gate was pulled shut again. Then the village went about as if nothing had happened. Maybe in a few hours they would return. Maybe it was the last they had seen of them? Only time would tell.

Garry was concerned for his brother he wasn't himself. His body language was all-wrong as if he wasn't in control. At first when they came through the Gateway his eyes had a slight orange tinge to them, now they were glowing with an inner power, the light radiating out of them was almost blinding. He kept walking back towards the Gateway then away again as if there was an inner struggle going on.

Garry went to grab him at one stage to give him a shake to try and wake him from his ramblings, muttering to himself in a strange tongue, but when he touched him he received a static shock, not powerful, but strong enough to make it unpleasant, and not to want to do it again.

Then in one split second Glyn was not so much as falling to the ground, but more like pulled. His body fell quicker than it should have, hitting with a soft thud. He lay totally motionless, his body perfectly still, no more mumbling under his breath, it didn't even look like he was breathing.

Garry forgot all about the shock he had just received, and was quickly at his brother's side, kneeling down, checking on his pulse. He let out his breath not realizing he was holding it in. There was a pulse, a very slow one, too slow. He wasn't a doctor but he knew a pulse of any kind was better than none. He rocked back on his thighs and let out a long breath. What was he to do?

His brother lay unconscious on the ground in a strange; what could only be described as different – alien - world. They had no food or water. He hadn't the faintest idea as to what he was going to do next.

He checked for what seemed like the tenth time that his brother still had a pulse. Then he got back up to his feet, which were unsteady due to the pins-and-needles running through them. He stumbled to the side before he caught his balance, stretching his hand out to steady himself. His only plan was to get his brother back through the Gateway, take him to the large chamber, and wait. The National Trust, college or whoever the people were would be there in the early hours of the morning. Any place was better than this. It was too quiet here, he had heard no birds no small animals, no noises whatsoever. That was the scariest thing about this place, the silence. All he wanted to do was go back.

That's when he realized what he was leaning up against when he had stopped himself from falling. His out stretched hand was resting on the wall, the very part of the Gateway he had only moments ago walked through as if it wasn't there. Now it was as hard as any wall he had ever touched.

This couldn't be happening. Not again, the way back had been blocked from the first door they had walked through in to that strange chamber. Now they were blocked from returning through this one. But hadn't his brother put his head back through? Put his arm through and grabbed him? There must only be one particular way back, only one section of the wall. He started to feel around the surface, but to no avail they were truly trapped in whatever place this was.

Garry let out a long string of obscenities at the top of his lungs. He then came to rest back on the ground next to his brother. He tried to get some sort of reaction out of him. He was now resorting to quite rough jabs of the fingers to the rib cage, something his brother couldn't stand when conscious. But still to no avail.

That's when he heard it, a loud sound ringing through the silence of the still air. Quickly recovering from complete shock, he jumped to his feet. No pins-and-needles now; a mass of adrenaline was surging through his veins, washing them away.

Charging towards them from the trees were four Lanks.

Garry was at a complete loss. One minute trying to work out what to do, the next four what could only be described as upright lizards, running on their strong powerful rear legs, and their long whip like tails thrashing about behind them. They were also carrying a collection of weapons, which they were holding over their head, ready to deliver a deathblow.

What could he do? Run. Run where? What would he do with Glyn? He couldn't leave him here! Then again he wouldn't be able to carry him either! He pulled the eight-inch blade out from inside his jacket and held on to it tight.

No one ever believes they would be in a life threatening situation, but everyone daydreams about how they would handle such an event. Fighting heroically and fearlessly, defending against hordes of attackers. But when a situation arrives the body goes numb, the brain closes down. Which Garry now found to be true, he was now at a complete loss. So he just knelt down and wrapped his arms around his brother in a comforting embrace and waited with his eyes shut. If he was lucky it would be over quickly.

He just wished he could wake up from whatever nightmare this was.

12
The Monitors of Death

They were now ten minutes drive away from Whitchurch, which sat on Dartmoors fringes, near Tavistock. They were slowly approaching the house from the east side, coming to a stop before the first fence. The vehicle could have easily punched its way through the rickety barrier, but this one was out looking on to the road. A broken fence would alert people to the fact that someone had gained entry. They didn't want some over zealous local to pass, see the fence and call the police out to investigate. The last thing they needed was an interfering local police officer getting in the way.

As he was thinking that, the noise of a small car could be heard approaching from around the bend in the narrow road. Everyone stood watching as this small green vehicle approached, and then started to slow down, pulling up next to the Captain after passing the large army truck. The passenger's window wound down and the Captain leaned down forward in to the car.

"What's the problem? Has your truck broken down son?"

Looking in he saw whom the voice belonged to; a little old man, who was just able to see over the steering wheel, was turned to one side looking at him. The old man pushed his bifocal glasses back up the bridge of his nose with his nicotine stained fingers. Ash was sprinkled all over his brown corduroy trousers. His green cardigan was way too big for him, as if he had shriveled up over the years and hadn't yet had time to replace his wardrobe.

"No Sir. We have a much different problem." The Captain looked over his shoulder at Doc who was just pulling out another syringe from a small plastic case on his arm. The Captain slowly nodded no.

"There was a breakout up at the prison sir," he said looking back at the old man once again.

"You mean up at Dartmoor Prison, the big one in Princetown?" The old mans hands tightened on the steering wheel. His old skin stretched over his white knuckles all his veins standing out like an old road map. "I've heard nothing on the radio son?"

"Only a low risk inmate. About to be transferred to an even lower risk facility," he answered casually. Trying to make out this happened all the time.

"Oh dear..." The old man looked around at the countryside as if the prisoner was standing on the other side of the road.

"Nothing to worry about sir, that's what we are here for. Best if you keep your windows done right up, and all your doors locked until you get home sir. Not that he's dangerous," he said leaning in to the car window a bit further. "Not in the slightest, but better safe than sorry." With that the Captain stood and turned as if to say, *conversation over, be on your way.*

"Thank you sonny," with that he wound up his window. The noise of the doors clicking shut could be heard. Then the car drove off into the distance at a slightly faster pace.

With that over and out of the way, Brains reversed the vehicle to give Flatfoot and Babe space to kick and loosen the main support for the fence section, which they were about to pass through. The truck blocked what they were doing from any other passers by.

Once it had started to rock in its foundations, Flatfoot pulled a small device out of one of his many pockets on the side of his jacket; it was about the size of a wallet, upon clipping and punching certain areas of the device a small round blade shot out the end, protruding about three inches. Reaching into a pocket under the one he just removed the cutter from; he removed a cable, connected it to the bottom of the cutter and released the rest, he then popped open his thigh pocket and joined the wire to a connection on a black flat pack; a lithium battery. The blade sprang to life making a slight swirling sound as it revolved. Then he proceeded in cutting the other two fence panels away from the loose one.

Within only a couple of minutes they were driving through the hole. Then the panel was lowered back into the ground. They raked the earth around with their fingers to get rid of the tell tail signs of sawdust caused by the cutter. Both then jumped over the fence and into the back of the all-terrain six-wheeler truck and were off again.

There were another three fences on the way to the house. The next was barbed wire. It needed clipping, the loose wire pulled to the sides so the truck could run through. The other two were just wooden, like the first fence. Unlike the first these were approached slowly, the bumper resting against the fence. Pushing with the powerful engine and the large tired grip, the fence fell slowly and in a controlled manner to the ground, with the vehicle then simply driving over the top, the wood buckled and splintered under the machines weight.

The truck came to a rumbling stop in front of the large impressive main door. They all exited one at a time. Some closing the doors, others rested their heads on their hands, just staring at the door that lay in front of them. It was an impressive sight, almost twenty feet high and about ten feet in diameter, looking like an army could churn out of it any minute. It was an ominous and powerfully fear inspiring image.

The Captain stood directly in front of it. Removing the black glove from his hand, he then began to run it over the surface of the door, feeling the texture, the power. "Brains if you would be so kind."

Brains came to stand beside him. With the others still standing back alongside the vehicle. All had been debriefed about what to expect; about the door and the general look of the place. Mainly from Peterson's description, but also from the one they had already uncovered in Kigoma, Africa. But that one was hundreds of feet under the ground and completely incased in rock. The one that lay before them had taken on the appearance of a large house, and a strange deformed one at that.

Brains started to fish through the pouch on the side of his trousers, removed a piece of flexible pipe, which he rested on the ground. Swinging the black pack off his back, he started to unzip it pulling out a piece of equipment about the size of a small hand held T.V, which was more-or-less what it was. He started to screw the flexible pipe into the end of the small monitor. Pulling a few other parts from his bag he attached these also. Finally he held in his hands a complete all-purpose viewing device, with a long cable on the end, with a small fiber optic camera attached. This could be inserted into the small crevice and view what lay on the other side.

The door was way too thick to drill through, and they weren't sure how it would react.

Flatfoot now came to take his position beside his brother. In his hand was a small yellow canister. Unscrewing it he knelt on the mud packed ground on one knee and turned his body to one side so his nose was pointing the other way. Then he began pouring a small amount on the ground in front of the door, on to the stone supports, where a small plume of black pungent smoke began to rise in to the air. Once it had cleared a small hole was visible in the flagstone flooring that ran the length of the door. Then pouring the rest into the hole he watched it eat its way underneath. Once the smoke had cleared a gap of a few centimeters deep had burned through the stone rather than the wood. There was now enough room to push the camera through, after water had been poured down to clear the way.

The camera was pushed beneath the door, when it became loose on the other end he knew that it had passed completely under. But the screen only showed static. He fiddled with a few buttons on the front of the device, and wiggled the attaching wire. Still to no avail the screen was still inert.

The Captain tapped Brains on the shoulder. "Boost the power," Brains had forgotten he was standing so close, looking over his shoulder.

Brains got to his feet and walked around to the back of the truck. Opening the rear door he removed a small black generator and the box next to it. Returning to the house he placed them both on the ground and started getting the generator up and running. It was a small compressed standard military generator with enough power to run a small field base, with a battery pack with enough juice for just over sixteen hours continuous use. It was connected to a transformer, which was in the other box. He didn't want that much power blowing all the circuits that were on the small delicate surveillance apparatus.

Once they were joined together and running as close to speck as he could get it, he once again turned on the small monitor. First it was the same as before - just static. But this time when he started fine tuning it a picture started to form; hazy at first but then slowly clearing, not to a perfect picture, it was still grainy and lines running horizontally along it, but a picture all the same.

"Captain. Sir, a moment please. I think you will want to see this."

The Captain had moved back and was taking a general look around at the door and surrounding house. He had no idea that Brains would have it up and running so quickly. He came and stood behind him once again, looking over his shoulder, peering down at the small screen. Now he also couldn't believe what he was seeing.

Rather than just the other side of the door they were seeing the other dimension: another world that was through the Gateway itself. The Captain was expecting this that's why when the camera didn't work to start with, he had told Brains to get more power running through it. The picture had to travel a long way. In reality the wire was only four foot long. In real space it was connecting the two worlds. But that wasn't what was catching their attention; it was the two bodies lying on the ground, one hugging the other, with the four creatures charging towards them with weapons raised above their heads.

"OPEN THIS DOOR NOW," the Captain was shouting at everyone in general. "Brains the door, now." The Captain stood back as if waiting for Brains to simply reach up and turn the non-existent handle to open their way.

"But Sir, the proper way to open it will still take me almost an hour to set up, with all the equipment," Brains said while still staring in to the monitor, at the creatures that were within twenty foot of the young men.

"Flatfoot blow the door. Now!" He knew there was nothing any of them could do. Deep down he already knew the answers they would give, and knew that if he ordered them again they would do as he asked. But he was just snatching at straws. There was nothing worse than watching somebody die, and knowing there isn't a dam thing you could do about it. The face of his small beautiful child filled his vision, as he remembers clutching his youngest to his soaked chest.

"Sir setting a control explosion of would take twenty minutes to set up alone, and would let everyone within a couple of kilometer know we are here. That's if it would have any effect at all," Flatfoot said, looking around at everyone with pleading eyes, sweat glistening from off his shaven head.

They all stood around Brains as he hunched over the camera. All were staring at the sight that lay before them. All knowing there was no way of reaching them in time. All having already seen far too much death in their lives, and in one way having become so accustom to it.

"What the hell are they doing there? How did they get through?" But no one was listening to the Captain; he was now just venting frustration. All eyes were transfixed on the monitor – watching, waiting. They were about to witness the young men's impending death. There being nothing they could do to help them, except watch in morbid fascination.

13
Unleash the Power

Garry had his eyes shut tight against what he knew was about to happen. But then his hands started to vibrate and tingle. Opening his eyes he looked down at his brothers' body, which was starting to move. But not the movement of a waking person, but rather his body was starting to levitate up off the ground, slowly rising skywards. He now completely let go and moved backwards on his knees away from the body, which was now a good five foot off of the ground. Spark's started to jump from the dark earth to his brother's limp torso, becoming more intense. The body was now completely covered in what could only be described as electricity, racing up and down Glyn in a fierce show of power.

The Lanks, being either intent on their attack and not noticing, or just not caring continued onwards unstoppable at an amazing neck breaking turn of speed.

That's when it occurred.

A large ark of electricity; ashen in color, flared out of Glyn's body, emerging upwards into the shape of a dome covering him completely; in one split second it raced outwards in an increasing circle, growing with every second. It hit the Lanks head on. Not just stopping them dead; in a bone crushing slam, but yanking them through the air, throwing them backwards at an alarming velocity. As their bodies flew through the air they shook uncontrollably in fits and spasms, the noise of tendons snapping could be heard over the top of the phenomenal crackling electrical power, which was being unleashed.

The ark of power suddenly stopped as fast as it started. Glyn's body fell back to the ground with a soft thud. Garry reopened his eyes. The sheer light given off was blinding, as he rubbed them he started to look around. His brother lay back in the same spot as if nothing had happened. If it weren't for the ground around him steaming, he wouldn't have believed it himself. Where the cocoon had finished - around the edge of the powerful ring - the ground had a deep grove burned into the very earth. The tall standing stones had now been scorched and blackened. The metal dragons were still steaming as small electrical bursts randomly ran along their surface. A few banners still smoked. The skeletal remains around the gateway were now charcoal in color.

The four Lanks lay in a jumble of body parts, their appendages were sticking out in all directions, with steam rising off of them. Pools of sticky looking liquid were starting to gather around the still blubbering, crackling bodies.

Garry slowly got to his feet, and stood over his brother staring down at him. His senses still in a state of shock, not being able to fully comprehend what had just happened. He then turned and walked over to the creatures that lay on the ground in a smoldering heap. As he got closer the smell was almost unbearable. But his curiosity was stronger than his sense of smell, so he carried on forward, coming to stand as close as possible without getting any bodily fluids on his brown trainers.

They were well and truly cooked, was the only word he could think of to describe what had happened to them. Their skin was all stretched and dried. Bones stuck out in some areas, this looking all-brittle. Their mouths were wide open, stretched from their final screams of pain. Their tongues hanging out the side, all blistered, still bubbling, with liquid running off of them. The most depressing sight though was the black holes where their eyes once belonged. Now only empty sockets where the pure power running through them had made their eyes boil and pop, what remained were just the black staring orbits that were still smoldering.

What were they? It was now hard to really tell. He had seen them running towards him, but they were just a blur. They were obviously part intelligent, for they had made and wore clothes, and were wielding hand made weapons. These were still all intact. The blinding force had not affected them in any way. Some weapons had been dropped, others were still held in their mummified hands, now dried like concrete.

That's when he felt their presence. Similar to when you are walking down the street and you can feel someone looking at you, as you turn you see them just looking away. But when he turned around they were still nearby. Two people just stood there, just out of the covering of the trees; one young man and a woman both staring across towards him and the creatures at his feet.

He wasn't sure what to do. They had weapons in their hands, only small, but still lethal daggers, both holding one in each hand. They hadn't moved towards him or retreated back into the bush; they just stood motionless. Maybe they had witnessed the sight only moments before, and were now being wary. At least they weren't attacking; he didn't think his eyes could hold up to another assault like the last.

They started slowly moving towards him, still cautiously at first, and then picking up speed as they came closer. Garry moved back towards his brother just incase. He walked around the side of his brother and knelt down, still being able to see the two strangers walking across the clearing. He also had one of the long spears in his grasp that he had taken from one of the bodies.

They came to a stop next to the fried bodies on the ground. The woman kicked out with a leather ankle boot, hitting one in the knee, which then disconnected from the joint and fell to the ground in a wisp of smoke and dust motes. They then started to confer in an undertone that he couldn't quite make out from where he was. The woman looked over at them both as if to check they were still there. She turned and started to walk towards them, still with the deadly looking knives, one in each hand.

His hands slightly raised the spear.

"What nationality are you?" Long gaze. "DO...YOU... UNDERSTAND...WHAT...I..."

"You don't have to shout I'm not deaf or stupid," Garry answered, his hands now wrapped tightly around the spear, as he moved it back and forth between the two newcomers.

"Then why didn't you let us know this when we approached you from the clearing?" She was now only a couple of footsteps away from them, the spear inches from her chin. But her hands, that held the knives, lay limply down at her sides.

"No offense but we just arrived here on the second class fight. Already we've been attacked by some friends of yours," Garry said pointing behind her with the head of the spear.

She turned and looked around as if she had forgotten what she had just walked passed. On looking back at him she said, "They are no friends of ours. They are, for your information, called Lanks. Get use to the sight of them for you will be seeing a lot of them from now on." She now slid the knives back into their sheaths on her thighs, and knelt down next to his brother, after pushing the spear away from her general direction.

"How long has he been like this? Since you came through, or after the little fire work show?" She was pressing her hand on his forehead.

"He went like that just after coming through the wall here," he said pointing his thumb over his shoulder.

"So it was you who killed the Lanks? Impressive. You will become powerful once trained correctly." She was now removing a bottle from a pouch on her belt with her long delicate fingers. The bottle reminded Garry of Poppers, a strong smelling chemical that he and his bother sniffed when drunk, which made almost anything seem funny; it gave you a mad head-rush and feel very high for about two minutes before returning to normal.

"I didn't do this, my brother did."

"You are mistaken. One can only defend ones self if you're contuse to be able to channel the Life Force." She then opened the bottle and started moving it back and forth under Glyn's nose, but to no avail he didn't as much as stir. "That's unusual, this usually works. We have stronger at the village." She clipped the lid back on and got back to her feet.

"What were you trying to do?" Garry asked looking at the pouch she had just put the bottle back into.

She motioned to the bottle. "This usually brings them around; it's simply a collection of herbs and minerals. Some, when they come through the Gateway, can't take the shock to their system, so they pass out. But he's gone in to too deep a trance for this to work. We will take him to the village and leave him in the hands of the healers." She had now turned around and was signaling to the young man, who was by all accounts keeping watch from the limb of a tall lanky tree. Garry hadn't even seen him leave. Then in one supernatural bound the young man jumped the forty foot distance to the ground in one leap, and then sprinted across to stand next to the young woman.

She removed two metal poles about a foot in length each from the mans pack, then a rolled up ball of dark green coarse cloth, flipping the ball it unwound into a length of fabric about six foot in length and two wide, with little channels running down the each side. Then by squeezing the pipes in the middle the ends shot out to reveal eight-foot long poles that were telescopically bundled together. These were pushed through the channels on the sides of the fabric to complete the stretcher. They then placed the stretcher on the ground next to Glyn's body and lifted him across onto it.

Garry wondered were the materials for the stretcher had come from, it looked military. He didn't realize that the American government had sent thousands of probes through the other first Gateway that they had found. Once the final probe had been sent through, with explosives on, the explosion had drawn some hunter's attention. They found piles of charred metal and material - some still useful. Everything that could be reused was shipped to the village, where it was then fashioned in to useful equipment. The material for Lakes top had come from a weather balloon. The metal for their knives had been beaten and fashioned from the casing of a droid meant to read soil samples.

"You grab the rear, I'll lead the way. Raven will keep watch as we walk." With that she lifted her end of the stretcher and stood there waiting for Garry to lift his end off of the ground.

"What's going on? Where are we? Why -"

"Look. I know you have a hundred and one questions burning to get off your chest, I will try my best to answer what I can, but we need to keep moving." She nodded her head towards the Lanks. "More will be on their way any minute. Or worse. We have to get to the village before the light starts to fail." She looked skyward towards the swirling mass of boiling pewter clouds above. "We should have at least two, possible two and a half hours of travel left in the sky, so we better get moving. The village is not far, but there is much that can happen to delay us."

Garry picked up his end of the stretcher. Then without saying another word they started moving off in to the direction of the hills in the distance; with Lake taking the lead and with Raven running on ahead to check the way was clear, his head snapping back and forth trying to see everything at once.

Garry was sure they were being watched: not so much from roving eyes but from the very ground itself; as if this whole place was aware of them being here.

When they had entered the trees he realized just how desolate this place was. No animals running for cover. No birds flapping from tree to tree. No leaves rustling as animals foraged in the undergrowth. There was nothing. All was quiet. If it wasn't for meeting these two strangers - and seeing all the skeletons at the Gateway - he would have sworn this world was desolate.

That was until it something flew through the trees from their left, without any warning or noise. It flew straight towards them; diving straight for Glyn's comatose body.

14
Move the Writing

All six were gathered around the small monitor, looking at the sight before them. In the distance four creatures were running at full speed toward the two people huddled on the ground.

Then something peculiar happened.

One of the young men leaned back, while the other started to rise slowly in the air. There was some sort of activity from the ground beneath him; bolts started to bounce back and forth from the ground to the body. Then the monitor died, the screen went blank not even any static, with a small plume of smoke trailing out the monitors casing.

There was silence for a few moments while they all gathered their thoughts together. The Captain was the first to talk. "Brains make ready the equipment, get this door opened. I want some answers to a few questions, and the only way to get them is from that side," the Captain said slamming his hand on the door. He then walked away and started to unload some of the equipment they had brought with them all the way from Base Bravo.

The Doc was checking his supplies incase there was a patient waiting for him on the other side of the door. Babe was helping Brains set up the apparatus. In the meantime Flatfoot and Hopper checked out the rear of the building. Soon they were back; bring news of another door around the back, which was similar to, but smaller than the one they were trying to open now.

"That ones okay don't touch it or interfere with it, that's the one the scientists are interested in. It's no concern of ours; it leads only to the Gathering Area. This is the only door we need to worry ourselves with." That was it. They were all trained to well to question his decision, especially after the little episode moments before, so they both went to help the others get the device set up.

After seventeen months of studying the scientist at the Kigoma, Tanzania site had come to unlock the secrets that the door held: it was operated by electrical discharges. In some cases with the smaller of the two doors, the discharge off of a human body could open it. But the larger one would need quite a boost to get it to *swing* open. Once it was open whatever passed through couldn't be retrieved, they had lost untold hundreds upon hundreds or research machinery and probes. But all sent back particular amounts of visual and biological readings, all to piece together the secrets that lay on the other side.

The whole site was sectioned off from the surrounding area. Nine foot thick and twenty foot high concrete walls, with high watchtowers and turrets, fitted with Heckler and Koch machine guns with 40mm rounds. Also four M2A2 Bradley Linebacker vehicles with Stinger launchers patrolled around its parameter incase anything airworthy - biological or mechanical came through the Gateway. These were also accompanied by four M1A2 Abrams tanks. And all were there for the so-called protection of the scientists inside from the rebel gorilla group's active in the mountain passes of Kigoma, even though the Tanzania authorities said the area had been politically stable for many years. But they were there to stop whatever might come out of the Gateway.

Once the Gateway had been opened from this side the American private group, so called The Trust, became a paranoid organization and had almost every conceivable type of firepower heard of. The main door had a heavy four foot thick titanium bombproof barrier that could be lowered down over the Gate once it was open in case of problems. There were four large automated mounted FN Herstal's .50 cal. M3M machine guns on large arms that would swing in to place if the need arose. Also, two hundred Special Forces soldiers were on hand, with one hundred on duty at any one time, patrolling the area inside and out of the so-called Mineral Research base.

Then the nightmare happened.

It was a normal routine day while sending through yet another droid, which would inflate a large balloon once it got to the other side then releasing it into the sky, where it would then take readings from the lower Troposphere and Stratosphere. This was the twenty-second to do such readings, but research was what they were there for and money wasn't a problem. They could send a thousand through to read the weather if they wanted to, as long as they got results. But when the machine passed through the connection was instantly lost. They couldn't explain it. Every single one they had sent through so far gave perfect readings. They were just putting it down to a faulty droid when they entered.

Later once the digital video footage was reviewed they realized there were ten Lanks and two Moregones; the Lanks bigger cousins. The Lanks with their speed quickly fanned out attacking anyone in their path, swinging their razor sharp weapons in deadly arcs. As for the much larger Moregone it started to smash up machinery with its powerful calloused fists. There would of been two causing destruction if it wasn't for the fast reflexes of one scientist, who smacked the button to release the three tons of heavy shielded door, which proceeded to drop crushing one of the slower Moregones and two of the Lanks.

All had become too relaxed over the almost twenty mouths of study. Because even though it was all kept up and running they had become complacent, even through it was still run as a military operation. But because they hadn't come up against any opposition before, then they weren't expecting to. If anything they believed the world to be void of any forms of larger life, never once seeing any creatures apart from insects and an abundance of plant life. They believed it was in the first stages of an ecosystem and that the larger animals hadn't come along yet.

Also the very fact that they couldn't retrieve anything made them believe the door could only go one way. They had a shock when they came through. Tens of millions of dollars worth of equipment had been destroyed. Twenty-nine scientists lost their lives, along with all eight of the soldiers in the large room where the Gate was situated.

The four large automated FN Herstal's .50 cal. machine guns quickly took out the Moregone, because of its slow reflexes; the Lanks because of their speed and agility were harder to take down. Most of the damage though wasn't done by the one Moregone or by the Lanks, but rather by the automated .50 cal. guns as they tried to track the fast moving creatures. Seventeen of the scientists, plus three of the soldiers was gunned down by so-called *friendly* fire.

It was put down to a pocket of gas that was disturbed from the drilling for the minerals, it supposedly leaked into the research room full of scientists and military; who were helping with the complex machinery. All in the room collapsed due to the gases, which had a dissolving affect on the flesh. So when all the bodies were transported back to there particular countries they wouldn't be opened and the truth found out. Large red biohazard stickers adorned each metal air sealed coffin.

The room was shut down for almost three weeks while new machinery and different guns could be fitted. The guns had tracer put on them, all working in the room had tags hung around their neck so the computer could tell the difference between them and the intruders, and not just follow a target regardless of anything getting in the way.

But as soon as they opened the door again they were attacked the second time. This time only two Lanks got through, both were caught by large nets that were raised from beneath, the nets then gave off a powerful burst of electricity knocking the Lanks out. They were then placed into two separate cages, which were built after the first attack. The blast door was quickly lowered stopping any more from entering. But now they had two live creatures. The ones that got through before were slightly worse for wear after being pumped full of thousands of .50 cal. bullets; in some cases completely obliterating the subject that was hit, leaving only parts of the animals intact, but very much dead. There were a lot of DNA samples, almost everywhere, particularly on the metal walls.

That was until the scientist working on the other part of the Gateway worked out what it was the large room done. What the secret of the swirling writing in the middle of the room meant. What the substance coming out the top of the seven pillars was, and what implications it had.

The Gateway was then ordered to be shut down. The Gateway was opened one more time; briefly, to release a small robot packed with C4 explosives to block the entrance from the other side. For they had found the room operated without the Gateways involvement. That even though they both went to the same place they both operated independently of each other. The Gateway was too much of a risk to remain open.

But thing's didn't go quite the way they planned it. The robot did get through safely, but the charges must have been placed in the wrong location. Once the explosion went off it didn't only stop the Gateway from working, but part of the circle on top of the mound - where the cloud developed from - must have been damaged. As soon as the Gateway was shut down the room almost stopped producing the swirling mass of orangey cloud. It was now down to an almost trickle. That wasn't good enough for what the Trust wanted to use it for. So when the next Gateway was found there was to be a group of people sent through to shut the other side down properly, to make sure the ring on top of the mound wasn't damaged.

The equipment was now all set in place. The vehicle was repacked. All were in position ready to start the machine. Doc, Babe, and Flatfoot took up flanking positions ready for the off chance that something would come through. The Captain was in the truck sat behind the FN Herstal's M3M machine gun, which stuck out the top just behind the driver's position, and it was loaded pulled and ready to rumble – with its large wide .50 cal. bullets strapped together in a long metallic snake, that folded in to the large munitions case. There wasn't much this monster couldn't stop.

Brains was crouching down in front of the electronics machine, which was positioned off to the right of the door, mainly because of common sense, they didn't want something to barge out and trample the machinery, plus they need to pass by it; they could pass through the Gateway but not the piece of equipment.

Hopper was checking the five wires that ran from the apparatus to the door. Each held on with a sticky substance that came out of a metal tube, which by all accounts would hold the wires on, while still allowing the electrical impulse to run through it into the door. The whole thing was checked and rechecked to make sure everything and everyone was in position to start the machine up and running.

It was just coming up to 0800, on a cloudy October morning. Because the sky was cloudy it made it quite gloomy. They had now been awake for almost twenty-three hours apart from a short nap on the plane over, the nap wasn't that long due to having to change into the British uniform, plus the sorting out of the equipment. So all should have been tired, and with no prospect of sleep anytime soon. But the task they were about to undertake was making adrenaline rush in all of them, they were more awake now than they had ever been.

"Everyone hold your position," the Captain called over the top of the noise the machine was making. It was reasonably loud; it was a powerful piece of equipment and trying to cover the noise it made was not an option. This was the only way to get the door open.

"Let's get that thing open people," the Captain shouted from the truck, to be heard over the load humming noise the machine was making. The machine had been operating for five minutes now; they were waiting for it to warm up; they didn't want it packing up in the middle of the sequence. The machine started to hum a little louder and then things started to change on the doors surface.

The door started to move, not in the sense of swinging open, rather the writing on the door started to shift around, making you want to squint your eyes to make sure you were seeing it right. The words were starting to move around on the surface of the door, they were joining up to the word next to it, so that they were all blending together, until the whole surface had completely changed contour.

There were now just seven large strange ciphers on the door surface, nothing legible; they didn't look human, was the only way they could think of describing them; more swirling, sweeping lines and dots than letters. Even though they were large letters you could still see the other words making up the shape, these were still swimming about. Then these started to move in to the center of the door, starting to over lap each other until they were all sat on top of one another. Then the words started to break up again, starting to stretch out over the complete surface, until it was once again completely covered. Then the writing kept going until there were no gaps left. The door was now a completely flat surface resembling a metallic ponds face.

They all stayed in their positions. It had taken thirty-seven minutes to get to this stage from when the monitor went blank. The last picture they saw was one person on the ground and another levitating with the strange creature's running towards them. But now there was only the noise of the generator humming in the silence of the air, with a slow drizzling rain starting to fall.

A wind picked up and scuttled dead crispy leaves around in a small cyclone, then it changed directions, hitting the Gateway, the leaves simply vanished thought the strange substance.

They all knew what they had to do, all had been briefed.

Brains jumped in to the truck and started it up, then started moving it slowly forward at a snails pace towards the Gateway. The bumper was the first thing to enter and then slowly the rest of the truck disappeared into the flat clear unmoving surface.

Babe, Flatfoot and Doc stood quickly; one by one they marched through the wall, their guns up ready. Babe with her F2000 Integrated Weapon System; Flatfoot with his P90, and Doc with a simple Sig Sauer P250 DC handgun.

Only Hopper and Brains was left behind.

Hopper then slapped the machine on the side, making a door slid open revealing a space holding a long cylindrical object. Which he proceeded to pick up and walk over to a rock, lean down and pushed the device in to the boggy ground, where the top flipped open and a small rod shot out, which then unfolded into a minute antenna array, which spots of rain bounced off. Then it proceeded to send a signal far up above the Thermosphere twenty-two thousand kilometres above the earth surface and rebound of a Rhyolite satellite.

Then Hopper raised his weapon of choice, a M60 E4 Commando, and calmly followed the others.

Brains then, with one grab, pulled all the wires off the door, wrapped them around the equipment, picking the now switched off machine up he proceeded to walk calmly through the portal, with the other hand holding his P90. Like all the others he didn't even take a last look around, even through he knew he would never see this world again. Then he was gone; disappeared through the barrier into another world.

Now the electrical pulse had stopped the door slowly started to revert back to its former state. Within minutes the whole place looked like it had been deserted for along time. The only clue that anyone had been there was the wide deep tire marks on the ground left by the M35A cargo truck, which even at this moment were starting to be washed away by the now steady stream of pouring rain, which was getting heavier by the minute. The wheels furrows would soon be washed away.

If you looked closely behind a granite rock you would have seen a small piece of equipment, which now it had sent its powerful signal to be bounced of the satellite, was starting to fold itself back up into a smooth pewter canister, like a flower at sunset, then it started to rotate in the ground, slowly getting deeper and deeper. Within a minute or two the device would be hidden from view. The gateway would be back to its original state. All would be quiet, as if no one had been here.

15
Questions

It flew towards Glyn's body at an alarming rate, faster than could be possible for a creature that small. It was a winged beast. Standing no more than a half a foot tall, with a wingspan of fewer than three feet. It had a long slender neck, an oval shaped head, small pointy ears and large liquid eyes that gave the creature an intelligent look. It had slender arms with four fingers, with rounded ends no nails of any kind. On the end of it's long slender legs were three large toes for hanging on to branches. Like most things in this place it had a tail, which tapered at the end into a fork to stabilize it while it flew.

It swooped down and shot straight between Lake and Garry swooping close to Glyn's body.

"WOW! WHAT THE FUCK WAS THAT?" Garry shouted almost dropping his end of the stretcher..

"Quiet, or you will frighten it away," came Lake's mild rebuke. She had stopped to see the creature turn about thirty yards in the distance and turn back towards them. Lake was now talking in only a whisper. "It is thought to be lucky to see one of these creatures; they have a small amount of magical power, and are very rare. Their skin is prized by the Circle and they would give anything to have one."

"The Circle? What is the Circle?" Garry asked as he followed the creature with his eyes keeping his body as still as possible. If he had to describe it he would say it looked like a baby dragon.

The small scaled creature made honking sounds as it glided around on the thermals. Its whip-like tail snaking behind it.

"All will be explained by Coben when we get to the village."

"Coben? Who's Coben?" Garry asked now looking at Lake.

"Yet more questions. All will be answered soon. But for now be silent because your voice can carry a long way in this place, we don't want to draw any more attention to ourselves than we need to."

With that the small winged dragon circled in the air and flew back towards them. It swooped low over them and circled above Glyn's body. Then it suddenly stopped beating its wings and let itself glide down to rest on Glyn's chest. It then curled up in to a ball on his chest and wrapped its wings over itself, to cocoon it from the outside world, then in all intents-and-purposes looked like it was going to sleep.

"Don't move a muscle," was all Lake could think to say. The fact that this creature was now resting on this young mans chest and was now going to sleep was beyond her comprehension. These creatures are so rare they are hardly ever seen let a lone physical contact. They normally stay well clear of humans.

She didn't want to disturb the creature but they needed to get back to the village, so she decided to keep going. This was getting more confusing by the minute. Was this some kind of omen? A sign? But it wasn't her place to question Coben or any of his decisions; many times she had done a particular scouting trip and not fully understood the meaning for it until much later. Things are not always what they seem.

They started moving off at a slower pace; the creature didn't stir or even seem to take any notice of the fact that the stretcher was in motion. It used its long pink forked tongue to clean between its stretched open toes.

They moved quickly over the terrain. Through the woods without being attacked or hindered in anyway. This, if anything, was more disturbing than a hunting pack of Lanks. They knew what actions to take, how to react to them, their patterns even the way they would attack. But the silence was more than they could stand.

For over an hour they marched across a diversity of landscapes from wooded areas that had strange images carved in to soaring trees, the lighter wood below the gloomy bark was standing out in stark detailed contrast. Once an ancient civilization had spent generations carving them and then simply vanished. Now vines and weeds were the only inhabitants of these towering grotesque statues.

They traveled over a vast marshland that disappeared off in to the flat distance on either side. Plumes of greasy olive gasses were floating up from iridescent oily sea green water, with strange four winged insects the size of humming birds seemingly feeding of the gas itself, or possibly off other small microbes. But there seemed to be markers indicating the hard land with which to cross the swampy earth; as if a pathway leading to the Gateway had been warn down over time.

The party soon left the wide but narrow stretch of marshes that then became an arid wasteland; where nothing grew. It seemed strange to go from such boggy earth to cracked mud in a matter of a few hundred meters. Soon their footsteps were kicking up columns of scarlet dust that was now covering them all and filling their nostrils and mouth.

In the distance they could see the hills where the village was situated, and behind them the apparently endless mountains, the snow covered peeks and the impassable cliffs and ridges, and deep dark bottomless gorges. And most ominous of all; the Temple of the Sky, which stood out owing to the powerful storm - making it look like a constant sheet lightning tempest.

Raven was now carrying Garry's end of the stretcher, giving him a rest. There was no need to run forward and keep watch because you could see for kilometers in every direction. There were no trees or shrubbery, nothing just an odd rock scattered here and there. The only visible inhabitants of the cracked mudflats were strange flat beady eyed spiky lizards that scurried along on thin elongated legs and rippled their dazzling neck ruffles at them as they passed, while also stamping their little feet in irritation.

Raven had commented on the creature that rested on Glyn's chest. He and Lake also talked about the day to day running of the camp with Garry, telling him about the wall which kept out all the creatures, even the winged ones. The wall apparently covered the whole village in a kind of invisible protective dome. Which so far nothing has got through, that is so long as it's up. They told of the time then the wall was lowered, and how they were tricked into doing so. Also he was told how the wall was maintained, about the magic needed to control it, and where the power came from. How every ones Life Force was used in keeping it running.

There is a large hut where twenty people can lay down all at once. They go into a kind of trance, using all their energies in keeping the shield up and running. Once the shadow gets quarter way around the old twisted tree that stands in the middle of the village - by the hut - then it is time to change, so they were getting some rest. After one sitting they would get a day to recover. Garry worked out that it was about six hours on then forty off and also he worked out that there must be at least two hundred in the village, give or take a handful.

They also talked about Coben. How wise he was and what a good leader he was for them all. But then it came to the crunch.

"If you don't mind me asking, how did you both get to be here?" was Garry's question, which seemed to make them both turn very quiet and solemn.

Lake was the first to become composed from the question. "Sorry for the silence, but we try not to think about it much, about what we left behind. Sometimes it seems like that life was just a dream, that we were born here and lived all our life here. That the other world doesn't really exist, but was a fragment of our imagination; our dreams."

Raven started talking. "Once I had a job, a good one, down in Silicon Valley. You know America?" Raven said as if he hadn't spoken the word in a long time. "Some friends decided to go on a trip. We were all mad on pot-holing, you know crawling around in caves on your belly and that sort of stuff," he said with a sad tone in his voice, his vision sort of glazed over thinking about his other life. Something he's been trying to avoid lately.

"Those were good days. We really enjoyed ourselves you know? Sort of as a group interacting and all that sort of stuff, we really got on well. That's why we went together as a group. We decided on Africa, Kigoma to be precise. We had been going through the mountains for a while. Days just flew past. It was getting near the time to go home, and we had heard about one good place from a few locals we had got to know in our time we had spent there. They told us about one cave that went so deep that if you dropped something in it you couldn't hear it hit the bottom. We were there in as the saying goes hook line and sinker. How could we miss a calling like that? That was why we were there. It would be our last cave of the trip." Raven then went quiet and lowered his head.

"That's when we found the God forsaken thing. We had been going down for what felt like hours, but I guess it was just a couple hundred-foot, maybe. Anyway, there was the direct route straight down the main shaft, which was gaping open to the elements, which had smoothed off the fissure making it like glass - making it treacherous. But next to it was a smaller cave which we guessed ran down parallel to the main shaft, so we went down that one. The rest, as they say, is history." He then looked at Lake who had also gone quiet; she had probably heard this story once already.

"That's when we found it, a huge door under the earth, hundreds of feet under the ground. It was giving off a kind of light which illuminated the whole area around it; it was freaky yet beautiful if you know what I mean? I couldn't just walk away from it, I had to touch, see what it does and why it was there." Now he was shaking his head from side to side. "All I had to do is walk away, why me, why couldn't one of the others have gone in first . . .

why me? Why?" He had lost it now; he was starting to cry with heart-felt sobs, causing his whole body to shake.

Lake put her end down, just as Raven had, and she walked back and put her arm around him.

Then turning back to Garry she said, "We all had different lives before we came here, we all had different name - different objectives in life. Now we give ourselves new names, mine was once Kathy, Kathy Porter. Raven once had a different name his name was Jason Kelly. We both had different outlooks, different views. Now our main objective is just to stay alive, and work out where our next meal is coming from.

"Now I'm afraid you have the same fate as us, trapped here. Trapped with no way out, except through release of death." She looked sideways at Raven. "And before long you will be longing for death, as we all do."

16
We Are Not Alone

Brains was the last to get through the Gateway. By the time he got through the Captain was out of the truck and around the back checking on all the equipment, in case of damage while passing through the Gateway.

Hopper was hunched over a machine terminal that he had set up in the back of the large cargo vehicle, flicking and clicking buttons up and down. Listening through headphones to some source or other that only he could hear. He had finished the final touches, it was now operational. A small antenna array now slowly rotated on top the trucks camouflaged roof.

Flatfoot was going through the boxes in the back of the truck, all being numbered and stacked; interlocking each other. He was pulling large textile sacks, full of cables, from the dark green plastic bubble containers, and then lining them up next to some other gear and small devices he had already pulled.

Doc was going through all his medical equipment and checking his supplies. So far they were the only biological subjects to pass through the portal, as well as medicinal and other manmade chemicals. Doc had to check that the supplies hadn't chemically changed during the transfer through.

Babe was standing behind the large mounted FN Herstal's .50 cal. M3M machine gun, which was on top of the truck, just in case of any problems. Her sharp iceberg blue colored eyes continuously scanning the distant tree line; trees that looked similar to Pine Ponderosa's and Red's, Scot's, a scattering of Yellowwoods and Scarlet Oak's - and all the while trying to ignore the strange look of the Gateway itself.

They could see the bodies of the creatures all twisted and smouldering, but the two young men weren't there. They were trained well enough to follow their orders, do what they knew they needed to do, which was to check all their equipment, make sure it still worked. Then they would check out the bodies, see what happened to the young men. See if their bodies were around here somewhere. They already knew it would have been too late to stop whatever had happened. An ambush could be hiding perched behind the large standing stones.

Stones Babe noticed that looked almost identical to Stonehenge's Bluestone standing stones, but not the Trilithons, because they had no lintel stretched across the top. But still standing about twenty or so feet tall, and she guessed must weigh close to fifty tons each. She had once visited England's famous site, built during the Neolithic period in European History; which stands twenty-five kilometres from Salisbury in Southern England. She also noticed there positions, making the Gateway seem like the Heel Stone, the centre of Stonehenge's circle.

All was well.

Nothing had yet attacked.

Once all the equipment was checked and double checked, they rallied around the back of the truck with Babe still stood up behind the .50 cal. machine gun, providing essential cover.

"Are the devices in place Brains?" the Captain asked.

"Yes sir all locked and loaded." Brains was referring to the fence perimeter he had just set up. With over three hundred foot of cable all running back in to one machine which would alert them of any activity around the Gateway, which stretched as far as the woods all the way around, this side of the stones. Once anybody or anything crossed over that line, an alarm would be set off, and also indicate what direction the intruder was advancing from. He had also set up claymores, tucked under the large monolith that circled the mound, with trip wires stretching from stone to stone - adjusted so the large stones would tumble sideway, blocking the way.

The Captain seemed satisfied that they were safe for the moment. "Babe, fall in."

Babe climbed down out of the truck to stand with the others. "Yes sir," was her only response when she came to stand besides them, now holding on to her short stocky matt black F2000 machine gun, which looked very similar to Flatfoot and Brains P90's, but being a 5.56 Bullpup, which is fully ambidextrous without having a modification.

"All right this is how it's going to be. Babe and I will erect the tents. Flatfoot and Brains, now the alarm is in place, set up the guns. And Hopper, get us all some radios sorted out, in case of any problems and we get separated. Doc you get over and start to check on the bodies or whatever they are. I want a full report on them, and what in your opinion happened to them."

With that there was no questioning or chatter between them, they all just got on with what they were ordered to do.

The Captain and Babe unloaded the three tents and other supplies from the truck, and then started to get the area looking more like a military encampment. The tents were ICS one man, three season, free standing, double walled tents, in woodland camouflage, put in a triangle configuration with the entrances pointing outwards, so if there was a problem they all wouldn't come crashing out in to each other. In the middle of the tents was some of the bubble-box equipment. The cargo truck was parked directly across the path of the Gateways entrance. They couldn't get back again, and they didn't want to put it to one side and obscure their vision of the woods; the towering standing stones were already limiting the view.

Flatfoot and his brother Brains unloaded three large crates from the back of the truck and started to put together the equipment that was inside them; two guns per box plus their power sources. The machine guns were M60D Enhanced, with 7.62mm standard ammunition that can penetrate light armour. They were big enough to slow anything down which got in there line of sight – anything that the claymores didn't finish off. The power source had a main supply of reserve energy - for night. By day they were powered by large solar powered panels, which were made from a light foldable material, which unfolds itself across the floor during the day, and closes back up by night like a large deformed metallic flowers blossom.

The M60D's were mounted and set in twos, back to back; so two guns could run on one battery and the same laser guidance system. These were also set out in a large triangle formation around the whole mound of the Gateway. So that the three sets of two guns could cover the whole area.

Hopper sat in the back of the truck. There were still quite a few boxes and other sacks still stacked up against one side. Hopper was opening a couple of the smaller boxes he had brought along with him.

There were nine small devices in the one box on the side next to him, and enough spares to build another two if needed, or to be used to repair the others. They were small throat microphone devices similar to an Otto set, favoured by SWAT. At only 13oz they sat snugly in to one ear and then wrapped around the back of the ear, so it was held firmly into place. Coming off the bottom of the device was a small wire that ran down the side of the neck and was attached to an elasticised cord that ran around the oesophagus, with a small device that sits to each side of the Adams Apple, so when you spoke even very softly it could be picked up.

You activated it, to give a response, by blowing into a small mouth piece that sat clipped to the lapel of your jacket. It also had a small tracking device set in to it, which could be picked up from a nine mile radius.

The hand held piece of equipment he was now working on and checking looked like a thick black rubber clad palmtop; this could pick those signals up. Each radio transmitter was now being registered under each of the six-different names so they could work out who was where.

Doc on the other hand had a job of working out what the mess was. Was it the creatures running towards the men? Or was it the young men?

As he got closer he could see the appendage's sticking out in all sort's of direction's what could be called feet, arms and heads. All in a tangled pile as if thrown back together by some powerful violent force. The bodies were what could only be described as reptilian. They were burnt almost beyond recognition. He remembered the photos of the creatures that had gotten through the first Gateway and attacked the African Kigoma base. These were; as far as he could work out; the same.

Their bodies had been pumped full of electricity. All the signs pointed to this. The blistering of the leathery skin, the burns, the fluid oozing even now from out of their bodies, the snapped tendons the blistered tongues. But where had the electricity come from? It would need tens of thousands of watts to produce this kind of damage! With at least twenty to thirty seconds of continued application to get the bodies this bad.

All he could think of was a lightning strike. But the ground around them would be scorched. There was a burnt area but it was in a huge circle, which started by the Gate and spread out to where the bodies lay – just this side of a standing stone. Whatever caused it had a lot of punch behind it, and the way the ground was charred showed that it was sustained for a while. But it couldn't have been lightning because the circle was too large, and if the lightning was that powerful then the bodies would simply be a bubbling puddle on the ground. Besides, if the atmosphere was that unstable the probes sent through the other Gateway would have picked it up. Wouldn't they?

The only thing those probes showed were heavy cloud layer, not electrical storms and freak random weather conditions. Besides, the lightning would in all probability strike the top of the mound rather than some object lower to the ground. Mind you, they did have metal on the tips of their spears, and their bodies did have metal chain-mail on them, so it could have been attracted to this. Plus they didn't know what the huge bowl on top of the mound was made out of. It could be metal.

But he had seen the effects of what a lightning strike could do to a body. Once you had seen it you would never forget the sight. On the soldier he had autopsied everything metal had melted to the body: his dog tags had melted to his chest, and his belt buckle had melted to his belly. Not to mention his gun, this had become an extension of his twisted, blistered hand.

He didn't bother to take any samples he already knew what these creatures were. And by the look of things and by counting the body parts, he decided there were four of them.

But no young men that they had seen crouched over each other. Had they done this? Hardly, he thought to himself. But he would have to pass this information over to his Captain, let him decide what had caused it, and what to do about the missing men.

The Captain and Babe had finished unloading equipment and raising the one man ICS tents, and generally organizing what would be their central base for the next few days, or so they thought at the time.

The signal had been sent by the small device Hopper left behind on the ground, just before they all passed through the Gateway, which would've bounced of the satellite and been intercepted. Even now the small off shoot of the American government, the Trust would be making moves to gain control over the area from the British Government.

Once they were there, the first thing they were going to do was send a probe through to gain information from the Captain's team. This was the first time a human team had been sent through, and before shutting the Gateway down - from this side - they had a lot of research and surveillance to do of the general area.

Even though nothing could be sent back, the information would be carried via the probe, which would be sent through by radio signals, because the only thing that could be passed back through the Gateway was radio frequencies.

"Right people listen up," the Captain called to get everyone's attention. "You know the score and why we were picked. What we do here will make history. You all have your assignments, and tests to be carried out. We have forty-eight hours in which to collect all that information. But first we need some nutrition inside us, and some sleep. Babe, Flatfoot, and Brains will take the first sleep shift, followed by myself, Hopper and Doc."

They all nodded.

Flatfoot and Hopper started unwrapping silver foiled bags they had just pulled from a blue container, and started to prepare the food over a small portable food warmer, while shaking their heads as they read what the contents contained.

"You think with the billions the government spend on military equipment, and training us, that they would come up with a better way of feeding us." He held up a silver aluminium bag and examined its label. "Beef and custard! What the hells that all about? Do they think we are on a fucking space ship? We got room for two bags they don't have to put them both in to one. Bloody cheapskates."

They both shook their heads; every time it was their turn to prepare the food they always had this conversation.

Babe started getting the sleeping mats in to position in the tents. Once that was done she started to walk around the clearing, careful not to go to near the perimeter fence or tripwires, and started to take pictures of the general area. They knew about the area around the first Gateway, but this was the first time this area had been seen. Not even probes had been sent through this one. In a way she was grateful it was the same as the first and not coming out at the bottom of an ocean or the middle of a scorching desert. This was one of the risks they had to take, one she was glad worked out fine.

She tucked her blonde hair behind her left ear and continued taking more digital photos.

The only obvious difference here was the general look of the Gateway itself. The first was just a bare mound. This one look like it had been transformed in to a kind of religious temple. The symbols carved around the grey Gateways wall, the metal dragons that seemed to be protecting the entrance. Small ceremonial shrines littered the earth with numerous skeletons placed in piles. Tall bending flag staffs were flapping in the breeze, these looking like Tibetan prayer poles, with long lines stretching from one to another; colourful yellow, blue and green square flags flapped in the breeze, having become tattered on the ends. And the tall pillars of stones that reminded her of Stonehenge; the only difference being that these were covered in strange alien marks.

Babe stood just admiring the colourful flags. "*Dar Cho*," she muttered. *Dar* meaning increased life, fortune, health and wealth, *Cho* meaning all sentient beings.

The Captain rolled his eyes at Hoppers and Brains conversation; he had heard it a thousand times before. Well at least it felt like that many times.

He then turned to Doc. "Doc if you would like to join me." He then started walking off towards the truck, closely followed by the teams Doctor.

Brains left Hopper grumbling to himself about tight-assed politicians, and went around and double-checked the perimeter fence, claymores and guns.

The Captain lifted himself up and sat on the floor between the two open doors at the rear of the truck, with his feet hanging over the side.

Doc stood in front of him.

The Captain asked, "So what did you make of the fried pile over there?" He said tilting his head to the direction of the mess on the floor off in the near distance.

"Well they are definitely the same creatures that came through the other Gateway."

The Captain nodded his head, as if to say yes. "What about the way they died?" He asked, looking at Doc as he took a gulp from a warm drink that Brains had handed to him as he walked past. He tried to work out what the drink was meant to be. But wouldn't dream of asking Brains for fear of a long speech about the taste buds of the cooks, that supposedly made this to be full of protein and other valuable and essential ingredients, but forgot to add the important component called flavour.

"Electrocuted alive - fried. But the amount of power needed to do that would be phenomenal to say the least," he said scratching his head messing up his perfect hair.

"So you're saying whatever did that could do it again?" He tipped the drink out on to the ground. He decided he wasn't thirsty; he would never be thirsty enough to drink that.

"I don't know what could have caused that. But whatever it was is still out there, and could come back," the Doc said looking around as if to emphasize his worry, while wiping some brown sludge off his trousers that the Captain just poured away.

"Whatever it was has long gone, and as far as I can make out from here it must have taken the two people we saw with it," the Captain said, while looking at Babe as she stood to one side taking pictures of the huge bowl on top of the mound that issued the orangey smoke.

"Correct. The men's bodies weren't in the jumble of parts over there. And I see no blood or tell tale signs of any other struggle," Doc said, now trying to remove the brown sludge from his hand, with not much luck. He was thinking to himself that he could use some of this to cover over wounds: it would kill any bacteria he knew of.

"So you're saying whatever it was protected the two young men, and then took them somewhere?" He had his brows knotted together in perplexity.

"With the limited information I've got from checking the ground over, and checking the signs. Yes." He shook his head up and down, as well to emphasize his words.

"Then that settles it. I'll send two people, Brains and Flatfoot to check around after we all have eating and rested," the Captain said as he jumped back down to the ground, careful not to land in the drink he just poured away.

"But that's not part of the orders, is it Captain?" Doc asked looking at the Captain for a response.

"No you're right it's not. But when we were sent here we were supposed to be alone. The only other person that has passed through the Gateway as far as the Trust knows is Jason Kelly, who walked through the Kigoma Gate. So I want to know how they got here. More importantly if they're here, how many others is there?"

17
A Time to Stand

They had been walking in silence now for about half an hour, all lost in their own thoughts. The hills in the distance were getting closer by the minute, the mountains behind becoming lost behind the mound of the steep rise.

Lake was the first to speak. "There is our village," she said, pointing to the hill in the distance. Where you could just make out some sort of settlement but they were still to far away to see it clearly, because the dull pewter clouds seemed to suck the colour and sharpness out of the landscape.

"It will take us just over another hour to reach its protective walls, and then we will all be able to rest," she said, looking over towards Garry, waiting for a response. He offered none; he just rubbed his stubble covered chin with a dirt incrusted nail; his thoughts wandering off to a hot steaming shower, and how much he needed one. His hand wandered from his chin and brushed red dust out of his short cropped brown hair.

"Then you will be passed over to Coben. He will then answer any of your questions, and tell you a little more about this place you now find yourself."

"You mean about our new home?" was Garry's response. It carried sarcasm and was meant to hurt. But Lake was in the same position herself years ago, she knew how he felt, knew he needed to release the anger at something, someone.

But at the same time the response annoyed her, because years before there was no one at the Gateway to welcome her; to walk her to the village. She had taken over a week to find the settlement, and she was near deaths door, having survived on what she could find. She had been confused as to where she was, and her friend who had passed through with her had been ripped apart by a reptilian type creature. She had only found the village because she had heard someone talking, and then followed the group of people to the hill, never approaching them because of being so scared, hungry and half crazy. It had taken her months to heal and learn to trust anyone.

Garry looked at Lake. "I'm sorry, I didn't mean for it to come out like that, honest." Garry was now shaking his head from side to side. "I've only been here half a day and I'm already referring to this place as my home."

He now looked at his brother just lying there. Still, motionless, eyes shut, body ridged. With what he could only describe as a small or baby dragon lying on his slowly rising and falling chest.

Lake and Raven had now gone back to being alert. They were coming up to the edge of the wastelands.

Raven had changed places with Garry so that he could walk on in front of the group once again.

They had just one more river to cross in order to get to the foot of the hills. The river wasn't that wide or strong, but it was very deep and the water was icy cold. If you fell in it your body wouldn't be able to sustain itself for very long, the cold would kill you in less than a minute. If not the living weed at the bottom of the river would wrap around your ankles and hold you under until you succumbed to the cold or drown. Then the carnivorous plant would consume its catch.

They approached one section of the river that had huge trees, felled and lying across it, from one bank to the other, with huge boulders anchoring them in to position. The trees were lashed together by thick vines, and looked stable enough to walk across, six or even seven abreast easily.

But Raven approached it wearily, his soft footfalls hardly even bending the grass.

"The ground around the river is dangerous, many creatures come here to drink and cross this bridge. We have to approach it carefully," Lake said in a whisper.

Raven approached cautiously, slowly. Sometimes Lanks were known to wait in ambush for people to make the crossing, knowing it was the only bridge for a long stretch in every direction.

Lake and Garry, who were carrying Glyn on the stretcher held back. All seemed quiet, too quiet. This place normally waited until you got close to the village before it attacked. But even so Lake had never known it to be this quiet for travellers, and for this long. She was starting to get a bad feeling about all this. Was something bigger scaring off all the other predators? And what had happened at the Gateway? Whenever someone passed through normally only Coben could feel the wave. But when these two passed through the whole ground shifted, it was even felt as far as the village.

And what had happened to the four Lanks? They had seen the light while approaching the Gateway, but had no idea what was causing it. To find two young men there with the bodies of the Lanks fried. And to round it all off Garry said Glyn - the person who had been unconscious since coming through the Gateway - was supposed to have done it.

If that were the case then he would be more powerful than Coben and everyone in the village put together. She just wanted to pass them over to Coben and get rid of the responsibility.

Raven was inching closer to the bridge, slowly making his way forward, always wary of what is around him. He was now almost up to the bridge when something detached from the shadows.

A creature jumped out from under the section of bridge that rested on the embankment. Raven jumped back in surprise, making his body lighter, he somersaulted backwards and landed ready for attack ten foot away from where the creature jumped out at him. Both knives appeared in his hands, knuckles stretched tight over the bones as he gripped the carved handles. One foot placed in front of the other, in a fighting stance. But upon seeing it properly he relaxed.

It was only a small type of forest animal, not to un-similar to a small Shetland pony. But it had a long ivory horn protruding from on top of its head; some would have called it a unicorn. But it was almost jet-black in colour, and had a long mane of pure white hair and a powerful stout body.

Even though it was only small, one had never been known to attack a human before. But some have witnessed it using its long horn to scour a Lank straight through. Someone from the village even said that one had come to his aid, when Spitters had attacked him. The unicorn had kicked the Spitters with its powerful hind legs breaking their necks; always keeping its back to them, so it couldn't be caught in the eyes by their blinding venom.

Garry's response upon seeing the creature was pure surprise; he lowered his end of the stretcher and made his way forward.

The unicorn, upon seeing him, started to make its way towards Lake and Garry.

Lake having lowered her end of the stretcher put her arm on Garry's and gave him a curious look. But Garry just shrugged it off and carried on walking towards it, with a child-like look plastered upon his round face. It was the first time he had smiled since arriving in this world.

"Their kind has never been known to hurt us, but we have never purposely approached one before," she said sternly.

But Garry's eyes were wide in excitement. "It's amazing, the old stories are true. Unicorn's do exist."

"Yes, we have witnessed the fact that the creatures from this world can pass through the Gateway in to ours. Then probably like us can't get back again. It's not unlikely that some of these have passed through the Gateway and have caused the stories about unicorns. They do grow much larger, and range in all different shades of colours. They are even endowed with small amounts of magical powers," Lake said as she stayed back with Glyn by the stretcher.

The unicorn came and stood just out of Garry's reach. It flicked its head back, causing its mane to flick back behind it.

Garry reached out his hand and patted the creature on its flanks. The unicorn seemed to enjoy the attention and rubbed itself against Garry, not to un-similar to a cat. It then flicked him with his hindquarters knocking Garry sideways. The unicorn then reared its head and neighed.

"Find that funny do you?" Garry asked getting back on his feet.

"Careful, they are powerful creatures," was Lake's warning.

"Its okay it's just messing around - playing with me."

Raven looked over towards Lake, and hunched his shoulders. "We don't have time to play I'm afraid," came Raven's warning. With that he turned his attention back to the bridge.

Garry gave the unicorn one more pat on the nose, and then started to make his way towards Lake, picked up his end of the stretcher and then they both started to make their way to the bridge.

The unicorn, which still wanted to be the centre of the attention made its way over to them.

Lake carried on trying to ignore the creature, until that is; it put its snout towards Glyn lying on the stretcher. Which for some reason made the little dragon uncoil its wings and look at the unicorn, which had its nose mere inches from the small dragon.

Lake and Garry stopped moving mainly to see what would happen. But the little red dragon simply flicked its long pink tongue out as if to lick the unicorns nose, then curled up and went back to sleep.

The unicorn in return gave the small dragon a lick with it's over large tongue, soaking the small creature. Whereupon the dragon stretched, and shook the saliva off its body. Then gave the unicorn a stare then turned around a couple of times, made itself comfy by pushing down with its small rounded toes, and settled down to rest. With its wings around its body, its tail wrapped over itself, but this time it kept its head poked up, looking where it was going, as if to check to make sure the unicorn wasn't going to give it another bath. Its little tail still flicking, showing it was starting to get annoyed.

Lake gave up trying to work everything out, and just started to keep on walking towards the bridge. With the little dragon now wide awake watching where they were going. The black unicorn following behind at a steady trot.

Coben was going to get a shock when they reached the village.

The only thing she was now thinking about was what else would they pick up on the way? If only she knew, she would've probably jumped in to the river rather than face it.

Coben was standing under the lookout tower. He had felt the group's presence coming up the side of the hill, but was unsure about what else he could feel.

He knew two people had passed through the Gateway, and with Raven and Lake that should make four. But he could feel the presence of six life forms making their way towards them. It took a lot of strength to stretch his powers to the limit to check on them, and now had given up and was relying on the sight of the watchman to give him more information.

The watchman had the *gift* of sight; he could see for kilometres and pick out objects others would miss. He was now describing what he could see to Coben. He said that there was one walking in front, who he knew as Raven. Lake was behind him carrying the front of a stretcher. Because they were zigzagging up the steep hill he could see a young man at the rear of the stretcher, and someone lying upon it. That person wasn't moving in anyway.

But the thing Coben wanted to know came next.

"There's a unicorn walking alone beside the stretcher." The watchman turned to look at Coben, and shrugged his shoulders.

"You mean it's attached to the side of the stretcher in some way?" was all Coben could think to ask, and was now wondering why they had spent time capturing a unicorn? Plus why were they now bringing it to the village?

The watchman was now shaking his head. "No it's not tied, just walking along beside them," the watchman said shrugging his shoulders once again. He then looked down at Coben, seeing the same confused look he knew would be mirrored on his own features.

That's when the watchman called out, making Coben jump and have to steady himself on the towers wooden barrier.

"DRAGON! DRAGON!" The watchman was shouting at the top of his lungs, while loudly ringing a large metal bell next to him, and then pointing in to the far distance.

All Coben could see was a small dot on the distant horizon, but he knew the watchman wouldn't be wrong.

The dragon was the most powerful creature this place bred. They ranged from around two foot tall, right up to their larger cousins, who have been seen to grow up to thirty foot in height from head to foot. Not including their tails which could be anything up to another twenty foot long, covered in spikes and tipped with a powerful scissor blade, that could either pick you up or cut you in two. Their wingspan could measure up to ninety feet in diameter. They always lived and hunted alone, because they were so territorial. An adult dragon's territory could range up to a couple hundreds square kilometres. One hadn't been seen around in these parts for as long as Coben could remember, and he had been here for a long, long time. They usually stay well clear of the plumes of cloud rising from the Gates.

As far as Coben could think the village had never been attacked by a dragon, so they wouldn't know if the magical shield would hold up to the onslaught of such a powerful and magical beast.

They were attacked all the time by other smaller flying creatures; they would give up trying to get through. Some just sat in the trees waiting for someone to venture out, so they could have easy pickings.

But Coben knew it wasn't coming for the village. Its intended target was on its way up the hillside. That made Coben's mind up. These that had passed through the Gateway were the ones foretold about in the ancient prophecy, which he was now playing over in his mind: *One would come and bring destruction, but two are needed to bring about order.*

The unicorn started to go crazy, rearing up in to the air and stamping its hooves on the ground. It was also running around them, digging large chunks out of the soil, which was being flung high up in to the sky.

At first they all started to back away from her. That was until Raven realized what the unicorn was making a fuss over.

"DRAGON!" He shouted at the top of his lungs, one hand pointing in to the distance.

That one word from Raven made Lake's heart freeze. She had never seen one before but had heard too many stories about them not to panic now. She franticly searched the sky until she saw it. It was now large enough to pick out details on its wings - the translucent material that was stretched across the powerful wings was reflecting the hazy light through them.

But from what she had heard the dragon wasn't as large as it could have been, possibly a wingspan of no more than thirty, thirty-five feet across. But still large enough to kill them all, and carry their bodies away.

The creatures were possibly one of the most intelligent of all the animals in this place; they were known for their intelligence and also feared for it.

Lake was franticly looking around; she had walked up this hill hundreds of times and knew there was nowhere to hide. Fear now took away any logical thought she had. She was looking for somewhere, anywhere to cover them.

But the hill was just grass and stones. That's why the village was on top of this hill, so they could see anyone who tried to approach; the same was of the other side. The only cover was sparse woods on each side, but the coppice was too great a distance to cover before it would reach them.

She also knew that the village watchmen would have spotted the dragon, and that they wouldn't lower the power over the protective wall, if anything it would be strengthened. She could envisage many more people laying down, joining their life force to raise an even stronger protective cocoon.

They were on their own.

She lowered her end of the stretcher, as did Garry.

Raven was standing his ground over to one side as if to get the dragons attention away from the others. Ravens hands were swinging wildly in the air like a windmill.

But it was ignoring him and diving directly towards the others, with its two piercing, intelligent yellow silted eyes set on the body lying unmoving on the stretcher.

It swooped past on its first run. Gliding almost gracefully over the top of the strange gathered group, as if getting a better look at the lot of them, as if checking for something. It started another climb to start circling around and make its final approach. Its long claws sliding out from their protective sheaves; long and glinting in the light as if made from shining metal.

The unicorn was rearing up on to its hind legs making a powerful display, but to no avail, the dragon ignored it.

Lake stood over the body of Glyn, with her daggers in each hand. Pitiful weapons against something so large and powerful. She could make herself invisible to the creature, and that option was still open at the moment. But she had seen a lot of strange things happen today, things she could not explain. For some reason - now the initial shock had past - she was feeling different. She had a strange feeling, something she hadn't felt in a long while; it was hope.

Raven must have felt something as well, because from where he was he turned his head to look over towards Lake. She could swear she saw a smile slowly spread across his face, as if to say, *I know how you feel.*

The dragon was wheeling its huge body back towards them in a large circle. It was now setting itself up, going for its final approach, heading directly towards Glyn on the stretcher.

Garry was in a state of shock. But some how he knew everything would work out. Hadn't Glyn's body sent out a powerful shield of energy to protect them both last time? Surely this was more powerful, more dangerous than those Lanks or whatever Lake had called them? Surely he would be protected again?

But as the dragon got closer Glyn's body still laid motionless, unmoving, and uncaring.

The only movement from Glyn's direction was the small dragon on his chest, which had been watching with its small intelligent eyes the whole situation unfold before it. Now instead of watching the little creature uncurled its petite wings and stretched them out ridged. It opened its little mouth in what could only be described as a long yawn. Then - in what appeared to be a blur - shot off of Glyn's body into the air flying in the direction of the oncoming behemoth.

18
Charge

Brains and his brother Flatfoot had been briefed about their assignment. Finding the two young men, then report back to the Captain via the radio headsets they were now both wearing.

They had been fitted with all the equipment they would need for the trip. Both had rucksacks on their back filled with various equipment they would need for tracking and defence. As well as food supplies to last the two days they were going to be gone. Two days were all they were given to accomplish the job at hand: locate the two missing men.

Both were the best at what they did.

Brains was the best they had in the field of tracking. He had already found the trail from which the group - as he said - had started from. Being asked what he meant by group he then went into detail describing the markings on the ground, how at least three or four people had been walking around in this area before they had got there. The ground was all scorched and where it had been trampled, was all flattened in to different patterns, different shoe sizes. When they started off in to the direction of the hills in the distance, two were walking in a line, as if to cover their tracks to make out there were less than they wanted someone to know. Or two were in line carrying something or someone. All because there was no blood it doesn't mean that one of them wasn't hurt.

Upon hearing Brain's theory the Captain was going to send Babe as well, but upon reflection he need as many as he could here to do the experiments and he was already sending two people off when he wasn't suppose to. So in the end it was to be only Brains and his brother.

They started off in to the direction of the hills that could be seen rising in the distance, which had dark foreboding mountains in the distance behind them. Both had their weapons hitched over one shoulder with the barrel pointing down towards the ground so movement through he pines and yellowwoods would be easier. The rifle could be lifted in to firing position within a matter of seconds, the butt clipped on to their flack jacket, so even if they removed their hands it would hang in position.

Both had slept and were now alert, the only thing putting a damper on the situation was the sky; the clouds continually circled over their heads. But there was one good point. The sky reaching plume of cloud rising out of the top of the Gateway was an easy point of origin to find there way back to. Far better than any marker they could have left.

Each had a small camera mounted over the same ear the radio was attached to, it was very small, smaller than a match box, and slightly thinner. Hopper had attached them to their radios for reconnaissance, saying that they might as well take advantage of the situation. The Trust wanted a mapped out picture of the area around the Gateway, and that was what they were doing in a sense. Also the rest of the group could see what was happening to them. So as well as hearing what they were saying, they could also see what they were doing.

Because there was only two of them and they weren't carrying anyone they made good progress. The trail the others made was easily followed, they hadn't gone to any length to conceal there direction, as if they didn't care if they were followed, or the fact that no matter how hard they tried, something or someone would always know where they were, where they were going.

Brains would swear the line they were following was like a path, walked upon so many times always in the same direction - a route leading between the Gateway and what? These questions would soon be answered he was sure.

They followed the path for almost an hour before they started seeing any real signs of indigenous life, creatures larger than bugs and other insects. They started seeing all sorts of flying creatures. A few larger land dwelling animals not to un-similar to wild pigs and deer, all in someway similar to creatures from back home, with only slightly different, an extra horn, longer legs, bigger ears. But the main obvious difference was the animal's pelts; they were covered in a leathery hide, reptilian skin.

The other main difference was the flying creatures they had seen. None were bird like in anyway; they had no feathers. All were a type of flying lizard of some description or another; as if most of the animals on this world had originated from reptilian ancestors rather than mammals. The evolution chain had gone down another link, or was still at its first stages.

They had just been capturing images of the towering tree sculptures on their headsets, which would be recorded back at the base; while both commenting on how the carvings looked like dragons made in different relief's, when something caught their attention.

The trees and bushes in the distance were rocking back and fourth violently, as if a large animal of some description was about to come crashing through. Then it did.

It was huge in comparison to anything they had seen so far. It must have stood twenty or so foot tall. They recognized it instantly from the photos of the attack on the other Gateway in Kigoma. One had gotten through while the other was flattened too a pulp by the Gates heavy titanium door. From the surveillance footage from the Gate Room they saw how powerful they could be, but also how slow they reacted.

This was what the villagers called a Moregone, large powerful, but slow. But now when it turned towards them, slow was the last word they would have used to describe it. It turned its huge head in their direction, focusing in on their location, its small eyes zooming in on them. Then it swung the rest of its body around to follow its line of sight, its powerful tail tumbled a small Scot's sapling as it swept in a large half circle - the noise was deafening. Its nose twitched as if wasn't too sure about them. It rested its hand on the limb of a pine tree and pulled the needles out of its line of sight, waiting, staring, the sound of the limb ripping free from the trunk of the tree was thunderous. Then it raised its head up in to the air and gave a mighty roar. The very ground vibrated, they could hear it making its way through their bodies making their very bones vibrate. It was like a jet engine warming up before take off.

Then just as suddenly it stopped, and then shook its head causing spittle to flick all over its own shoulder. It then turned its large head back towards them, then in a blur - of flying leaves and snapped tree limbs - charged directly towards them.

19
Fallen Giant

The small dragon sped towards the larger behemoth, a mere insignificant bug in comparison.

The larger sickly yellow coloured Dragon opened its mouth as if to just swallow the nuisance whole. But just at the last minute the smaller dragon, which had been shooting towards the lagers head now swerved, shooting off to the right.

The larger creature just ignored the smaller pest and carried on towards the people on the ground. Until it realized what it was about to do. It flung its huge head to the side, using its long neck to try and catch it, snapping its razor tipped mouth shut, but it was too late.

The smaller creature tore through the membrane that was stretched between the wings powerful muscles, leaving a tattered hole, with flesh flapping around the now spreading tear. The wind rushing against the wing was now tearing the rest of the membrane apart. Also as it passed through it left behind a ring of magical blue flames, which was now being fanned by the wind, spreading out in to a larger ring. Burning tattered flesh hung in large chunks.

The dragon was in excruciating pain. It's wing now useless. It started to veer off to one side, spinning in the air. Now instead of gliding towards the ground it was falling, unable to support its own body weight. Like a burning tree crashing to the ground it struck. It fell short of its intended target by a long mark, hitting the ground with bone crunching speed, churning up a large trench as its body slid along, with rocks and dirt flying in all directions, tumbling over and over. The sound of the creature's scaled flesh slapping the earth was deafening.

Then it came to a halt. The dragon started to slowly move its head a few feet off the ground; its wings twitching in spasms. Smoke still rising from the body. One whole wing was now nothing more than tattered flesh and blackened bones: the smell was overpowering.

The group stood motionless, not comprehending what had just happened. One minute flying towards them was certain death, the next it was laying in a smouldering heap.

But the creature was still alive. It was a powerful beast; left lying there long enough it would start to heal itself. Not many creatures would approach even an injured dragon, all an injured dragon was, was a more aggressive one. The dragon even now was trying to get to its feet, even after everything it had just been through.

But not for long.

The unicorn reared up on to its short but powerful hind legs, flicked back its mane and charged at the wounded behemoth.

The dragon concerned with its own pain, and trying to get back to its clawed feet didn't see the unicorn coming until it was too late.

The speed that the unicorn moved was astonishing, tearing up tuffs of grass as it charged along, bounding across the distance. Until it reached the dragon where it preceded at full charge to bury the full length of its horn through the underneath of the dragon's head, piercing through the soft under jaw straight up through the skin and muscles, ramming straight through the skull in to the brain. It started jerking its head from side to side, doing as much damage as possible. It then pulled its horn out of the now still corpse of the fallen dragon, and began to roll on the ground, wiping the blood off of its ivory horn.

The small dragon slowly circled the body of Glyn; that still lay motionless on the stretcher on the ground. Then stretching its wings out it slowly glided down coming to rest on Glyn's chest once again. It looked around at everyone before settling itself back down. Then it closed its wings over itself once again and went to sleep.

The unicorn came up along side them, looked around and spotted the small dragon on Glyn's chest again. Gave a neigh, lowered its head and simply started to graze on the long grass.

Never before in all his days is this God forsaken prison had Coben ever witnessed anything to compare to the sight that just transpired before him. He stood along side all the others from the village staring at the now fallen and utterly dead dragon.

It was just lying there. This once powerful creature was now nothing more than a smouldering heap of flesh and cracked bones, all due to a small flying creature that he couldn't make out from here, and a unicorn.

He was now positive that these were the ones the ancient prophecy talked about; in his mind there was now no doubt. He knew that others around him were coming to the same conclusion. All were looking at Coben, what was he now to do?

"Lower the shield; bring them in to the village." The walls hadn't been lowered to retrieve someone from that far a distance for longer than some could remember. Not since the time of the full out attack on the rear of the village by the Lanks.

The protective wall was lowered; ten ran to their location, another forty fanned out, in a protective circle around them. Many were now feeling almost invincible from just witnessing the slaughter of the fallen dragon; being one of the most feared and powerful creatures this evil place bred.

Some however were still a little uneasy about the whole situation; when his place gave you hope it usually tore it away from underneath you the very next moment. Some searched the sky checking that other dragons weren't on their way, or a battalion of Lanks weren't storming up the steep hillside.

The small group were brought through the main gate. The wall rose around them again to give them a simmering blue protective cocoon.

The stretcher carrying Glyn was taken straight to the Healers Hut, and then laid before the healers. Garry was still at his side watching, waiting. He had a lot to tell his brother when he woke up.

Coben stood to one side talking to Lake and Raven, talking in an undertone, and looking over towards Glyn on the stretcher. Lake was just nodding her head, her hair having come lose and trailing around her face. Ravens hands were a windmill of activity, while trying to explain everything at once to his leader.

The unicorn was taken to the stables and given food and water.

The small dragon now identified by Coben as a Fire-dragon; which was fully grown, and never before seen up this close, unless on a trophy shelf of one of the Circles walls.

Even now it was still lying on the young mans chest. Not asleep, though it was still curled up. It was awake and very alert. The healer wasn't sure what she was to do. Could she touch the dragon? Move it to one side? She needed to put her hands on Glyn's chest, but the Fire-dragon just lay there staring at them all, its wide penetrating eyes were unblinking.

Then as if reading their minds the small dragon stood stretched its wings and in one swift movement was flying up to the rafters of the large healing hut, and settling itself down, grabbing hold of the beam with it's three toes of each foot and swung up side down, with it's wings now tightly wrapped around itself, very similar to a bat, with its long neck extended, still looking around the room at everyone, now directly above Glyn's comatose body.

The healer placed her hands on Glyn's chest and lowered her head, closed her eyes, and went into Glyn's very being. She started to move her mouth. Words issued forth slowly at first then becoming normal. "There is so much going on in his body. He is in turmoil inside. Once he passed through the Gateway he was endowed with powerful gifts unlike any I've seen before. To powerful for him to absorb." She started to rock from side to side, her hands trembling on his chest.

"He knows what is happening to him, he is aware of all that transpires around him. He is trying to control the energies he has absorbed; it swirls around inside him like a god's tempest." She then became ridged, her arms locked straight, her head snapping up, and her eyes were now open, with only the whites showing. Then her voice changed to that of a man, a powerful booming voice which didn't so much as come out her mouth but issued though her whole quivering body.

"ALL THAT COMES THROUGH THE GATEWAY BELONGS TO ME. BRING HIM TO ME, OR YOU WILL ALL BE DESTROYED. YOU HAVE FOUR CYCLES TO GET HIM TO MY MOUNTAIN, OR MY WRATH WILL TRULLY BE SEEN. DO NOT MAKE ME UNLEASH THE POWER OF THE CIRCLE ONTO YOU." Then the healer collapsed in to a heap on the floor, shaking uncontrollably. Three others women ran to her and started ministering to her needs.

Coben was standing stock-still, thinking things over. No one had said a word to him. All knew not to disturb him while he was thinking. Except Garry.

"What the fuck was that all about? I said -"

"All will be explained to you," Coben said as he turned and walked toward the door. "Please follow me to my hut."

Noticing Garry was now looking at his brother Coben added. "Do not worry Glyn is okay he hasn't been hurt. He is still; let's say sleeping, given time he will awaken. While he's in that state nothing or no one can harm him."

Coben now put his hand on Garry's arm. "Come there will be food and water in my hut. We will eat and quench our thirst, and all will be explained.

I will answer all your questions." He then turned and left. Coben just hoped that while walking to his hut he would be able to work it all out himself.

20
Fine Tuning

Flatfoot and his brother Brains stood motionless, not quite comprehending the fact that a huge creature was charging towards them at an alarming rate; one that they wouldn't be able to out run. One that had the power to crush them in one blow, turn their bodies in to a pulped mess on the ground. And they didn't know if their weapons bullets would be able to penetrate such thick leathery skin. Or simply anger the beast more.

The creature's head was swinging from side to side as it charged, spittle flying in all directions. The ground was being churned up by the sheer weight of the being charging across it. Its bulky body was tumbling small trees as if they were nothing more than mere brittle twigs.

Then just as their composure was starting to return, another ear shattering bellow was ripping through the air. This time from behind them.

Turning they saw another Moregone stood there with its head in the air letting rip on its vocal cords.

Flatfoot put his hands over his ears against the sheer noise, which seemed even louder than the first.

Brains ever alert grabbed his brother and started to pull him towards the bushes. Realizing what was really happening, before his brother squeezed the trigger on his P-90 and irritated the beast even more. The first creature wasn't reacting to them but rather to the fact that another behemoth was imposing on its turf; it's territory.

The second was now down on all fours, raking at the ground with its front forearms, flinging the dirt in all directions. It then kicked its feet firmly in to the ground behind it. Then in one movement flung itself forward with astonishing speed, flinging all the dirt behind it up in to the air with such force and speed that it ripped its way through the trees behind it, leaving a couple bushes stripped of its leaves, and the bores of trees stripped of bark.

The two powerful creatures were charging straight towards one another. A cloud of dust and soil was being thrown high up in to the air. Swirling masses of debris were flying in all directions.

One small piece - possibly a rock - caught Flatfoot in the side of the head, striking the radio, shattering it along with the camera; also taking a chunk out of his ear, which was more messy than painful.

Brains, now having a firm hold of his brother, started to pull him through the bush and out in to another clearing, where they started to run to the other side for cover, disappearing in to some thick thorny vegetation that resembled Hawthorn.

The last thing they heard was the smack of flesh, as the two huge creatures hit each other at full speed, full on.

"Captain. Captain Sir, I think you would want to see this?" Hopper said who was now crouched down in front of the radio and camera surveillance equipment. No one was manning the station because they all had their own projects to get on with. More so now two of the team was on a different assignment.

Hopper had been outside, taking scrapings from the black metallic dragons that stood guard around the Gateway; until he had heard the control panel beeping.

Flatfoot or Brains could call them at anytime making the equipment beep. However, they had not; they were too preoccupied with their current situation. The reason the beeper went off was the fact that one of the headsets was now un-operational, due to being shattered by flying debris.

They realized that it was Flatfoot's camera and radio that wasn't working, so they punched up Brains frequency. The picture was all fuzzy to start with, then slowly it started to clear, but no sound as yet was coming through.

The picture on the screen before them showed Brains running full speed through some very dense undergrowth. Their fear of having lost Flatfoot was soon put to rest when Brains head spun around looking back the way he had be running, and while he done this they caught a glance at Flatfoot being dragged alone by his arm. He looked a little dazed, and the side of his head was bleeding in to his thick black hair, with no trace of the headset. So that would account for the lack of his picture. But the fact that he was all right made everyone relax a little.

"Hopper get the sound working on that headset, I want to know what's happening out there," the Captain said, walking back and fourth behind

Hopper's workstation.

"The trace program for the sound is coming through on another frequency. The headset has a fine tuner on the top of it. One of the branches must have reset it as he's running through the scrub," Hopper announced, while now rebooting the sound card frequency getting the computer to run through all the frequencies on the small headset.

"I'm running a diagnostics and a frequency search; we should have sound within a few minutes or so." Hopper was now punching rapidly on the keyboard, bringing up all sorts of charts and programs on the main screen, with such speed it was almost impossible to follow what he was doing, and the fact he was talking at the same time was phenomenal to watch.

"The program has been running since they left, it's been recording the entire picture output for over two hours. The only reason it wasn't displayed on the screen was to save power." He was now finished with the rebooting of the sound, which would now search for the right frequency on its own.

He now brought up the picture catalogue of the last couple hours. The screen was sectioned in to two halves, one for Flatfoot and one for Brains; their names were above the pictures coming off their particular compact cameras.

"Has that got sound on it?" The Captain asked.

"They are both recorded on different matrix levels, the sound only needs about a tenth of the space needed to record the picture, so both are separated and stored individually so if there is a problem with one, then the other will still keep recording. And they are both coming in on different frequencies. The power needed to join them both together once they meet again at the machine doesn't warrant the power output, which could be used on a different task or level."

"Just a no would have been adequate," the Captain said, leaning over Hopper's shoulder.

The pictures started to go fuzzy and show a close up of Hopper's face.

"That's just a test to make sure both the cameras were operational."

With saying that the pictures swung around both looking at each other, Flatfoot on Brains screen and vice versa. The picture was running to spec. They then had the two checking the equipment that was going in their camouflaged packs.

At this point Hopper started to fast forward the picture running through the last couple hours of footage, to the point they wanted, which would roughly be about ten minutes ago. The picture then went still. Hopper had stopped the fast forwarding.

"What is it? Can you see anything?" was the Captain's question coming from behind Hopper's back.

"Yes Sir. They have stopped walking, because they may have heard or seen something."

At that the Captain leaned over and tapped the screen. "There, what's that?"

There in front of them, about thirty feet away was a large creature with its head raised in the air giving off a mighty roar. Well they presumed it was because the sound was being carried through a different system. The sound was still working at this point so Hopper started to bring up the sound and overlay it onto the picture. There was a ping from the speakers to say the alignment was just about to be completed. Then the whole back of the truck was filled with a mighty ear-shattering bellow.

Hopper quickly turned the sound down.

At that point the creature was just standing there looking at them; looking in to the camera, before turning its head slightly over to their left.

"What the hell is that?" was the first thing Babe had said since she had been standing in the truck along with them, forgetting that only the Captain was to ask the questions.

"I believe…" Hopper said, as he paused the picture, and then moved it in to the top right hand corner of the screen. He then brought the video footage up from the African Kigoma lab. Running a few seconds into the film, he paused it on a close up of one of the creatures that had gotten through, and then brought it along side the picture he had just taken off Brains camera. Punching another button the computer started to run a matching program, within seconds the match came up, 97% probable match. Even though everyone looking at the screen would have said they were the same.

Hopper continued. "There's your answer." He then turned the recording back on, showing the remainder of Brains footage. Now they had the sound they could hear as well as see the creature now charging towards them.

"Why are they just standing there?" was all the Captain could think to ask.

"It's a normal reaction to shock. The body goes in to confusion and shuts down for a few seconds. You know like in the films when someone just stands there while a bus is heading straight at them," was the physiologist Babe's expert opinion. She looped a stray strand of blonde hair behind her ear.

Then another roar could be heard from behind them, turning quickly - making those watching the footage queasy - Brains and his brother Flatfoot spun their heads towards another creature, which had its head bent back in a mighty cry.

At that they both headed off through the tangled undergrowth, and it was at this point when Flatfoot's camera suddenly went dead. Then within seconds the sound on Brains went off.

"Can you back it up a bit and slow the picture down for me?" The Captain asked.

"Yes Sir this is the top of the range baby," Hopper said while stroking the side of the large computer with a tattooed hand, as if it was the silky curves of a woman's breasts. After that he then started to punch away on the keyboard - rewinding the picture. Then cutting out Brains side and bringing Flatfoot's on the full screen. He then slowly started to rewind the picture and slow it down just before it blanked out.

Then that's when they saw the stone flying out of the corner of the picture; and making contact; the screen went blank, now only showing static.

"So we now know what's going on. They're both all right. We have only lost one headset. I believe we have more?" the Captain asked looking down at Hopper.

Hopper simply nodded his head yes.

"Good then all we need now is the sound up and running on Brains headset, then we can get in contact with him."

At saying that sound started to pump through the speakers set in the side of the computer.

"Captain. Captain. Anyone, is everything okay at your end? Repeat -" Came Brains worried voice.

Hitting a button Hopper spoke in to the mike that he had now placed on his shiny head. "Receiving you over, everything's fine. Copy."

"Damn you Hopper. What took you so long? We thought something had happened back there."

"Your head set must have been knocked, it reset your frequency. I've just got you back up and running again."

"Hell, if you only knew what we have just been through?" came Brains shaky voice.

"We know. We just looked through your video footage and saw the past half hour. Pretty hairy stuff," Hopper answered in to his headset.

"How's Flatfoot's head?" the Captain asked leaning in to the mike on

Hopper's head so he could be heard.

"He's fine. Just a cut on the ear. Lucky it didn't hit him on the other side of the head, because without it hitting the headset I think the projectile would have logged itself in my bro's skull, and done some nasty damage. Over."

"You're both okay then? Are you coming back or continuing? Over." The Captain asked.

"We are fine just a bit shaken up that's all, we are going to rest for a minute then continue. Plus I need to take a shit; I'm surprised it didn't come out just now." His reply ended in laughter, his comment had eased the situation.

They could now see the picture from Brains camera up on the main screen. His hands were up before his face, attending to his brother's ear. He had cleaned it up and was now placing cloth gorse over the ear and holding it in place with clear tape. The gauze would have a blocking effect, the blood would fill up the mesh, then dry, causing the blood to stop flowing which was always a problem when it was a chunk missing, because if it was a cut the cut would seal itself, but a hole needed help, which the gauze gave.

"Ok. Carry on as normal. But from now on Hopper's going to be watching your every move. Copy."

"We appreciate that Captain. Over."

"Carry on," the Captain said, now straightened up and put his arm on Hopper's shoulder.

"Call me if there are any problems. I'll be over checking the perimeter fence. Keep an eye on them. Also catalogue all the video footage so far. I think back home would be interested to see the creatures attacking one another. Because in the attack on the African base they were working as a team, but here they are territorial and fight among themselves." The Captain was now resting his finger on his chin, like he normally did when he was thinking.

"Like as if they were under someone or something else's control before," was Babe's answer to the Captain's unasked question.

"My exact thoughts," he said rubbing his chin. "And if that's the case, then whose control?"

21
What Prophecies Are Made Of

"Please sit. Rest you must be tired from you long journey?" Coben said as he pointed to the woven hemp mat on the floor, next to where another mat was laid out with some strange looking vegetables and some kind of meat on it.

Garry was about to speak when Coben spoke again. "I know you are very confused, and need some answers to a lot of questions which are laying heavy on your mind. You are also worried about your brother, but please.... sit." Coben spoke in a very accented English. But it carried warmth and knowledge in the way he spoke the words. He never raised his voice, never changing the tone, but you knew you would end up doing what he asked, sooner or later.

Garry went and sat down on the woven colourful mat where Coben had pointed, and went about massaging his feet.

"You can remove your shoes; I will not be offended by the smell." It was as if Coben could read his mind. Without any more words Coben sat down opposite him, crossed his legs, and lowered his head, then to all intense and purposes it looked as if he was saying a blessing upon the food. When he had finished Coben looked up at Garry, who felt guilty for staring at him.

Garry quickly pretended he hadn't seen.

"You seem embarrassed that I say grace?" Coben asked looking straight in to Garry's grey-blue eyes.

"No not embarrassed its' just that being here I thought -" Garry let the word hang in the air.

"You thought I would have given up on God?" Coben finished the sentence for him. "I am a Christian, and always will be. All because my surroundings have changed, doesn't mean I have to." Without saying anymore about it he took a piece of bread in his hands and broke it in two, handing one part to

Garry.

"Thank you, but I need -"

"Silence. Eat first regain your strength then we shall talk," Coben said as he passed what looked like a piece of chicken.

Garry took it gingerly, raised it to his nose and sniffed it.

"It is what we call a Screamer. It's an animal roughly the size of a chicken, but more like a lizard. It has wings but can't fly very far. It's called a Screamer because as you approach it in its hiding place it gives off a loud noise similar to a child screaming, to scare off its predators, because the noise that comes off of it sounds too loud for a creature as small as it is. The good thing for us is that it's easy to find because it gives itself away. Not being all that intelligent even after you have walked past it, it still screams so you then know where it is, and you have a meal." He said lifting a piece to his mouth and taking a bite.

Garry now licked the meat, which didn't really have any flavour.

"It doesn't really have a taste, but if you concentrate hard enough it can taste like chicken," was Coben's remark, which he said with a smile on his face.

Garry noticed this was the first time he had seen anyone smile since he got here. He gave a weak smile in return and took a large greasy bite.

They also had some greens that Coben explained grew on their own farm, which is inside the protective wall. He described how the food was grown.

A couple of the villagers have the power of speeding up nature. By concentrating on a plant or tree it would grow at an amazing speed right in front of your eyes. The *gift* was also useful when being attacked by a predator, creating a plant to spring to life and rap around the body of an on coming Lank. Because of the speed it would be running, its neck would snap by the shear velocity it was travelling one minute then coming to a complete stop the next.

Coben spoke about some of the other abilities the people had received when arriving here. Garry listened in awe as the god-like powers were described.

But all this was just pleasant talk, because Garry knew better than to ask any questions until Coben offered himself.

But also to his amazement Garry hadn't realized how hungry he was. It had been over half a day since he last ate, and he had now finished all the food set before him. He was feeling quite tired as well because he felt like he had been hit by jetlag. It was in the middle of the night when he and his brother had entered the strange house, but when he got here it was only midday. That was only an estimate because it was hard to tell what time of day it was being that the sky was always dull and overcast.

But now the light was dimming rapidly outside he was concluding that it must have been coming up to nightfall.

"You have been patient and have asked no more questions since we started our meal, so now I will tell you about the position you are now in, and what will come of you and your brother. Firstly your brother will be fine, given time his body will adsorb all the power that has been released into it and he will once again awake as if from a relaxing dream, or more to the point a nightmare. You yourself also have been given a gift, but it will take time for that gift to manifest itself, some gain it straight away, others take a couple days or even weeks before it manifests, but it will come." He then stood and walked over to a bowl on the side and washed the food from his hands. Then he gestured to Garry to do the same.

Without a word Garry rose and began to clean his hands and face, the water was refreshing, and he splashed it up over his face for the second time, just to feel the sensation of the water again. Accepting a cloth from Coben he then dabbed dry his face and hands.

Coben then handed Garry a cup and began to poor himself and Garry a cup full of red coloured liquid from a wooded caved jug.

Then, lifting the heavy lizard skin flap on the hut he stepped outside, keeping the leather flap up until his guest had walked under, and then he let it drop.

Walking around the back of the hut there was an open area with a circle of crude wooden seats. They had grass weaved cushions on them, and Coben picked one up and started to walk over in to another smaller clearing. Garry watched Coben then did the same; he picked up a seat and proceeded to carry it over to where Coben had placed his. Putting it down a couple of feet away from Coben's, but facing the same direction - looking out over the top of the village and down the hill in to the direction he had come only an hour or so before.

From their advantage point at the top of the hill where the village was situated, they could see over the one whole side of the settlement. People were going about their every day business, and preparing for the onset of night.

The sky was going a slight reddish colour over on the horizon directly in front of them. They could also see that there were about twenty or so villagers on the other side of the protective fence, all huddled together around something.

Seeing what Garry was looking at Coben spoke for the first time since they had left the hut. "That is the dragon which was slayed by your friends the unicorn and the fire-dragon, only an hour or so ago, the flesh is still warm I would think?" At that he lifted the drink to his lips and took a sip from the cup he was caressing in his hands.

"Ahhhh... this drink is so refreshing, it is a wine made from the berries of a Spike tree, and they are very difficult to harvest, so the drink is very prized among our village. Please drink." He said lifting his cup in the air as if to emphasize the fact Garry had one in his hand as well.

"The meat from the dragon will feed this village for over a week, and the skin will go into making shields and clothing. Its teeth will be made into weapons. Its claws will be kept by the healers, because one small scratch from them knocks a person unconscious for hours. But its blood will be poured out upon the ground, because all blood is sacred here, even it's," he said waving the cup towards the dead dragon.

"Its head will be raised on a tall pole, as a warning to other creatures of this world."

Coben's tone then changed in to his business voice. "See those plumes of what looks like smoke in the distance?" He waved his hand over towards the horizon. But there was no need; it was the first thing Garry had noticed when coming out of the hut.

Coben continued. "There were four of those Gateways. We don't know why, but one was shut down. We take hope from that, and try as hard as we can to shut down the other three. But alas..." Coben let out a long deep breath. "It take's all our energy just to stay alive in this world. Let alone trying to close them," he said once again pointing at the Gates.

"They are connected to our world, by what means we don't know? But the fact that all the people here came through one of them proves that point." He took another sip.

"There use to be only one of those Gateways until he came through."

Garry didn't ask who the he was, knowing that Coben would come to that part when he was ready.

"See on this world, this dimension, whatever you care to call it, was run by those called the Holy Ones. These beings were the religious people in charge of the inhabitants of this world, they worshipped the Gateway, and the life giving energy that it poured continually into their world.

Garry pictured the gleaming bones, the tall standing stones and flapping flags around the Gateway. It did indeed look like a shrine or religious area of some kind. Only religion can use death so casually.

"They look like us, need all the things we do, food, water, a God. They passed sacrifices through the wall, in which you came out of. Things from this side can enter but we cannot leave. Anyway, they had been doing this for as long as any could remember. Who had made the original Gateway no one knows or cares. It has been there for thousands of years, and the people indigenous to this world had worshipped it, by means of the pious Holy Ones.

"That was until some time ago; no one knows exactly when; when two brothers entered through the Gateway, while they were all worshipping before it.

"The people were dumbstruck. The Holy Ones weren't sure what to do. Then just like yourself and your brother who had stumbled on to the Gateway from the other side, they were also confused, and didn't know what was happening to them." Coben then leaned forward and scratched some itch on his knee. He continued:

"Then one of the brothers collapsed. They were then taken to the Temple of the Sky, which was situated on the inside of a colossal mountain. There one brother tried to wake the other, all under the scrutiny of the Holy Ones," Coben once again scratched at the stubborn itch.

"After that the story becomes a little confusing. There are many different opinions as to what happened next, but the most reliable is this: When the brother who had collapsed awoke he proclaimed to have been sent by the God whom they had been worshipping for eons.

"He then killed or imprisoned his brother. This we are not sure about. But he told the Holy Ones that he had sent him back to tell their God how faithful they had been over the years.

"Then he took control of the whole order of Holy Ones, and announced he was now their true ruler." Coben stood and without a word went back in to the hut, returning a moment later with the jug of Spike tree wine. He then went to refill Garry's cup but upon seeing it still full went and retook his seat, and then poured another cup of wine for himself. After taking a sip he made himself comfy in the chair then continued.

"The power he obtained coming through the Gateway was unlike anything the Holy Ones had ever seen before. Believing their God sent him they put him in an elevated position. He asked them how the Gateway worked.

Thinking it was a test they openly told him all the Gates secrets which had been passed down from generation to generation of Holy Ones, they told -" He turned to Garry. "You really want to try that wine; it is refreshing to say the least."

Garry who had forgotten he was even holding a cup, looked down in to his drink. It was red in colour and had what looked like corky bits and small red petals floating in it. But so as not to cause offence - but mainly so Coben would continue - he took a sip. It was refreshing and surprisingly nice on the tongue.

He raised his mug to Coben and gave mocking cheers! "Very nice," was all he could think to say.

Coben then turned back facing the mountains in the distance and continued his story.

"He; we say he because no one knows his true name, or where he originally came from, or even which Gateway was the original. Personally I believe it is the African gate, mainly because of its appearance.

"Anyway he then knew how the Gateways worked. He was told about the special stone, which made the Gateway possible.

"He then put the hundreds of thousands of people to work, in huge quarries, where they were to look for the stone to make more Gateways, to bring him more power. They erected three more Gates all in different locations, and he is still looking for more of the rare stone, especially now one of them has been shut down." Coben stirred in his chair to make himself more comfy, he then reached out for a log and placed it under his feet as a footstool.

"Even now after these long years the quarries are still there; seven of them now. Huge gashes in the land stretching for kilometres at a time. Generation after generation, being born in to nothing more than slavery, but knowing no different from the life they had been born in to." Coben turned to his side to see what reaction this had had on his guest.

Garry was just staring straight ahead in to the distance, which was getting darker by the minute.

"The Circle," he continued, "is his way of controlling the people: his people," Coben said the last bit in a mocking tone.

"All those of the Holy Ones were imprisoned. Only the young from the religious organization were kept in his service, so he could mould them in to what he wanted – brainwashed with greed and offers of supremacy.

"He has endowed them with powers to keep control of the 'followers' he likes to call them. The older Holy Ones slowly started to die off. Slowly he wiped out the past.

"He controls everything in this world; the Circle, the people, and even the animals. The only things he can't, and doesn't control are us." He poured himself more drink from the carved wooden jug, which was now empty. He put the empty jug on the ground next to his chair.

"See he can't stop others from coming through the Gateways, not without destroying them, and he can't do that because he needs the Gates power, because he needs his power to control the Circle, and his so called 'follower'. He hasn't the energy to control us as well. So he mutated some of the creatures of this world, and endowed them with intelligence enough to do his will. These he uses to fight against us all the time. It's easier to control them than it is us."

Garry now asked a question for the first time. "Has he lived so long because of the power he holds?"

"I am two hundred and ninety-nine years old, in two mouths and four days. I was fifty when I stumbled through the Gate, hiding from those pursuing me." Coben lowered his head; the memory of why he was running was still as fresh after so many long years.

Then he spoke again. "See, all those that live in this world die through old age. We -" he said sweeping his hand over the village "- all of us that come through the Gateway die only when we have are lives taken from us. Murdered, killed, call it what you will. But you will stay the same age you are now for as long as this place lets you live. So, the misery of this world, the so called 'followers' all in this village and others like it will continue like this until the prophecy has been fulfilled." Coben now turned to Garry.

"The prophecy?" Garry asked. After everything he had heard the word prophecy was bound to come in to it sooner or later.

"The ancient prophecy was supposedly scratched on the wall of the prison cell where the Holy Ones were being held, until they died. The last one scratched the words on the wall just before he passed away.

"He had all who saw it put to death, but like a virus the word spread until all knew the prophecy. The last thing the Holy Ones left this drying world was..." Coben paused, and then continued. "*One would bring destruction, but two are needed to bring order.*" Coben looked Garry directly in the eyes. "You and your brother are the two mentioned in the prophecy. You two alone will destroy the Evil One, the Dark Lord who now rules this sickened world. You both will bring about the release of the 'followers' and bring about order and peace."

Coben then stood up, and with a slight wobble righted his chair, looked over to Garry straightened himself up and waved his hand over the village.

"But all that can start tomorrow, because tonight we have a dragon to prepare."

"Prepare?" Garry asked, confounded that he could change the subject at the drop of a hat.

"Prepare for the celebration, because tonight the prophecy starts to be fulfilled. And I do love a good party."

22
To Do or Not To Do

It took them sometime before they found the original trail, which they were following before the incident with the two Moregones.

They had run in panic and they had paid the price: with time. They were hoping to catch up with the group and the young men before dark, but now because of the detour it was getting late; night was closing in fast.

They stood at the edge of a clearing looking out over a barren wasteland that ended in the distance at the foot of a large hill. The hill was maybe a couple of kilometres away tops. But the fact it was getting dark and they would be out in the open didn't fair well with them. They could have used artificial light, but while crossing the barren land it could attract all sorts of predators. The last thing they wanted was more exercise, having to out run something else that might consider them an evening snack before bedtime.

Besides both were wet and smelling of marshy moss and stagnant water, after taking wrong footsteps in the fading light. And the green rising gasses was attracting clouds of buzzing insects that kept flying over to investigate them.

Brains had a powerful set of binoculars held up to his face scanning the distance. He believed he saw some sort of light issuing from the top of the hill. But in this dimming light and at this distance it was hard to see anything.

So he now lowered down a pair of PVS-7D generation 3 night vision goggle/binoculars. He slowly started to focus the 40 degree view finder in on to the hill in the distance. To his amazement he could see blazing fires on the top of the hillside. Also many fuzzy green outlines of people, some sitting around the huge open-air fires, others that he would only describe as dancing around. And all this was happening in some kind of fenced in area. Also there were squat looking mounds he would have sworn were some kind of huts. There must be hundreds of people living at the top of that hill. Even with all the creatures they had seen and witnessed, they were still out in the open, with great fires to advertise their presence.

The two brothers decided to make camp at the edge of the clearing for the night, before they reported back to the base camp via radio. They knew the camera was being left on, on the other end but because they had met no more problems Hopper was now outside preparing the camp for nightfall along with the others.

Flatfoot and Brains had all sorts of instruments and equipment to set up so they could be safe during the night. They picked one section that had thick bushes around a small area that was far enough away from the greasy water as possible, and then with their Ka-Bar Night Raider knives hacked their way through into the middle that was practically empty. The bush was a kind of donut ring, with a green canopy over the top, with a practically clear patch in the centre. Here they set up camp in the seven-foot area, roughly a circle.

The area they had climbed in through was then put back in place. A hole about three feet across was cut so they could enter the thick bush. This was then pushed through the holes of a camouflaged net, and then secured on the inner side. So they now had a small entrance. Once it had been pulled back into position, and fastened, it would be almost impossible to see that the bush had even been tampered with from the outside.

From Brains backpack they took out a ground sheet of water proof material, not the sort that crackles and makes irritating; but more important; loud noises. This one was designed to be water proof, but also silent and manageable, like rubber.

They then removed a thin but strong, dark green almost black material, which was also water proof and strong. This was put over them like a dome, going from the ground right over the top to the other side, on the inside of the bush. Now with this secured, and in place they could light their torches and it wouldn't be seen from the outside of the thick tangled vegetation.

Then all around the inside of the bottom of the bush was pushed small cylindrical objects, which were all connected to one electronic box. If anything got to close and started to rip away at the bush to get at them, then these devices would emit magnesium flares lighting the bush up like the sun itself, confusing and hopefully blinding the creature, or creatures that were attacking them, to give them time to get a safe distance away.

With all this in place and secured they could now send a message back to base camp.

BEEP... BEEP... BEEP...

"Get the Captain." Hopper asked Babe. He was outside working on the spotlights that would flare to life once the M60D machine guns tripped on, when the beeping was heard coming from inside the truck.

Babe was helping him in his assignment, but now she was sent to get the Captain, who had been dry shaving.

Hopper climbed inside and positioned himself in front of the computer monitor. He was just punching up the information sent when the Captain accompanied by Babe, and Doc entered the truck.

The three of them stood hunched shouldered looking over Hopper's back at the Zenith 25" plasma screen.

The camera was still switched on but they were not communication by voice, now that they had set up their camp they didn't want to give themselves away by making any noise. The message was comprised of written text, along with recorded pictures, down loaded from an extra attachment that clipped on to their night vision binoculars. It read:

Report: We have located the camp we believe the two young men were taken. The trail leads straight in the camps general direction. The camp - or from the size of it we should say village - is situated on the top of a hill: seven kilometres *northwest of your location on alignment 123-17, there is a lot of activity in the village at the moment. We are still in the nine-mile circle area of the location beacon in the remaining headset, if there is a need to join us. There is some picture reference to our position point, which has been sent with this written message... Awaiting your reply.*

"Get the recording up and running," was the Captain's next request.

But Hopper was already bringing the format up on the flat screen.

The picture was rather fuzzy because of the distance and the limited light, and also because of the power output of the binoculars.

The picture showed the top of a hill, slowly being zoomed in to. Four fires could be seen burning, with an eerie green flame. With a large number of people moving around the four focal points and some were stationary.

"Hopper can you sort the picture out a bit, make it clearer?"

Hopper started his fingers racing over the keyboard. Then the picture was pulled up to the full size of the screen. A small box then appeared. With the mouse, Hopper enlarged it over a group who looked like they were sitting down. Once the box was in place he punched a command key and from the top of the box a line slowly started to move downwards. As it went the picture became clearer, taking out and refining the pixels so the objects would become more distinct.

He repeated his process a couple of times until a clear picture could be seen. Even though it was all in a light green colour the picture was very apparent.

In the square they had cleaned up a group of people, males and females, all sitting around, and by the look of it they were celebrating something. One even jumped up pulling another with her, and started to dance around a bonfire.

"Send a message back, tell them to hold position. Repeat to hold position. We are leaving to join them first light. Repeat first light we are packing up and meeting them at *123-17*. We will follow the beacon to their current position. They are not to approach the hill in anyway. Repeat stay in position we are coming to join you. Out."

The Captain looked around at Babe and Doc. "This was never covered in our debriefing; we are doing it off our own backs. Our orders are to stay here and do experiments until the Gateway is secured at the other end.

"But they never knew there would be settlements here. From the look of the village there could be more.

"The two young men got through, we got through, who's to say more haven't?"

Hopper swung his chair around to face them; he rubbed his hand over his face then over the top of his shaved head. "Captain, I believe I speak for us all when I say let's go have a look."

"We could all be court-marshalled for breaking a direct order," the Captain replied.

"Yeah, but how are they going to do that sir? They can't call us back through. And they definitely wouldn't come through to court-martial us," Babe replied.

"We owe it to whoever is out there, to see what the situation is sir," Doc chipped in.

"Then we go check the village." The Captain looked at them all one at a time.

"Yes Sir," the three replied together.

"Hopper send the message back. First thing in the morning we are packing up camp, and joining them."

23
All-Aboard

The night was getting along.

Flatfoot and Brains had sent their report with the visual references, and had received the reply. They weren't sure what the response would be. They thought they would be sent orders as to proceed with surveillance or hold back while the visual footage was being studied. But the orders that came back didn't so much confuse them, but completely shock them. The last thing they thought would happen would be for them to all pack up and come and join them.

But at the moment that was the least of their worries. It was now pitch black outside, because of the cloud cover the light from what could only be described as the moon was not getting through as brightly as it could.

The night was also quiet, to quiet; as if all the animals knew better than to move around at night, unless you were a predator. But there was always a larger animal than you out there, so even the predators had to tread carefully.

It had been over two hours since they had sent the message back to the main base.

All they could do now was wait for the others to join them in the morning. They were to take turns catching sleep. One sleeping, while one staying awake, having to always be alert to what was going on, on the outside of their sheltered bush.

There wasn't much you could do in such a small space, but they were trained to stay in positions like this for as long as their food and water held out. They had food and water for two days, even though they were to be met in the morning, anything could happen. They could be stuck out here for the two days waiting for the others to arrive.

But that was just negative thinking. If the Captain said he would be here first thing in the morning, then they would be.

It was time to wake his brother up. There was no other way to do it. Flatfoot nudged his brother with his foot. They were laying head to toe, so as he nudged his brother his foot was on his brother's head, rocking him slowly to wake him without making him jump, or shout.

But Brains didn't jump. He hadn't been in to deep a sleep. When on these sort of operations you couldn't fall in to a deep sleep. Besides it takes three hours for the body to go in to what's called REM, Rapid Eye Movement; where your body goes in to a deep dreamless state, so much so that you could touch, and in some cases shout at the person and it wouldn't even so much as make them stir.

So they only slept for two hours at a time, on and off all night. The only problem with that is your body is not moving from the position you wake up from, so it would be easy to fall back to sleep again, it was only strong will power and practise that keeps you awake. They had both excelled in their sensory deprivation courses.

Suddenly Flatfoot thought he had heard something, off to the right hand side over his shoulder. He waved his hand above his head to get his brothers attention. Then waved three fingers over his shoulder to point in the direction the noise came from, the sign to show he had heard something.

They both held their breath, and opened their mouths wide, to be able to hear better. It could only be a small foraging animal looking for food. Or it could be some one from the village; maybe they spotted them making their way across the wasteland, and were coming to have a closer inspection.

Who or whatever it was, it wasn't welcome.

Flatfoot had his hand hovering over the switch for the magnesium flares. They both had pulled their goggles down over their eyes. There was no point setting the flares off if it was going to blind you as well.

The silence was deafening, they could swear the noise of the hearts beating would give their location away. Seconds turned in to minutes, minutes felt like long drawn-out hours.

Flatfoot let out his breath not realizing he was holding it. He needed to wipe the sweat off his forehead, but one arm was tucked under his right hand side. The other was resting on the switch; he couldn't afford to move either of them.

Brains was reaching inside his backpack that was lying on the ground beside him. Slowly so not to make any noise he pulled out a small piece of equipment; it was a 24oz Thermal Vision Tag-7 Goggles, that would pick up any heat signature within a thousand meters of their location, with the thermal sensitivity of 100 mk. The only reason it wasn't already on was because they didn't know whether anyone in this area could pick up the electrical output it gave off.

He raised it to his eyes and turned it on. It took a few seconds for the equipment to warm up, and then when it did the picture was confusing. There was what could only be described as shadows walking around outside the bush, they gave off no body heat, and you could see the trail they left as the air was disturbed. It took a couple more seconds for this to register in his brain.

The reason the machine didn't pick up their body heat was because they were lizards: cold blooded. They took heat from their surrounding area, but if it was cold, so their bodies couldn't absorb the heat so they gave off no heat residue.

All this took no more than five seconds to comprehend, but even that was to long. They were upon the bush within seconds, tearing at the leaves with their long clawed fingered hands, issuing no sound, silently trying to get to the two warm bodies inside.

At that same moment they started their attack Flatfoot slapped the activation button. The problem was he still had the Thermal Vision goggles on, because he hadn't had chance to change them back for the darken ones. Even with his eyes closed tight Flatfoot could feel his eyes watering, burning even. Also the heat the magnesium gave off was intense. Whatever the Lanks hadn't stripped away was sent up in a quick burst of severe white flames.

It was all over in an instant. Even though the flames had taken out the first wave of Lanks there was just too many of them; one wave after another came running forward, climbing over the burnt fallen bodies of their companions. It was over in a matter of minutes.

Flatfoot and Brains both tried to stand and pull the P90 weapons to bear, but it was too late; there was just too many of them.

Flatfoot felt many clawed hands lifting him into the air: strong clawed hands, like clamps over his arms and legs. He felt their strength; he knew they could crush him in an instant if they so desired. As he turned his head to the left he could see them doing the same to his brother. But his brother wasn't moving. Flatfoot hoped he was just unconscious. Because there was nothing he could do for his brother now, he had to just hope he would be all right; there was still a chance, even a slight one, the Lanks hadn't killed them outright, which they could have done dozens of times over by now.

Then Flatfoot caught sight of where the Lanks were taking them. Maybe forty or so foot away from the bush they were hiding in was a cart. The cart had a large cage on the back made out of wooden poles - thick wooden poles; even by looking at it Flatfoot knew if they were put in it they wouldn't be able to get out again until they were taken out.

The cart had only two wheels, large cumbersome looking things that didn't promise a comfy ride. Pulling the cart was a two legged, dark grey creature that had the oversized body of a frog; it was covered in lumps and warts, and walked on its hind legs, with short clawed arms at the front. It had no neck to speak of, it's head just blended in to its body. It had two huge eyes that swivelled independently of one another. But the most prominent feature was its mouth; it must have taken up half of its face, a toothless maw, which was constantly opening and shutting. This suggested that it had walked a long way already, and was even now trying to get its breath back. The creature was probably a little larger than a shire horse, and just as much bulk as one, and it was strapped to the cart by two poles, chains and thick hemp rope.

But the main thing that got his attention was the middle-aged man that had his hand on the creature and was now patting it in a reassuring manner. The handler didn't sit on the creature but rather led it by the rope, which was attached to the underside of the creatures harness.

The man didn't look any better off than the creature did. He wore torn scruffy clothes and his hair was unkempt and long. He had a beard that went down to his chest, and was all matted with twigs and bits of leaves protruding out, as if he had fallen and hasn't bothered to brush himself off. Even though he couldn't have been any older than forty or so, he looked much older and fore-longed. He looked a pitiful sight. His eyes were glazed and the spirit of life had long since gone from them, leaving him an empty shell, being no will left to fight back against his captors.

Even in the predicament Flatfoot was in he felt sorry for this slave.

But then as he was being carried closer he noticed another man off to one side. He was sat on what Flatfoot could only describe as a unicorn. Looking like an ordinary horse, well muscled, and a long black mane that was tied back in flowing braids. But the most impressive thing was the large ivory horn protruding from the middle of its eyes. The unicorn was the size of a standard horse back home and was a jet-black colour. Almost invisible against the darkness of the night, the outline of it was mainly picked out by the cloak that the man was wearing upon it - this draped down over the unicorns sides and hunches. The cloak was dark grey, but still lighter than the colour of the unicorn, and the night around him.

Nothing could be seen of the man apart from the hands that were holding the reins, which looked like they were covered in a kind of chain-mail gloves. His face was covered over by the hood of the cloak; all that could be seen was the wisps of his breath being caught in the cold night air. But his feet could also be seen, and they looked like they were covered with overlapping metal plates, that ended in a wicked looking curved hook.

He hadn't spoken, or moved his head towards what was going on. Rather he had his head down. He didn't even seem to notice what was going on around him, as if he slept sat upright. But the hands gripping the harness gave his awareness away. He radiated pure confidence, even though Flatfoot couldn't see any weapons. Then again why would he need any? By the looks of things he controlled the Lanks.

But that was the last thing he remembered seeing as the Lanks threw his brother into the cart. Then as they threw him in, his head struck the side of the wooden cage. He felt no pain, just darkness as he slipped in to the sweet blissfulness of unconsciousness.

Their bodies were stripped of all belts and pockets emptied of all contents. Pockets ripped as over sized clawed hands pulled at the zippers and poppers. Then the door was lashed in to place, leather pulled tight, and salt water poured over it, making it impossible to open without a knife to cut it.

The lone rider then with a small almost unnoticeable nod of his head sent the Lanks scurrying off in to the cover of the night. Then the lone rider moved off in to the darkness, with the cart lumbering slowly behind.

24
Dance Until the Light

The festive spirit was well underway.

Garry felt slightly guilty that he was actually enjoying himself while his brother still lay in a deep comatose state.

But Coben laid his hand on to Garry's arm for the third time in as many minutes, and told him his brother would be fine, given time and rest.

The people of the village were dancing around the immense fires, while eating the flesh from the fallen dragon. Even now the skin lay stretched over the tall strong poles in the distance drying. A symbol of the power of people united. The village had a lot to celebrate, for now in there presence was the two the prophecy talked about; whom the prophecy promised – their salvation.

People had been going up to Garry all evening, some just touching him, others just staring. This was a strange experience for him, in a sense it was like being worshiped. His brain still hadn't quite taken in all that had happen so far today, and now with all the attention he was being given he felt drunk with power; the six cups of spike tree wine wasn't helping matters either.

The night was moving on, people were shouting and dancing, linking arms and skipping in great circles around the blazing fires. The people's spirits were being lifted up along with their voices.

"It has been a long time since I have seen the village so happy," Coben stated, leaning over shouting in to Garry's ear.

But Garry gave no response. It wasn't a question, more of an observation, so he saw no reason to answer, but just kept staring out over the village as he enjoyed the night's revelry.

Before everyone lay a banquet fit for a king. Wooden bowls filled and overflowing with many colourful dishes, vegetables of all kinds, strange limp yellow leafed greens, bloated orange things that oozed flame coloured liquid, and a large collection of fried, roasted, and steamed fish. Garry wondered where the river or lake was.

Coben had a lump of tender red meat in his hand, and every now and then he would take a bit from it. Coben had explained to Garry that it was the meat from the fallen dragon. Once when Garry went on holiday to Turkey he had eaten wild boar meat, it was very tender and it easily fell apart in the mouth. The dragon was very similar. He had expected it to be tough and chewy.

Then Coben stood and raised his arms, as a sign he was about to speak. It took a couple minutes for everyone to settle down. Then after a few minutes the village was standing staring over at their leader.

Coben Hathanen opened his mouth and was just about to speak when someone shouted from his left. Startled that anyone would interrupt Coben, who was about to talk, the whole villages attention was drawn over to the offender, who had his hand raised pointing out in to the far distance. All their eyes followed to where the person was pointing. Then they all saw what the ceremony was all about.

In the distance a great blinding light was rising from the ground. It flared white-hot for about four seconds then faded away. Even from this distance some covered their eyes. Those that didn't had dancing spots before them.

The village became silent - waiting.

Some continued to stare at the point the light originated from, which was just on the other side of the barren wasteland, a couple of kilometres in the distance. Others were now talking between themselves; some had turned towards Coben and Garry waiting for an explanation.

Coben turned to look down at Garry but he was also looking towards Coben for an answer. But Coben had none to give. He could have guessed; then again anyone seeing the blinding light could have guessed about its origins. But Coben wasn't in the business of guessing: lives depended on him getting the right answers.

"Lake, Raven come with me to my hut, if you please." Then turning to walk away he suddenly turned back as if remembering something. "Garry, I wish to speak with you also." Then he turned his attention to the rest of the crowd who were still staring. Whispering.

"Dance on, the night is still young." With that the four started to make their way towards Coben's hut.

Some went back to dancing. The music in part started up again, but the festive spirit was now lacking somewhat.

People were gathering in groups talking about the light, speculating. Others were far too drunk to care and went back to flinging their bodies back in to their attempt at dancing. But all in all the spirit of the night had been dampened.

Like this place always did when you thought you were winning - taking hope, it would pull it out from beneath you in one foul swipe.

Flatfoot kept his eyes shut. The pain behind them was excruciating. He was disorientated to start with. He remembered lying on his back hitting the flare switch, which seemed even brighter due to having the wrong goggles on, it succeeded in momentarily blinding him.

He remembered the onslaught of the Lanks, and then that was it. With his eyes still shut, and a little sore, he tried to reach out with his senses. He now realized he was moving, a slow side to side movement that he could only guess as a truck or cart of some kind. Then his nose picked up the sent of straw, his skin starting to itch, he was lying on his back. He could only guess where his brother was, or how many Lanks were sitting around waiting for him to show any signs of movement. But at the same time he couldn't stay like this indefinitely.

The cart was moving on the way to somewhere. So he didn't have long to waste. He swallowed, tasting blood. He ran his tongue over his lip and found it puffed-up, but the bleeding had stopped which suggested he had been out for at least an hour or so.

He slowly opened his eyes waiting for them to adjust. It was dark. He could see the reflection of a torch to his right. Slowly turning his head he could make out the wooden bars around him and the body of his older brother to his left. Then the hazy memory returned, of how he had been tossed into this moving prison.

Brains was lying on his front with his head against the side of the cart, but his back was rising and falling in slow shallow movements. He was breathing that was at least good news. But what sort of state he was in was another matter.

He lay there taking in deep breaths letting his body completely awaken. He mentally checked himself over, apart from the bleeding ear from earlier, and the headache, which even now was starting to reside, and the swollen lip, he was in good shape, no broken bones, just a lot of bruises.

He wiggled his hands that at the moment seemed foreign to him. His entire conscious was around his senses, sight, smell, and hearing. But now he went to move the rest of his body it seemed out of proportion. It took his brain a couple moments to realign itself. He slowly moved his toes, and then gradually tried moving his head to one side, lifting his neck slowly to see what the light source was issuing from.

The handler of the creature had the ugly beast travelling behind a light, which was hanging from a bending pole so the creature could see the way forward. The creatures night vision was obviously not as good as it could have been, so he made a mental note that this creature didn't usually travel around at night-time.

The creature was also overly tense and didn't like the night travelling. The handler was doing all he could to settle the creature down as he walked along beside it.

Twenty minutes or so later he awoke again.

Realizing he must of slipped back into unconsciousness. He realized he must have hit his head harder than he first thought.

He tried to move his head again to see if he could spot the lone rider on the back of the unicorn. But as he tried to move his head in the other direction the pain was unbelievable. He fought against fainting again. Slowly he moved his head back to where he started and closed his eyes. He relaxed his whole body and tried to calm down.

The last thing he needed was a neck injury. But common sense saved him; his hands and feet were fine. No numbness anywhere in his body, just pain. Pain was good. If it went numb he had a problem. But so far all of his body was screaming out to him. The pain was almost unbearable, but it was there.

He stayed still for a few minutes then slowly, this time so slow it didn't seem like he was moving at first; he started to look over again towards the unicorn rider. He could see him just in the light coming from the handler's lamp. But he was way off to one side, no sign of the Lanks. But then why would he need them, now they were in no state to try and run free. He could barely move, let-alone run. And his brother still had not so much as moved.

The rider needed no light as if he knew the way, as if it he travelled this way so many times, or was following some sort of different vision, as if using some other sight.

His head was down not looking where he went, as if the unicorn was leading the way. It was not reassuring because he looked like he was in complete control, not a good sign for them both.

The road - if it could be called that - was getting smoother. From the light sent from the lamp he could no longer see the trees or bushes so he realized the path was opening up, becoming more spacious, as if riding out onto a plain or grassland.

Time was ticking by, he knew that given time the Captain and the others would turn up and see what had happened and follow them.

He just hoped it wasn't an all-out attack, and that they weren't fighting for their life as well.

25
The Temple of the Sky

All was getting done.

The truck was almost full, the gear was easy to store away, it was designed to be easy; to get out as quick as possible. There were only a few things left to pack in to the large, hard bubble boxes.

They were also destroying all proof that they had been there. But the huge scorch mark around the Gateway was better cover than they could of hoped for. The area was so badly burned that there was no way of knowing that anyone had been here.

They moved quietly all knew what had to be done; they were all getting on with their jobs assigned to them. It was taking just a little longer because the two brothers weren't here to help.

Babe was thinking to herself. What were they going to do after the project finished? They would be packing up to move out to destroy the Gateway. But what then? What were they to do? She had never thought about what they would do after, where were they to go? She knew there was no way back. But what if there were others here? Others like her; like them. They were going to have to make a life here, but all-in-all she had not contemplated the future.

"You okay there?" The Captain asked, putting his hand gently on her forearm.

"Yes..." She had a far away look in her eyes. "Sorry, my mind was else where." She looked down embarrassed, before continuing. "I'm okay now, a little thinking, nothing more."

"Thinking can be good, but it can also distract the mind," he said taking his hand off her arm. "Keep busy, that all I can say. It works for me," he said as he turned and started to walk away.

She called after him. "Wait its just -" Her words trailed off. "I'm sorry," she looked down again. "It's just, I never thought this far ahead. I -" She stood tall and seemed to shake herself off. "Sorry Captain. Just a little self-pity I'm okay now," she said turning back to what she was doing before.

"It's okay Babe, we're all thinking along those lines: me included." He helped her lift a box on to the back of the all-terrain vehicle. "That's why I came to you first. I know we are all thinking the same, if we didn't we wouldn't be human." He winked and walked away.

Doc was stacking his things in to the containers they arrived in; these were shock proof and fire resistant. You never knew what the vehicle would get involved in, and no matter what happened to the truck; the medical supplies would be needed when everything calmed down, or even cooled down, in the case of fire. He was working fast, but he knew what he was doing. That was until Hopper came over and tapped him on the shoulder.

"Damn you fool," Doc said spinning around, doing a good impression of Mr. T., and not realizing it. "Don't ever sneak up on me like that," he had a stern look on his face, as if to say: *If you don't believe I mean it then read my expression.* His hand had also instinctively gone to his Sig Sauer side arm's handle.

"Look we haven't heard from Flatfoot or Brains this morning," he said completely ignoring Docs first reactions.

"So, have you a point to this? I'm busy." Doc grumbled, turning his back to him, while clipping the catch back over the guns handle, and then finishing packing the delicate apparatus.

"It's over an hour past sunrise. If you can call it that." Hopper had turned around and was looking at the dim light coming through the thick churning cloud layer.

"If you think there's a problem then talk to the Captain." That was it as far as Doc was concerned. He wasn't in charge and didn't want to be. It wasn't his problem. The medical supplies were, and at the moment he was being interrupted while trying to do his job.

Now Hopper was in a confused state. He was great with computers but when it came to making any decisions it wasn't his strong forte. But he thought Doc would tell him it's okay to approach the Captain, or would go there himself to tell. But now he wasn't certain. But he had a strange gut feeling. Then again that could probably just be the strange surroundings, or the mishmash of food the two brothers had cooked the evening before.

So he went back to his job, reeling in the cable that connected the M60D's machineguns together. The cable started to smoke. He took his eyes off the cloud billowing out of the top of the Gateways hillock, down to what he was doing. He hadn't reeled it in already. "Damn that was fast," he muttered to himself. "I must have lost track of time." But if he thought more about it, and touched the wire he would have realized it was hot from the speed it had been wound up.

The bleak sun started to rise, trying to push through the thick cloud stratum.

Flatfoot shivered with the cold. He had been in and out of consciousness all night, but now he was fully awake, aching from head to toe but awake. Even his neck was feeling somewhat better, he could now roll it either way, and his whole body had almost recovered. Which was a stupid thought because after the beating he had received he should have been laid up for days, but only hours later he was feeling better? The pain was still there in certain areas, but all in all his body was recovering remarkably fast.

He now rolled over onto his stomach, looking at the animal keeper, who was up in front walking along with the revolting frog-like beast. The creature was exhausted, its warty body covered in slime like sweat, bubbles popping on its wide mouth.

The horseman was well ahead, just the rattle and jingling of his unicorns harness was the only sound coming from his direction. The rider still rode with his head slightly inclined towards the ground, giving him the impression of being a hunchback, or a very old man. Flatfoot had no idea; he could be both or neither.

Now he wasn't looking at the roof of the cart he could see where they were being taken. Up ahead across the grassland, looking between the hills they were now passing through was a huge mountain, colossus in size, shooting up out of the land surrounding it, as if the earth itself was rejecting it, pushing it away. It stood alone with no other mountains or hills around it. The top of it was lost in the haze of the cloud cover, it was an incredible sight. Lightning was sparking off the sides, bouncing back and forth from the mountain to the clouds, a continuous firework display of phenomenal elemental power.

The animal handler looked over his shoulder for the first time. He looked at Flatfoot, staring in to his eyes, realizing his passenger was now awake he came to a standstill.

The creature was completely oblivious and kept walking forward, by the time the creature had taken a few lumbering strides the man was now standing next to the cart. He then matched the carts movement walking along side.

Reaching down below Flatfoots line of sight under the carts side, he withdrew a ladle. Flatfoot presumed he had just scooped it from a bucket of some sort. The man put his arm through the bars and held his hand out.

Flatfoot just stared at the brown murky water.

The man looked at him, grunted, then took the ladle back and took a swig, showing Flatfoot what he should do, as if Flatfoot had never drunk from a ladle before, and in the process showing off a collection of blacken teeth. He offered it back again, but now Flatfoot had seen from the mans actions that it could be drank; ignoring the colour he took a sip. It was muddy, but it had been a while since he had any water, and even this was better than nothing. He pointed at his brother. The man stared, as if deciding what to do. Then he pulled the ladle out, sank it back out of his line of sight and pulled it forth, full once again of cloudy liquid.

Flatfoot tried to sit; putting all his effort in to it, he just managed to. He reached across to his brother and pulled him towards himself, turned him over and rested his brothers' head on his lap. He then took the ladle and started pouring it over Brains cracked lips, wetting them at first; rubbing the water around with his finger tip. This would bring anybody around, the sense of water, but it had no effect. He slowly poured some into his brother's mouth, slowly letting in run down his throat by gravity. He didn't want to drown his brother with a ladle of water, but he knew his brother would need it, and he wasn't sure when their next chance of a drink would be.

The handler turned; stared at the unicorn rider as if he had been given instructions. He put his dirty rag covered arm back through for the ladle, received it and dropped it back in to the bucket with a plop. He leant close to the bars and stared at Flatfoot long and hard, looking at all his clothes, and Brains clothes to, as if trying to decide who, or what they were.

But when Flatfoot went to speak the man held his finger up to his lips and looked sideways at the lone rider. He then turned sharply and jogged to the side of his slowly bounding creature, which didn't even give him a sidelong glance but just kept lumbering forward.

The riders head turned in their direction, his hood waving around his hidden face, plumes of fetish breath catching the chilly air, rising up around the cloaks edges. Seemingly uncaring he turned back to the trail; his chain linked covered hands gripped the bridle harder.

The rocky outcrop started to close in around the cart, as the wooden contraption started to bounce and judder over mud and sharp flint like stones.

Tall dreary trees overhung the imposing rock face, their misshapen leaves brushing against the cart as it passed; depositing the accumulated dew. Scrawny bushes clung to any crevice; all dripping a musical symphony from the mornings heavy mist. Long rope-like vines, with small white flowers, crawled over most bare surfaces; here and there the thin stalk would bulge in to a vast sack, where the clinging vine had collected the misty morning rain water to feed it during the coming day ahead. Here and there scuttling creatures darted from root to stem to leaves, their small armour cased bodies glinting in the morning dew.

They seemed to be going through some sort of deep ravine; possibly following some ancient riverbed. The outcrops veered straight up, sheer walls of solid impenetrable rock.

Flatfoot's only hope was that part wasn't going to break free and completely crunch the cart they were in. But from the position he was now in he was watching where they were being taken. The ravine suddenly opened right up, and the mountain was now the full forward view. Nothing else could be seen apart from this mammoth outcrop of rock.

Lightning was almost blinding the closer they got to it, dancing more wildly. They were only a short distance now; possible an hour or two and they would be there. The lightning was making Flatfoot worry; it was striking everything, the mountain the soil, digging up huge deep furrows of steaming ground and tossing it high into the atmosphere - earth flying - monument to the lightning's awesome power.

But he realized he hadn't of worried, the lone rider, showed his first signs of movement since he had been leading the cart up ahead. He slowly let the cloak drop down from around his arm, then extending it outwards from his body.

Flatfoot could see the chain mail glove that tucked into overlapping plates of armour, which was the same that covered his feet, was also running up his arms. Small, thousands of intricate links held the plates together, almost to small to see, only the small amount of diffused light, and the blinding effect of lightning showed the small links up, otherwise it would have looked like a metallic armadillo. The metal plates also had delicately caved images imbedded in to them, but Flatfoot was unable to see what they depicted.

The rider stretched his arm out as far as he could; parallel with his body, then he proceeded to stretch his fingers out wide to their limits. Nothing seemed to happen at first because of the blinding radiance the lightning was giving off. But then on the tips of the riders fingers a blue light started to glow, faint at first but getting stronger and stronger until it was almost impossible to look at. Then in one blinding movement it arched upwards and outwards, covering first the rider then the creature and its handler.

The creature jerked as the light passed through it. The man completely ignored the light as if it were an everyday occurrence.

It then passed over and thought Flatfoot and Brains, encompassing the whole gathering. A blue dome of crackling luminosity, which made the hairs on Flatfoots arms stand up; hair stated to rise as if being rubbed by a balloon. The straw in the cart started to swirl and dance about; making little whirlwind movements, even without the aid of wind, but then everything became clear: a huge boom echoed; ear shatteringly loud, the light was also dazzling.

The handler did all he could to calm the creature by pulling some sort of coarse cloth hood down over its head possibly covering its ears and eyes; the creature seemed to calm down, then the man started to guide it forward.

It then dawned on Flatfoot what had just happened. The random lightning bolts had struck them. He looked across at the rider who now had his hand clenched in to a fist with his arm over his head, the blue light billowing forth keeping the arch over them all, the lightning played over the arch once more making Flatfoots hair stick straight up. Apart from that he felt on other ill effect.

They travelled like this for more than an hour, unharmed, through the lightning storm. Huge chunks of the terrain was still flying up round them, until they got to the side of the mountain. This to Flatfoot just looked like any other part of the sheer cliff walls, which ran as far as the eye could see in all directions, left, right and straight up. Wondering why they had arrived here he looked to the rider to see what was happening.

The rider moved forward, the unicorn lowered its head and proceeded to slide its horn into a breach in the wall, its mane being tossed by the ferocious winds. It wasn't until then that Flatfoot realized the horn was slightly different on the end, sort of distorted. Then he realized why, as the horn slid into the fissure the ground started to shake. A collection of runes started to appear on the rock, glowing in a wide arch, yellow light poured from the ciphers. Then a section of the side of the mountain started to fold in onto itself.

Unbelievable amounts of energy would be needed to move this heavy solid rock vault-like door, and yet it slid like it was on ice, revealing a long excavate passageway in to the heart of the very mountain. Gigantic pillar-like torches burned on both sides of the tunnels walls running the length of the passageway. Cobwebs of crisscrossing thick chains arched overhead and down the walls around the burning columns. The flagstone flooring looked like it had bones and skulls imbedded in to the design, crushed and pushed down hard by the unknown forces. Towering statues of men leant against the walls between the flaming torches, wrapped in chains and leaning slightly forwards; weapons held in stone hands, eyes simply bored holes in the granite figures.

The unicorn pulled its horn free, and moved forwards down the tunnel, leading the frog-like creature, its handler, and the two captives down into the mountains gapping chain wrapped mouth.

26
Drive By

They all now sat in their particular seats.

Babe was driving, with the Captain sitting next to her. Doc was sat in the back of the truck looking thought the screen as to where they were going. Hopper was at the computer terminal watching the route that Flatfoot and Brains had taken the day before.

All were nervous, they had not heard back from Flatfoot and Brains. And to make it more worrying, their one surviving transponder was either broken or not within range. This was more puzzling, because they wouldn't have left the vicinity without telling the Captain first. So it was anyone's guess where they were.

Little did they know that the one remaining headset had been turned off for the night in case anyone from the village; that they had spotted; had the equipment needed to track electrical apparatuses. Besides the transponder wasn't working, because of damage from the Lanks. And even if it was turned on, they were to far away for the transponder to be picked up. But of course the Captain and his team didn't know any of this.

They all had their own thoughts on what had happened, but all sat quietly. Only Hopper was talking, telling them the route that the others had taken. Going over the film and seeing the general area. This was a bit tricky because the brothers were on foot, and were travelling through rough terrain. Whereas the large cargo truck had to go around certain areas because of simply not being able to go through, or over certain patches on thick bushes that the other two just hacked through. But to make a route big enough for the truck to get through would take all day.

"Go left at the top here by the rocky outcrop; the one with the petrified white tree clinging to it.",He looked back at the computer screen to check he was right. "Now swing around left and follow the line of lanky pink blossomed trees," Hopper said.

They were getting close to where the pair had met the two Moregone's, near the vast clearing where the beasts had fought the titanic death battle.

"There should be a clearing up around this tree line somewhere," just as Hopper said that it panned out in to a wide short grassed glade. Small floating blossoms like dandelion seeds danced in the air.

Thick, what looked like long-pined fern trees, but much more spindly and fragile looking, covered most of the area, with a few large towering, thick oaks. But right in front was a large open grass patch, with big furrows of meadow ripped up and littering the area, and more or less in the middle of the clearing was the loser of the great battle: a large mound of now putrefying flesh. Thousands of armoured insects buzzed and zipped around the carcass.

As the truck started to pull up, a number of small creatures scampered off in to the thick undergrowth, and a few reptilian-flying birds took to flight up in to the branches of the nearby trees, to sit patiently for them to move on so they could get back to their banquet.

But one creature didn't move.

At first they couldn't see it because it was hunched down behind the bulk of the fallen giant. But as it lifted its head to see what the noise was all about they could see it clearly.

No one recognized it; it wasn't a Moregone, or a Lank (not that they called them by their given names) but something that walked on all fours - a quadruped. And now it was raised up onto its rear thick muscular elephant-like legs to look over the carcass of the Moregone, in order to see them. It wasn't huge by Moregone standards, but it looked powerful. Large chest muscles rippled as it raised itself. It had a short neck but ending in a big wide oval head.

As it looked over chewing on a chunk of wet dripping meat, they could see row upon row of large ivory teeth, with two long protruding tusks, which it had used to tear the tough dead skin. Its two eyes stared straight at the trucks shining windscreen, a tail came in to view, which started to thrash about, similar to a cat when it gets agitated, but this one was over three metres long and covered in barbs and with what looked like a small boulder on the end.

"Captain," was all Babe said.

"Reverse... slowly," the Captain replied.

There was no need to check the area over. They knew what had happened here, and the last thing they wanted to do was to shoot down a charging beast defending its meal, wasting ammo, and making a lot of unnecessary noise.

But as they started to reverse the creature lost all interest in them, and lowered itself back down to its meal, as if nothing had happened, its two long tusk ripping away a couple meat covered ribs that it started to chew loudly on.

They continued on, following Hopper's directions.

They passed the strange tree carvings that looked surreal and strangely out of place.

After leaving the forest behind, they then came upon the swampland. Slightly boggy but nothing the truck couldn't handle. Once or twice Babe mistook a patch of muddy water for solid ground. But the truck was built for this sort of environment, and all it done was making for a bumpier more interesting ride. But at the Captains orders Babe stayed well clear of the plumes of greasy green pillars that wafted up here and there. The windscreen wipers were on full, clearing the strange humming bird sized insects away, which seemed to just ram the windshield head on.

Then they reached the first stretch of water. The watercourse was dark and running fast, to fast for them to judge its depth. So they had to pull up along side and get out of the truck to judge the best place for crossing.

In their video footage, Flatfoot and Brains had found a kind of stepping stones crossing, which lay in front of them, but there was no way they could use that. It was just out of the question.

Doc made a small joke saying, if Babe got it up onto two wheels, like she seemed to have been doing most of the journey so far, they could get across it easy.

No one laugh. But he did get a vicious sidelong look from Babe, which made Doc snigger.

Doc and the captain now walked along beside the truck, with weapons up and ready.

Babe slowly drove along the side of the water following the Captain as he checked for away across.

Hopper now sat in the area above the steering, with the powerful FN Herstal's .50. cal. machinegun, training it around in an arch, scanning the bushes and few trees that grew close to the waters edge.

It didn't take long to get to a part of the river where it spanned out into two small tributaries rather than just one. Each was shallow enough to slowly drive across.

All clambered back into the vehicle and carried on over the small channels to the other side of the watercourse. It then opened up into grassland, which had a few trees here and there, and large mounds, which looked like termite hills; these reached up to twenty foot high and in some cases looked almost paper-thin. They drove past all these on their way to the beginning of the wasteland. Where they started to come up upon the area where Flatfoot and Brains should have been waiting for them, at location 123-17.

Flatfoot and Brains weren't there, only a burnt up mess of leaves and charred twigs, and many burnt twisted carcases. But what they did find were two other people, looking around the same area: waiting for them.

27
Float the Time Away

Either Flatfoot fell back into unconsciousness, or he was put back into it. Which he wasn't sure, but he believed it was the latter so he wouldn't recognize the way out again. Not that he was dim-witted enough to try and get through that lightning storm on his own. Besides, when they made their way down the long torch lit tunnel the chains seemed to spring to *life*, stretching and crisscrossing over and over in a circular motion behind them, completely barring the way, making an impenetrable metal barrier.

He sat himself up. There was no longer any straw underneath him. Only icy cold stone, which had a slightly sodden feel to it, damp, sticky, and because the stone was chilly it was making him unpleasantly cold. But he didn't get up just yet. He was letting his eyes adjust to the light; it wasn't much but just enough to dispense the darkness.

He was in a chamber of some kind, more likely an incarceration cell of some description. He could see the wall he was up against, which went about a meter to his right and stopped. It met another wall, which ran in to the distance about five or six meters away, before the darkness swallowed it. The wall running to his left did likewise, disappearing into the coldness.

He could hear water dripping, an endless harmonious melody. It reminded him of Chinese torture, where the victim was tied down and an endless drip was positioned to fall continuously onto his forehead, drip... drip... drip... This would either drive the person insane, or eventually bore an opening through to the brain.

He then realized where the light was coming from. Next to him on the floor was a small stone, no larger than his fist, but it was glowing with some kind of inner light. He gingerly put his hand out to it; it got warmer the closer he stretched towards it, his hand sort of cupped over the top, the heat was so welcome, it was so warm, and he wondered why he hadn't noticed it before, then again he had only just started to look around.

For some reason, he wasn't sure why he put his finger out to test; the stone was only slightly lukewarm to the touch.

Then he heard it, a kind of muffled noise. Someone was coughing, over to his left. It suddenly dawned on him, his brother was, or should be in here somewhere as well.

He grabbed the pebble and started to crawl along on his hands and knees. He didn't want to stand because he still wasn't feeling a hundred percent, his head still felt fuzzy and disorientated.

Shuffling along on his knees, taking the light with him, he realized even with the light he couldn't see the ceiling. But he could feel drips hitting him, as they fell down from above, and no matter how high it was, there had to be a ceiling somewhere. He couldn't feel a breeze, and he was sure it wasn't rain that was hitting him, so the ceiling was there just out of sight. Besides there was a ceiling, because the air was too stuffy, as if no fresh air had blown through the chamber in years.

He wanted to call his brother's name, but he didn't know how far the room stretched, and wasn't in the mood to find out if they were the only occupants. Then he noticed movement. He slowly made his way towards it, with the stone stretched out in front, trying to see as far as he could. Another movement, this time to his right, but it sounded more like small clawed feet scuttling along.

He didn't know what passed as rats here, and didn't really want to find out, but whatever it was had scuttled off in the other direction, which as far as he was concerned was just fine. He just hoped it wasn't going to get a bigger friend.

He could see what was coughing now, it was hunched over, and facing the other direction. As he came closer he realized it was his brother Brains camouflaged clad back. He quickly crawled to his brother's side and put his hand on his shoulder.

"Its okay bro, it's only me." He laid the stone down next to them, and used both hands to roll his brother over.

His brother was shuddering uncontrollably. He didn't even recognize him, his eyes were rolled right back with only the whites showing, with white spittle flecking from the corner of his lips, his neck twitching to the side. He clawed at Flatfoot, with twisted, distorted fingers, and pushed his brother away. Then he tried to clamber off in to the distance, but he was shaking too badly, gave up and dropped to the wet floor, still quivering.

"Bro don't worry its going to be okay, I don't know how, but I will get you sorted out."

Just then he heard it, off to one side just next to where he had awoken. Footsteps, at a steady pace coming in their direction. Also now he could just work out a light, getting brighter and brighter, from the same direction, just out of his line of sight.

He looked back over his shoulder just to the right of his original position there were some bars, which now he had moved along, he could see. They were strong looking as thick as his forearm. Also that was the direction the noise and light was approaching from. Was it a guard? The turnkey?

He pulled the glowing stone closer to himself, and rested against the back of his brother, who had now stopped shaking and was laying still, and just giving a violent twitch every now and then.

As the light was approaching it was illuminating the cell he and his brother occupied. The light flickering off the smooth metal of the bars; reflecting in pools of what could be water, then gleaming up across the stone walls. As the light became brighter he could work out the size of the area they were in: it must be easily forty-five by forty-five foot square, with the bars off to one side, where the light was issuing. He could also see the other wall where there was a huge dark, could be wooden door. Many chains, thick and thin, dangled from the ceiling and manacles swung slowly from side to side; the light glinting off the metal surfaces. Also piles of what could be rags or bodies littered the corners and floor area.

Flatfoot couldn't quite work it out in this light, but the worst thing of all was a large heap in one corner. As far from the light as it could be, it looked like some kind of beast, but as far as he could tell it wasn't moving, to his relief.

"Luckily for you it's dead," came a dry voice. "It was a Moregone. Such a shame."

The voice startled Flatfoot, he knew someone was coming, but looking around the room he missed their approach.

The figure stood with the light stretched out in front of him, so all Flatfoot could see was a shadowy outline, because of the light glaring in his eyes, reflecting off the bars smooth surface.

"Someone forgot to feed it." Then came a small brittle laugh. The laugh as far as Flatfoot was concerned went perfectly with the voice. It was low, issuing from the chest area rather than the mouth, spoken slowly, deliberately as if it wasn't use to this form of communication.

Flatfoot looked at the figure holding the light. Then as he was watching the bars disappeared before his very eyes, one minute there the next, nothing vanished. That is until the man stepped through, and the bars sprang back in to existence.

Flatfoot wasn't sure if it was the trick of the light but the light seemed to move away from the person. Then he noticed, it was.

The figure stood there with hands held together in front of him, and the flaming torch just held suspended in the air, just off to one side. So he had a perfect view of who stood in front of him.

The being was dressed in a long, dark cloak, which went right to the floor; the ends were slightly worn and dirty from being dragged on the ground. He had a pure white stock of long hair, pulled back, he must have been at least fifty years old, and he had the face of a mortuary attendant, the sort that didn't have to pretend to be bereaving. But the most alarming was his eyes, no iris just jet-black like holes, with a slight glimmer of orange glowing in the core.

The cloak he was wearing hung open, loosely hanging down from his thin shoulders, underneath he had on what looked like a full suit of body armour made from the same metal plates, similar to the unicorn rider, and he could now pick out the pictures that rested upon them: each piece was covered in what looked like scales, carved into the metal. All the plates interlocked perfectly, a master craftsman's greatest work. He also had an elaborate belt, with a buckle that looked like a long thin dragon that was twisting upon itself, with a sphere held in one clawed hand.

But from the stance he knew it was a different person to the one who brought him here. The other crouched this one stood tall, tall and imposing, powerful - regal.

"What is wrong with this one?" The white haired man asked, nodding his head towards Brains.

"He's... he's not well," Flatfoot answered. He didn't know what else he could say. He could have jumped the man in front of him. But he was still a little light-headed from everything that had happened. But he wouldn't anyway not after witnessing what he just done with the bars, and also the torch floating beside him was testament to his power.

"I sometimes forget how weak and easily damaged your kind is." His eyes dipped as if the conversation was boring him, or if he was just about to take a nap: a purposefully lower of the eyelids.

Flatfoot didn't know what to make of it.

"You have quarter of a cycle, to awaken him." Now he opened his black-hole eyes, with their glowing orange star and looked directly at Flatfoot. He moved a hand inside his cloak, and removed a cobalt blue marble, perfectly round, shining from the light given off by the torch. He held out his hand and let it go. It just held there, floating just like the torch.

Then behind the man there was movement, and without looking around the man signalled with the same hand, and the bars once again vanished.

This time a bedraggled old man came hobbling in. He was completely naked apart from a frayed loin cloth. He was all skinny and black with dirt and grime, looking like a bag of bones, all elbows and knees, unkempt hair, all matted, with a bitty beard down past his chest, almost a comical figure, if he hadn't looked so pitiful. He was limping with a gammy leg, all blistered and swollen at the thigh. He was carrying a tray of some kind; he hobbled past the stationary man and nodding as he did. Then he placed the tray on the ground in front of them both, with a quick look at its contents. Then a flash crossed his face wondering if he would be able to snatch anything off it without anyone noticing. But he must of thought better of it, because he then quickly like an animal turned on his haunches, and was gone back out the way he had come, without even bothering to stand but scurried off on all fours.

On the tray was a jug filled with green liquid. A plate with what appeared to be some dry bread and lumps of fleshly yellowy-red what looked like small uncooked chicken livers.

"Eat, drink, and refresh yourselves." He pointed at the floating marble. "When this touches the floor you will be taken for an audience with your new lord. He has much to ask you." Once again the brittle laughing started. The man then turned and left, with the flaming torch following closely behind, as if connected by an invisible cord.

The bars materialized back in to place, looking as solid and impregnable as ever.

All was once again quiet, with just the endless sound of dripping water and rattling hanging chains.

The glowing stone in front of them just about illuminated the tray of food. But also it illuminated the floating marble. This as he watched started to gradually float down towards the floor, at a steady pace. To fast as far as Flatfoot was concerned.

28
Ladies First

The two strangers were just standing there.

If the Captain didn't think it sounded too strange, he would have sworn they were waiting for them. A young man and a young woman both stood in the charred remains of what looked like a bush in its former life. They didn't move. As the Captain and the others exited the truck; except Hopper, who now sat behind the machinegun that was perched on the vehicles roof, pointing it directly at the two people.

"We have been expecting you," was all the woman said, as she started to move towards them.

"No offence, but come no closer," the Captain said. He had his left hand outstretched and was pointing at them. "I take it you are from the settlement located over on that hill over there?" He said gesturing with his head to behind Lake, and Raven. His right hand was resting on his Steyr Pistol M-A1 Series, with a small laser sight beneath the barrel.

"Good deduction Sherlock, where else would we be from?" Lake answered, while flicking an insect off of her leg.

This remark puzzled the Captain. "There aren't other places here like that one?" He looked back towards Babe and the others.

The young woman ignored him. "We haven't got much time, do you want to help your comrades or not?"

"You have them?" The Captain asked.

"What would we do with them? You see them in any of my pockets?" she said putting her hand on her hip and leaning into it.

"No offence but we are not getting anywhere here," the Captain said walking closer, his hand still on his sidearm.

"We all saw a blinding light coming from this direction, around just after sundown." Raven said, speaking for the first time.

"So you haven't taken them to the village?" The Captain asked.

"Are you in charge?" Lake questioned. "Because you are either stupid or you're not listening." She started to walk around the area. "See these?" she said kicking at the charred remains of a barbequed Lank. There were almost a dozen all piled up, all twisted in their dieing throngs of agony.

"These are what were trying to get your friends," she said kicking another. "But there were obviously more, because the others succeeded in taking them away," she announced, pointing towards the furrows the cart had made in the soft ground.

The Captain pointed. Babe went over to investigate the tracks.

Then from on top of the truck Hopper joined in the conversation. "Am I the only one thinking this, but, who are you both? Where did you come from?" Hopper asked climbing down from the machinegun, after smacking the safety catch on, and clipping down the bullet guard. "With that I don't mean the village or whatever it is." He then paused and stared straight at Raven who had been standing in the background.

"And you mentioned Sherlock Holmes," the Captain stated, meaning it was a word associated with back home on earth.

"You!" Hopper pointed. "You're him aren't you? You're Jason Kelly, who disappeared through the first Gateway?" He waited for an answer.

So did the Captain, now that Hopper had said that, he recognized the young man from the photograph shown to them from the debriefing. He only looked slightly different - a little thinner and more muscular.

Raven just nodded sorrowfully.

"You, what's your story, how did you end up here?" The Captain asked now looking back at Lake.

"I am the same as all the others," she said sweeping her arm in a wide circle towards the crown of the hill. "We all came through the Gateways, and are all trapped here just like you." She looked at them all.

"How many others are there?" The Captain asked.

"In the village there is just over two hundred of us," she looked down, her voice lowered slightly. "All trapped here." She looked back up again, and regained her composer. "We are to take you back to the village with us."

The Captain was about to say something.

Lake cut him off. "There's no point chasing after your associates. There is no way you would be able to get into the mountain without our assistance."

"Why would you want to help us?" the Captain asked.

"Because it's in our interest as well. Look we know you have probably got a hundred questions," she shook her head. "How many times have I had to give this speech this week?"

"You have seen the other two that came through just before us, haven't you?"

"They're also in our village," she said while nodding yes. Then looked at Doc for the first time and said, "You're a quiet one aren't you?"

Doc said nothing but was just taking in the whole situation.

Lake looked back towards the Captain. "Look we are wasting time, we know where your friends have been taken, but you will need our help to get them back." She looked back to Raven. "In our village we have a leader called Coben; he will fill you in on everything. He will answer all your questions about this place." She said gesturing with her arms around her.

"He will tell you where your people have been taken." She shook her head again. "Funny we had to go to the mountain anyway," she gave a small laugh. "Excuse me, I'm a little tired and this has been a bizarre couple of days – even for this twisted place."

She looked towards Babe, who had wandered back from the direction the cart went off in.

Babe looked around. "So what'd I miss?" she asked.

"We will fill you in on the way to their village," the Captain said looking around towards the truck. "Well there's room if you want to show us the way." Then he turned and opened the passenger side door for Lake. "Ladies first."

29
The Time of Meeting

The small stone had almost touched the clammy floor; hanging in the air on an invisible cord, slowly moving closer to the inevitable. He didn't know what to expect when it kissed the flagstone, but he knew there was nothing he could do about it except wait. That was one thing he was now good at - waiting.

His brother hadn't so much as stirred, or even given off any signs to show he was even alive. He was though. Flatfoot had been checking him every couple of minutes, trying to get some response out of him. But so far to no avail.

Flatfoot had eaten some of the food. The reddish kidney type meat wasn't as bad as it appeared; it tasted like warm thick jell-O. And the green juice had the same quality as what was called a Mexican Custard Apple. He could eat it with relative ease. He had travelled extensively around Latin America, and much of their cooked meat was a guessing game. There wasn't much the Latinos wouldn't eat. Besides he didn't know where his next meal was coming from, so he took advantage of this one, this could be his last. But then again you never know. He didn't know what this so called Lord wanted with him, with them. Didn't know if he would be put back in here again, and like the poor creature - or whatever it was in the corner - forgotten about.

That's when he felt the strange sensation.

First it was a sort of low rumbling sound, which didn't come from anywhere, just a slow deep tremor, which seemed to emanate from the very walls and floor around him. That was until the light stared to pour down upon them. Like thick liquid it started at the top of the walls, which now the light was shining on them he could see how far up they started.

The ceiling was high, very high. It could have been about thirty meters to the top. The walls went down at a slant, like a pyramid shaped apex small at the top, getting wider as it came down to the chamber below. Down to where he and his brother were waiting.

Flatfoot quickly took his eyes off the trembling walls and looked at the small marble; it had now reached the flagstone flooring and just rested there. So this was it, the meeting of the so-called Lord. Whoever or whatever he was.

By the power shown by one of his aids, he didn't really want to meet the boss, but he knew he had no choice.

The ceiling was now getting wider at the top, light spilled in, it was almost blinding after the semidarkness he had gotten used to.

Then he felt I slight vibrating through his body. All over like the feeling he got being surrounded by the powerful force field, protecting them from the lightning. But he couldn't see anything. He felt like something about him was changing, and he couldn't explain what.

Then he understood what was happening. Slowly he started rising heavenwards - his body being pulled up. He had no power over his limbs in any sense of the word; he was like a puppet being pulled up by its strings.

He looked over to his brother who was still unconscious, once again there was nothing he could do for him, accept watch as his brother also started the ascent up towards the blinding light.

For some reason, he wasn't sure why, he was looking at the walls on the way up, and wondering how many others had been in the same position as himself: watching the same walls slowly slip by.

As he came closer to the top, he realized if he reached out he could grab the side, but there was no point in fighting something he couldn't control. This wasn't the same thought as those that came before him. Because he could see the scrapping of, and broken off fingernails running up towards the last part of the journey, with long dried trails of blood running up from them.

As he came to the top, the light was almost unbearable, and for the first few seconds he couldn't see anything. He was aware from some sixths sense that he was completely clear of the top of the gapping hole, but he couldn't hear it shutting again, so he presumed he was simply going to hang there during the meeting, and he was fully aware that he could be dropped back down at any given moment.

Things just seemed to get better and better, he thought to himself. Can it get any worse? That was until he opened his eyes. After they had adjusted to the brightness, and he saw the surrounding chamber, he realized, yes it could get worse, and it just did.

As his eyes adjusted to the light he could see the outer laying of a vast round chamber, massive in size. Straight before him was a throne enclave, elaborately carved out of the solid stone, and as it veered around the walls shot off behind and then came back around in a circle. The walls were just visible from where he was because of the distance they were from him.

He looked down the hole he came out of it was pitch black, with a circle encompassing the top, also elaborately carved in runes, which as you looked at it the surface continuously moved so you couldn't focus on the pattern.

Three huge bonfires burned around him, supported by colossus metal bowls that stood upon piles of twisted distorted animals and humans, carved from the same granite type rock that the chamber was hued from - one behind, and one to either side. He could just make out where the ceiling was. Gigantic stalactites hung from the darkness above; so long he couldn't see where they joined at the top. He could just make out walkways and platforms suspended by chains and thick hemp ropes. The stalactites were being carved in to different forms of a man; faces in different posses and positions.

But that wasn't the reason Flatfoot was frightened. He was twenty-four and not many things scared him, not after the things he had been through during different assignments in Kosovo and Iraq. But what lay before and around him petrified him down to his very core, freezing the very marrow in his aching bones.

Around in a big circle were twelve men, the Dark Lords henchmen. They all stood, on smaller platforms, carved just as strangely as the one he now floated over, with shifting changing patterns, which if you stared at them to long it made your eyes water. The appearance of these figures standing around him didn't so much scare him, but rather, the appearance of the so-called Lord did, it made him want to curl up, and plummet back down into the darkness below.

30
Revelations

The truck had arrived at the gates to the large compound, or village as the others called it.

The journey up had been interesting to say the least. They had traveled across the wasteland, a complete desolate place where nothing grew, only a few stones scattered about here and there. Stones Babe managed to hit a number of times.

Then they reached the fast flowing river, but this one unlike the last had a wide truncated bridge running over it; huge fallen trees lashed together. The vehicle easy crawled over this wide obstacle.

You could feel the nervousness of Hopper, as Babe slowly inched the vehicle over the fallen giants. His nervousness was almost palatable.

Several times Lake looked sideways at him, wondering why he was clinging to the armrest of the seat. They made it across with only one hic-up, one of the huge gripping wheels had slipped on the wet bark, but the other nine kept the truck on the bridge and they soon righted the situation. It looked like Doc wanted to vomit. Hopper was even wondering if Babe had done it on purpose to shut Doc up. Babe had a wide smirk etched on her face.

Then came the steep hill. It had a scattering of undergrowth all over it, which was no trouble to the powerful cargo truck, but the steepness was; it had to continually zigzag all the way up the hill.

Raven was giving them directions over the terrain. His excitement for being inside a machine of any kind was obvious; he was like a child with a new toy. Especially Hopper's computer terminal, he could hardly take his eyes off it.

The others understood, he had been trapped here for a while now, and anything that reminded him of home, even a truck was a welcome break to the madness of this strange world.

In no time whatsoever they were at the gates of the settlement. Waiting, as they swung open slowly, huge wooden structures held together with vines and mud, which didn't look like it would withhold a few people more-or-less an army. They were large but poorly made, with gaps you could push your arm through, but as they were waiting for them to swing open, Lake explained about the magical field that surrounded the village; including the gates. This made things even more complicated for them all. But as she already said, Coben would explain everything properly once they got inside.

They were soon within, with the gates swinging back in to place. People started to appear from everywhere. Hundreds; men, women and children of all ages, all stood in tattered clothes, a mishmash of remnants of what they entered the Gateway wearing, and what had been added or replaced over their time spent here. The over all appearance was that of a refugee's camp. At least the people looked well fed.

A few stood out.

One was a black man; his skin was almost purple it was so dark. He was tall and wore a long white garment that reached down to the soil; he had his hands closed over themselves in front resting on the paunch of his rounded stomach. Next to him stood a man they had seen before, but only briefly, it was the person gripping the body of another, the first sight they got, as they looked in the monitor, a spectacle they would never forget.

All around the clearing they had entered were huts, of all sizes and descriptions. Circular, square, and long rectangular huts with two holes in the roof for the escaping smoke from the fires. All built with the same material; thick wooden branches for the sides, covered in mud, leaves and straw and thinner branches for the roof, that had been covered over with turf; a great insulator and extremely waterproof. Firewood was stacked against every hut, under small lean-to's to keep it dry. The huts clung to the sides of the hill, with thin mud paths running between them, these looked like they were brushed regularly. Small stones lined all the paths as a kind of border; the people were trying to bring some kind of order in to the chaos they now found themselves.

Clothes dried and flapped in the wind between the wooden buildings. Dogs chased each other and barked, running around in circles, or playing with the children.

But what caught everyone's attention was just to one side; a massive building, more of a hall, huge living trees were used as its supports.

The Captain decided this was the meeting hall, or where they all ate their food. But he was about to find out.

Coben came forward and introduced himself; the man next to him wasn't introduced just followed along side them in to the Great Hall, as it was called.

The hall was as the outside suggested - huge. An impressive display of workmanship, one that left you in awe. It was immense inside, it was a meeting place and an area where the whole village could sit and eat, and be protected from the weather: because once it started to rain it rained for weeks at a time.

Hopper and babe were told to stay and watch over the truck, they all seemed friendly enough but they had learned before never to trust a friendly face, because they were normally being that way to lull you into false sense of security. But they hadn't of worried, the people were glad to see them, and were friendly. All asking questions about the situation back home on earth.

Soon it was very relaxing, people bringing them food and drinks, and chairs appeared so they could sit. Before long Babe and Hopper were sat on their seats with a group of possibly a hundred people all sat around on the ground, some were standing, leaning against huts or even the truck, listening as Babe described to what had been happening on the other side of the Gateway over the last couple of years.

Hopper told them who were winning the latest Super Bowl, which made a few shout out, and others slap the backs of those around them with sayings like: "Told you they would do it". Also: "What did I tell you?" And: "No way!"

Others shot questions out. "Who was the president now?"

"Had there been any major wars?"

"What are the latest fashions?"

All stupid questions in the general sense of things, but Babe and Hopper knew what it meant to these people around them. So they answered all of the questions being thrown at them.

They soon started to ask their own questions. They found out that a few had entered through the Gateway over the past several months, but only Raven had made it all the way to the village. The others died trying: killed by this cruel world, before they even understood what was even happening to them.

That was until the two brothers entered.

They were told about how the ground moved when they entered through the Gateway. And about the dragon, the way it had been killed. They were told about the prophecy regarding the two brothers who would enter the world, and how they were to put an end to all the suffering.

More food was brought as they were told about the powers gained through entering in to this world. Both Babe and Hopper looked at each other when they were told this. Hopper explained how he had wound the cable in so fast he thought he had lost track of time, he looked down at his tattooed hands, and just a small, "Wow," could be heard escaping his lips.

Soon the sun slowly started to fade, dipping down behind the distant mountain range. People started to peel off from listening or taking part in the conversation, and started to move away, to get things prepared for the onset of the night ahead.

Hopper showed a few of the younger men around the vehicle, how it worked, the engine compartment, simple things that these people lapped up like it was the first vehicle they had ever seen; for some, it was. But he understood this was a familiar thing to them, things they thought they would never see again.

Babe showed a little girl how to braid her long hair in to a complicated design; like the one she was wearing. She discovered this little girl had been born here, and that her mother had also been born her. But her grandmother came through the Gateway over sixty-eight years ago, and she was twenty-three when she came through, but her daughter now looked older than her and had a child herself.

She was told about how if you came thought the Gateway you remained the same age, which shocked Babe, and that if you where born here you aged as normal.

It's was almost dark now, burning lamps started to appear all over the village, raised on tall wooden pools, illuminating the whole area. The scales on the dragons stretched out leathery skin glinted in the flames flickering light.

The Captain and Doc had been inside the large hall for a few hours. Babe realized they must be learning all the things they have and probably more.

Torches were also lit all around the clearing with the truck parked in the middle. Hopper was just thinking about getting the tents out; and having them all set up; when the Captain, followed closely by Coben, came out of the archway leading from the Great Hall.

The Captain walked over to them. He looked around the clearing as if seeing it for the first time, he saw Hopper in the back of the truck by the tents. "No need for them," he announced. "We have a hut set aside for us." He pointed over to a shelter just on the edge of the mud packed main square, and then looked at Coben. Coben nodded as if to say, *yes that's the one*.

"You can leave the truck there, no harm will come to it I promise. It is well protected under the canopy of the shield," Coben stated. He stood in the same position again hands crossed in front of himself.

"We can get ourselves cleaned up and refreshed, and then we are guest at a meal thrown in our honour." The Captain gestured to the hut.

Babe went first. Then after Hopper had secured the back doors he punched in a security number, which he had changed once acquiring the vehicle. It closed the power down for the night, also locking and securing all the doors and setting an alarm.

Once inside the hut they noticed there were six cot type beds, all spaced out, with a kind of woven hemp partition down the middle obscuring two beds out of sight of the other four. A fire was burning steadily inside a pit with stones around its outside, warming the huts interior; and it was also the huts only light source. The floor was brushed compacted dirt.

Once Babe had thrown her stuff on one of the beds on the other side of the partition, she walked back out in to the centre of the hut, and sat down close to the fire.

The Captain was on the edge of his bed, head in his hands.

Babe looked at Hopper. Both looked at the Captain.

"Where to begin?" was all he said. "So much to brief you on," he started laughing. Then he looked up. "If only the Trust knew what they were getting involved in." He thought shaking his head.

"Doc is looking around up at the infirmary, to see if there's anything up there he can help with? Not that they need help, some of their powers go well beyond explanation."

"We know all about this place Captain there's no need to go over it all again, all the villagers were more than helpful in telling us everything that's happening," Babe announced.

The Captain looked up. "Well that saves a few hours," he said, once again giving a forced, weary laugh. "Tonight we are to eat our fill, rest and get ready for early morning," he said looking at them both. "No alcohol or whatever constitutes as liquor here okay?" He was still looking at them.

"Because tomorrow morning first light, along with a few others, we are going to make our way to the Temple of the Sky, to where Flatfoot and Brains have been taken." He put his head back down in to his hands.

He described all that Coben had told him about the world, filling it bits the villages either didn't want to tell them, or simply didn't know. All about the so-called Lord and the power he exerted over this world. About the two people who came through the Gateway just before them. He told them about the prophecy, about everything.

When he finished they too were sat on the edge of the beds, looking in to the warm flames with their own private thoughts. They thought learning about this place from the Trust was hard to take in. But what they had just learned from Coben; about this world; made the Trust's information seem childish in comparison. The Trust knew nothing about what was really happening here - nothing about this so-called Lord. Nothing about how this world effected their own.

Plus two of their own were being held by this mad man, who wielded godlike powers. And first thing in the morning they were going to get them.

31
The Lord

Flatfoot felt helpless just hanging there. With no way of moving he was held fast. He felt like a rabbit caught in the headlights of an on coming truck - helpless and paralysed, unable to even form words.

He looked to his right. Brains was just hanging there like a dead piece of meat on an invisible hook, head lulled forward, with no discernable signs of life in his body. Spittle was running from the corner of his twisted mouth, this was the only sign to show his body still held a mockery of life. Whatever those creatures did to him really messed him up.

His brother knew that before Brains went into his teens he used to have violent fits. But Flatfoot was too young to remember everything, and there was nothing anyone could do for him. Doctors gave up, institutions wouldn't accept him. That was until he went through adolescence, and his fits stopped, and he hadn't suffered from any since. That was until now.

His brother didn't know what he could do for him. Apart from the fact there was nothing he could do for him: at this moment he couldn't even control his own body, more-or-less help anyone else.

But Flatfoot was really trying to divert his mind, anywhere apart from having to stare at what lay in front and around him.

The sight was out of some grotesque sadistic horror movie. His brain tried to avoid thinking about it, diverting his attention anywhere except to stare at these mutants. Deformed figures that could once have been called humans, the sight was stomach turning, he had to keep fighting back bile that kept rising in his throat.

What he presumed was the Lord - as they called him - was in fact three people, all sat in a row, on a elaborately caved throne, which was raised on a dais, back splashing in to huge intricate carvings running up the stone wall behind, like nothing he had ever seen before, fanning out around the sitting figures.

But the figures were the reason for his uneasiness. Three forms of men, sat together, joined at the shoulders. The ones to either side had one arm; the other was missing where it joined the body in the middle. The figure in the middle had no arms but was joined by the shoulders to the two next to him.

The figure in the middle was staring straight at him. It had huge deformed thyroid eyes, but its mouth and nose had been sewn up: grotesque stitching could be seen, depriving the figure of its other two senses.

This became apparent when he looked at the remaining two figures. One had a mouth, but its eyes were just empty sockets, and its nose was sewn up like the first.

The third was displaying a nose with wide nostrils, stretched to their limit, held open by wire wrapped around the side of its face. It to had sockets where eyes should have been, and its mouth was also stitched closed.

They were decked out in elaborately embodied clothes, which seemed a mockery after what had been done to their bodies. Long flowing golden garments covered the rest of their body. Only the upper body, the head and arms near the shoulders were left uncovered.

Each wore a type of facial crown. The middle one had a golden mask, which was oval, and stretched out before it, hooked over its ears; which Flatfoot realized all three had; then the mask bent back around, with spikes pointing out in an elaborate display of fine craftsmanship, reminding Flatfoot of pictures of ancient Aztec facemasks. The two on either side had similar; but made of silver; with less on the showy display of intricacy, but still elaborately made. The masks were strange because they were simply wire frames, not covering any of the features at all, but simply a protection of some kind.

The two bodies on either side had slim white arms, delicate, with long fingers, and elaborately painted nails, which must have been four possibly five inches long, which started to curl back on themselves – which might explain the face guards. The overall display was impressive but more importantly disturbing. It looked like a demonic form of the trinity: three in one.

Around in a circle were the twelve men, all wearing long flowing greyish-brown garments, the same as the visitor that had come to see them earlier in their cell. But theirs were all pulled together; nothing could be seen of who wore them. Their hands were tucked behind their backs, and the hoods were pulled up over their heads, with their heads bent forward. Not even their feet could be seen. The cloaks went down to the floor, resting on the small platforms that they were standing upon.

All were mumbling a mantra.

Flatfoot couldn't work out what they were saying; it was a sort of chesty noise, which seemed to travel through the ground as much as through the air. He could tell this because on the flooring all around him - and them - was a kind of dirty gritty sand: it covered as far as his eyes could see, and at the moment it was vibrating, dancing. The sound was also getting louder.

Then all of a sudden it stopped.

The sand went flat.

The silence was deafening.

Out of the corner of his eye Flatfoot caught movement from the throne, he had been looking around at the standing figures, but now his head snapped back in to place, looking at the three figures, which were starting to rise.

It was an unsettling sight, as the three stood at once. Then they parted. The two figures to the sides stepped sideways, separating from the middle one. The shoulder joints slipped out of socket, with a sickening popping sound. The flesh quickly reclaimed its position; within a fraction of a heartbeat the three figures all stood separate.

The two side ones had a shoulder bone joint sticking out, but the flesh had sealed the wound, leaving a dirty white protruding bone. The middle figure stood, armless, rounded shoulders wrapped once again in their fleshy clothing. The middle one stayed motionless, while the other two started to circle around the pit which Flatfoot and his brother was suspended above. Their eye orbits deprived of eyes were swiveling about, looking around even without the benefit of eyes; they were taking in all his and his brothers' details.

Then there was another movement coming from over to his left. A figure walking, it was the first time Flatfoot noticed this figure, then again it could have been walking from the far end of the chamber for ten minutes and Flatfoot wouldn't have been able to see him, because of the distance. But now he was coming in to focus, he could tell it was the same person who came to see them in their cell earlier, he walked with purpose and intent, his cloak open billowing behind him as he walked towards them. In his hand he carried a staff, a long slightly twisted piece of wood; or so it seemed from where Flatfoot hung.

The middle deformed creature moved to meet him, armless; walking towards the oncoming figure.

Flatfoot's first thoughts were on how weird it looked for an armless person to walk, the upper body swung side to side, in a mockery of movement.

That was until he noticed what the three figures were sitting upon. Now the middle one had moved he could see what was behind them. What he presumed to be carvings was in fact another individual. If it could be called that. He presumed it was once a man, in the sitting position. He had sort of, well, the only way he could describe it was melted into his rock throne. It looked like he hadn't moved in hundreds of years, and had become part of what was around him, blending and becoming one with the stone.

What he thought at first was carvings were the very walls of the cavern joining up with this being. His arms were outstretched and spread out, as if opened up with a razor sharp knife, with the veins becoming rock, joining and blending with its surroundings; mineral and flesh now one. His fingers were akimbo and sunk into the stone as if it was made of putty. He was kind of suspended on the wall. He had completely lost all colouring, and had changed to a kind of mummified dark putrid grey. His legs were in the sitting position, and also twisted to almost beyond recognition. His head leant forward, mummified remains of a cranial cavity hanging by the same shreds connecting him to the rest of the wall.

Then the being next to him on his left with only the mouth left open, whispered in a low grating voice: "Behold the Lord." Pointing with its one arm at the mummified remains hanging suspended on the wall behind.

As it did so the head slowly started to rise. The only sign that there was any life left in this decomposing body.

All twelve of the figures standing in the circle dropped to their knees. So did the man who had just walked towards them. The three misshapen figures merely lowered their deformed heads.

Flatfoot looked once again at the suspended figure, presuming the movement was from the wind. That was until its empty eye sockets started to radiate a bright, almost blinding, orange glow.

32
The Writing on the Wall

Once again there was a large meal going on, and once again the food being consumed was provided from the body of the fallen dragon. Its meat had been spiced, grilled, roasted, and prepared in many different styles.

This time, because the air was slightly colder than the night before, all were eating inside the dome-like Great Hall; the monstrous creation of wood and straw, and splashing of mud here and there. Complete trees were bent over, leaning towards themselves. Their thick bough was used for the main support frame, with the branches still connected to the main trunk of the tree; these were bent and woven between other branches of the other huge trees, smaller entwining branches and mud filled in any other gaps. All together these made up the majority of the arching building. If you were told about such a place you wouldn't believe it would stand.

As the Captain looked around he believed, after everything he had heard about this place, that it just might be held up by magic as well.

"Another helping?" This brought him out of his daydream. Before him stood a young woman, with long blond platted hair and creamy complexion, she was about eighteen. But he couldn't be sure, this young lady standing in front of him could well be twice, or even three times his age. She held a wooden bowl full of the most delicate part of the dragon, which had been marinated in Spike tree berries; its tongue.

"Thank you. But no I'm fine thanks." He gave her a pleasant, tooth filled, smile. She reminded him of his late wife when he had first met her.

The guests were positioned at the top of a collection of heavy carved wooden tables, raised slightly higher than the rest. The Captain didn't believe this to be because those on the top table saw themselves as better people, or deserving of an elevated position; but rather, so they could be seen and heard better as certain thing ascertaining to the running of the village were talked about.

Next to Coben was a young man he recognized from seeing in the small monitor, while watching creatures charge towards him. He was introduced as Garry: one of the two brothers, who had come through the Gateway in England just a matter of hours before them.

They were told about his brother Glyn who was in some sort of coma, due to entering this strange alien world and about the fight with the dragon. He felt like he was in the pages of some fantasy book, everything was so surreal.

Also Babe, Hopper and the Doc were sitting up with him. Babe and Doc were in a deep discussion with Garry, while Hopper was flirting with the young woman who had just spoken to the Captain; he was showing her some of his impressive tattoos. But the Captain didn't think Hopper knew what was in the wooden bowl, because he had so much of it stacked onto his plate, mainly to keep the lady from wandering off to serve someone else.

The meal had been going on for at least an hour. All was relaxed and informal. They ate inside like this every time it was to cold, or wet to eat outside. Or possibly Coben wanted to show off their greatest feat of work.

And everyone was learning something new.

The Captain was having a long relaxed chat with Coben, about the day-to-day running of the village, and what sort of organization goes in to it. Also about this world, the way it works, the way it controls the animals here, and the way it draws power from their world; Earth.

All this was learned mainly from a cave not to far away from the village, down the other side of the hill, towards the Temple of the Sky: the original home and spiritual place of the Holy Ones, but now the residence of the so-called self-proclaimed tyrannical Dark Lord.

The Holy Ones not knowing what was to become of themselves, because the man, who they first thought of as being sent from their God, was nothing but a fake. They realized this too late. But they couldn't explain where he had come from, but they recognized that he was pure evil.

It was too late they had already told him about the secrets of the Gateway, and the workings of it. So they went about putting all this down in a cave, scratched and painted on the cave walls, all done in picture form; and in secrecy.

The story of his arrival, the way he took charge, and the way his brother disappeared - everything. The only thing not there was the last thing they wrote down, that was the prophecy. But other things were there to, things

Coben couldn't explain, couldn't begin to understand.

There was the picture of their world. But also linked around it was six others all joined in a large circle, with only one small strand joining each to the next, with a sort of arrow pointing one way.

Coben had his own theory about it. He had spent years going each day to this cave. The thousands of pictures made up a story. He had a theory that he now shared with the Captain.

He believed there were seven worlds; all join by gateways, or portals. They weren't meant to be a Gateway for people, just what they drew through them.

The original builders travelled through them, but now the gateways had been forgotten, fallen upon by unsuspecting people such as those here in the village.

But the main purpose was not for travel, even though at one stage it was used for that, possibly to transport different races from one world to the next. Now it was used as a sort of equilibrium between the seven planets. Each drew certain products or even by-products; a surplus off of the other world; and like-wise the next one along drew off the one before, going around in a continuous circle. Each supplied the next world with what it needed, each given the surplus of what it produces.

He believed earth had a surplus of something in the soil itself, something that controlled the ozone. Something this world needed. He believed the layer of cloud covering his world was a compound taken from the very substance of our planet. A compound that mixed with the vapour as it came through the gateway, and poured in a steady stream towards the sky. Creating an unnatural ozone layer, but one needed to let life survive on this world.

All was satisfactory and running according to its designer's original plan – whoever they were?

That was until the so-called Lord, went and had the people indigenous to this world dig for more of the stone that made up the Gateway. In time three more were produced, drawing more power than was required, more power than what it was suppose to.

He believed this was why Earth has so many problems: the ozone depletion, earthquakes, volcanic eruptions, freak random weather fronts and drought and famine, all because this world was slowly draining their own dry, making Earth unstable. All simply because the Lord wanted more power.

Coben was asked where he believed the magic came from and why it was so strong in this world. Coben's answer was simple and made sense.

He explained that the Lord came through a long time ago, no one was really sure when, but he had been here a very long time. Over a few thousand years ago, in human folklore it was said there were people able to do similar things to what could be done here. For example Merlin; a powerful magician. Also legends were full of stories of powerful sorcerers, witches and warlocks, history was riddled with them. Possibly Greek mythology was examples of normal humans with powerful magical abilities, being classed as gods. Coben said he believed there was a time when these things did actually take place. Magic was as common then as it is here now, but only certain people could control it, could use and direct it.

But because after arriving the so-called Lord had the other Gateways made, it drew more than it should of, until the power dwindled and disappeared. After time it became a myth, only believed to be tall stories.

In 1320 – Coben explained - the church, at the request of Pope John XXII, officially declared Witchcraft as a heretical movement throughout Europe. In 1541 witchcraft was outlawed and made illegal in England. Showing that the magic was still around, but dwindling, even in the 1600's.

The Captain wandered how Coben would know all these dates.

But as Coben said, all you have to do is look around and see it was true, and because he's pulled through more power than was meant for this one world, the magic was in surplus, everyone here gained some kind of magical ability.

His other theory was that the Gateways only swung one way, for people indigenous to this world; they could travel a certain way through the Gates. That's why they used to sacrifice things through the Gateway, and why once we passed through we couldn't return. Because as he said before, they only swing one way.

The only way you could get back to Earth; as far as Coben believed; was to find the other Gateway in this world that joined the next in line, and travel around, through the others back to Earth. Meaning if you wanted to get home you had five other worlds to bypass. Also once there you would have to find the other Gateway that joined the next world in line. A world was a big place, but he believed he knew where the other gateway was on this world.

He told the Captain what the plans for the morning were. How the Lord had spoken through the healer, and what he demanded. He was going to do as he was asked. But also in the party that was going to take Glyn and Garry to the Temple of the Sky was going to be Coben, Lake and Raven, as well as the rest of the Captains team.

First thing in the morning they were all going to leave, to see if they could find Flatfoot and Brains, and see if the prophecy was really about to be fulfilled.

33
The Meeting

The head moved slowly with a kind of jerking movement, until its empty eye sockets were fixed on Flatfoot and his motionless brother.

Movement to his left-hand side caught Flatfoot's attention, but he could no more turn and look away, as he could break the bonds that held him levitating over the dark hole.

Even though the head was decayed and was a pitiful sight, its eye sockets were staring not so much at him, but he would swear it was looking straight through him, reading his every thought and intention. He could feel an uncomfortable tingling feeling behind his eyes, as if his very thoughts were being syringed out.

"WHY WERE YOU SENT?" A deep booming sound.

It took Flatfoot a few seconds to realize it was words; he ran it over in his head and realized what was being asked of him. But he didn't see the forms mouth move, if it could be called that.

Then he came to understand what the movement was to his left.

The humanoid figure of a man that was sitting to the left of the grotesque display was relaying the words from his Lord, moving the only feature on its face, its mouth.

He turned to look at the middle figure, it was standing ridged staring straight at him, and its eyes were now shining bright orange.

"What do you want with us?" Flatfoot managed to squeeze out from his burning lungs. His head was beginning to spin from all that was transpiring around him, and the pain behind his eyes was almost knocking him unconscious.

The hanging head seemed to take in the question Flatfoot asked, and then completely dismissed it to being of no relevance.

"WHAT IS WRONG WITH THIS OTHER ONE?" The hanging head

had now turned to face Flatfoot's brother.

But Brains was in no condition to answer questions, he was in no state to even be breathing by the looks of him; head lulled forward, spittle running down over his chin, dripping into the oblivion of the black pit below.

The one armed freak, which was sat to the right, was now moving towards Brains. It reached over and put its thin out-stretched arm towards the limp hanging figure. Then, using its long curved nail it scratched a deep wound in his brothers cheek. Blood dripped, but no other movement in response, not even a flinch.

The richly dressed hunched over humanoid turned to look at its Lord, and appeared to shrug, which considering it only had one shoulder was quite impressive to witness.

"WHAT IS WRONG WITH THIS ONE?" Asked a second time. The head looked back at Flatfoot for an explanation.

"He's not well…" Flatfoot tried to think of what else to say, what would he do to his brother if they found he was no further use to him?

"They are very weak creatures Lord. He will heal, given time." The voice was that of the visitor to their cell earlier. He was bowed down in front of the Lord. He must be some kind of adviser, Flatfoot reckoned.

"TIME…" The Lord seemed to mull this over for a few seconds then apparently came to a decision. "TIME IS ONE THING WE DON'T HAVE THE LUXURY OF," it said in the same booming voice, which took Flatfoot a few moments to comprehend.

But it was too late for any more words. As the Lord said this there seemed to be a shimmer coming from Brains direction. Then like a stone, no longer being supported Brain plummeted down, dropping uncontrolled into the blackness of the void underneath them. No scream of surprise, no swinging of the arms, nothing, just a noiseless plummet straight down.

For a few moments Flatfoot just stared, unblinking.

This couldn't be happening, his brother being dropped the thirty meters down to hard flagstones like a piece of useless trash. His mind did a somersault, he was no longer afraid, but rather he was now angry. How could he? Why? The anger was so much he couldn't put it into words, his face turned bright red with fury. His body went ridged. Then the pressure became too much. Before he had a chance to let his anger out; put it into words, his body started to shut down under the complete strain which was being forced on it.

But before he did his last thought was, *where were the others? Why weren't they here helping them?* "The first rule," he muttered: "Never leave anyone behind." Then he fainted; passing out.

34
Blind Leading the Blind

The air was completely motionless and had a cold crisp feeling; there was no wind, nothing to stir the air around them. There was nothing to distract them from their personal thoughts.

Time was getting on, it's was a few hours after sunrise, and if they wanted to reach the mountain before the four cycles was over, they had to leave today. Not that they were worried about the consequences, but they needed to look like they were doing as instructed.

Glyn had been brought out of the healing hut and placed on a stretcher on the back of a bulky farm cart. The wagon was large because it had to hold Garry, Coben, Lake, and Raven, as well as the stretched out form of Glyn. Not to mention all the food and other equipment needed for the two-day trip. That's if everything went according to plan.

It was being pulled by two large beasts, which up until that moment had been tethered up in the large pen to the right of the clearing. Large ugly beast, quadrupeds with powerful beefy shoulders, which rose at the front, then lowered back down to the rear quarters, this gave it a kind of large bulldog affect. They had large round faces with thick wobbling folds of skin, but with small eye that seem in stark contrast to the rest of their bodies. The main difference apart from the obvious size was, rather than being covered in fur, like most of the creatures of this world, it was covered in a thick leathery pelt, not to unlike a rhinoceros. The first creature had its heads lowered and was grazing on the flora around itself. The other, which stood the same height, was just standing rock still looking straight ahead; anticipating the journey it knew was before it.

Coben was talking to a short Chinese looking man, who Garry knew to be called Yang Lu. A good listener and he showed all the qualities Coben does. He was a good choice, as far as Garry was concerned, to be left in charge.

He was pointing to certain areas of the village, giving instructions. It became obvious he was to be left in charge while Coben was gone, and Coben was making sure he left proper instructions.

While all this was going on the Captain and his team were also preparing for the journey ahead: sorting once again through their equipment.

They were to follow along behind the others, and at the last moment they were to peel away and enter the mountain through an underground entrance, which had been pointed out by the wall drawings in the cave left by the Holy Ones.

Brains wasn't around, so they had lost their map and topography expert. So in his absence Hopper had been sent to the cave. He took along photo equipment, which was then attached to the computer on returning. The result was a complete map of the underground passageways and tunnels under the Temple of the Sky.

They were told about the continuous lightning storms and that without proper protection it would rip their truck asunder in the blink of an eye.

The tunnels weren't big enough for the ten wheels cargo truck, but they could carry all the equipment they needed on their backs. The Captain had asked for a guide, but as Coben had pointed out, no one had been through the tunnel network, so sending one more person wouldn't help the situation. Besides they would have Raven and Lake to help them along.

All was almost set.

The sun, which they couldn't see, must have been climbing over the mountain ranges in the distance, because the sky became that little bit brighter.

A huge flock of reptilian flying creatures flew overhead, caught some sort of updraft, or purely by instinct cart-wheeled around and headed off towards the distance, letting out loud squawking noises as they went, all rearranging themselves in to a huge V shape pattern.

Some of the villagers had come out to see them off. There were no farewells, no hugs, and no tearful goodbyes. It just wasn't done; you never let yourself become attached to things here, because nothing stays the same, it was always changing; always-different problems arising. Tomorrow will bring something else to worry about.

Coben now stood before everyone that was about to leave.

"Can I have all your attention please," Coben was standing with his arms out stretched, making a pulling motion.

Those fussing around the cart, as well as and the Captain and his team, stopped what they were doing and came forward so they could hear properly.

Coben continued, "We will be setting out first, taking the lead. Then Jethro and the others will follow in the truck, at a distance." He nodded to them, and then looked at the Captain who had turned a little crimson from Coben using his first name.

The Captain took his cue, and continued. "We will stay back in case of there being any watchers placed along the trail. We will be far enough away to be able to use some of our tracking devises. We will not let you out of our sight," the Captain announced, he then looked back at Coben for him to carry on.

"It will take just under two days to reach the mountain, if we make good progress. In that time we don't know what we will run into. We are expected, someone or something might be sent out to take us part of the way. If that happens don't look behind, don't make it obvious that there is someone following us."

They all shook their heads in response.

"What happens if we are attacked, will you come to our aid?" Lake asked looking at the small gathered military group, who bristled with automatic weapons, grenades and foldable rocket launchers.

"From what I have been told," he said looking at Coben, "the prophecy is known by this so-called Lord. So he's not so much afraid, more intrigued. He's so pompous he doesn't see Glyn as a threat, as I said, he's more intrigued than scared. He thinks he is immune to everything around him including the prophecy."

Coben nodded his agreement. Then he carried on, "He will not destroy Glyn or us. He wants to see who the prophecy has picked to match against him."

Coben now looked over to Babe.

Babe turned to talk. "He has no enemies, in the sense that no one can match his abilities or skill. So he sees himself as all-powerful. It's simply called the *God Syndrome*, because he sees himself as a God. Probably also thinks he's immortal in the sense that he can't be killed." Babe looked back towards Coben.

"So as you can see he will want Glyn alive, to inspect his prize as it were," the Captain announced.

"But what about us?" Lake asked looking around. "He didn't ask for us?"

"That's true, and if we meet no resistance, then you all, apart from myself, Garry and Glyn, will travel through the underground passages with the Captain and his team," Coben replied.

"But we are sort of winging it a bit, not all will fit in the truck, not with the extra stuff we've packed in," the Captain said leaning against the side of the bulky wooden cart as he munched on an apple for breakfast.

"Well time is upon us, we have to leave now." Coben looked towards the distance as if looking into the future. "Time is of the essence."

Without another word all finished off what they were doing, and climbed aboard their particular transportation. Without a fuss, or farewells they pulled away slowly, with the cart in front, bouncing over the rough terrain, jolting everyone onboard.

Following at a snails pace was the truck, heading down the other side of the hill, away from the plumes of billowing smoke, off into the distance towards the Temple of the Sky.

35
Greed

Isabel Deerwood sat at her computer desk. She was looking at her nails, thinking it was time she had them manicured again. She was deciding on what colour she should have them done: maybe French style this time, or maybe a little symbol, possibly a diamond or flower?

It had been a quiet morning.

She sat on the fourth floor of a non-script red brick building, situated in Baltimore. It looked like a small run-of-the-mill local newspaper company: which it was. Apart from the one small out cove, this looked the same as all the rest in its section, along with another eighteen small tables all enclosed in chest high partitions, which tried to give the impression of privacy.

Isabel was busy running a program through her work computer; to download and de-encrypt the algorithmic message she had received. It was a slow process, one that would take her computer a good three, possibly four hours. Then it would be re-encrypted and sent on along the line to the next computer in the line of higher echelons.

It had already taken two days to get to her, through six other computers similar to her own. After her computer it would go straight to another, which she had no knowledge of. She didn't know and didn't care where it went or what information was encrypted on it. She had done her job, helped her country. Or at least believed she had.

Four months ago two men approached her, both were perfectly dressed in suits, but she was no fool. They might have had expensive new Armani suits on, but the standard issue army boots gave them away: just like the German type men wore in Diehard 3.

But Isabel said nothing, wanting to hear what they had to say.

They told her she could be useful to her country, if she wanted to help. They explained an elaborate story about service men stuck in other countries, needing to get information home. Spies she was told. They needed people all over the America who could use their computers at work as camouflage, so the message could be sent through, going through four possibly five computers before it got to the eighty-six-acre headquarters of the National Security Agency's Cryptologic Strategy Facility, in Fort Meade, Maryland, where it was then redirected to its final destination; the Trust's headquarters.

She was told she would be in no danger, it was standard operation, but would rather no one else know apart from her.

Isabel agreed after they explained that she would be compensated monthly for her troubles. So she tock them to her work place, when all had left, and watched as they swapped her computer for an identical one.

They had explained how it all worked, and how the money would be deposited. Then thanked her for her service to her country, and disappeared.

Now the program had finished. She had done just like they had shown her, re-encrypted it and sent it on its way.

Time to take a long lunch break and pop down the road to the manicurists - she could afford the little luxuries.

Next stop, it went to a tall building that sat above the Trust large underground bunker. The head quarters of the Government off-shoot, in a sleepy little suburb block in Manhattan New York City, away from prying eyes. It was under a huge cleaning company; a front for what lay underneath.

The National Security Agency use to be the new, secret organization that was kept under strict secrecy for as long as possible. Even though it was established in November 1952 by President Truman, it was still referred to as No Such Agency, until Hollywood started to integrate its name into their films; the FBI and CIA were old news. So a new agency needed to be formed - step in the Trust, with its unlimited Government and private funding, with no accountability to any other world agency. It soon wiggled its way free of all government holds and stood on its own.

The encrypted message rested for no more than nine minutes before a meeting was called, people brought in. Within less than six hours private Lear jets were diverted, schedules adjusted. Now the twelve directors of the Trust sat around the long oblong dark mahogany table.

"The message has been received gentlemen," James Patterson said, leaning back in his chair, and taking a long drag on his fat Cuban cigar, then blowing the blue smoke towards the ceiling.

"They passed through the Gateway just over two days ago." He flicked the head off of the cigar, missing the large thick green tinted glass ashtray.

"But there's been a problem gentlemen. One I need your opinion on." He took another long hard drag on his *Hija de Cabañas y Carbajal y Cía,* Cabañas cigar.

The other eleven stared at the red glowing end of his thick cigar, waiting for him to continue.

"The purchasing of the land around the site is underway."

Some gave a sigh of relief thinking maybe that was the problem, but upon that being dismissed they once again drew their brows in to frowns.

"We received another message a day after they had entered the Gateway, from shall we say our insurance." He chuckled to himself at some private joke. "We have been instructed that there has been more than just the one person known to of entered the Gateway." He leaned forward in his chair; it creaked under the weight of his obese body.

Now all eyes were burning in to the top of his bolding head, as he relit the large cigar. Sitting back once again; to the relief of the chair. He blew another long plume towards the ceiling fan.

"We have had another report from our man." He picked a piece of steak out from between his teeth and placed it in the ashtray. Fettuccine with steak and zucchini was one of his favourite meals. And he wasn't pleased when he was called away from dinner with George J. Tenet, the director of the CIA. *The food,* he mused, *was better than the company.*

"Apparently there is a whole village of people on the other side. All have been taken through one of the four Gateways." He placed the long cigar in the ashtray, and crossed his grey vicuna *Kiton*; seventeen thousand dollar suits arms on the polished tabletop.

All just sat staring at him. None uttering a word.

Then in one movement he lifted his fat arm and slapped his big hand down flat on the tabletop. Making most jump.

"So what are we going to do ladies and gentlemen? But that's not all." He drew his hand back and placed both on his lap.

"There are four Gateways, we control two. Or will in…" He looked at his watch, "four hours time." He picked up his cigar once again and began to refill his big lungs.

Those around the table realized he was referring to the purchase of the land around the second Gateway.

"That means there are two more Gateways out there, which we need to find." He looked around at their faces, before continuing. "The easiest way is this," he looked to the left, as he did so a door opened and an army officer walked in.

"Gentlemen you all know of Colonel Madera?" The Colonel was a notorious Black Ops officer that done anything to complete his mission, regardless of the number of body bags brought home. Saddam Husayn had been captured by Madera, but only after losing forty-three of his Special Forces team to Husayn's personal guards.

All turned to look at the figure just walking through the door. He didn't stop for hellos or hands stretched out to be shaken. He walked passed them all, and stopped at a blank wall at the end of the long table.

"Lights!" The Colonel said.

A man dressed in army uniform - which the others didn't see enter - lowered the lights.

Madera went straight in to his talk. "Here we have four columns of smoke, each rising from the top of a different Gateway." He was now pointing to the surface of the wall, which had a still picture superimposed over its surface from some hidden projector.

"We calculate each is about six or so kilometres apart." He clicked something in his hand. The picture changed, in its place a three-dimensional wire diagram showing the topographical map of the underlying terrain of the area.

"As you can see once the trees have been removed the ground is even and movement over this region will be easy." He nodded his head and the lights came back on. He stepped forward and put the switch on the table.

"To save time, plus not knowing who else will find the Gateways, it has been decided that another team led by myself will enter the Gateway, the very one situated in England, and gain control of the other two portals." He reached behind himself and unclipped a small device off of his green belt, and placed it on the table also.

"This is a Radio Frequency Emitter, on a level four matrix pattern, sending off a continuous relaying encrypted algorithmic code; which will be sent broadcasting on 224.8662 UHF, which is the same frequency as our Rhyolite satellites, which will then move and hover in a geosynchronous orbit over the sites." He poked it with his finger. "In other words gentlemen, in layman's terms, placed near the two unfound remaining Gateways it will give off a radio wave pulse which can only be picked up by one of our Spy satellites twenty-two thousand kilometres above the earth's surface. "As you all know the only thing which can return through the Gateways are radio waves. This is what will be picked up by our satellites." He looked around to see if that had sunk in.

"It will show the location of the other two Gateways, pinpointing them within a couple of inches here on earth." He looked over towards Patterson.

"So Colonel Madera will travel through the operational Gateway and locate the other two for us. He leaves within minutes, with another one hundred and forty men in order to achieve his directive." He looked around to see if there were any questions. None were forth coming.

"At all cost those other two will be ours. Look at what we have achieved with just one; soon we will have all four." His smile was unnatural, as if he had studied a book on how to but never had the opportunity to try it out.

"We are lagging gentlemen; we are no longer ahead in the arms race. Russia is no longer a threat, but now China and some other eastern countries hold a nuclear arsenal. It is even believed Libra, and South Korea are also nuclear capable, as well as our other more distant friends. You know of whom I speak; who have weapons and technology that we couldn't even begin to imagine.

"But soon no nation, or world, will stand against the United States of America, not when we have a weapon with far greater destructive power than anything they could possibly envision."

36
What Dreams Are Made Of

The time had melted away.

Flatfoot was no more conscious of how much time passed, as he was aware if it was night or day outside.

His head was thumping to the sound of his own heartbeat. The blood pumping it through his ears, the noise was all he could hear. Please let this be a nightmare, where he could awaken back home in the comfort of his bed. But no such luck.

His eyes opened and he let them adjust to the amount of light filtering through them.

He wasn't in the cell as before. This one was more airy, light, and had a more lived in feeling.

His head was pounding but apart from that his body felt perfectly rested. No pain.

What was happening now? Where was Brains? Had the fall killed him? Where were the others? So many questions, and who was going to answer them? Not him that was for sure, at the moment he didn't even know what was going to happen to himself.

His eye adjusted, he could now take in the complete room. The sight momentarily startled him. Lavish wall hangings were draped all around, depicting images and landscapes that could have been from back on Earth; beautifully sown tapestries with intricate weave. Light wood tables of strange shapes, some were so long they needed eight or so legs to support them. Perched upon them and draped down over there edges were weird and exotic fruits; varying in colour and bulbous shapes. Strange glass structures rose from the tables which had the fruit hanging from them. Long plush luxury seating areas adorned the walls, these being crammed with hundreds of silky pillows of all shapes, sizes and colours.

He lay in a huge four-poster bed, larger than any he had ever seen. The posts went all the way to the ceiling, which was made from a kind of glassy rock, which admitted a kind of soft pink light. The bedposts didn't so much as go to the ceiling, but join it. It was made from the same substance as the ceiling, walls, and the floor. The posts were adorned with huge embroidered fine pink silky material, draped from one to the other that gently shifted in the nonexistent breeze.

The room could have come straight out of a storybook. The riches and the beauty were phenomenal. The sheets pulled up around him were just as lavishly decorated as the rest of the room; thick heavy fabric that had more embroidery sown into them. When he lifted them, he realized he was naked, and had been cleaned; even his nails had been cut.

Was this a dream? With all that had happened nothing at the moment would surprise him.

That is until one section of wall melted away and a figure walked through.

He knew that all this was just an illusion; he knew that this person couldn't possibly be walking into the room.

He believed he was still on the alien world, in this mockery of a sick stricken planet, and he knew he wasn't dead. He didn't believe in life after death, so he knew this wasn't real.

The person walking through the wall had been dead for sixteen years, so he knew this was a kind of mind trick, but at the same time his mind was hoping it was real, wanting to believe what he saw; because he really missed his mother. When she had passed away all those years ago, both he and his brother were taken into care. They didn't even get to go to the funeral, but were both whisked away by Social Services.

The shock of seeing his mother made him pass out.

He awoke a few moments later, and sat bolt upright. The fast movement made him queasy but he didn't care, he thought at first he had been dreaming, but no the room was still there. He quickly looked around to see if the figure was still around. He spotted her in the corner readjusting some large blue flowers in an extraordinary fashioned vase.

"Mom?" was all he could say, the words stifled in his throat.

She turned around to look at him, graceful movements, like a dancer. His mum had never danced in her life, but the movements suited her, made her more beautiful than he ever remembered.

"No baby," was all she said, while moving closer and sitting on the end of his bed. "I'm not your mother." The figure moved her hands to point at her own body. "But does this body suit your wishes?"

He was confused, he knew deep down that this couldn't be his mum, but to see her was a blessing and he didn't want it to end. Not yet.

"Who... what are you?" He leaned forward and touched her arm, it felt different, unlike flesh, but he couldn't explain why.

"I am whatever you want me to be." She held him and lowered him back down onto the soft pillows, then pulled the sheets up around him.

"I am your helper, if you wish to call me something. I am to make your stay here as comfy as possible, and enjoyable." With that the figure in front of him changed shape, no longer was it a middle aged woman, but a young teenage girl, around nineteen possibly twenty years of age, with a perfect body, with all the right curves, a full head of blonde hair, and a voice like silk.

"I am whatever you want me to be." She stood and spun around, the flimsy material of her clothing swishing in the air, clinging to her sculptured body.

"Is this body more appealing?" She gracefully sat back on the bed.

"How can you... what are you?" He laid his hand over his eyes. He knew this figure, this image, it was what he always dreamed about when he was younger, his teenage minds fantasy. Every teenage minds fantasy, but normally the figure wasn't wearing clothes.

"The Lord wants you to heal, wants you to be comfy." She flicked a lock of stray blonde hair over her left ear. "He was harsh with you, and he is sorry." She shifted on the bed, making herself more comfy, moving closer. Her thigh now rested against his arm.

"He is not use to dealing with people from your world."

"My brother... my..." his voice cracked at the though of what had happened.

"He is resting also." She started to fiddle with the silk draped around the bed pillars. "He will be fine. He is in a room such as yours, and has a helper too, to also help him recover from his journey."

"I want to see him," he said, started to raise himself up on his elbows.

"You are in no fit state to go anywhere, that's why I'm here to look after you," she said with a beautiful smile, while flicking her long curved eyelashes. She stood, walked around the bed and started to tuck it in, straightening out the fine sheets.

"All will be okay you'll see. And once you are fit the Lord wants to see you again. See how you are? See that you have everything you need?"

The thought of seeing the Lord again made his stomach turn.

"You are hungry maybe?" She turned and waved a delicate hand. Where there was nothing, now stood a long table arranged with selection of all his favourite food, and drinks; even served in the same type of dishes his mother had used. Even the same faded blue tablecloth.

His mind was doing somersaults. Why did the Lord need to talk with him when it was obvious he could just read his mind, as he was doing now?

"Mmm, your favourite... meatballs." She put her finger in the bowl and pulled it out covered in sauce, then proceeded to lick it off her finger in a sensual way. One small drip landed on one of her half uncovered bosom. She moved closer, putting her hand on his arm. Wiggling her body closer to his.

"Or maybe there is something else you fancy instead?" she asked, using one delicate finger to wipe the sauce away, but all she succeeded in doing was smearing it over her large rounded breast and soil her lacy top. So with a, *Oh dear, silly me* look, she pulled the top up over her head, letting her bosom swing back down into place. She then crossed her arms over her chest, cradling her bust, pointing her two large cookie sized nipples in his direction, and gave him a wide teasing smile. Then she raised her left breast in one hand and started to remove the sauce with her alluring pink tongue, leaving a luscious tantalizing smear.

37
Stop All This

They had been travelling now for over several hours, and the scenery had changed very little. Just long rolling hills and lush grasses. The fields could have been from back home, the only difference was the animals, reptilian creatures of all descriptions. The further they got from the Gateway the more wildlife they saw.

Flocks of strangely shaped reptilian creatures cart wheeled in the air, picking up small insects as they went. And many of the strange leathery birds sat high up in the brittle branches of the thin trees, squawking at them as the cart lumbered past.

Time rolled on.

All were fidgety in the wagon.

Garry sat next to his brother, watching him for any sign of movement.

Coben sat up front with Lake and Raven on a long wooden plank that was raised above the flat back, from which the animals could be steered.

Time passed, nothing changed. The panorama did a little.

The truck was well behind them, and could not be seen with the naked eye. But the Captains team had them on the computer. Hopper fitted a small device to the wagon before leaving. It could pin point it within a few inches, up to a hundred and twenty kilometres away. Not that they ever planned on lagging that far behind.

In the distance there was a huge herd of grazing animals, there must have been thousands all hunched down grazing on the short grass that grew in this region. They were strange bipeds with huge mouths, chewing as they slowly ambled along.

There was also long grass to one side, with predators trying to sneak up on the unsuspecting grazers. From their elevated position they could see a group of nine animals circling a mother and newborn calf.

They passed a selection of oddly shaped trees. With huge broad trunks that veered in further up towards its top, until finally it shot out into an explosion of colour and foliage. Grazing on the top most leaves were tall, leathery bipeds, with long articulated necks, twisting this way and that, getting at the foliage, ripping it from the branches with their long bright green tongues. They looked like giraffes, but had six long triple jointed legs.

One tree though looked slightly different to the ones besides it. Garry stared at the tree trying to figure out what was different about it. That was until one of the long necked creatures moved over to it, to chew on its high braches. But as its tongue touched the leaves the tree changed. No longer standing tall, it was now wrapping its branches around the now struggling creature that had tried to eat from it. The trees roots pulled themselves from the ground and wrapped around the creature as it struggled for its life. It now looked like a huge wooden spider clinging to its prey.

Garry continued to watch in morbid fascination until he could no longer see the strange struggle.

Time marched on, nothing else interesting happened. One hour bled into the next, time soon moved past, letting their minds meander.

Then out of nowhere small six legged creatures started to run at the wagon. Hopping up on their strong back legs trying to get a look at what was on it.

Garry instinctively pulled back his feet and tucked them beneath himself.

"Its okay they will not harm you. They are just curious of us, and what we are doing," Raven said.

This seemed to relax Garry a bit, but he still didn't put his feet back over the side until the little creatures got bored of their game, and scampered off into the undergrowth; jumping all over each other as they went, disappearing into the bushes in a big jumble of small bodily parts.

Time seemed to drag on even worse, the night was slowly pulling its veil across the clouded sky, and everything started to become grey and shadowy, with long steaks of purple on the distant horizon.

They didn't stop the truck, but ate on the move. Lake removed a woven hemp bag and pulled food from it. Garry recognized it as the same meat he had eaten with Coben; Screamer he believed it was called. They also had raw vegetables that grew in the village gardens, and hard coarse bread, baked fresh that morning.

While all were digging into the food Garry spoke for the first time in almost five hours. "What's this place like we are going to?" Garry shouted out over the low rumbling and creaking of the wooden wheels, to no one in particular, just a general question.

Lake looked at Coben.

Coben simply stared straight ahead. He wiped the crumbs from his mouth and started to answer. "It's where the ancient Holy Ones once resided." He pulled the reins to one side to get the beasts to go around a small mound, rather than over it.

"It is a huge mountain, unlike anything you would ever have seen, or ever will see again," he said looking over towards Lake.

Lake continued. "Its top rises into the clouds," she said. "Because of punching through the cloud layer it is constantly covered in violent lightning storms."

The cart bounced to one side as the wheel caught a tree root protruding from the earth that Coben didn't see in the fading twilight.

"The mountain is colossus; it is more of an ancient volcano than a mountain. It is hollow now and is over forty-three kilometres wide inside, from wall to wall." Coben let the size sink in, before continuing. "I told you about the seven quarries where the stone for the Gateways are dug from."

Garry turned around to look at Coben while he talked, and bit off another chunk of bread, nodding yes, to the question.

"Those seven quarries are inside the mountain."

"Wow!" Garry stated, spitting crumbs over Ravens back, and then shaking his head from side to side.

"It is no more than one giant prison," Coben continued.

Raven brushed himself off, picking crumbs from his hair.

"So if this mountain sticks up through the cloud layer -" Garry let his words hang in the air.

"Yes it's true, and it is as you think. The cloud layer stops the dangerous rays from this world's sun from entering and killing all on the planet. But because the cloud layer is not there, all who labour inside the mountain live very short, painful lives. After only a few years they die." Coben's grip tightened on the reins.

"All those that are indigenous to this world are slaves as I told you. On the western side of the mountain are huge cities where the people are bred like animals, to work, live and die inside the mountain."

"And because of all the lightning, once you are inside there is no escape, not that they run away, where would they go?" Lake said looking sadly at the passing trees. Pulling at a branch that over hung them, stripping a few leaves off, and watched them lazily drift down to the ground, but the darkness soon swallowed them.

"But we have ways of getting into the mountain, by way of the underground passages." Coben announced, as he took a drink from a wooden cup, just handed to him by Raven.

Lake took the cup from Coben, and then offered Garry a drink.

He took the cup and looked at its contents, a yellow liquid with brown bits floating in it.

"It's made from the roots of a Putjia plant, the leaves and stalk are poisonous, as some sadly found out after just arriving here long ago. But after watching animals dig down to the roots and chew on them they realized they could be of some use. Now we grow them for this drink. And lately we found that the leaves once ground up, mixed with water, and placed on a wound stops it from getting infected and speeds up the healing process."

It was almost completely dark now, with the clouds all but a dark patch over the sky. No flying reptiles travelled the night sky, in fear of becoming a larger creature's meal.

Raven took the reins from Coben, while Coben made himself comfy for the night.

Lake was already fast asleep leaning on Raven's shoulder.

As soon as they found a sheltered spot they would stop during the hours of darkness.

Garry turned back to look at his brother, and pull the blankets up around Glyn's neck. The thought once again crossed his mind: *how are we both going to stop all this?* Especially, he mused, when his brother hadn't even woken up yet.

38
All Ready

All was complete. The Colonel and all his men had arrived eighteen hours earlier. They were now standing around the area of the second Gateway.

The land around the base was now the property of the American Government; or rather one small part of it that most didn't even know existed.

Colonel Madera was ready, as well as his one hundred and forty Special Forces troopers who were going with him.

As well as himself and his men, there was an extra three hundred and sixty-one personnel on the grounds. These were all the technical staff needed to get the place up and running, and monitor the entire goings on in, and around the Gateway. They had arrived in two huge Antonov 225 Mriya heavy-lifting transportation aeroplanes, carrying all that was needed for them to have the base up and running within sixteen hours of landing.

Most believed that there was only one An-225 in existence, because of its huge size and cost. But it was the largest plane in the world, weighing a staggering five hundred tons, and capable of transporting two hundred and fifty tons; being that it was 18 meters high and 84 meters long, with a cargo space of 6.4 meters wide, 4.39 meters high and 35.97 meters long, with a staggering wingspan of 88.4 meters long. The Trust had the finances to have whatever they desired; they owned three.

The small military base between Widecombe in the Moor and Manton had never seen so much activity. It was now the short-term property of the American army, who was in the process of changing a few things around, and repairing the damage from a mysterious explosion.

All British army personnel had been removed, with the Trust officers placed in there positions instead. All was up and running as if it had been there for years.

Most of the equipment had been transported forty minutes away, on top of eight large 35 ton flatbed lorries, four had fitted into each Antonov 225, preloaded ready to drive straight out and directly to the Gateway. The equipment created the huge dome that now covered the strange deformed house Gateway and surrounding area. Its colossal white surface could be seen for kilometres; it was already the talk of the neighbouring village of Whitchurch. Many were parked in their cars on the roadside trying to see what was going on around the erected dome. But armed army personnel kept them from getting to close.

The villagers were told that this was an historic area, that remains from prehistoric English life had been unearthed. That the dome was there to stop the weather from eroding the precious site away, while the area was being studied.

No one thought to ask what the army was doing there. But if they did an explanation was all ready for them.

Also an area of two kilometres around the house was out off limits to all aircraft, as well as newspaper helicopters, to stop unwanted photos. Only the Trust aircraft could get anywhere near the area.

This was the worst case scenario, the Gateway being in a built up area, and in a free country. At least in Africa, once the Government was paid off, you knew that was the end of the story, that you wouldn't get people snooping around. Africa had enough problems without checking up on every so-called research base.

England was different. Everyone thought they deserved to know what was happening in their own backyard.

So far it was all going smoothly and according to plan. All who worked under Madera knew what was expected of them, nothing but one hundred percent at all times. It was a finely tuned operation and everything was going according to plan, and so far all deadlines had been met.

The Colonel now stood in the operations main control room; this was located in the outer ring of the dome. Here all the electrical equipment and sensitive apparatus was held, which monitored the activity of the Gateway and surrounding area.

The Colonel was looking at the front Gateway to the house. The door was all wired up. All machines needed to check and open the door; as well as monitoring equipment; was positioned around and had been attached to it.

"Is everything ready for deployment?" The Colonel didn't even bother to look at whom he was talking to; he kept his eyes on the Gate.

"Yes Colonel. All is in place. All ready to go, sir," said a small military man sitting behind a large plasma touch screen monitor, who was speedily moving his hands over the screen, giving off some new order that only he could fully comprehend.

"Good… good." He turned to the officer behind him. "Get everyone ready and in position. I want to leave within the hour." The Colonel had his hands behind his back, clenching and unclenching them, holding onto a small faded photo.

"Understood sir," the officer said saluting. Then turned on the spot and marched out of the room, his heavy boots resounding off the metal decking.

The Colonel had only one thing left to do before going; he was waiting for a radio transmission, one he couldn't afford to miss.

39
Roger Roger

It wasn't what could be called a hard journey, just tedious. The landscape changed very little, and apart from the mountains in the distance there was very little to concentrate on. It became hill after rolling hill, valley after long dull stretching vale. Even most of the creatures didn't want to come this way.

Raven picked up the small transceiver, which Hopper had given them to keep in contact.

"We are stopping for water. Roger. Over."

Hopper lowered his head. He was regretting that he had given the thing to Raven rather than Lake, because of the annoying way he used it, always saying Roger, Roger, or some other annoying phrase he had heard in a film at some point, believing this is how the military actually talked to one another.

"Received," he said, looking over to the Captain who had a smile on his face, knowing how much it was getting on Hopper's nerves.

"Can I send an electrical boost through this thing? Please?" He looked sadly at the Captain. "We could blame him and say he dropped it or something."

The Captain gave off a short chuckle. "Best not in case it actually comes in useful at some point."

"That's if he doesn't wear the batteries out first," was Babes input to the conversation, this made the Captain laugh once again, and made Hopper slap his forehead and wipe his hand over his shaved head.

Just then the radio buzzed to life once again, filling the back of the van with Raven's voice. "We have found a river. Over. We are going to refill our water bottles, and have a short rest. Roger. Over and out. 10 – 4."

"*Rubber Duck*," Babe said, giggling.

It had been a few hours since they all awoke and set off once again across the terrain towards the mountain.

Hoping that they were not being watched, or followed, Hopper had snuck across during the night and had spoken with Raven, leaving him the two-way radio. "But only for use in an urgent situation." He had stressed that point. He had to sneak to see him mainly because of all the commotion and haste in setting off, he had forgotten to hand it over then.

Now he wished he hadn't bothered.

Babe had to take the small handset off of Hopper and reply for him. "Understood, will stand by. Copy." She handed the handset back and slapped Hopper on the back in a reassuring manner.

"Don't worry if by some strange coincidence he changes into a mutated monster, you can have the privilege of shooting him between the eyes," Babe announced.

This got a sideways glance from the Captain, but seemed to cheer Hopper up.

The Captain was taking a turn at driving the vehicle, and now slowly brought it to a stop under a dense section of large leafed bushes that had outsized blue flowers that wilted down to the ground.

"Okay people we have a timeout. If you need to stretch your legs feel free, but I don't have to remind you to be on alert."

All nodded.

The sun was quite low in the firmament, from what they could guess, because of never actually seeing the thing, just a sort of light smudge in the clouds above them, defused by the dense swirling cloud layer.

"Hopper, what does your readings say about this area?" the Captain asked looking over his shoulder. Now he had parked up, he was standing in the back of the truck.

"Well it's a bit strange. There's a sort of electrical discharge coming off from around here somewhere. It's sort of screwing the readings up a bit," he said, while his hands flew over the keyboard.

The Captain turned to give him his complete attention. "What do you mean, there's a kind of discharge?"

"Well in some places there are different rocks that give off different radiation levels. For example, in Devon where the Gateway was situated - the place called the Moors - gives off a kind of radiation called radon. This comes from the granite in the area under the ground, in some places it gathers and becomes strong enough to effect electrical equipment."

"And you just happened to know this?" came Docs remark.

"Its my job to study the areas we go into in case there's an anomaly that I need to know about, that could effect the running of my equipment. So yes I just happened to know," he was looking at Doc waiting for an argument.

"Well I don't know about you lot, but I'm going to take a shit in a bush somewhere." With that Doc straightened his camouflage jacket, brushed off some imaginary lint, then opened the back door and jumped to the ground, slamming the door behind him.

"What's eating him?" Babe asked looking at Hopper.

"I have no idea. He's tuning into a right grumpy twat lately that's for sure," he said punching away at his keyboard, and taking a bite out of a ration chocolate bar.

"He's just feeling the stress more than us, that's all," came the Captain's mild rebuke.

Doc walked some distance from the truck, down a small incline and onto what looked like a dried up river bed, with just a small trickle running down the middle, possibly something to do with the river the others had stopped at.

That made him realize even though the sky was constantly covered in clouds it hadn't rained yet. This was only his third day here, but from the look of the clouds it should have rained long ago.

Little did he realize that above his head a huge tempest was brewing.

He looked around to check no one had followed him. Realizing he was on his own he pulled his rucksack off, and opened it up, taking out a small device and laying it on the ground. He then took several other things from his bag and laid them on the ground next to the first. When he had finished assembling the six pieces of what looked like surgical equipment together, he had one bit left. He took his watch off and unclipping the winder and pulled a long fine cord out, adjusting its length he clipped it into the object he had just assembled. It was now ready to use. He attuned the small switch on the side and waited.

He didn't have to wait long.

"Ah, I see. It's you," came a crisp sharp voice.

Doc felt like saying, "Of course it's me, who did you expect, the fucking Easter Bunny?" But he didn't. Rather he listened to what was being said.

"What information have you got for me?" asked the voice.

Doc looked around once again; it always seemed much louder than normal, when he was listening to it out in the open.

"We are on our way to the Temple of the Sky."

Silence. Followed by, "Good… good." As if he was thinking of something else.

"What do you want me to do?" Doc looked around he thought he had heard a twig snap; leaves rustling.

"Carry on as planned. We have talked this through; there is no need for changes now. I will be through within the hour, and will take control of the whole situation."

Doc stuttered at first. "S-so I'm t-to carry on and do as you asked?"

"There is no need for changes now. You know your orders," announced the stern reprimand.

Doc ignored it and continued, "But if you're coming through can't you do it?"

Then behind him came another sound.

He looked. Zilch, nada.

"But I'm a medic!" came his whisper, as he turned his attention back to the conversation.

"Yes and you are also a trained killer. So don't whine like a fucking Girl Scout. You know your orders. Do not fail me. I want the whole team dead before I get through the Gateway."

Before Doc could answer the radio went silent.

"Be careful. The river runs very fast in this area, it will pull you under and you would freeze to death within minutes, or the weeds on the bottom will entangle you and hold you under," Coben said warning Garry.

Garry looked up. "Wow this place is just a bundle of laughs isn't it?" he said mockingly, his shoulders hunched.

"I know you are not unintelligent. I was just giving you a small warning; some have been lost to rivers such as these, because they became complacent."

The river Doc sat at almost two kilometres away, met up with two others to cause what the others had stopped next to.

Garry scooped up the water into a kind of leather skin sack, which held a surprising amount.

The cart had stopped and they were all out of it. Coben was now chatting with Lake pointing off into the distance, towards the heading they were all going to go off in once their rest was over.

The large creatures were untied and were now drinking from the river. One was even wading out. It was unconcerned about the power of the currant, and the numbing coldness, because of its size and powerful body and the thickness of its hide.

Raven was sitting on a small rock cradling the walkie-talkie receiver in his hand looking at it; waiting for it to sound, or possibly thinking of something to say.

That's when they heard it, a loud thunderous noise. The earth started to shake. The river even started to pulsate, the water being tossed into the air from the vibration.

All looked around trying to work out from what source or direction it was coming from. Then they could see from the distance what the noise was.

From the vast grass covered plain, running towards them, was a herd of creatures, thousands of them, all running with their head down, charging. It was hard to judge their height because they were leaning forward sort of using their own weight to propel themselves onwards towards their destination.

Coben took control, shouting, "Everyone into the trees. Take cover." He was waving his arms to get their attention away from the spectacle that was charging towards them.

Garry grabbed Glyn with the aid of Lake and carried him towards the tree line.

The beasts of burden were confused. The one drinking by the water was looking around panicking. The larger one that was in the water was thrashing around, unsure of which way to dash.

Everyone was now crouched down in the bushes and under the trees taking cover.

The cart and the animals had to be left where they were; there was no time to move them. No time to react other than running for cover.

That's when they arrived.

About twelve foot in height, covered in thick leathery skin, a dark patchwork of sea green and coffee brown colour, with two large strong legs, with a long powerful neck, short arms out front tucked up underneath themselves, and a long thick tails behind for balance.

There was more than the eye could count, all running off at an angle to them, causing an immense plume of dust to rise high up into the sky.

Coben was annoyed at himself for not noticing the dust kicked up by these beasts earlier, which would have given them some kind of pre-warning. For a minute Coben believed, as so did the others that the creatures would bypass them on the other side of the river. When suddenly in one swift movement; which reminded them all of a flock of birds; the creatures changed direction. Now they were charging towards the watercourse, heading straight towards them, in an unstoppable stampede.

40
Sitting On the Fence

The tunnel was long and dark, going down, deeper and deeper. Water dripped constantly from the ceiling. Moss squelched under foot, making walking slow and precarious.

He rarely came down this far, but he had someone to see, he hadn't seen them for a long time. But things change, things had happened.

He walked with his cloak open billowing behind him, his twisted staff in his hand, the same torch burning in front of him, levitating, shining off of his scale etched breastplate, and showing up the slippery path ahead.

But he needed no torch that was from force of habit. He had walked this way thousands of times over the years. It was exactly the same; nothing had changed in the narrow damp tunnels. But things had changed above, and he felt he needed to talk with them, see if they knew what was transpiring far above them, in the world of the living.

He knew no one would be following him; why would they, they never do. He was one of his Lords most trusted advisers. If only they all knew what he knew?

He had been walking down for sometime. The tunnels becoming colder the further he got from the heat of the roaring fires in the main chamber.

He turned a few more corners.

It was a complete labyrinth down under the mountain. If you didn't know your way nor had a map you would easily get lost. But the map was his memory, engraved over the years.

Small areas this far under were populated by all manners of strange creatures, which had adapted to life underground. Some were human, but had long since changed into light fearing, scavenging creatures, which hunt and fight among themselves.

But they scurried away as he approached with his torch. Only once had they tried to attack him. He left a large number of them dead and many more wounded. They hadn't tried anything since.

He came to an underground lake where large stalactites hung from the ceiling, with soft light issuing from some florescent mosses growing high above.

Sounds of splashing could be heard from some unknown source, possible bits of the cavern roof falling into the dark waters, or some aquatic animal of some kind. None ever bothered him.

The other end of the cavern was far away in the distance; to far and to dark to see the other side, even with the light issuing from the caverns ceiling.

He lifted his staff into the air. Its texture strange and moving, you couldn't tell if it was writing or pictures. The carving changed as you looked at it. It was a gift from them, for his service.

As he lifted it in to the air it shimmered with an inner light and power.

Under the surface of the water effervescent bubbles started to rise, followed by faint lights starting to glow, they got brighter as they came closer to the choppy surface. Small foot sized stones floated out of the cold dark watery deep.

He then placed his foot on the first, as he walked along leisurely from one to the other, the ones in front came into position just before his foot touched it and as his foot lifted off one, it went dark and began once again to sink into its watery abyss resting place.

It wasn't long before he reached the other side, the stones having led him to a small enclave in the wall where the water lapped. It looked the same as all the rest of the cavern face. The light from the ceiling reflecting from the water was making an optical illusion on the wall, if you didn't know where the gap was you would never find it. Not that many, if any, ever came down this far, or attempted to cross the murky – some say bottomless - lake.

He entered the opening into yet another tunnel. But unlike the rest of the tunnels this one was well looked after, protected. Magic kept it clean. Torches burned on the walls leading down into the belly of the mountain deeper and deeper, far underground. So far even the Lord never bothered with these lower areas. He had far too much going on above ground to worry about the icy depths below.

He came across the large double doors, lavishly carved with intricate patterns of unusual animals of unknown origin. These animals seemed to have a kind of fur growing on them, instead of leathery skin. Also they were in unusual surroundings. He had once asked about them, he was told that these doors depicted life on another world.

The doors silently swung open on their own, as they normally did as he approached.

A grotto lay before him, not as large as the one up stairs, but still imposing.

Huge copper vats with swirling green flames sat on top of four large carved creatures; the same as on the doors; each facing a different way, north, south, east and west, carrying the huge copper basin on their wide powerful shoulders. There were two vats, one to either side of the large pool, which was full of metallic looking liquid that was rippling and bubbling.

All about on the walls were large tapestries, depicting images of people worshipping at the Gateway, how life once was: a time long past, but not forgotten by some.

Thousands of candles lay on every possible surface; cracks in the wall, ledges, all over the floor, apart from a small trail leading up to, then around the pulsating pool.

The Lords advisor walked along the path and set himself down in the kneeling position before the shimmering liquid. His body armour making the only sounds other than the crackling and hissing of the thousands of burning candles.

He stretched out his arms, and put his hands palm up, head now lowered, eyes closed.

The surface started to swirl, become unsettled, gathering into the middle of the pool, drawing all the metallic liquid into the centre, and then separating. It slowly rose up becoming a pillar of darkish fluid: all done in eerie silence. Slowly a shape started to become apparent, until there was a figure resembling a humanoid stood on the surface of what had now changed to a substance resembling water, now they had removed themselves from the pool.

Now stood on the water itself, floating, was a figure of a tall man, or rather the impression of a man, with long flowing robes, cowl over its head. Head lowered. Hands pressed together.

The figure spoke; it was the voice of a hundred voices overlapped, not quite in unison, you could catch the tail end of what a few of the voice said after the others had finished.

"ALL IS GOING WELL... *ing well... well*?" It didn't as much as walk, but floated across the surface and moved over the rim of the pool. It didn't seem to touch the floor rather hovering above it a few inches.

"THEY ARE ON THERE WAY... *there way... way*?" It turned and floated across the candles, as it did they went out and relit after he had passed over them.

"THE PROPHECY HAS ALMOST RUN TOO COMPELETION... *completion.*" It stopped next to a tall stand which had a book perched upon its top. It silently waved a hand across over the books thick delicately painted leather cover. The book flicked open, ancient pages creaking under the stress of being used so infrequently.

"ONCE THE PROPHECY HAS BEEN COMPLETED, OUR SOULS WILL REST... *will rest... rest.*"

The Lords adviser stood tall and looked into the direction where the figure was standing, leaning over the book.

"Once the prophecy has been fulfilled?" the adviser asked.

"ONCE IT IS FULLFILLED, THEN WE, THE HOLY ONES CAN GO TO OUR REST... *to our rest... rest.* OUR SOULS WILL HAVE PEACE... *have peace.*"

"What is it you wish me to do, in order to help you?" He crossed his arms over his chest as a sign of complete submission.

The figure wavered in the air, becoming a blur before coming back together again.

"THERE IS ONE THING NEEDED TO BE DONE IN ORDER FOR THIS TO COME ABOUT. THIS IS WHAT YOU WILL DO... *will do... do.*"

41
Hallowed be Thy Name

The room was much colder than he remembered it. He knew that it had only been a little while that he had slept. Or had it?

Flatfoot tried to move his head but it felt stuck. What was happening?

Suddenly his head became free and the darkness retreated. It was light again. Fresh cool air once again blowing around the confines of the room.

He sat up in bed.

Now a window had appeared. The frame was huge and intricately carved. It was more of a picture frame than a window: covered in golden trim and intricately carved overlapping flowery petals that entwined there way around the outer edge. All made from the same glowing pink stone-like substance.

He pulled back the sheets, heavy though they were, and walked over to the newly formed window. Flatfoot peered out. It was a sight he knew all to well. One he had seen many times. It was the view from a postcard he used to have pinned on the wall next to his bed at St Catharine's Orphanage. He always promised himself that one day he would be staring at that view from that very hotel window, as he now was. Was he in a hotel? He couldn't remember signing in. How long had he been here? The world seemed confusing to him, everything blurring into one moment.

He sat back on the bed, his hand touched the sheets, and it didn't feel right. How could he afford a room like this? And where was his brother?

His mind was all cloudy, confused, tired: was it tiredness? He wasn't sure he couldn't concentrate.

He went to stand but his feet gave way from beneath him. The room became blurry. For a split second the room was gloomy. He was held fast, his head restrained, his arms and legs were firmly held and locked in to place.

The next moment he was lying on the floor of the room again. The floor seemed colder than he remembered it. His hand felt the texture, it was all wrong.

"Pull yourself together mate," he whispered, trying to gain some kind of control. He felt high on drugs. Only once had he indulged himself, when very drunk, to try an E. tablet. The sensation was similar to what he felt now; unbalanced, queasy and completely out of control. He hated that feeling.

The world flickered for a moment; it went in and out of focus; it all distorted and came back into clarity, the room bending like the reflection in a cheap carnival mirror.

He was suspended from a wall, his whole body held fast, in a kind of cocoon; a sticky substance holding him in place. The only part of his body he could move was his head, only slightly but enough to see around him.

To his left another person was suspended in the same type of dark sea green, pulsating membrane. To his right hung his brother, held as fast as he was, with his head dangling forward. This time instead of spittle running from the corner of his mouth it was blood. Eyes open only a fraction with only the whites showing that had red veins mapped all over them. Tendrils from the green cocoon were slowly spreading out, crawling there way over his face.

Then a deep voice issued from the right, "This one is awake." The person who said it was just coming into focus.

"He is much stronger than we thought he would be," said the second foggy silhouette.

Flatfoot's eyes were going in and out of focus. For a moment the figure came into vision, it was the young lady who had nursed him, or had she? His mind was just working through all that was happening to him.

"You are right; it was all just an illusion. You were never in that room, you were here all along," as she said this, her figure blurred and came back into focus, this time instead of a young lady a hooded figure stood before him.

One of the Circle as he remembered them, those that were standing around in a ring in the throne room. But this time he could see his face as he looked up towards him. The person was strikingly handsome with strong features, square jaw and high cheekbones. But the most outstanding feature; just like most things in this world; was his bright shining eyes, burning with an inner orange intensity.

"This one is useless," the figure standing next to him said, while pointing a long sharp object at the person suspended on his left. As he said this he swung the instrument upwards and cut along the cocoon that held the body in place, as he did so the person dropped to the floor below with a sickening thud.

It was a man, or what was left of him. His head looked normal, but the rest of his body had been completely sucked dry. A skeletal carcass lay on the gritty floor, skin pulled taught over the now brittle bones. The fluid that was left was now seeping out of all the minute holes all over the cadaver; thousands of small puncture wounds.

As Flatfoot looked up to the two halves of the now split cocoon, he noticed thousands of small tubes that must have been inserted into the body, draining its body fluids. They were now swinging around frantically, with little opening and closing mouths on the end, with hundreds of tiny razor-sharp teeth, looking for more nourishment.

The shrouded figure to one side swung a long hooked instrument that stuck through the corpses shoulder, and then proceed to pull the skeletal remains of the man along the floor, depositing him down a dark dank pit.

Flatfoots body suddenly became all itchy; now his senses were coming back. He could feel all the worms penetrating his body, wiggling deeper; slowly sucking the life from him.

How long would it take? How long had he left? He didn't know. But he did know that if the others didn't come soon, he would be like that pitiful sight that was tumbling down the blood soaked hole.

Flatfoot had never believed in God; how could he, he always reasoned, after everything that had happened to him and his brother in their lives. And he hated those people that only prayed when they needed or wanted something. Like if you found you had a terminal illness, and your faith in God suddenly awakened.

But that's exactly what he started to do now, saying the first thing that came into his head. Something he was taught at the orphanage, taught until he memorized it. With each word he used to get wrong, he would feel the bamboo cane; quickly lashed across his naked back, impartially portioned out by the Father who was taking the prayers that morning.

He closed his stinging eyes, and slowly started to recite the words he had memorized in those awful circumstances. Even now he still couldn't get the words right. "Our father who's in heaven. Hallowed be his name... thy kingdom come... thy will be done, in heaven as it is on earth..."

Unbeknown to Flatfoot, the length of his last few dieing moments all depended upon the Lord and his hunger. The pods were an extension of his body, after having blended into the walls of the Temple hundreds of years before when he became one with the mountain. And at the moment the Dark Lord was ravenous, because he knew what had arrived through the gateway and he needed all the strength he could absorb in order to meet the challenge headlong.

42
Rag Doll

The Captain's group could hear the rumbling even from where they were. From where they now stood; to one side of the truck they could see an enormous cloud of red dust reaching high into the cloudy sky.

"Hopper, can you see what's happening down there?" The Captain asked looking over the crest of the hill down onto the wide stretching plain. Where even now the cloud was getting closer to where the others location was situated.

"It looks to me like a large herd of animals, sir." Hopper passed the binoculars over to the Captain.

"Carnivore, herbivore, what do you think?" The Captain looked around to Babe, who was the sort of unofficial animal expert; in the sense, she was the only one who had any idea about them, which was more of a childhood hobby, from hours of sitting in front of The Discovery and National Geographic channels.

"Don't worry; I would say herbivore, mainly because of their number. No way could a group that large live on meat alone, they simply wouldn't survive."

"I just hope they don't get trampled to death that's all," Hopper stated, looking in to the distance.

The others looked at him.

"You're such a pessimist," said Babe.

"Well think of it, they're all moving at what fifty, sixty kilometres an hour. That's some speed, and that many as well. The others would just be mowed down where they stand." He shrugged as if to say, *it's not my fault.*

"But if they all crouch down won't they jump over them, you know like in stampedes with cows and such?" the Captain asked, once again looking at Babe.

"At home yes, but we are dealing with different species, we could only guess at what they would do."

"Well there's nothing we can do apart from hope they'll be okay," the Captain announced, walking back to the truck.

"What do you mean nothing we can do?" Hopper questioned.

The Captain turned and looked at him. "By the time we get there it would be too late. Plus how do we know this Lord person hasn't sent this. This could be a test of some kind. I just don't know. But I do know we are going to sit it out until Raven gets in touch with us on the radio."

As if to change the subject the Captain looked around. "Where'd Doc go? He must be deaf as well as constipated or something. Babe go and look for him will you? Tell him to give it a shake and get back here."

Doc had just finished taking his radio apart and stashing the equipment back into his knapsack when he heard a noise again. He looked around but as before saw nothing, so as before he simply ignored it. He had too much on his mind at the moment to worry about a small foraging animal.

He hooked his pack back on his shoulders and set off in the direction of the truck. They would be concerned about his time spent away from them, they were all so meddlesome, and he couldn't wait to rid himself of them. Even though he wished it wasn't him that had to do it. But orders were orders. He had been integrated into this group from the beginning; by Madera. And each day he had to give a full report about its progress. He had been having second thoughts about the whole situation; mainly because he thought when he came to this world he would never see the Colonel again. Now he had just found out that Madera was on his way here.

He hadn't realized he had walked so far from the truck.

Movement caught his eye to his left. He pulled his small matt black Sig pistol from his belt and held it at eye level towards the bushes in a double handed grip. "I know you are there, come out." It was a wild shot; chancing that if someone was there they would give up so easily.

A figure came crashing through the undergrowth; leaves and branches flying.

"Put it down dipshit. Do you think that if I was trying to sneak up on you I would be crashing around like an elephant?" Babe turned back around, heading back towards the truck, and the others. "Pull your finger out, let's get back." Then she mumbled, "Why the hell would you want to walk this far for a shit, I don't know. Maybe you have an embarrassingly small pecker?" She started to push her way back towards the direction she had come, parting springy branches with one gloved hand, while picking twigs out her blonde hair with the other.

It was all over in an instant.

One shot too the back of the head. And like a cloud of death, her blood sprayed outwards. Babe was flung forwards, her body dead before she even hit the leave covered ground. The terra firma was now saturated with her blood, soaking down through into the roots. Her body was still twitching. She lay like a rag doll tossed into the bushes; her body twisted at an unnatural angle, because her cadaver was no longer limited by living limitations.

The shot echoed through the trees. Reptilian creatures took to flight.

The gunshot was deafening. Doc didn't really think. He knew what he had to do. He would say she surprised him. It was reflexes.

The others would be confused, upset. He could, and would use that to buy himself some time, to work out how to get rid of them as well.

The trees parted, but instead of the others it was young female who walked through. She was stunning in appearance, having the sublime body of an exotic dancer. She had thick curly long jet-black hair, so black it almost looked blue, like the wing of a raven. She looked Latin American in appearance; her dark brown eyes shining almost black, like two stones of obsidian. She was dressed in what looked like a lizard skin dress, a dark bottle green colour; that rode high on her thighs, showing off her long smooth legs that ran unadorned down to her bare feet. She came out of the bushes and looked down at the body of Babe, staring at the hole through the woman's head that was the size of a tennis ball; because Doc's ammunition were hollow tipped.

At the same moment the other three pushed through the trees on the other side, all with weapons up and ready. They took in the situation.

Hopper quickly knelt down besides Babe's body, his fingers reaching out, but not able to touch her, just holding back, not capable of comprehending the situation, just staring wide eyed at all the blood and brain matter that was splattered on the leaves and branches.

"What happened?" the Captain asked quickly. Keeping his eye on the new arrival that just stood there not saying a word, presuming she had done this. His firearm was levelled with the woman's torso, the red laser point over her heart.

"She's dead," Hopper announced, lowering his head, tears stinging the corners of his eyes.

"She snuck up on me. I… I was s-surprised I reacted. M-my gun went off.

It was reflexes."

For a few split second's confusion rained down upon them all. They had presumed this stranger to be responsible, but now they realized it was Doc who had done this?

"But she was shot in the back of the head." Hopper whispered. Then turned, standing in one movement. "IN THE BACK OF THE FUCKING HEAD!" he shouted.

Doc looked around. Suddenly he lifted his gun and pointed it towards the Captain and squeezed the trigger.

The mysterious young lady lifted her hand. In one quick flash Doc now lay on his back breathing hard, his body in convulsions, his pistol dropped to the soft soil without a sound.

The Captain had seen what Doc was about to do, and had no time to move or react. All he could do was close his eyes; he was going to join his beautiful wife and children. Seconds passed.

Nothing?

He opened his eyes and looked at his chest where the blossoming red hole should have been, where the blood should have been pouring over his jacket. But the bullet was suspended in the air a matter of inches away from his wildly thumping heart, and then it dropped harmlessly to the leave strewn ground.

The young ladies knees gave way; she collapsed forward, her shoulder hitting a tree bough that twisted her as she fell, she landed on her back, her long curly hair fanning out around her.

Doc was just lying there shaking. Blue sparks rolling over his body, which died away, as it did he fell into unconsciousness with a final twitch and a glob of spittle from the corner of his mouth.

"What the fuck is happening?" the Captain shouted to no one in particular, once the shock of what just happened wore off. With that he laid his hand on the area the bullet would have entered. Reaching down he picked up the bullet, it was still hot to the touch.

Hopper had tears running down his cheeks as he looked away from Babe towards Doc. Then in a flash he was on his feet and lunging towards the team's medic, kicking him in the ribs, blows after blow, landing one or two in his face.

The Captain was quick on his feet, pulling Hopper away. "That's enough." He wiped the sweat of his face. This was the last thing he expected to happen, and the last thing he needed. "I said ENOUGH! Hopper!" He pulled him away once again, pushing him backwards with all his strength.

"Tie that bastard up. And check him for any more concealed weapons." He looked at the doctor and whispered, "*Primum non nocere*," which was Latin for, First Do No Harm, an oath all doctors took. He wondered where Doc went wrong.

He turned and looked at the fallen, twisted dead body of Babe. He then slowly removed his jacket and laid it over her. Turning around he looked at the young woman that has just saved his life. Why? Who was she? What was she doing here? But at the same time he was bloody glad she was. There were a few questions that needed answering. And by god he was going to get them, one way or another.

The Captain just hoped that Coben and his group weren't doing as badly as them?

43
Sweeping Clean

The Colonel didn't understand how the Gateway worked, whether it worked by magical or scientific means, but more importantly he just didn't care, so long as it worked and got him from A to B, which was all that concerned him.

He was now standing at B.

He held no gun or any type of weapon in his hand - he didn't need to, his Beretta 92 model was still sat in its holster with the popper in place, because fanning around him were his one hundred and forty troopers. All in complete combat attire, each a walking deadly arsenal. They fanned out in a large semi circle of two groups, all in the crouching position. Powerful P90 machineguns resting against their shoulders, aiming out towards the tree line: watching for any type of movement: waiting, seemingly uncaring that they now found themselves on a different alien world.

The Colonel strolled down the middle as if on a picnic outing rather than a tactical deployment.

Now they had set up a perimeter the rest of the equipment started to pour through the Gateway. One at a time eighteen vehicles started to churn out of the grey wall, one after another they came until all eighteen had deployed into a semi circle, nine to each side.

They were about the size of a typical family saloon car; they had eight wheels, four to either side of the pivoting axel that broke the vehicle in half. At the front was a dome, which now it had passed through the Gateway, was opening up to display two large mounted XM-214 Microguns, with six 5.56mm barrels, each to either side of a small missile launcher, which carried eight, small two-pound explosive tips ground to air missiles; similar to the Dragon 2 Weapon System. Also a small but powerful collection of antenna and miniature satellite dishes rested just behind the main weapons section.

On the back end were two large rectangles boxes, back to back. These both held forty high-density canisters, which could be jettisoned high into the sky. They also had a red biochemical warning sticker attached to each.

There was a small section between the front Microguns put aside for a driver, but these machines were almost fully computer controlled, with the driver simply monitoring and giving small orders every now and then.

Now these were set into place, the troopers pulled back and started working on two other vehicles – the supplies and sleeping quarters - that had only just passed through.

Last - but by no means least – was the crème-de-la-crème just scraping through with mere inches to spare; this was the largest of the weaponry. It had thirty-six wheels, eight to each of its four sections, all separated by large pivoting axels. The four large sections now started to fold up into place. On the back of each section was machinery, which even now was starting to click to life, rising up as if to touch the heavens. Each section held two hundred and forty missiles. With all four sections this made nine hundred and sixty small experimental ground-clearing scatter, high-pressure detonators: aptly named the Earth-Destroyer.

As soon as it cleared the Gateway it didn't delay; it turned towards the direction it needed to point – southeast; projector 14-137 - and proceed to release one section of its arsenal. Dozens firing at once, row after row, shooting into the distance high into the cloudy sky. Once hundreds had been released they flew into the distance gaining altitude high over the dense forest, towards the direction of the next Gateway.

After all on the first section fired, the silence was deafening. Dense thick smoke hung in the air like morning mist. Everyone was now waiting. The fully automated machine now seemed to be waiting.

Far in the distance small dots could just be seen, hanging silently in the air, their small fuel propulsion tank now having run dry, they silently carried on climbing until they could no longer carry on their momentum, gravity then started to pull them back down to the ground, just like they were designed to.

Once on a downward motion the missile casings parted and jettisoned to the sides. This released a smaller projectile, which because of the counter weight began to turn facing the right direction. Another smaller booster then came into play, to speed the falling detonator on its way. Also a slight change on the tip of the weapon, it was now rotating at an incredible rate of speed. Moments before impact a third booster gave it that extra jolt needed, along with the rotating end to punch its way through the thick foliage, severing tree limbs, ripping bark from the trees, and digging themselves deep into the planet crust, up to eight foot down.

All waited. All held their breath.

In his hand the Colonel had a small trip switch. He pulled a cigar from his mouth and rolled it around in his fingers and then putting the end in his mouth again he bit the stump off and spat it to the dense smoke swirling ground. Putting it back into his mouth he lit the end, taking a long deep drag he held the smoke in his lungs, and then blew the blue plume towards the sky. He looked at the burning end and smiled. He always had time for a good Cuban cigar; one that Patterson had handed him just before he left the Trusts underground bunker. He put it back into his mouth and took one more long, deep drag and held it, as he released it this time he flicked the cigar into the distance towards the forest, as it hit the terracotta coloured soil he pressed the small red switch he held in his palm.

The troopers around him took their P90 rifles and released them, the linked hooks caught and they simply swung down against their torso, now hanging from their flax jackets. They then lifted their left arm; underneath was a foot long black rubber cartridge. Holding the small lever they pulled the handle down, a long black strip released itself from the casing, unfolded and spread out, like an awakening flower. From their kneeling position they then clipped the handle onto their boot. Now they had a screen between them and the impending blast.

But still nothing seemed to happen.

Then all of a sudden a sonic boom pierced the air. Starting from under the ground, first pulverizing the tree roots, then sending the blast skywards, and shredding the trees from ground level up, the blast being directed upwards turning all the trees and vegetation into a collection of splinters and dust, mixed with flying burnt soil and superheated shattered stones. The scientists predicted that the underground blast would be equivalent to a 4 on the Richter scale, over a five kilometre radius.

The detonators had two sections; the second now came into play. The first causing total destruction, the second blasting it all out of the way.

The primary blast didn't affect those around the Gateway anymore than causing the ground to sway slightly, making the vehicles wobble on their tires, because of being directed upwards, but the second scattered the debris, causing it to fly in all directions. First came a strong humid wind, then the fragments of trees and small crushed rocks.

The noise of stones could be heard pinging off the large transportation vehicles metal sides, and the flimsy shields on the troopers arms, these swayed under the onslaught but held together.

Within a matter of four minutes all was over.

Where a forest once stood was now a clearing: a long stretch of scorched, blackened land, having a large channel slashed through it, with nothing but smoking topsoil. To either side the vegetation was flattened, branches twisted and ripped from the trunk, small isolated fires still ablaze, with burning leaves still floating down from the sky.

"Move out," shouted the Colonel as he tucked the remote switch into his breast pocket and patting it as if it was a prized procession.

The troopers moved to the two trucks that came through the Gateway just before the Earth Destroyer, and started to unpack the equipment needed to shut the Gateway down safely without harming the basin on the top.

Then the eighteen armoured machines started to roll forward, in single file they moved, into the direction of the newly formed trail towards the third Gateway. As they moved along the two sections of launchers on the rear-end came to life, these jettisoned small round canisters high into the Troposphere, in a large spread pattern in the direction they were heading as well as to the sides and behind. Once they reached their appropriate height the canisters compressed and exploded, or more accurately popped, causing a light yellow coloured liquid to spray out and slowly rain down to the ground, in a misty drizzle, covering the trees, grass and everything around.

All had donned their masks, leaving their eyes uncovered just covering the nose and mouth in a small collection of tubes and filters.

Small animals - which had been scattered by the noise of the explosion - were racing around, and flying creatures were also scattering in all directions. That was until the micro droplets released by the canisters started to enter their respiratory systems. Within seconds of inhaling the substance the creatures started thrashing about, bodies convulsing on the ground, flying creatures plummeting from the sky.

The bio-technicians at the base had been working on a chemical weapon from the moment they had caught the couple of Lanks coming through the first Gateway. The bio-weapon was mainly a respiratory weapon, but given enough time, if it fell only on the skin of an animal, it would over a period of a few hours have the same desired effect.

It didn't affect humans by touching their skin, but they didn't have time to iron out the problem of it still affected their breathing, not anywhere as lethal as the effects it had on the creatures here, but still enough to cause respiratory problems and slow them down: hence the breathing equipment.

The large Earth-Destroyer once again started to rumble off into the direction of the second section of trees lying between them and the next gateway.

The troopers moved out in a five-group formation.

The eighteen launchers slowly carried on towards the third Gateway firing all the way, jettisoning their deadly poison cocktail into the atmosphere.

As they all moved off a controlled explosion shook the ground behind them, as it closed the Gateway down, leaving the still curling plume of orangey smoke rising into the sky. The smoke didn't seem so dense, but none of them noticed as they proceeded on their way towards the third Gateway on their list.

44
Time of Truth

The Captain held his firearm level with the stranger's chest.

"I will not harm you; your threat is momentarily subdued," her words, even though they were understandable, were heavily accented with Spanish.

It had all happened so fast. Babe was now lying next to him, dead.

Doc lay unconscious on the floor after killing Babe, then trying to shoot him.

His head was spinning.

And now the stranger who had collapsed was getting back to her feet. She was still obviously weak, but she was still able to talk. She leaned against the bough of a nearby tree, to steady her weak legs. She went on to say, "I heard your truck pull up from the grassland into the scrub. He came out of the back of the transportation," she said pointing at Doc. "So I followed him," she said this with no thought to the fact of invading his privacy. "I was a little behind when I heard him talking."

"To Babe?" The Captain asked, thinking he could get to the reason why Doc had shot her.

"No he was alone." She kicked the bag on his back. "He was talking to someone through some sort of metal device."

The Captain looked around to Hopper.

Hopper shrugged, wiping tears from his face on the back of his hand.

The Captain's mind was doing summersaults. Only the day before he remembered her asking what they would do once the mission was complete; now Babe was dead. But he had to put that aside, hard as it was, he still had others whose lives were depending on him. He hoped he wouldn't let them down as well. He had already let too many down in the past. He shook his head, clearing his thoughts; it was not the time to dish out the blame. That would come later, along with the nightmares; if he survived.

But Hopper had heard what the strange woman had said, and was now crawling over on his knees, to pull the straps off of Doc's bag, but just then he looked back up at the young woman.

"Its okay there is no charge left in his body, you can safely touch him."

Hopper proceeded to pull a knife from a concealed place and cut the straps off. He opened the bag and pushed his hand in, pulling out a collection of medical apparatus; Tissue forceps 14cm, dissection scissors 12.5cm, hemostatic forceps 16cm, plus more that he didn't recognise still resting in the bag.

"He shouldn't be carrying those things around on him, there delicate," the Captain announced frowning.

"But no radio?" Hopper announced.

The Captain looked over towards the stranger as if to say; *well what's your explanation for that then?*

"Wait a minute these aren't quite right." Hopper was turning them around in his hands. "They got little clips and sockets on them, and if you could believe this they look electrical in a way."

"Once he had finished his conversation with whoever it was, he pulled all those bits apart," she said pointing at what lay in Hopper's hands.

"So you're telling me that's a radio?" the Captain asked.

"Wait a minute I think she may be on to something." Hopper was looking at the end of each of the pieces of equipment, then sliding one piece into the other. "I think we are cooking with oil here. These are positive and negative receptors."

"Meaning?" the Captain looked puzzled.

"Meaning it's a jigsaw." Hopper was now clipping and adjusting different parts until all the bits had been assembled together.

"It's not pretty but it will work." Hopper turned the thing over in his hands. "That is if there's a power source." He turned the bag inside out, a few small items dropped out, but nothing that could be a battery.

"Roll him over," the exotic looking young woman said.

Hopper looked at the Captain.

The Captain had now lowered his side arm to point at the ground. He just nodded his head in answer to Hopper's unasked question.

As Hopper rolled Doc over she leaned down and grabbed hold of his watch. A blue flash jumped from her hand and split the watchstrap, she then handed it to Hopper. "Here is your battery." She was looking at the Captain as she handed it to Hopper.

He turned the watch around in his hand, and then he pulled on the only part that could possibly fit into the small hole that was left. The winder came away and with a long cord clipped into the small remaining socket. As the battery clipped into place the apparatus came to life, static, loud and crackling filled the small glade.

Hopper turned it over thinking he must have missed the tuner, but as he did the static cleared, being replaced by a male voice.

"Has it been completed? Are they all dead?"

It was a voice the Captain recognized all to well.

"We are now on your side of the Gateway. When will you be joining us?"

"Hello, Madera. Long time no see. I thought you had retired?" the Captain asked, staring at the radio as if being able to see the speaker.

If the Colonel was shocked at hearing anyone's voice apart from Docs he didn't sound it, rather he took it all in his stride.

"Why, hello Captain Stokes. I take it the miserable weakling has failed?"

The radio went quiet for a few seconds then Madera's voice filled it once again. "Congratulations, but then it doesn't matter now. I'm quite a busy man as you can imagine, but I'm sure I can arrange a welcoming party for you Captain. In fact it would be my honour, for old time's sake. See you soon Jethro, old friend," the last few words were said in a mocking tone of voice.

Then the radio went dead. The watch face then started to revolve, with a small red light clicking on.

Hopper, out of reflex or a sixth sense, threw the receiver away from himself into the bushes, as it hit a tree it flashed a brilliant white with a small controlled explosion, not enough to kill a person outright, but enough to remove the appendage holding the device, and cause them to slowly bleed to death.

The Captain stood still tapping his chin with his finger.

"I take it he's a friend of yours?" the stranger asked.

The Captain looked over at her, as if seeing her for the first time. "Who are you? Where are you from?" The Captain kept his eyes on her.

"My name is Misho, and I live about a day and a half travel from here, up on the boundaries of Black Peak Mountain." She pulled a piece of raven-black hair from her eyes and pushed it back behind her ear. "The reason I'm here?" She looked at her feet as if unsure. "That I'm not a hundred percent sure about. But so far all is coming true," she stared at the Captain.

"True?" He asked.

"My dreams. For months I have been having strange dreams: visions. They told me to meet you here. I put it down to the sickness I had; delusions from the fever, or just to this mad twisted place." She motioned around with her outstretched hands.

"But I had to see. Had to know. Who would have guessed that I wasn't going mad?" She sighed. "But in a sense after what I have just witnessed, I wish I was going crazy."

"You say they, who are they?" Hopper asked, looking around to see if the Captain was thinking the same thing.

He was, because he started to shake his head as in saying, *yes whom?*

"The Holy Ones," she stated. "Who else?"

45
Shaken Not Stirred

The noise of stampeding feet was deafening.

They couldn't move back any further. They only hoped the trees would give them some sort of protection against the onslaught of the charging barrier of beasts.

Now the animals were closer they could hear the front ones making loud honking noises, so the one behind knew which way they were travelling, so they could follow. Now they were on a direct path, and were soon upon the river. They didn't slow down; rather they sped up to give them the boost they would need in order to jump across the wide expanse of water.

Now his attention had been brought to it, Coben noticed the banks on both sides of the watercourse had been worn down, creating two wide stretches of sandy banks.

Thousands were headed their way. Hundreds at once were now leaping the river. Their huge bodies easy cleared the stretch of water. But not all made it; some were tossed out of the way, bodies tumbling into the churning water, accompanied by huge splashes shooting up into the sky, droplets falling down all around, small rainbows filled the shimmering air.

The animals did this each day, going back and fourth. In the morning, while it was still cool, they ran out on to the vast grasslands - the wide-open plains. In the afternoon, as the heat picked up, they charged back to the cover of the forest, to the protection that the trees gave, not just from the heat but also from the stalking predators.

Now as the sun was rising, even though it was behind the cloud layer it was still impressively hot, it was almost unbearable, like a warm shawl draped over the body.

So these creatures were once again making the trip made twice a day, everyday for their whole lives. To reach the tree line, for some nourishing leaves and the cool protection they offered.

But this time an obstacle lay in their path.

The cart was abandoned on the opposite bank, just left where it was, having no time to move it out of the way.

Instinct is what controlled the beast's movement. Instinct is a powerful force. It made small lemmings charge over huge cliffs to their death, because thousands of years ago, before the continental drifts lifted the tectonic plates up into mountain ranges, their ancestors ran along flat ground. Instinct made a salmon swim thousands of kilometres, across oceans, up streams and into lakes just because it was what was done, never did their small brains question these facts.

And these charging creatures were also running from instinct. They saw the wagon and the belongings around it but their brains didn't register them, rather they plunged onwards all as one, single minded straight ahead regardless of the obstruction before them.

Their bodies were bulky made up of mainly muscle. They tore through the wagon as if it wasn't there. But the obstacle took its casualties. Some got their feet caught in the shrapnel tripping them up. Once one had fallen it caused a chain reaction, causing those behind to trip into them. Beasts tumbled over each other, crashing to the ground, rolling to the side smashing up against the one ahead. Most regained their footings, but some were trampled under the onslaught.

The effect was a kind of huge organic multiple pileup.

Before some had the chance to stand, others rammed them at alarming speed from behind, causing them to snap their necks; adding more obstacles to pile into.

Before long the cart was removed, it was now smashed up beyond all recognition.

Now the creatures could uncoil their bodies from themselves and carry on with their journey.

The two beasts of burden that had been untied from the wagon were also caught in the middle of everything that was transpiring. The one on the riverbank panicked and started to run backwards and forwards trying to dodge the oncoming behemoths. It was hit continuously in the side and being knocked to the ground then trampled on. Exhausted, unable to pick up its body weight, it lay in the same place, thousands of feet pounding on it left their mark. To weak to stand its heart gave way.

The second that had swum out into the river was used as a stepping-stone. Hundreds of powerful clawed feet catching hold of its head and shoulders and propelling them forward. Soon it succumbed to the same fate as the other. Hundreds of claws ripping its flesh, blood spilling into the murky water. Weak and bleeding, and unable to keep its purchase on the riverbed, it started to drift along with the strong current. Its body got caught in a small inlet in the river. To tired; and having lost to much blood; it lay in the water not being able to pull itself free, it slowly gave way to the cold and closed its eyes letting out its last ragged breath.

Within a couple of minutes they had not only lost most of their belongings that they had brought with them, but also the two beasts of burden with which to pull them.

But at the moment that was the least of their worries.

The creatures were still passing by at an alarming rate. The wind being churned up from the speed their bodies whipped past was buffering them against the foliage.

One creature, which had snapped its neck while running into the fallen creature in front, flew across the clearing and slid along the ground, flesh slapping the grass, churning up a heap of tufts and rocks, causing a large cloud of dust to billow into the air, it came to a halt only a few feet away from where they were all hiding. The bulky creature's body was still twitching in spasms.

They tried to wave the dust out of their eyes, brush the mud and twigs from their clothing, and out of their hair.

Then the dust started to settle.

All had gone silent and still.

The shaking ground was settling.

They could hear the last of the creatures retreating into the large wooded area to their left.

Once all had died down, the wind stopped and the dust settled, the carnage could be seen. The area was scattered with their equipment, fragments of the cart lay everywhere. Splinters of the wagon were even now, along with leaves and small stones, flittering to the ground.

A couple animals that had been hurt to badly to move, or had their necks broken in the pushing, were lying on the ground around it. Their bodies at odd angles to their necks. All had succumbed to the buffering and pushing. Another two were still thrashing around, still enough life left in them not give up the fight. But not for long.

An adolescent Moregone came crashing through the trees, and charged at one of the thrashing creatures. At full pelt it landed its clawed foot into the creature's ribcage, smashing open its chest cavity, then burying its head into the deep open wound, pulling out a mouthful of warm quivering innards. The Moregone then tilting its head back tipped the flesh down its wide throat, the blood was spilling down around its mouth dripping onto its shoulders, splattering the dusty ground.

Coben and the others moved back against the tree line, as far as the vegetation would allow them. And they just hoped that once the Moregone had finished that carcass, it didn't move onto the one that they were hiding behind.

But they need not have worried, because a huge explosion rocked the land, causing all to catch their balance. Even the Moregone had to climb back up from one knee. It also caused the Moregone to run off back into the direction it had come leaving its meal unfinished.

But for some reason they would rather have contended with the Moregone, rather than whatever had caused that mighty explosion.

46
The Chase Is On

The vision in front of them faded out. They had all witnessed the unfolding of the actions before them. All twelve of the Circle now stood waiting for their Lords wishes to be spoken.

The ground didn't rumble as he spoke. The figure hanging on the wall didn't move. Rather he used his three grotesque slaves to pass on his wishes.

All were sat connected together. Just one figure was doing the speaking.

"More have come through, bringing with them powerful weapons of mass destruction."

All listened intently. Eyes transfixed - unblinking.

"They are moving towards the third Gateway. One was shut down one hundred and fifty-eight cycles ago. Only moments ago they shut down the second." The trinity waved its two emancipated arms as if to emphasize its words. "They are now heading towards the third Gateway: the original Gateway." It laid its hands on to its laps. "I don't know how the original Gateway will react to being shut down."

They stood as one and started to pace, a sadistic sideways cancan. If it weren't so disgusting it would have looked funny. The three figures looked like they were listening to some kind of inner voice before they spoke again.

"It leaves only two operational channels."

All twelve listened. None stirred. All knew the Lords powers came from the Gateways. But they didn't realize he was dependent on them.

The figure continued. "You will all leave at once to the third Gateway. Protect it at all costs. Destroy all those around it. Spare no one." The three figures then spun around.

"Destroy all their blasphemous machinery. Destroy everything, reduce them to mere ashes." The figures sat back down. All three heads leant forward as if in sleep. This marked the end of their instructions.

All twelve of the Circle bowed to the hanging figure of their Lord. Then turned as one, and made their way towards their goal. They were ultimate killing machines, with no conscience and no remorse. Once unleashed none would return to the mountain until their purpose had been fulfilled. But first they had a vast army to organize.

The Dark Lord was feeling something deep down, an emotion he hadn't experienced in thousands of years, it was something he had to check through his ancient memory for - it was fear.

47
Matter of Fact

They gained their composure.

The explosion had come from the direction of the second Gateway. They could only guess as to what was transpiring there.

Coben was starting to organize everyone, sorting out what had been left intact. What could be salvaged. Most of it was beyond repair, crushed to pieces by large heavy pounding clawed feet.

"What...?" Lake was looking over across the plain beyond the river, something had caught her eye. Now everyone was looking in that direction, everyone could now see what she was staring at.

"Another stampede?" Raven asked.

"There's no more behind it, it's just a lone rider," Lake answered.

At first Raven wondered at her reference to lone rider, he then realized what she meant, her eyesight was better than his. He could also now see a person sat on the creatures back, now he gotten use to the distance.

Garry stopped wiping the dust off his brother face and clothing, and stood looking in the direction everyone else was staring.

All unconsciously gathered into a tighter group, seeking comfort not realizing it, waiting for whoever this was. Was it a messenger from the Lord?

"There's a young lady riding that thing."

All turned to look at Raven wondering how he could possibly see that far. Doing so they realized he had salvaged a pair of binoculars from the wagon, which Hopper had given him.

Not realizing all were looking at him he carried on. "Wait..." It seemed he pulled them closer to his eyes as if this would help him see better, you expected red rings around them when he pulled them away, because of how tight he was holding them to his face.

"The Captains with her." He pulled the binoculars down and stared at them all. He took an involuntary step backwards after realizing everyone was staring at him.

"What?" Raven turned suddenly, thinking they were looking at something behind him.

Lake snatched them from him and put them to her eyes. "He's right. What's going on?"

"All will be explained once he arrives. I'm sure," Coben chipped in to calm them down.

They didn't have to wait long. The creature could run at an extraordinary speed. Soon the binoculars were no longer needed; all could see them both clearly.

The beast was coming up to the rivers edge.

They were wondering if it could make it across with two people on its back. But they needn't have worried; it didn't even seem to notice their added weight. In one mighty leap it took off from the opposite bank and propelled itself through the air, tail waving behind it. It landed softly for such a huge beast, catching the riverbank with its clawed feet, swinging around and coming almost to a complete stop in front of them all.

As the creature approached they all took a few steps back, thinking it was going to crash into them.

It had a huge squared off head, flat on top with small orange eyes. A wide flat mouth, which was open taking in huge, gulps of air. Its flat teeth were large and grey, rounded on top for chewing the grass. Its long black lumpy thick tongue lulling out of the corner of its mouth. It had small hands at the front clenching and unclenching. A tail waging like a dog, looking as if it wanted to start off again, or possibly it could smell its own kind that had just passed through; or more probably the carcasses of the other beast lying around on the ground was making it uneasy.

The Captain gave off a loud moan as he dismounted slowly. "You think riding a horse makes you walk like a crab. You know nothing. Awwww." He was bent over massaging his rear.

"What's the problem? What's happening?" Garry blurted out.

Coben put his hand on his arm. "Give him time, all will be revealed," Coben said looking at the female still sat on the back of the creature.

"Hello, Misho." Coben gave a small gentlemanly bow.

"Good day, Coben Hathanen." She slightly lowered her head in response to his bow.

"I'm not sure if it could be called a good day -" Coben started to say before Misho interrupted him.

"You are all still alive!" She looked around.

It was to the point and Coben had to concede it was true.

"I see you still have your unusual outlook on life, Misho."

The Captain looked from one to the other before speaking. "You know each other?" the Captain asked. He waited for one to speak.

Coben talked first. "We know each other." He looked over to the Captain then back to Misho. "Good to see you again, my daughter."

"Likewise, father." She once again bowed her head, causing all her black hair to cascade down around her face; she flicked it back and sent it flying over her tanned shoulders.

The Captain went to open is mouth to say something, then closed it again, opened it, closed it. Nothing could surprise him in this place anymore he decided.

Misho flicked her hair back once more, and swung her legs around over the creature's head, and jumped down lightly to the ground.

"Did you hear that explosion?" Raven asked which as soon as he said it realized how stupid it sounded. Of course they had all heard it. The dead could have heard it.

"Coben could we speak please?" The Captain motioned with his hand over to one side.

The others grouped around Misho. He could hear them starting to chat with her, asking questions.

"Daughter?" The Captain asked.

"Yes my daughter. I didn't know you had met her. How and when?" It was Coben's turn to ask the questions now.

The Captain went ahead and told Coben about Babe. At first there wasn't much of a reaction. But the Captain realized that death was all around Coben, just another thing to get use to in this place.

Also he explained all that had happened about Misho appearing and what she had said, and done. And how Misho was going to get them to the mountain, and that the others were on their way in the cargo truck. It was just that the beast was faster over this kind of terrain.

He told him about the Colonel, and what he was now doing. And that the so-called Lord would have other things on his mind at the moment, so the least of his worries were this lot heading toward the mountain.

At the moment he didn't think it was worth telling him that there were some others being sent to find them. But he believed they would be in the mountain by then out of their reach. Nor did he mention his previous relationship with the Colonel and how he had known him before.

48
Revenge Is So Sweet

The Lords adviser stood in the corner, watching the proceedings unfold before him: listening to all that was being said. The wall was cold against his back, even through the cloak and linked chain mail.

Time was moving on. He knew the right moment would arrive, the entire Circle were to leave the mountain and head toward the third and original Gateway.

This would leave the Lord unattended; the Circle would not be here to defend him. Plus now two of the Gateways were inoperative, all was falling down around the Lords ears; his power was growing weaker by the hour.

Given time the adviser would take action.

Time was something he had. Time was something he had learned to respect.

All he had to contend with was the freaky threesome. Nothing for him to worry about, but still even though they looked like a demonic joke, he knew they were still not to be underestimated; powerful magic accompanied their twisted deformed bodies.

The Circle started to file out of the room, with one minded determination; they filed past him unconcerned that he was stood in the deep shadows.

Now all he had to do was wait.

He played with the object in his hand. The object the Holy Ones had given him. He stroked it; the time would soon be here. It would soon be time to use it.

He had dreamed of this moment for such a long time. Ever since the Lord had sent his only daughter to the mines. He wasn't an adviser then just a poor background attendant. But over time, with patients and hard work he was in a position to make a difference. Soon he would have his sweet revenge, so the soul of his daughter could eventually be laid to rest: and most probably his along with it.

Flatfoot was slipping in and out of awareness. He could no longer feel his body. He didn't know how much time had passed since he had been hanging in the gruesome life-sucking pod.

Every now and then movement had drawn his attention to someone else being cut out of their cocoon, their lifeless bodies falling to the ground with a sickening thud.

The stench of death was overpowering. But he needn't have worried; soon his body once again fell back into the bliss of unconsciousness.

Time passed: there's no stopping it.

The Circle was not around to cut the now useless bodies from the casings, so no sound brought him around form his sickening sleep that was slowly draining the life from his withered body.

Suddenly there was some movement, and he couldn't tell if he was dreaming or awake, but he swore he saw the same man who had come to him in the cell; he seemed to whisper something in his ear, something about *it not being long now, things are in motion.*

Flatfoot seemed to see the figure move off into the shadows of the cavern. In the distance he could just make out the three huge red fires burning, now blurry in his weak dieing vision.

Walking towards him came one of the demonic trinity. He couldn't tell which one. His head was swimming too much from lack of energy: lack of life.

The figure lifted its one single arm and using its long twisted painted nail it scratched along Flatfoots forehead. No blood ran from the deep lesion.

The beings deformed head twisted to stare – void of eyes – at the reaction. Muscles behind sown eyelids moved over empty orbits, regardless of no eyes. After a penetrating visionless stare it stalked back towards the fires.

There was hardly any life left in Flatfoots body; just enough to keep his brain operational: his body had died many hours previously.

But for some reason he wasn't worried, his mind was relaxing into complete peace. He ignored the deformed figure stood before him. All he could hear repeating over and over was the words of the lone figure that had walked off, with his cloak billowing behind, and its scaled chain mail glistening in the light of the fires. Saying to him in a quiet voice as he walked off, "Have no fear; you and your brother will rise, the prophecy is soon to be fulfilled."

The Captain now stood with Coben, over to one side of the others; he was talking in an undertone about everything that was transpiring.

The others had arrived with the truck and all were in a tight group. Sadness was the order of the day. Babe's body was in a black body bag in the back of the truck. Even those that didn't really know her were shocked at her being killed by one of her own companions; someone she trusted with her life.

The Captain had asked Hopper and Raven to dig a hole for her grave. There was no way back for them, and as he pointed out even if it did sound callous that there was no point dragging her body around with them, she deserved rest; that much he could do for her.

Hopper had picked a quiet spot under an unusual tree, with its shadow hanging over the soft springy grass, the light playing through the foliage. It looked like a weeping willow, but its leaves were much longer and had small bright yellow buds all over it. The water lapped past only ten foot away. Even given everything that had happened it seemed a quiet and peaceful place. Hopper knew Babe would have loved it.

He, along with all the others, stood quiet for a few moments, all remembering Babe in their own way. Coben said a few verses from the Bible, remembered them from what seemed like a lifetime ago. Once all that knew her had said a few short lines, it was time to fill the grave in. They would have liked more time to say their peace, acknowledge everything she had done, and to talk about the obvious gap that was now missing from their lives. But time was one thing that was going against them. If all went well, they knew that they would soon return to this very spot to build a more fitting tomb for their friend.

Once all had been done Hopper laid his hand upon the disturbed earth and said a few words quietly under his breath. Then sat down next to the grave waiting for the others to decide what was to happen. Tears ran freely down his cheeks. *To have loved and lost, is better to never have loved at all*; he remembered the proverb. Strange that now she was gone he was willing to show his true feelings, but never when she was alive.

What a dumb fucking saying he decided, then cried some more.

After a few minutes he slowly moved off to start carrying the large stones over to place on the soil mound, so no large foraging animals would disturb her eternal rest.

The Captain had asked Coben if there was anyone with the power to bring life back from the dead. Coben shook his head sadly, and pronounced that there was no one that powerful, and even if they could, would you want to bring them back to this place, to this existence?

Doc was still unconscious in the back of the vehicle, and would be out for a while yet, Misho had pointed out. A few times the Captain had checked on him. Twice he had kicked Doc hard in the knee cartilage, to check he wasn't fretting sleep; no one could pretend through that excruciating pain. Also he was keeping an eye on Hopper to make sure that Doc would be around to interrogate.

But at the moment Hopper seemed to be too preoccupied to worry about retribution. Hopper seemed to be paying some kind of penance to himself, by not allowing anyone to help with lifting the heavy stones. He ambled back and forth, shirt off, muscles and tattoos bunching under the stones weight.

A voice besides him brought the Captain back to the moment at hand.

"You are telling me everything aren't you?" Coben asked. It wasn't said in an angry tone, but rather it had sadness to it. "For instance, you said the explosion was from the second Gateway?" He let it hang in the air, waiting for the Captain to finish the sentence.

"You are right. I needed to sort things out in my own head first before I could tell the others. Some of it I'm telling only you." He seemed to shrink in size, stooping his shoulders and sitting on a nearby rock that was protruding from the sun baked earth.

"It's a long and sad story I'm afraid, but one that now affects us all. Something that happened sometime ago, something I thought I had put behind me: I wish it were behind me." He rested his head in his hands. The sadness flowed from him like the light from a lighthouse.

"I was married, had two children, beautiful bambinas." He lifted his head and his eyes had a glazed look over them. Tears formed and flowed freely.

"We loved to sail. How the children loved the freedom of the open sea, the wind in their shining hair. Their laughter." He looked away. "Little Mermaids I called them," said while wiping his eyes.

"My wife - a cherub that had fallen from the very heavens above - pure and beautiful. She loved to sail as well, loved the freedom." He seemed to gain his composure and stood straight and started to walk around a little, his foot absentmindedly kicking the rock he was just sat upon.

Coben didn't say anything, he knew that Jethro was building the story up and would speak when he was ready.

"We had our own boat, called *Freedoms Voice*. We went out weekends on her, and on holidays we took her around the coastline.

"We decided that for this; the final trip before we sold her to get the bigger boat; we would take her down to Kingstown a small place on the island of St Vincent, in the East Caribbean. We had been there a few times before, and the children loved to see the parrots. See they always wanted one but Katharine," he looked up. "That's my wife. She didn't believe in keeping birds in cages you see, so the children loved to see them flying free.

His voice became a whisper. "Hanna and Autumn. Beautiful, just like their mother. Beautiful." He sat once again on the stone and changed his voice to matter-of-fact.

"The storm was a complete freak; no one could've foreseen it. One of those once a century things. Warm air from the Caribbean, catching a freak cold front coming up from the Florida Keys, a natural phenomenon they called it. Even marvelled at it." He gave a shrug, and a small grunting noise.

"I was the only one to survive. My wife and oldest daughter's bodies were never found. I was holding tight to Hanna, thinking I had saved her. I was to exhausted, cold and injured to even notice she had died in my arms." Another tear ran down his cheek.

"You see it was a complete blow to all the family and friends. Kate's mum was so shocked from not only losing her only daughter, but also her only two grandchildren, that she became very ill. She died within four months of hearing the news." He stood again, walking around.

"My father-in-law blamed it all on me. The accident. Losing his wife, daughter and grandchildren. Saying I was to well trained to let such a thing happen - take me unawares. The finger was pointed at me and me alone." He walked around and turned to face Coben.

"Colonel Madera is my father-in-law. It has become personal. He will do what he was sent to do. Then he will hunt me down, for what he believes to be my fault. He's using this as an excuse to get to me, to take his revenge."

49
Forward March

Darkness started to fall over the sky. Clouds that didn't have much light in them anyway started to lose their dull brightness.

They were on a straight-line projector, straight towards the third Gateway; nothing could stop them, apart from the failing daylight.

The Colonel motioned for one of his troopers to approach. "Get all the transportation to make a ring, get everything ready for nightfall." The Colonel then proceeded to look around the clearing they had made; he gave a small lopsided smile.

"Once all are in place send five of your best to me." He didn't even bother to look at the man knowing he was still standing there, because he hadn't dismissed him.

"Yes sir." No questioning or anything, just pure obedience, just the way he liked his men.

"You may depart, carry out your orders."

The trooper didn't make a noise. Didn't motion to say he heard, but just disappeared. He knew when he turned that he would be gone. He turned slowly. The orders were already underway.

The large Earth-Destroyer was folding down its weapons, while the eighteen smaller vehicles were making a circle around it. Besides the Destroyer were the two long transportation trucks, which would hold the sleeping men; a hundred at a time, while forty stood guard. The men swarmed around these machines while organising the encampment, like ants around the queen mother.

While the camp prepared for darkness the five soldiers came forward, those that were about to be debriefed about their new assignment: to bringing back the corpse of Captain Stokes.

The Colonel tuned slowly looking at the diminishing light, pulled a cigar from his breast pocket and lit it, taking a lung full of smoke and releasing it slowly, whispering, "Revenge is sweet; sweet indeed." Then his eyes opened in a moment of internal struggle and deep underlying madness. "I'm coming for you Captain."

Eight hundred Lanks scratched at the floor with their clawed feet, rearing to get going. They could already taste the human fleshy tissue and blood in their mouth; the sweetest of meat; man flesh.

All were in battle formation. All were in groups of fifty, each with a leader up front; each following a gaudy crudely stitched banner on a long pole. All with their different weapons of choice in their hands, spears, shields, nets and long pitch forks. All milling around jostling each other.

Their sour smell of excitement and anticipation was making the unicorns uneasy.

At the back of the group were fourteen Moregone's. Huge bodies, front arms swinging back and forth eager also to get moving. Each had an armoured human slave attached to their back, on a small saddle between their shoulders, chained into position, to steer and control the docile beasts.

All twelve of the Circle sat upon their mounts up front. Twelve jet-black, fully grown unicorns. Heads swinging back, their manes flying around them. Also keen to get moving after being cramped up in their stables, and also from being so close proximity with all the wound up Lanks. Their armour plated hooves scraped impatiently at the ground.

The forty foot gate was almost open now, the huge wooden doors slowly lumbering across the ground.

They were to make their way out the other side of the mountain, through the great cities that bred the slaves for the mines. Across the Great Plain of Sabion towards the third and original Gateway.

The doorway now swung the last few meters into its locked position, a great reverberating sound announced its yawning maw open.

The great procession started to move out; all churning out the mountainside like a foul sea. First existed the mounted unicorn riders then the jostling Lanks, all pouring out one after another; a long line of death. Followed closely by the fourteen huge Moregone's, the riders holding them in position, holding the magic in place to keep the Moregone's under enchantment.

Hooves scraping the flagstones, armour rattling, clawed feet clicking, as well as weapons clanging together made a deafening hubbub of rolling noise that preceded the advancing army.

This side of the mountain wasn't being constantly bombarded with lightning. The huge cities were built onto the side of the mountain itself, perched on its steep ridges, having colossus columns coming from the ground reaching towards the heavens, up towards the cloud line. These had constant lightning bolts flaying off the top, rather than the lightning striking the ground, hitting the cities and destroying the Lords slaves.

Outside the cities children milled about. They were all slaves, not old enough to work in the mines, leaving them for a few more years to build up their strength.

Women milled around; all were pregnant, all were breeders for more workers, a constant breeding factory. Ten children were born almost hourly. So vast was the cities areas where the children were sent, sent to get them ready for their short brief painful lives.

At the age of nine they were forced to work. If they were strong, or just lucky they would see their tenth maybe even twelfth birthday, but very rarely.

Running through the main city the main causeway was a long straight flagstone avenue. This is where the army slowly made its way. Being watched constantly by the children and women who leant out of windows, or standing in the dark doorways holding crying babies.

The cry of women giving birth could be heard from different directions.

Monstrous fields lay around the cities, large enough to feed all the inhabitants, worked by pregnant women until they could physically work no more. These muddy fields produced green vegetables to accompany the meat: the steady quantity of meat that was wheeled out of the mountain daily, small bodies thrown into the wagons, deformed by the radiation that came through the open sky. Nothing was wasted here. The meat from their dead children would give them the strength they needed to push out the next generation of bastard slaves.

Very few men could be seen; those that were around were busy producing the next workers. Once they were too old to do that they were also sent into the mountain.

The long procession continued on, giving a small change in the otherwise dull, short lives of those watching.

Small children ran around the streets. Watching, paying attention to all that was passing. Apart from the few that didn't move in time, mowed down by the unicorns, trampled under hoofed feet. Or those that were curious and came to close to a Lank, that quickly picked them off, supplying the excited beasts with a brief meal as they continued forward towards their goal.

The next stop, the original Gateway, to protect it at all cost.
A battle, unlike anything seen in this world before, was about to unfold.

50
Rain On Me

The darkness closed over them all. They had found a large cave, which Misho knew about.

They had been travelling for a few hours until the darkness was getting to oppressive, and to dangerous to travel under.

Misho had made an alarming ear-piercing noise, which at first had everyone thinking she had turned crazy. Until they realized what she was doing. A few Grass People as Misho called them, stuck their heads out of the forest opposite and looked around in alarm. But noticing the group of people there, and one of their own they came bounding over. First sniffing at Misho's animal, then coming to stand beside it. Misho then seemed to whisper into their ears, and they settled down.

"What were you saying to them?" Garry asked.

"I was asking if it was possible for them to give us a lift to the mountain," she said, then turned and proceeded to stroke them on their long leathery necks, as if talking to the animals was an everyday occurrence for her.

Garry turned and shrugged his shoulders at Raven who was giving him a blank stare.

"Okay then, Mrs. Doolittle," Garry said in a mocking tone. Then again, he reasoned, with all the powers he had seen over the last few days, why wouldn't someone be able to talk with animals.

"These are free animals. They need not do anything for us if they don't want to. My friend here," she stroked her own animal. "She stays with me at her own choice. She gives me lifts around to where I need to go, and I protect her from predators. We both benefit from the arrangement." She then turned away as if no more needed to be said.

So they now all had transportation.

The ride was bumpy and it took a lot of strength and skill to stay upright as the Grass People bounded along. They could jump large obstacles that the truck had to drive around; many times they had to stop for the truck to catch up. The others couldn't wait for the small breaks, letting the blood drain back into their backsides.

They made good progress, before they stopped ready for the onset of night.

The mountain had come into view. All stopped and stared at the spectacle before them. No words could describe the vast mound of rock jutting from the earth; none spoke, all just looked on in trepidation. The lightning was constantly striking the ground around about the colossal mountain, flashing off the sheer walls and ripping across the pitted earth.

They then moved across into the caves besides a gorge that ran along into the distance. It looked like an old riverbed, which had been cut into the land, hundreds of metres deep.

They settled into a cave just on the lip of the chasm, overlooking the drop, with a large ledge to one side giving them access. They had all settled inside, welcoming the rest. The four beasts lay on the ground at the cave entrance, also enjoying the respite. They had made it just in time, because a constant steady stream of heavy rain had started to fall almost the exact instant they had entered the cavern.

"Are we resting on an old river bed?" Hopper asked. No one seemed to want to answer, considering he wasn't asking anyone in particular. "So with this rain we're not going to get washed away are we?" He looked at Misho this time; bearing in mind she picked the cave.

"Don't worry we are safe," that was all she said, as she continued to open a cloth bag she had lifted down off of the beast she rode. The bag, Garry noticed, was made out of light material, possibly from one of the many weather balloons sent through the African gateway.

"What my daughter means is, yes, eventually the water will rise and fill this cave, but that will be many days from now, we will not be here then." Coben turned and looked at his daughter who just nodded her head as if to say, *I just said that.*

She then took a brush out of her woven sack and started to unsnarl her long dark curly hair, with her head forward, while starting to sing a soft hymn under her breath to herself.

Raven was helping Hopper start a fire; to roast the meat of a small animal Misho had knocked down with a boomerang she had at her waist. It was similar to a deer but covered in a light blue leathery hide.

Hopper commented that being blue against the green backdrop of the grass it was bound to get picked off sooner rather than later buy a predator. Whereupon Misho pointed out that it was a foraging animal living mainly on grass, and on what berries it could find. But it stayed close to the river by day kneeling down in the water against the rushes and weeds, cooling itself, coming out only at night to feed. It must have become separated from its family and wandered about the plain, where its hide was in stark contrast.

All were pretending to be immersed in what they were doing. All were in a sober mood. Still saddened by the death of Babe; none yet ready to talk about it.

Doc's body was still tied up and laid on the ground over in one chilly corner: still unconscious. Misho apologized for knocking him out so strongly. Whereupon the Captain stated that if she hadn't he would've probably shot him. This way they could question him on what was happening, and about what he knew.

All sat around now eating from the tender meat of the small animal. None really had an appetite, but all needed the strength to accomplish what they were going to do in the morning. Tomorrow they were going to make their way, a little distance from here and enter the underground tunnels of the mountain to find their companions.

All sat around chewing and picking at their food. All mulling over their thoughts.

The rain continued pouring down outside, a steady stream of constant hammering water.

Suddenly the Grass People all got up as one, and started to move off into the darkness.

Garry jumped to his feet. "They're leaving?" He pointed out to no one in particular.

"They are free to go. As I said they're here by their own free will," Misho said this without looking up from brushing her hair. "They will be there when you wake in the morning. You have just eaten, they also need to eat." With that she put her brush down, adjusted the mat she had rolled out and laid on, pulled a lizard hide up over herself and closed her eyes.

"Will it rain all night?" the Captain asked, waiting for either Misho or Coben, or the other two to answer.

"Once it starts to rain it continues to rain for days at a time, sometimes even weeks." Coben looked down at the meat he was chewing and threw it into the flames, causing it to spit and crackle, with a display of sparks flittering up to the caves high ceiling, dancing embers flittered down to the cave floor.

"Time to now rest," Coben muttered, he then rolled over and made ready to sleep, pulling a thick camouflaged Mummy style sleeping bag over himself, a gift from the Captain. He believed it was once babes.

"Hopper; you and I will take first watch." With that the Captain stood and walked over to the cave entrance, while pulling his pistol from its holster and clicking off its safety.

He didn't catch the movement over his head, as a Lank quickly pulled itself back away from the over hanging lip.

The Lank was slightly different from the others; this one clung to the side of the rock face with its four arms. It was obsidian-black, for night travel and prowling, and it was slightly thinner for more speed. It also carried no weapon of any kind, and if you saw its head you would say it was slightly deformed, because it had larger eyes and ears. But it was just a different kind of breed: one created for surveillance and reconnaissance. One sent out before a marching army.

51
Behind You

The army of Lanks made their way towards the third Gateway, moving throughout the bitter cold night. The darkness was oppressive, but it did nothing to prevent the onslaught of the creatures, with their blood lust. They jostled for position, following their particular standard. They had limited intelligence, but they knew that before the next day was out they would have their fill of warm human flesh.

In front the Circle didn't converse; they didn't require words or polite chitchat. They had their orders, as one they headed directly towards their objective. Eyes fixed straight ahead, their intent playing over in their minds eye.

At the back the Moregone's were itching to attack anything put in their path. Their huge hands clenching and unclenching, pulling at trees as they passed to relive built up tension. The magical enchantment was doing its job of holding the powerful creatures back from attacking and scattering the Lanks in front.

At the rate they were travelling they would arrive at the original Gateway by dawns first light.

The black scouting Lank had crawled back from its concealed position. It fluidly crept back up the rock face and jumped down a small lip to the rock-strewn ground. Couched like a frog, it turned its head upwards; it was looking for something, its large eyes scanning the gloomy sky. Rain washed over its dark skin.

Catching its attention a large reptilian creature swooped downwards at an alarming rate of speed. And in a blur, using its long back scaly legs, grasped the Lank by the shoulders and latched on with its long powerful claws, hoisting its passenger, soaring into the fading night sky, swooping off into the far distance. Before long it was nothing but a blurry dot on the distant horizon.

The two beasts flew over the long line of the rallied army below, unconcerned with where they were heading.

A couple of the Circle raised their heads, their faces being drenched with the pouring rain. They could sense the creatures far above. But they had nothing to do with their orders. Heads lowered, hands gripping the reins, eyes facing their goal, they continued on their way.

The large flying creature; known as a Velvet dragon, because of its dark purple pelt, which was almost black; knew its location, knew the area it was heading towards. Before long the creatures were veering towards the Mountain, bypassing the front because of the constant lightning storms it headed off around the back towards the cities, then gliding over the metropolis down below, flying high above it all, beating its powerful leathery wings, taking its passenger soaring above the city walls, over towards the mountains sheer cliff face.

Rising higher.

It seemed to be heading towards an overhang. The rain pouring down, slapping against its wings, whipping hard against the creatures. The wind buffering them, swinging them off course so it had to fight to get back on target. Soon it was swooping in. The lightning flashing against its back, lighting up the air around it, momentarily picking out the details of the two beasts.

A gaping opening could now be seen under the overhang. The flying creature fought against the wind and the relentless hammering rain and headed towards it.

Then just before it reached the aperture it released its grip on the Lanks shoulders, letting it drop down towards the gapping abyss, the Lank seemed to just plummet. Then just moments before hitting it flayed its arms out stretched akimbo, which against all probability slowed it down enough, just before it hit the hard wet surface.

The Lanks hands gripped the slimy rock; the water was running down the mountain in small rivers, a waterfall pouring over the ledge. The Lank slipped on the wet surface, but caught itself on the lip. Its four arms and two legs scurrying around on the surface like a hairless spider. Then swiftly it disappeared under the waterfall down into the darkness of the mountain.

Before long it would be in the large throne room passing on its information.

But instead of meeting its Lord, the first person it encountered was the Lords adviser. The last thing it saw was a long twisted piece of wood being raised into the air then come crashing down with bone crushing force.

Hopper was leant against the wall listening to the steady downpour; lost in his own thoughts; fighting off sleep. It had been a horrific day. Few days you can look back on and know that they changed your life forever: this was one of those days. *Everyone dies* he thought, *but few really live!*

The Captain was over to one side cleaning his Steyr MA1 handgun he carried: having taken the bullets from the clip, and was now pushing them back in. Sleep deprivation was something he was use too. Not just through training, but due to loss of his loved ones. Sleep brought nightmares; even now.

Movement and a slight sound caught his attention behind.

"Hopper," he whispered, but before the words left his lips he was on his feet looking back into the caves recesses. Hands crossed over each other, one holding the gun, the other the flash lamp, shining it into the darkness. If anything it made the shadows seem darker.

Another movement caught his attention.

Hopper came to stand next to him, his automatic heavy M60 E4 wedged under his muscular arm, training it towards the direction the Capitan was pointing. He gave a quick look down at the top of his M60, checking the bullet casing. It was big, but the weight was worth the power. This weapon could stop a charging bull elephant, or shoot a depleted uranium bullet through a concrete wall.

The Captain knelt down besides Misho and touched her arm lightly. In a flash she sprung up on to her feet completely awake; she was use to sleeping lightly – deep sleepers only needed to be surprised once – deep sleepers died in their sleep. She was now looking the Captain directly in the face.

"What's the problem?" she asked in an undertone.

Others started to rouse from the commotion.

"How far does this cave go back?" He was not looking at her; rather he was looking down the barrel of his gun; the direction it was pointing, aiming it at the circle of light.

"I couldn't tell you, I've only been back so far. From what I know it opens up into a small cavern with a lake. There's no other way in, or out, back there," she said this while rolling up her things making ready to move out if necessary.

"I saw something move, something sinuous." The Captain started to wake the others that were still sleeping. Coben was already awake sat motionless, staring beady eyed.

Then before anyone could react a huge life form shot out of the darkness behind them. The creature must have resided in the lake because it was covered in dripping water, its body a pile of throbbing tubes and tentacles. It didn't roar it made no screaming noise as it attacked. All that could be heard was its body being dragged across the floor of the gravel-strewn cave.

Raven and Garry were facing the other way and didn't even notice what was happening until they turned around; it was like a slow-motion dream. The creature was oozing across the ground; their attention was caught by the Captain and Hopper firing their weapons into the sinuous mass. The sound of gunfire off the enclosed walls was deafening.

But nothing seemed to stop its oncoming charge. The bullets just disappeared into the liquid textured surface.

Garry and Raven picked Glyn's stretcher up and ran with him to the vehicle, getting drenched in the process.

Just then the Grass People returned and added their honking noise to the confusion, splashing about in the gathering pools of muddy colored water just outside the entrance, smacking their tails hard against the sodden ground, heads raised and bellowing.

This seemed to cause the oncoming heap to momentarily stop. It had no eyes that they could distinguish. But it seemed to stop and consider the flaying beasts. Then in one lightning movement; faster than it had moved perversely; it shot a long greyish olive tentacle out, latching it on to the top of Doc's head. A sickening popping sound could be heard as it crushed Doc's skull, covering the walls in brain matter and dripping blood. Then the tentacle covered his whole head, small hooks flicked out and grabbed hold of the neck. Then in one sudden yank lifted him high into the air, hitting his body against the stalactite speckled ceiling, and began to shake his body, separating his head from the bodies' torso. But before the body hit the ground more tubes and tentacles shot out at lightning speed, latching onto the rest of his dead body and pulled Doc into the tangled heaving mass.

Misho raised her hand and in a flash of intense light a bolt of blue electrical power sizzled out from her hand and struck the heap on one of its tubes. The tube dropped to the floor, as it separated from the body it turned to water splashing to the ground. All it accomplished was a blackened scorch mark, which didn't seem to cause any discomfort to the creature in anyway.

All this had happened in a matter of mere seconds, the others not being able to do anything for Doc, made a hasty departure, all clambering up the muddy incline to the open plain above the deep yawning ravine; their feet slipping on the loose gravel, which went plummeting over the drop.

Hopper wheel-skidded the all terrain truck up the slope - shaking its camouflage; branches and leaves cascaded from off it - the truck protested loudly. Hopper hoped he wasn't about to burn out the vehicles clutch. He had a smile on his face, after what had happened to Doc, whispering, "Couldn't have happened to a better guy."

Hopper was closely followed by the Grass People that were still honking at the top of the vocal cords.

It was an unorganised mad dash away from the sinuous predator.

All stopped at the top of the incline, breathing hard. Confused as to what just happened. Rain soaking them through to their skin in seconds, hair pushed flat against their heads, water streaming into their eyes. All having just being awakened from their slumber. It took a few moments for them all to come to their senses: the rain helped in this matter immensely.

But before they could come to terms with what had just happened, and evaluate the situation, they all noticed what was now surrounding them.

Out of the frying pan and into the fire.

52
Stand and Be Counted

The five military personnel had left, running off into the enveloping darkness. All had their new instructions, to bring back the body of Captain Stokes. Taking with them only what they would need to accomplish there new orders. They had the rough location from a small device, which was sown into the lining of Doc's khakis - a small mini transmitter.

They left behind the one hundred and thirty-five others, who at first light were going to close down the third – and original - Gateway. They didn't realize that none would be alive to accomplish this.

The Colonel was wide awake, he seldom slept. He was going over the orders for the morning.

The sun was just rising on the horizon, light spilling through the plastic window in his erected tent. He had a strong creamy coffee perched on the side of the folding table, his hand gripping the cups metal handle. It had gone cold without him even noticing; so deep in thought about the day's events that lay ahead, and while thinking about seeing Jethro's cold cadaver laying on the ground before him. His beloved son-in-law, who had caused the death of everyone he had ever truly loved.

Gunfire made his companions jump, which were sat around the table waiting for their new orders. The Colonel didn't even flinch. They all anxiously looked out the obscure plastic windows. The Colonel stared at his cold coffee, with its thick layer across the top, and poured it out on the ground.

Noise could be heard outside, people running about. Random gunfire was now echoing through the haze of the morning mist.

Huge spotlights flashed to life, turning the dim morning rays into bright luminosity. Halos of light could be seen glaring through the pouring rain.

As the Colonel stepped out into the stark bright halogen light, he could see his hundred and thirty-five men that were left, gathered around all in formation in a huge circle using the trucks bulk for cover.

The Colonel looked over into the distance that was made even darker because of the unnatural brightness around him. But he could see what the commotion was all about. For the first time since coming here he had a slight look of surprise etched his face.

In the distance gathering on the hill before him was an immense army. Hundreds of Lanks lined the bulging hills. Their arms clutching different weapons, now banging them against each other and their shields. All restless, awaiting the impending battle. Huge Moregone's were spotted around, raising their arms in the air and giving off loud cries that pierced the Colonel's ears even from their distance high on the hilltop. Riders sat on unicorns, silhouetted against the backdrop of the sun, which was just starting to shine through the thick cloud layer behind them.

Also silhouetted on long poles were the hanging forms of the five men which had moments ago been sent out. There now lifeless corpses hanging flaccid upon the instruments of their death, rammed clean through their bodies. Their heads were missing. Looking down the Captain could see their decapitated heads laying on the ground in front of the machines his men were situated behind. The heads had been ripped from the torso and then tossed down. Steam billowed off there gaping necks, where the cooling blood still issued. The men's eyes now glassy and wide with shock and pain.

A sign of what was to come. A symbol of the savagery of the encamped army around them, an army with no remorse, no pity, no compassion, and absolutely no understanding of the word mercy.

Everything suddenly went deadly silent. The creatures lowered their clattering weapons to their sides. All that could now be heard was the sound of the rainfall lashing down from the heavens, pelting the ground in its unrelenting torrent; soaking the severed heads, making small crimson rivulets of water run down the hill towards the Colonel's encampment, pooling around the vehicles wheels.

The Captain and all the others looked around, thinking it was a play of the light from the sun that was just rising in the distance.

Encircled all around them were ghostly apparitions, tall robed covered humanoids. These beings seemed graceful, even through they were not even moving. The rain was falling straight through their bodies, making them shimmer slightly.

No one moved or spoke; even the Grass People stood motionless sniffing the wet air, with a sense of unsettled unease about them.

The rain was thrashing down, pelting the ground soaking them all through to the skin. Deep muddy pools started to gather around their saturated feet.

Then just in front of the Captain a lone figure appeared tall and regal, like the others in the circle that surrounded them. The figure lifted both of its long thin arms, and its billowing robes flayed out like an enormous butterfly, flapping around itself. However you got the impression that the wind came from no living source.

"The Holy Ones," was all that could be heard, whispered through Misho's parted lips in reverent awe.

The Captain took one step forward to speak or make some kind of contact with these mysterious ethereal beings. As he did so a beam of intense light shot out from the raised hands of the one in front of him. The light was so intense everyone covered their eyes from the pure cleansing brightness. When the dots in front of their eyes resided the figures had disappeared, as if only a hallucination.

All that was left to prove they had been there was the Captains unconscious figure, lying in a cold puddle being pelted by the constantly driving heavy rain.

Now a soft whisper could be heard being carried on the raging storm. "THE TIME IS UPON US - *is upon us*."

53
The Light of a New Dawn

"Stand your ground, no one fire until my order." Colonel Madera stood facing the crude, but powerful army on the knoll.

He was overconfident. Then again he had the most up to date military weaponry available, and all at his fingertips.

A solitary figure came wandering down the hillside - it looked human, scruffy and dishevelled - he was clumsy falling down the hill rather than walking, crawling on all fours at some points.

All weapons in the camp were trained on the single unarmed shape.

He was a sad excuse for a human being. One of the many slaves took along to aid the army in anyway required. Today it was to delivering a message.

No one fired as he approached. None would, they looked at the Colonel as he un-holstered his good old American Beretta 92 handgun he had strapped to his side, and he then proceeded to walk out past the protection the vehicles were providing.

The pitiful human came to rest on his knees before the Colonel, then proceed to proclaim its masters wishes. "When the sun has risen and the dawn is no more, then we shall attack. None will be spared." The figure looked at the gun in the Colonel's hand longingly. He stared at the firearm as he continued. "Implore whatever gods you worship, because today our living god has pronounced your annihilation." The figure then put his hand out to the Colonel, lifting the hand with the pistol in it, resting it against his forehead and closed his eyes.

The Colonel looked up onto the hill at the army encamped against him. Then looked around at his men. Then with no emotion whatsoever he squeezed the trigger and watched as the messenger's head exploded outwards, like a blossoming burgundy flower. The lifeless corpse slumped to the ground, with what looked like a smile spread on the remains of his blood-spattered face.

Even though the pitiful figure wanted release from its existence, the Colonel was going to shoot him anyway, as a sign to those in charge up on the hillside.

"Their god. Ha!" He holstered his weapon, wiping some of the blood from his hand onto his slacks.

"The only god around here is me. I will totality decimate them all." He said, with a vein protruding from his forehead. He then turned and pulled the control for the Earth-Destroyer from his pocket and pressed the button to awaken the sleeping behemoth.

It happened so fast it took a few moments for them all to react. Lake was now kneeling down at the Captains crumpled side; gingerly placing her hand on his cold wet shoulder. She gave him a small prod. Nothing happened. She turned and stood facing Misho.

"You said they sent you. You said they were trustworthy." She spun back around to the Captain who was just lying there motionless, a pool of brackish water gathering around him.

"Everything happens for a reason," that was all Misho said.

Lake was about to twist around and scream at Misho, when she noticed movement from the corner of her eye. It was the Captain.

In one swift feat he jumped to his feet as if on elastic.

"Everyone mount up we are leaving." He started to move towards the truck and opened the door to clamber in. He was now also covered in sticky mud and waterlogged, but he seemed oblivious to all this, simply wiping the mud and water from his vision.

"What's happening? What's this all about? You were struck w-w-with -" Garry stuttered. It was all becoming too much. Things were making his head spin. He just wished his brother would wake up, he missed his annoying guidance. Garry also realized that he hadn't had a cigarette in over a day, and no longer had the craving. Besides his baccy tin was probably waterlogged.

The Captain cut him off. "I was shown a vision of what was transpiring. What we need to do. The prophecy was laid out before me and its meaning." He climbed up and jumped in and slammed the heavy door, then cranked down the window; the rain poured in but he didn't seem to notice, he couldn't get any wetter.

All were bewildered and a little dazed at the speed things were happening.

"We have only a short period of time, all will become apparent. Let's move people," the Captain shouted to be heard over the torrential rain that was hammering a staccato tattoo on the trucks metal roof.

The others stared at each other, and then one by one they started to mount their animals. The creature's warm body was welcome after the bitter coldness of the hammering rain. There was no harness, and no hair on the animals, so they squeezed the folds of leathery skin between their numb fingers; and gripped hard with their shuddering knees.

The remainder climbed into the revving vehicle.

The rain waterlogged the ground gathering in large pools. The wheels of the truck skidded through the puddles, leaving a long furrow in the soaked earth. They now headed towards the towering mountain.

The rain poured and the lightning flashed all around them. The weather was relentless and getting worse with every passing minute.

Flatfoot had never felt such a feeling of peace such like this before. His whole body was vibrating with pure gratification. He had a smile on his face. If this is what passing away felt like he welcomed it with open arms, he would totally embrace it.

Then he realized what the sensation was, it was something he had never experienced before and wished the moment would last. Around him, as he opened his eyes, he saw figures, ethereal images standing next to his brother. The ghostly apparitions were holding out their hands to Brains his brother, their colourful garments flapping majestically from some otherworldly breeze.

His brother's body started to glow. The cocoon holding him split apart shattering to the cold ground. The small tube creatures all dried up, lifeless, now raining down to the dirt covered floor, like a handful of thrown long-grained rice, tinkering on the cold stone surface. His brother's drained body started to reform, filling out, becoming the perfect figure Brains had never been able to attain in his whole life.

Flatfoot's head was still lulled forward. But his hands started to clench together. Suddenly his eyes popped open, and he looked down at his hands, then he slowly raised his eyes to meet his brother's gaze. His body was still being suspended but not from the tubes that were inserted into his body, but rather from the almost impossibly bright light radiating from him. But the light wasn't blinding you could look at him with ease.

The tall wraithlike figures around him all stood back, and then their bodies started to fade as they stepped back into the very wall itself and vanished.

Flatfoot went to close his eyes thinking that this was just another hallucination, another illusion from being so close to deaths wide open door.

That was until a hand held his chin and lifted his head up.

"COME BROTHER. THE TIME HAS ARRIVED." Brains voice was not loud but could be heard echoing through Flatfoots head as if he had spoke straight into his mind. The feeling was unnerving.

The cocoon that held Flatfoot suspended from the wall started to crack and fall apart, the tubes withered and fell to the soiled floor. The holes in his body healed over, and as his brother laid his hand on his arm the radiant light filtered through and passed over his body regenerating it, passing on its strength, its life.

With his hand still on Flatfoot's arm he pulled his brother towards himself. Flatfoot slowly floated down to the standing position. His feet were unsteady. He had no idea how long he had been hanging there.

His head was all woozy. He stood next to his brother whom he only moments ago presumed dead, and he himself being on the way to join him. Now his brother stood sturdy radiating a powerful light, filled with self-confidence. He had never seen his brother stand so straight and tall.

Brains then turned to him looking him in the eyes, and then spoke in his unnerving voice. "NOW THE PROPHERCY WILL BE FULLFILLED."

Then from nowhere the adviser - who had proclaimed their destiny in the cell earlier - arrived, and held onto Flatfoot's arm as his brother started to stride out towards the huge burning fires in the vast chamber of the so-called self-proclaimed Lord of this world.

As Brains walked off, his Body seemed to illuminate the whole cavern. Like a walking supernova he headed toward the heart of the vast chamber. The huge raging fires seemed nothing in comparison to his glowing supremacy. They started to flicker as he walked out towards them, the flames dancing in the glow of his body.

All around in the immense cavern a wind picked up out of nowhere, with words being carried on the wind. Whispers swirling around their heads, pulling at their hair, dancing in the flames. The voices echoed. "ONE WILL BRING DISTURCTION. BUT TWO ARE NEEDED TO BRING ABOUT ORDER - *to bring about order.*"

54
Whispered Regrets

Madera stood staring out upon the distant army. They seemed to be brimming with confidence. It was like an ancient battle ground conflict where a particular time had been picked to start the fighting.

"Stupid morons." They might have chosen a time but he hadn't.

He pressed the switch.

The bulky Earth-Destroyer came to *life*. The top slowly lumbered into place, lifting the firing mechanism in to position. Then one row after the other the engine of war spilled forth its hundreds of small arsenal, flying through the air towards their target that sat oblivious on the hill in the distance.

The release of the missiles seemed to announce a premature start to the battle. One group of Lanks broke way from the rest and started to charge down the steep hillside, running at full pelt, a blur of leathery greenish grey pelt. Their weapons hoisted high in to the air. Tails lashing about, the hook on the end ready to pierce the humans flesh tearing it from the warm bones. Death curdling animalistic guttural screams rose from their wide throats.

The first batch of missiles reached their destination and started to rain down. But not having time to make the proper adjustments the artillery fell well short, raining down on the first wave of screaming Lanks, instead of all that sat on the hillside.

At first they didn't see them coming, falling from the heavens, mingling with the down pouring rain, hammering down into the ground. The Lanks realizing what was happening and started to put their arms up, lifting metal plated and leathery shields to protect them from the falling objects.

The missiles were moving at phenomenal speed. They ripped their way into the ground. Whatever was in their way was pulverized, shredding through arms, shattering skulls, tearing through shields, splattering body parts all over the battlefield. The Lanks were falling one after another. Injured and flailing about on the blood-soaked earth. Severed limbs twitching scattered around. The battlefield was now littered with the first main fatalities.

The Circle having seen this weapon in action before, from the lord's minds eye, knew what was coming next. They raised their hands and produced a shield engulfing all those remaining on the hill.

The military hardware now blossomed to life, buckling the ground out from under the fallen Lanks.

The missiles were created to clear heavy laden areas of forest or buildings. As the first charge exploded upwards there was nothing to stop the amount of pressure released, only a few scattered dieing Lanks.

The plume of fire shot heavenwards, reaching far above the ground into the sky, taking the topsoil with it. A huge plume of dirt and small stones exploding high into the atmosphere. Then the second detonation came into play. It was meant to clear away anything left from the first detonation, but because there wasn't anything the explosion ignited the very air, meeting the rain, which was on it's downwards course.

From his position Colonel Madera saw what was about to happen. Having not thought it through properly to start with. Now he was reaping what he had just sowed.

"EVERYBODY GET DOWN," he screamed. With that he threw himself down behind the armour of one of the small chemical releasing vehicles, which had the soldier strapped into ready to head off into the fray.

The flames billowed over his head. Small stones and soil blasted against the sides of the trucks. The tent he had moments ago walked out of melted under the onslaught. A few of his men that didn't duck in time were blown backwards, their bodies coming apart; being flayed alive, becoming part of the burning wind that engulfed everything.

Most had the initiative to pull down their protective screen to take most of the heat and to stop the shrapnel.

Almost as soon as it came the superheated tempest blew over. Small fires burned around the area. Chard remains of a few of his men were scattered about on the ground, crisp and steaming, burned almost beyond recognition, twisted into unnatural positions.

The Colonel had one consolation he looked up and waited for the dust to settle, and see the remains of the attacking army, blown across the hillside. To his utter disbelief and pure amazement, when the soil finished its downward spiral and the stones finished landing and bouncing across in front of him, he could see the intact army still standing where they stood moments ago;

unscathed.

Where the stones and soil rained down over them, he could see a blue shimming as it hit their protective shield that they had raised over themselves. Six of the Circle had their arms raised above their head producing a blue haze that covered them all.

Once the soil came to a complete rest their shield was dropped and the remaining Lanks charged.

The Colonel groped around for the control of the Earth-Destroyer; this time he would reset the weapon, having the missiles land directly upon them. He found the controls remains melted to the outer shell of the truck he was hiding down behind - now just a blob of bubbling useless plastic.

The remainder of his troops climbed to their feet and saw the on coming assault. To their praise they all held their positions. But then again, where could they to run to?

The fourteen smaller vehicles, those still operational after the firestorm, came out of formation and started to move towards the on coming charge. The Microguns started firing round after round, thousands of bullets per second.

The second wave of Lanks that had come in to range was literally cut in half by the constant roaring machineguns, wave after wave sliced down, falling over each other, bodies piling up, blood soaring through the air. The Lanks following had to jump the carcasses of the ones in front, becoming drenched in their dead companion's vital fluid.

The ground still hot from the blast now started to run a sticky scarlet colour. Small tributaries running down the embankment towards the slowly moving vehicles.

The Moregone's now started to move into the affray, taking their place among the Lanks. The towering figures were standing out like trees among bushes, each carrying in their arms huge spears; complete small trees with the branches removed, sharpened at the end with stones pushed into the splintered bark to give it a counter weight. The Moregone's now hoisted these high above their heads, letting loose a volley of monstrous flying spears.

They flew through the air striking the small vehicles with such force and speed, that the spears weight and mass were carried straight through the casing and ripping into the metal machines framework, pinning them to the very ground. Small explosions erupted as the javelin pierced the radioactive battery compartment. Green explosions rocked the earth, fires breaking out all over the theatre of war. The screams of the drivers soon died away, lost in the mêlée of noise.

The force of the vehicles explosions was sending the Lanks that manage to pass the barrage of bullets, flying in every direction, and coming apart limb from limb.

Now everything was falling apart.

The small machines were being destroyed before the drivers even had chance to release there poisoned canisters from their back compartments. The few that were released did nothing to slow the onslaught, the poison evaporating in the flames from the many fires now burning around the battlefield.

One or two soldiers even exited the machines and were now fighting either hand-to-hand or using what weapons they had. None lasted long, completely overwhelmed by the opposing forces; now simply another mangled corpse on the battlefield.

One Moregone even had a vehicle held above its head, shaking the driver out. But the Microguns were still firing, and because of gravity the weapons slowly arched around to point downwards. The thousands of bullets, shooting from the twelve barrels sliced through the Moregones neck and chest. The towering beast collapsed the armoured vehicle landing on top of it.

The Colonel looked around in complete bewilderment. These beasts, these mere animals were decimating his superior forces. His machines were being destroyed one at a time, the few operational ones that remained were next to useless. One had even been pinned to the ground and was still operational but was spinning around on the lance as an axes and firing in all directions, even at his own men.

Madera noticed that not one truck had released one single missile.

The Lanks had now reached the frontline of the store trucks that were being used as cover for his men. The soldiers were standing up picking off the Lanks one at a time. His men were also firing 81mm explosive mortar canister into the on rushing creatures. Small red blossoms of fire were erupting all over the grassland in front of them.

One caught a Moregone halfway through the process of lifting a spear above its head. The canister landed right on a Moregone, hitting it square in the chest, it exploded, the force knocked it backwards; its upraised arm was blown harder upward ripping it from its socket, pushing its chest in, ribs smashing against its spinal column. Within seconds the gigantic Moregone was reduced to a pile of reddened pulp - blending in with the rest on the carnage lying all around it.

The charging Lanks now reached the line of trucks.

The Colonel was now fighting for his own life. A rushing Lank flew through the air - appearing through the curtain of pouring rain and smoke - placing its clawed foot on the truck in front of him, and pivoted about and slash down with its spiked club that it was carrying in its swinging arm. As it positioned its foot the Colonel raised his Beretta and fired three shots in quick succession into the creatures face. It was killed outright, taking off the crown of its head. But the gun wasn't powerful enough to stop the momentum the creature had gained. The Lank carried on flying forwards, now a dead weight.

The Colonel ducked.

The spiked club flew over his head, a rusty spike catching him racking a long channel across his brow and up into his hairline. Blood ran into his eyes. He threw himself to the smouldering ground wiping at his forehead, trying to clear his vision.

His men were doing no better. Each was desperately fighting his own battle. The mass of creatures charging was immense, barrage after barrage: eight hundred to their one hundred and thirty-five.

Some troopers who had spent their ammo and grenades hadn't the chance to reload, and were now using their short P90's machine guns as clubs to defend themselves. Some were reduced to using knifes, pathetic weapons against such an onslaught.

The Colonel was crawling around on his hands and knees, blood gushing from the open gash, running down his face, obscuring his vision. The rain was relentless; now blurring much of the scenery around him into what looked like a fading watercolour painting.

The sound of his men screaming in pain, or giving off their last angered shout of defiance before dying rang around him. The sound of the Lanks bloodlust cries soon drowned out that of his men.

Creatures were now jumping over him as he lay on the sodden ground, their intent on the still standing. He looked sideways at a solider that was still holding his ground, but not for very long. He was surrounded by Lanks all striking out at him with spears and clubs reducing him to nothing more than a collection of warm soft tissue spread over a large area.

The Circle who had been watching from a distance started to slowly make their way down the hill in a small tight formation ignoring the carnage of their own army around them. They were intent of seeing the complete destruction of their enemies that lay ahead.

From his position from under the now useless Earth-Destroyer, the Colonel was surveying what was happening around him. He could see the Lanks going around checking that all his men were dead. He could, from his position under the truck, see the oncoming group of cloaked figures on the unicorns.

And all he could think about was how he had let his wife and daughter down, and his two sweet grandchildren, by not reaping vengeance on the man who caused their deaths. With that in mind he reached up under the Earth Destroyer; he was hiding under; and unclipped a small metal hatch. Inside was a panel, which he preceded to punch in the code. He wiped at his eyes again, this time it wasn't to remove blood, but salty tears that were welling up. The code was eight digits long, two digits for the birth dates of his wife, daughter and two grandchildren.

As he punched the last number in a Lank spotted what he was doing and plunged a jagged lance through the calf of his leg, then pulled it back out intending to make the next strike a death blow. The pain almost blanked him out, but with the last part of pure spite left in his body he turned the red activation key.

"I'm taking you bastards with me!" was the last thing that passed his blood covered lips.

In an immense earth-shaking detonation, the large Earth-Destroyer self-destructed, igniting the remaining four hundred and eighty missiles, along with its bulky nuclear power core. The arching dome of intense radioactive fire arched outwards catching everything in its donut-ring shaped expanding path.

The trucks left standing were blown away like small matchbox toys; metal turning to liquid under the intense bombardment.

The Circle; who didn't have time to raise a protective barrier; had their skin burned from their bones, then in the same fraction of a second the bones blew away as dust.

The huge fireball expanded, and then in a split instant contracted, creating a towering deformed mushroom shaped toxic cloud.

Nothing was left within a thousand meters of the explosion. Up to four kilometres away the intense heat being blown on the superheated current of air stripped all trees off their leaves, catching the bark ablaze, flattening them in a huge expanding circle around from the detonation.

Looking back over the landscape all that could be seen was an immense bowl in the ground. Steam rising out from its circumference, as the unrelenting rain poured on to the scorching hot molten soil.

If you hadn't known what took place only moments before you would have had no idea of what had transpired here. There was nothing left that could be identified: bodies and machines were all obliterated, returning to dust from hence they came. By the look of it a huge meteorite could have caused the steaming hole.

All that remained hanging in the air was regrets and lost memories.

55
Road Rage

The truck flew past the tunnels they were to travel beneath.

Coben who was riding in the truck along with the Captain gave him a sideways glance, but said nothing. He had been told about the vision the Captain had seen in those split seconds, and Coben was still absorbing that information.

The Grass People bounded along behind following the truck. The rain was pelting down and stung the shoulders and heads of those on the fast beasts. Their faces were becoming raw from the wind and rain lashing against them. All held on for dear life.

The surroundings flew past in a cocktail of brown and blue hues.

Those on the beasts didn't have the benefit of listening to what the Captain had to say, so they had no idea as to where they were now heading, all apart from Misho who had travelled this way before. They were headed towards the far side of the mountain, to enter it by its main door, through the larger of the two joined cities.

The storm whipped relentlessly at the ground. Leaves and braches whizzed past.

The ground suddenly shook; the puddles seem to throw their water back up into the sky for a split second. A sonic boom pierced the air.

All kept their attention on holding onto the moving beast, grasping around their wet necks for any purchase they could. None gave the noise anymore thought. Putting it down to thunder that was raging all around them, as they drove the creatures forward.

"What was that?" Garry asked, from inside the comfort of the warm truck.

"If you asked me it felt like an explosion," the Captain answered. "But it's not coming from the direction we are headed so it's no concern of ours." He pulled the wheel hard to one side just missing a large skeletal decomposing carcass.

Garry wondered what the living beast would have looked like and what heights it would of reached, looking like it could have eaten a Moregone as a snack, and then used a tree as a toothpick. The truck now drove through a towering arch of bones, a creature's ribcage, now whitened by time and the elements.

Before long the mountainside came into view. All that could be seen before them was the vastness of the towering rock mass. Now as they veered around they could see the huge cities clinging to its sides as if seeking cover from the deluge of rain and howling wind. The lightning storm flaring off the top of the tall columns were giving off a spectacular display.

Even with the wind whipping their faces forcing them to squint, they awed at the size of the settlements.

The Grass People made bellowing calls, which couldn't be heard over the storm.

"He better know what he's doing?" Misho shouted at the tempest that was slapping at her freezing body, her black hair tangling around her cold face.

As they approached no one could be seen, all in the city were seeking shelter from the driving rain and unrelenting battering wind.

They all pulled up and stopped outside the towering city walls, which seemed pointless because the city gates were left hanging wide open.

"Garry you stay in the vehicle with Glyn." The Captain looked around. "You too Misho." He looked at the others. "There's room for two more of you. It's your choice." Staring at them one at a time.

"I'm coming," Lake said jumping in the back.

"I'm with you Captain, couldn't let you get in to trouble without me now can I?" Hopper said. "Besides that mounted machinegun has my name written all over it."

"Are you sure Hopper?"

Hopper just shook his head once. "That's my friends in there too," Hopper announced. He wasn't about to lose anyone else.

"The rest of you stay back behind these walls and stay with the Grass People, any problems and you get the hell out of here. Okay?" he said, shouting to be heard above the howling wind and the rain that was filling his mouth every time he opened it.

Saying no more he jumped into the truck and it wheel spun off. The trucks tail lights shining through the gloom of pelting rain.

The city was immense; having towering buildings that seemed to defy the laws of gravity, hanging dangerously off the side of the mountain, the buildings stacked on top of each other like a bundle of cards.

The machine rumbled through the open causeway. The wheels spinning on the smooth surface of the long road, meant for processions to show the Lords power. Now reduced to nothing more than a simple road, leading to the entrance through the front of the mountain.

Faces popped out of windows. Bodies appearing at doorways, trying to seeing what the noise was. Even though the wind buffered against the walls and rain pelted the roofs, they could still hear the noise of the truck, an unaccustomed sound in their meaningless monotonous lives.

The straight thoroughfare was longer than they thought. The mountain didn't seem to be getting any nearer.

Lanks that were left behind patrolling the city were drawn by the unexpected noise as well. Coming around the corners they weren't expecting a fast moving unfamiliar metal object to be rushing towards them. Some managed to jump to one side, other tried to attack the machine; these became nothing more than a bloody smear on the front of the large wide, tall bonnet. The windscreen wipers that were on full to compensate for the rain, were now also wiping the continuous crimson fluid splashing against the screen - arms, legs and parts of armour, would bounce of the strong wire mesh protecting the windshield.

People started gathering watching the machine shooting down the causeway. Some were holding their crying babies in their arms, having no understanding of what was happening, having no concept of what the vehicle represented. Inside the machine was their hope for freedom, the answer to the prophecy - their salvation.

56
Awaken

"The prophecy has been awakened," was whispered into Flatfoot's ear, as his body was pulled back towards the wall.

Flatfoot sprung around. His lack of energy forgotten. Anger and confusion now gave him the strength he needed to pin the adviser against the icy stones.

"What the hell is going on? And no prophecy crap!" His face was livid. Everything that had happened to him suddenly caught up with him, his body went limp and he sagged to his weak knees, feeling like his body had been filled with lead.

The adviser stood over him. Not looking down, but out towards the commotion that was happening in the large ordnance chamber. "I have waited for this moment for many, countless years." He took his hand off of Flatfoot's head and pulled a small object out of his robes pouch. The item the Holy Ones had given him. He grabbed his staff and pushed the object onto the crown, a small click announced it was in position. He then lifted his staff high in to the air and like a leader of a marching band he started to walk out after the glowing moving image of Brains.

"What... what?" with that Flatfoot's body slumped. He rested his back against the damp wall and watched in exhausted fascination as the two figures caught the attention of all in the immense cavern.

The outside walls gave way to the entranceway. The inner walls now surrounded the vehicle; the surrounding suddenly closing in giving the impression that the truck shot forward much more rapidly.

A long tunnel snaked its way into the heart of the mountain. Small side tunnels broke away to either side.

But the Captain seemed to either recognize the way he was going, or was travelling on instinct. Now inside the surrounding walls the engine was deafening. The large black wheels skidding and screeched around the corners.

Lanks poked their heads around from the side tunnels, which were quickly taken off of their shoulders.

The headlights were put on high-beam, bouncing off the slick walls, causing reflections and illusions. But the Captain knew exactly which way he was going.

The passageway suddenly opened right up into a huge hall, with many smaller sections breaking off, all big enough to take the truck. But he didn't even look around. He ignored the Lanks that were sat around a great roaring bonfire. At first it seemed he was going to charge straight through the lot, but just at the last moment he pulled the wheel hard to one side throwing everyone in the truck to the left.

No one had chance to protest or had the breath to do so, owing to being tossed around so violently.

The truck swerved once again, just missing a large crowd of Lanks that were disturbed from what looked like a meal of a small human torso. He managed to miss most but ripped his way through the corner of them, flinging their bodies to one side, spraying the screen scarlet once again.

Others were thrown backwards by the velocity of the large .50 caliber bullets that were randomly striking them, because Hopper was now stood up in the back of the truck, standing behind the powerful mounted machinegun; spraying the large bullets in a large arched pattern, trying to hit as many as possible – it only required one bullet per Lank.

Hopper had to duck twice, after spears ricocheted off the thick armour beside him. Taking his hands off the trigger and grip he pulled hard on a handle besides him, it pulled a bullet-proof shield up, making a shoulder high barrier appear around him, leaving a slit for his vision and for the machineguns barrel sticking out of.

The Captain veered down a small side tunnel, shooting down at alarming speed, clipping the corner sending the truck raking in to the sidewall, causing a waterfall of sparks flying up into the air. He pulled the truck sharply hitting the opposite wall causing the right headlamp to explode in a shower of glass; something all the bodies of the Lanks hadn't managed to do.

The walls seemed to close in. Then at one point they did. The truck shot through the opening hitting both sides. The screeching of metal was grinding on the ears. Then suddenly it opened up into a larger chamber.

The truck skidded to a halt, causing everyone to jerk forward.

The Captain jumped out, ran around the back and opened the back doors, pulling at the stretcher Glyn was lying on. "COME ON," he shouted.

But the others were not sure what he was trying to accomplish.

"We need to get him in there." He pointed at the bars to the left with the cell door left open.

The others shot out of the truck and scampered around the back, all trying to be helpful.

"I and Garry can manage this. You lot sort them out," he said pointing back up the passageway. At first they wondered what he meant, but turning they saw the tunnel filling wave of Lanks washing down upon them.

"What is the meaning of this?" The three figures stood as one, all still joined at the shoulders.

Brains carried on walking forward ignoring their objection. As he came close to the figures he raised his arms.

The three walked towards him were confused as to what the light was, which was radiating from his body. As they approached they were confident in their power to stop him. But suddenly from his raised hands appeared a beam of concentrated radiance, spilling out like a wave uncontrolled and moving forward towards the central figure.

Its two skinny white arms came up instinctively to ward of the assault, but they were like a flimsy sheet of newspaper trying to hold back a battering ram. The figure in the middle was hit squarely in the upper body flinging it backwards, separating it from the other two, as they were tossed sideways from the blast. They all flew apart at the shoulders.

The middle one lay on the floor, a gapping hole where his chest was only moments before, a small ring of fire still burning the remains of the clothes that was left hanging on its tattered body. Being weak and mortally injured it couldn't heal the wounds left by the violent removal of its shoulder joints. So blood spilled out of its two gapping shoulder wounds. Its head now lulled to one side as its life seeped away with its blood pouring across the cavern flooring being soaked up by the filthy sand. Its facemask clipped the ground, unhooked and rolled away.

The other two not being battered by the main blast started to pick themselves up from the floor, which was difficult with only one arm each - involving a lot of rocking backwards and forwards. The first thing they did was repair the holes left by the shoulders being violently disconnected. Blood from the holes covered their elaborate golden garments; which were still smouldering from the blast.

The first to gain his feet was rewarded with another blow, but this time by the adviser's staff, knocking it hard to the floor again. The adviser put one foot on the deformed beings long neck and turned it to one side; he then proceeded to thrust his walking stick into the missing shoulder joint, ramming it down with all his strength, down past the shoulders ball joint and into the chest cavity, rupturing both lungs as it ripped its way through them, jerking the staff side to side. As it tried even after all that to fight for its life. But its struggling soon became weak. Not once being able to summon magic to aid it. It died a painfully slow death, drowning on its own blood that filled its useless lungs.

The third was on its feet and summoning powerful forces to come to its aid. The floor started to blur, and rising up from it was a green miasma that started to orbit around Brains. His forward motion was not stopped as he carried on towards the figure on the throne.

Then the remaining triad clenched its one fist and its mouth flew open in a cry of rage, calling upon all its power to stop Brains forward momentum.

The jade coloured mist became more solid and in one movement shot inward towards Brains abdomen. But whatever its intent it didn't work. Instead it gathered into one orb and shot out towards the standing figure, and hit it square in the open mouth. The sphere was absorbed and its eyes turned from orange to green, then in a violent shudder its head expanded and popped with a sickening sound. Part of its silver facemask went shooting past the adviser just missing his left ear. The body devoid of its head relaxed and tumbled forwards, smacking the ground with a sickening thud, and there it lay with a pool of gummy blood gathering around its ripped open neck.

Then the earth started to quake and the roof started to tremble, loosening small stalactites causing them to plummet down around the two figures left standing in front of the throne.

Then a noise rose out of the very ground itself, starting in a slow deep booming voice and screaming like a man suffering asthma, "WHAT HAVE YOU DONE? YOU WILL BOTH DIE FOR THIS." The rumbling voice caused the sand on the floor to vibrate and dance high into the chamber.

Then in a whispered voice the adviser said, "No it is you who will breathe your last breath."

He stood in front of Brains and lifted the staff high above his head and brought it down with startling force, wedging the staff into the rock surface in front of the now stationary Brains.

The head on the wall started to raise its eyes that were radiating bright orange. Then the figure of the Lord started to move for the first time in a thousands years; he started to break himself away from the wall, leaving gaps where his body once hung.

57
Come Crashing Down

Garry and the Captain managed to carry Glyn through the cell entrance, over across the flagstones and lay the stretcher down in the middle of the chamber, with the ceiling rising way up into the distance far above them, as if they rested inside an ancient pyramid.

The Captain then leaned over Glyn and ripped his tee-shirt from off his chest.

Garry was looking around the room. Then noticing a large mound in the corner he jumped to his feet. "What the hell is that?" he shouted pointing over into the corner, wishing, and not for the first time, that someone had trusted him with a weapon.

The Captain didn't even look up from what he was doing. "Don't worry it died long ago." He carried on with his work.

Garry wondered how he would know that. But then again the Captain was doing a lot of bizarre things at the moment, since his interaction with the mystical Holy Ones.

In the hallway outside they could hear the fighting.

Misho was calling on her power to take out large groups of charging Lanks at once, spraying their body parts over the walls; their bubbling remains sliding to the floor. But every time she sent forth a surge of power it weakened her slightly, she could only keep this up for so long. She wondered what the Captain was up to, and she prayed that it wasn't going to get them all killed.

Hopper had leapt back into the cargo truck, and was once again firing round after round in to the distance, mowing down the charging creatures, aiming for their legs, trying to immobilize them, with the least amount of bullets possible; he only had so many bullets on the linked munitions, and they wouldn't last forever, and he was sure he didn't have time to change to the next one.

Time to find out.

His finger relaxed after the last depleted Uranium bullet left the barrel, making the trigger limp. His hand slapped the clip that released the metal linkage; it coiled falling into the truck. He then ducked into the back of the truck, pulling the bazooka from its Velcro harness and popped his head back out, positioned the green tube over his right shoulder, clipped off the safety, and fired down the long tunnel, without bothering to aim. Flames licked out the rear end as the single missile fired up and shot off towards the charging Lanks.

The explosion was deafening in the close confinements of the tunnel, the blast wave had only one direction to head – it washed over the cargo truck. Dense smoke and rubble replaced the wave of flames, pinging of the trucks metal bodywork. Hopper now had the precious seconds needed to change the linked munitions roll.

The Captain ignored everything and started writing on Glyn's torso. He used no marker, no instrument of any kind apart from his finger. Where he moved his finger over Glyn's skin he left a mark, strange written lines, swirls and circles: symbols of an ancient long forgotten language.

Misho's power had started up in the tunnel again, illuminating the chamber. Luckily, because of the gunfire, nobody could hear the names she was calling Hopper, after he had fired the bazooka without giving her any kind of warning.

Hopper's gunfire was once again reverberating throughout the passages.

"What are you doing?" Garry was staring at the marks left on his brother's chest.

He was being ignored. The concentration on the Captains face was transfixed; sweat pouring down off of him, dripping onto Glyn.

Garry was about to speak again when the Captain sat back on his haunches and stared at his handy work.

"What is it? What does it do?" Garry asked staring at Glyn's upper body with all the writing over it, which was giving off a soft cobalt radiance.

The Captain wiped sweat from his forehead, before looking across towards Garry. "I have no idea," he stated.

Then as if to answer their question the writing started to glow a radiant indigo. His body then became engulfed in the blue shimmering light and started to slowly ascend off the cell floor, his back arched, his hands and legs hanging stretched out, heading upwards towards the Lords large audience chamber.

Garry and the Captain looked upwards, watching the body rise towards the ceiling. The light surrounding him lit up the hatch above his head. Then in one burst of piercing light the hatch blew upwards, splintering in to thousands of little shards.

The Lords foot detached itself and came to rest on the sandy floor, pulling all his spread out veins and organs back into a sickening sight; as his body started to reform before their eyes.

The barrier behind the Lord, now he wasn't attached to it started to disintegrate, falling inwards; being pulled from some unknown force. Behind the wall was a bright emerald swirling mass; it could be seen pulling all the broken parts of the wall into its spinning cloud.

Brains stood his ground as if controlled by some other force.

The adviser, who had moved to one side, crouched away from the onslaught of power raging around him. Bits of broken rock and the sand from the floor were flying around in the wind being whipped up by the pure power being produced from these two beings.

The Lord was now almost complete. His cranial cavity filling with matter flying from the wall behind him. He was drawing his very being out of the mountain itself. His legs started to be wrapped in flesh, muscles inflating like melons, veins laying out there tracks on his arms and face. Hair starting to grow at an experiential rate, like fast forward photography. Eyes bulging with juices and mapping with veins, lips growing and glistening like fat wet worms. The Lord now drew his arms together clenching his muscles for the first time in aeons, and took a another slow step forward, as if unsure about how to use his organic body.

The Lord stood hunched over, head lowered, looking more like a towering demon rather than a god. Then like slow moving tectonic plates he raised his head, rounded his thick shoulders and stood tall and imposing. He now looked like a Greek statue carved from marble. His feet where set wide apart, his fists clenching and unclenching. He was once again whole.

The floor started to ripple, wave after wave, as the Lord pulled the power he needed out of the ground itself, to use on those insignificant bugs around him. Electrical discharges flared off his skin striking the sand and wall behind him. With each burst he seemed to grow a fraction bigger, his muscles swelling, and veins bulging.

Brains stood just staring at him as if he had no cares in the world. As if waiting for someone else, to arrive.

And just then he did.

The floor between the Lord and Brains exploded, splinters being caught in the mass of wind flying around the cavern, whipping past all their heads.

The Lord took a step backwards; his eyes open wide in bewilderment.

Brains stood his ground.

Glyn's body rose up between them, his hair flying in all directions, caught by the blowing tempest raised from the two beings. Then in a sudden build up of power Brains body seemed to adsorb all the power from the vast chamber, all the wind stop suddenly the sand and shrapnel dropping vociferously to the floor.

The electrical sparks crawling over the Lords giant muscular body stopped.

Everything then went deadly silent.

Then came the explosion.

Brains body poured out an intense beam of pure cool refreshing white light. It arched out of his body in all directions at once like an expanding donut-ring. Engulfing what seemed like the entire chamber. Then in what seemed like eternity in was all sucked back in and blew forward hitting Glyn's back arching his body against the onslaught. His arms and legs sprayed out into the shape of a starfish. The light carried on straight through Glyn but as it came out the other side it was a bright eye piercing sapphire blue.

The beam flew forward and struck the Lord squarely in the wide chest spraying his arms out akimbo, making him totter backwards.

And travelling through the light was the runes wrote on Glyn's chest, they seemed to slowly detach themselves and was leisurely carried across the blue light, being stretched across the space into the Lords body; one letter lazily tumbling after the other.

As the letters battered the Lord they slowly took him apart. His power was seeping away with every strike. Each letter causing more damage than the one before it. His body only just coming together was now being torn apart. Flesh flying, bones splintering. His body was flailing around like a fish from water, he was not able to defend himself, he was two weak from having the Gateways shut down. And he had no Circle or demonic trinity to defend him.

Then as the last rune struck his body it sent the last part of him soaring through the remainder of the wall behind him, which now his body struck it, it completely collapsed. The wall he was only moments ago hanging from, was now completely pulled inwards absorbed by the green swirling mass that had lay behind him, for who knows how long.

Glyn's body now changed its course and started to travel across the floor, floating over to the staff wedged in the ground. He levitated above the staff, the small orb on the top started to glow and the energy that was only moments before directed at the Lord was now being channelled into the twisted staff.

The ground didn't just start to rumble, but started to break asunder.

Down below the others were fighting the assault of Lanks. Until they were pulled up Short. One moment they were fighting for their lives, hundreds of Lanks pouring down the hallway, climbing over the rubble and their dead companions. The next moment the creatures seemed to waver in the air, forms shifting as if fighting to keep their shape. Then suddenly the Lanks disintegrated into a shower of dust, the momentum with which they were travelling caused the now grey residue to fly down the tunnel, the cloud it raised covered them all.

Garry and the Captain came out of the cell to a view of Misho and Hopper dusting themselves off. Both covered in thick lead-grey powder. They were coughing and spitting the dust from their mouths, rubbing it out of their eyes. They were just trying to come to terms with what happened, when the mountain started to quake at its very core.

"Everyone in the truck. NOW!" The Captain shouted at the top of his voice.

"What about them?" Garry looked up as if seeing into the chamber above.

"I don't think we have to worry about them," he shouted over the rumbling noise coming from all around them, as bits of rock started falling from the roof, as mammoth cracks started to run up the side of the tunnel walls like encompassing spider webs.

The orb was distorting everything. The whole chamber seemed to be drawn towards it. The sidewalls starting to crumble away. Massive chunks of rock started to fall down from the ceiling, and then being pulled along the floor as if by invisible cords, towards the staff.

Colossal stalactites cracked and fell from the ceiling; one pulverized a huge copper fire bowl. Another hit the other fire bowl on the side, sending a shower of flames and dancing embers high in to the air. A smaller one tumble and fell directly down the opening into the cell below, wedging itself in tight, cracking the floor, sending out wide crevasses in a web-like pattern. Large chunks of the floor started to drop into the chambers below.

Many human servants ran around, dogging the falling projectiles.

Brains dropped limply to the floor.

Flatfoot, who had gained control of his senses after seeing everything unfold before him, ran to his brother side.

The adviser climbed shakily to his feet leaning against the onslaught of the wind that was buffering around him, whipping his cloak high in to the air. Small stones pinging off his body armour.

Glyn still hung above the staff, providing the power for whatever the thing seemed to be doing.

The adviser waved his hands as if to catch Brains and Flatfoot attention. He then grabbed the staff from under Glyn's body and pulled it out of the ground towards himself.

Whatever chain reaction had started carried on after it was removed.

Behind them the wall had utterly crumbled, the swirling mass of emerald green substance could be seen now taking up a large section of the chamber, which only a moment ago was hidden by the wall made up from the now deceased Lords body.

The adviser shouted to be heard above the howling of the wind. "Look the Gateway which connects this world with the next in line." He waved towards the mass of green that was growing larger by the second.

Glyn's body was now lying on the shaking floor. His eyes started to twitch, his fingers slowly moving.

They all went over to him and knelt down following the advisers actions. Once they were all together he raised the staff above his head. A bubble of azure shimmering light covered them all slowly settling down to the trembling floor. Once it touched the vibrating sand it darkened and then shrunk in on itself. Cracks ran along across where they had just disappeared from. The floor gave way.

The whole mountain continued to be pulled into itself. The Gateway behind now drawing power from some unknown force - sucking everything in.

Epilogue
Homeward Bound

One month later...

Where to begin?

I remember small fragments, as if I have been in a shallow sleep.

I'm told I've been out cold! But as I sit now and look across the city I can remember clips as if from a movie preview.

Once the mountain started to fall in on itself most fled the taller buildings supported by the mountain sides. Unbelievably only a small handful perished in the debris.

There's commotion around me, the hustle 'n' bustle of new lives that I'm told are owed in some part to me.

We have had a lot to organize.

The people from the cities have been used to direction. Now they have their freedom they are not sure what to do with it.

Those who lived in the cities have welcomed those from the village. Their powers were looked upon with awe and astonishment. But even now their powers weaken, with only one Gateway now operational, after Hopper used explosives to safely close the fourth one down, leaving only the original.

The village from which Coben and the other came from has now moved into one section of the rebuilt city.

The forces of the now dead Lord have been reduced to nothing more than dust on their shoes. His other forces were now no longer a threat but have returned to their natural order of things. The Moregone's returned to the cover of the forests. The Lanks, created purely by his dark power, no longer stalk the land.

People can move about without worry of being attacked. Something all had never experienced before. So in a way losing some of their 'gifts' hasn't done that much harm.

Everything they say is completely different. I have to take their word for it.

I'm still getting use to this world. So different yet the blood that runs in their veins here is the same as back home. They all have the same feelings, emotions. All have new lives to reorganize.

The sky they say is also different. There was a thick cloud layer before they say. I think somewhere back in my recollection I can see the sky in my minds eye, when I first walked through the Gateway. But that could just be my imagination.

The sky now has only what looks like a very faint orange gleam over it. As if the sun was just starting to rise. But the thick clouds that hung across the sky continually have gone.

Now where the mountain once stood; stands a pillar; is the only word I can describe it by. It must be four even five stories high. A slow turning column of emerald green haze, with small flares of emerald light shooting out, then being pulled straight back in by the strong gravitational force. This green pillar is our doorway to the next world in line. The next one of five we have to travel through to reach home.

Above the pillar coming down from the sky is the water vapour, which was once the cause for the cloud cover. As the substance we call ozone comes through from our world, it mixes with water vapour drawn out of the atmosphere to aid its skywards journey. Now the vapour deposits the ozone substance and makes its way to the other Gateway, where it is sucked back down and passes through to the next world in line.

What the vapour is used for there we do not know. But soon we will find out.

This we are told by the Captain; or should I say High Priest. Yes he now represents the wishes passed on by the spirits of the Holy Ones. He's in charge of the spiritual well being of all. Something I'm sure he never would have thought would happen when he started on this mission. A position that has given him peace, and let him come to terms with his past.

Coben now runs the day-to-day things concerning the metropolis. Raven and Lake are staying to help him. Hopper, Brains and Flatfoot are to stay as well. They knew when they came on this assignment that they wouldn't see their homes again. This is their home now.

Most that passed through have decided to stay here. As they pointed out, they have been here for many years, the ones they loved and cared about long since passed away back on earth. Besides they have families of their own here now.

Only a few have decided to travel with myself and my brother Garry. Those that feel adventure running through their veins. Or just like my brother and me haven't been here long and want to see home again.

I'm sad to say because of all the activity since I have awoken I don't know any of them. But then I suppose I've got a long journey ahead in which to do that.

I'm glad to say Misho is one of them; I'm starting to like her.

So the three of us will travel with forty-seven strangers to see where the next gateway will take us - I nice round number of fifty.

I can understand why most want to stay, in a way I do. Now there's peace, those who passed through can enjoy it for eternity. But for me there's more to life than just its span.

There are people I miss at home, family and close acquaintances. And that magical place; home, the word that causes thousands to give up their life in war to protect.

But now I must go. I am being called by Garry. All have gathered, and are now ready to leave, pass through the Gateway to the next world in line.

There's many gathered around the pillar to see us off, knowing they will never see us again. Appreciative for what we have done for them.

I can see them all from my position on the balcony looking down towards the large green pillar. My mind churning over and over wondering, what does the next world have in store for us? Is it a world of peace? And how are we to find the next Gateway, to take us on to the next world?

But all will be revealed I'm sure. As we pass through the next Gateway.

Close the world. Enter the next.

APPENDIX 1

The Workings of the Gateway System

(A report compiled by Coben Hathanen for his own use)

I have studied the writing on the walls of the mysterious cave for some time now and here are my findings.

I believe in a time long past, entities with godlike powers, for some unknown reason, (apart to themselves) brought seven worlds together. They connected all the worlds by means of powerful Gateways, or Conduits, depending on how you look at it.

From my deductions of the pictures on the cavern walls, I have decided that it was purely for their own selfish purposes that they did this.

Let me explain what I have deduced.

Firstly, how the Holy One's found out this information, I cannot say. But I believe it was because of their spiritual backgrounds. The entities that used their world, such as they used our own, must have told them. Possibly seeing them as above the inhabitants of the others worlds, and decided to confined in them. Or possibly they told different groups on each of the worlds. And back home on earth it was explained, and somewhere it is written down such as in the cave here.

But let me get back to what I was first saying, about why they connected them all in the first place? I believe it was because their world was dying!

Like so many other races they also took to much advantage of their own world, realizing like our own, what we had left it to late to stop the catastrophic consequences of their own actions. They had raped and pillaged from their own world for far too long. Now nothing, not even their own powerful magic, could stop the downwards spiral of their world's ecosystem.

Their only answer - to leach off other worlds to balance out their own.

How they located the other worlds, it does not say. But it does tell of how they choose which world to go in what order. Through long studies on each of the other six planets they decided which one was to go where.

It talks about the powerful entities splitting in two. One group saying it was the only way for them to survive. The other group saying it was not for them to use other worlds as if they owned them.

It doesn't go into much detail; as if embarrassed that they as powerful as they were, were still fighting among themselves; but it does say something happened to those opposed. What happened to them? It doesn't state.

Now with these ones out the way, the remainder could draw on their powerful magic to pull the worlds together; join them by means of their magical Gateways.

It says that the Gateways could be used safely by means of traveling from one world to the next. This, as some of us has sadly found out, is true.

Why would they need to travel from world to world? This it does not declare. They had what they wanted, minerals, and other life sustaining compounds from the other worlds, to replenish what they had decimated on their own.

But what then happened to these powerful beings? Maybe they reside on one of the worlds still. If so why have they stopped traveling from one world to the other?

Or maybe like most races; even as powerful as they were; they destroyed themselves. Who knows? Not me, because the paintings in the cave don't go on to describe what happened after.

All I do know is they could still be out there. And if so, are they still at war with each other? And if they are what hope is there for us meager mortals if the gods fight among themselves?

The two brother's journey continues. Look out for book two of Glen Johnson's *World Two of The Gateway Series – THE KEYSTONE.* Here is the second books synopsis, and a foretaste of the first chapter.

World Two of the Gateway Series

THE KEYSTONE

It's a world of gods, untamed magic, sorcerers, dragons, vast desert plains, dry valleys and deep ravines; populated by humans and dwarves. A long dormant Kingdom has suddenly awoken, sending out dark armies of in-human beasts, controlled by a Black Keystone of ancient legend. The two races have to join together, as in times long past, but strong prejudice and hatred now separates them. The two brothers find themselves between raging battles, and join forces with an unlikely alliance of dwarves and humans, sent on a mission to find the mystical Red Keystone, their only means for survival; traveling beyond an immense wall, protected by symbols that are the answer to an ancient riddle. An old man and his dragon become their guides. But beyond the wall are creatures even more vile, ancient and powerful that have to stay contained at all costs, for the sake of all seven worlds.

Chapter One
The Black Death

Cries rang out in the still morning air, mixed with the shrilling rings of the alarm bells, mounted in the western valley pass. These give a forewarning to any impending danger. As suddenly as they started the bells were silenced, now only a fading distant echo.

The city was full to its limits. The four smaller cities of the Mountain Kingdoms had been called together to the main fortified city of Domisian; ruled by king Sosamon.

But only two groups had arrived just over two days ago, from the two northern cities, high up in the Domisian passes. The other two groups, from the two other cities; from the lower passes down south had not arrived as pre-arranged. This gave way to speculations and rumors. Which were proved true the evening after, when a small handful of around forty turned up at the gates of Domisian.

They were a pitiful sight, terrified beyond belief, in torn blood soaked clothes, having only just escaped with their lives. They spoke of a dark army of inhuman beasts, tall black, clawed creatures that walked on their hind legs, and how these creatures had attacked their city without warning or provocation, just as they were leaving to make their way to the fortified city of Domisian.

Most were already out of the city when the attack started. Those that had survived had already made it to the forest section of the trail, where they proceed to scatter and hide. Then after dark they regrouped back together and started to make their way towards the kingdoms capitals fortified city, only traveling at night.

As they made their way across the pass, they could hear the screaming echoing down the valley, right throughout the night, until finally it stopped. Then as they peered through the tree line towards their once home, they could see a red light glowing up the cold night sky, followed by the reflection by the moons light of a huge pillar of dense smoke, emanating from the remains of their once proud city, their homes.

This drove the refugees on, this and the fear of being pursued, until finally they reached the safety of Domisian. Some believed they were spared to pass on a message, the message of destruction - a warning of some kind.

The word of all this spread quickly throughout the huge city of Domisian. Panic set in. Some refused the safety the towering city offered, saying it would do nothing to stop the advancing army of dark demons. Many hearing their words - and seeing the fear in their eyes - fled along with them. Two hundred and seventy-four left all together in one large group, crossing the Hapsuim Pass, leading down towards the kingdom of the Plains, towards the city of Raemaner.

Those that were left behind - to fearful to run and to weak to fight - were placed into the old part of the city. The city was ancient, and generation after generation had added to it. It perched on a huge valley cleft, looking as if it was about to topple into the ravine below at any moment.

The city started before recorded time, by their ancestors, digging into the very mountain itself, also enlarging existing natural caves. These eventually; as time went on; spilled out onto the mountain ledge. Over the passage of generations of building and expanding, there now sat an immense, hand built fortified city, part inside the mountain, the rest clinging precariously to it.

The city also made use of three natural ridges that ran its entire length, making its outer wall, which was almost forty foot high, and two inner walls of thirty foot high. The city eventually made it all the way past the first two walls, having to stop at the tallest; then could go no further.

The city had three main gates, two were twenty-foot high iron gates that were bored through the first two walls, which until today hadn't been closed for as long as most could remember, they didn't even know if it huge eight foot high hinges would even move, time having corroded them together. But they were well maintained, and hardly squeaked when sixty men, using ropes pulled them shut. Then came the imposing outer cities main fortified gate.

Also as part of its strong defense there was a narrow bridge, what was the only means of access to the fortified metropolis. Naturally formed by waters long forgotten, which had eroded the valley below it, most of the mountain collapsed as its foundations were eaten away. All that remained was the narrow stretch of arced stone, making up the bridge, that joined Domisian to the mountain pass opposite; over a hundred meters away.

This bridge was the only way into the city, apart from descending a vertical cliff of over a thousand meters. The eleven tunnels leading out onto the Plains of Casos had been plugged up.

So the advancing army had to churn over this one bridge. The bridge was sixteen foot wide, and had a five-foot wall running both sides to stop people falling over the edge, as the mighty wind blew down the high ridge walls on either side.

Also as a line of defense, at the end of the bridge was a thirty-foot tunnel, which was bored straight through the thick wall leading to the cities gateway. Running all along this tunnels roof was slits, where arrows could be fired or hot tar poured onto the head of those approaching; as well as stones and other projectiles.

And just before the gateway a part of the bridge had been removed and replaced with a drawbridge, being over twenty-five foot long, leaving a gap dropping down into the darkness of the ravine below.

All this lead to the main gate three foot thick with metal spikes on the outside, over a foot in length, the mechanism for opening the gate was built by dwarves from the far away kingdom of Frondar. It operated on a pendulum mechanism, with eight tons of rock on a seesaw counterweight, making it impossible to open from the outside.

Even with all this protection the outer wall encircling half the city was crammed full of men holding crossbows, bow and arrows, and long javelins. Besides the archers were small terracotta pots full of tar, ready to be set alight, to send flaming arrows at the encroaching army. Also the middle section of the narrow bridge had been doused in tar, so as the army advanced the archers would, with a single arrow; set the bridge - and all upon it - up in devouring flames, stopping them dead in their approach.

All woman and children, along with the old and invalids were secured inside the mountains vast caves. With all the able-bodied men up and ready upon the battlements, ready to fight, to defend their loved ones, and their homes.

The valley passes bells had rang, where was the advancing army? All they could do is wait and stay alert.

The mist slowly creped over the valley walls, then being swept away by the light morning breeze, trailing off in long wisps into the hazy morning air, with the sun starting to rise from behind the opposite mountain range, the soft morning light was causing the first shadows to start appearing on the cities towering fortified walls.

Suddenly a horn could be heard, sounding out through the morning stillness.

Then just as suddenly hundreds upon hundreds of tall dark silhouettes appeared on the opposite mountain ridge, with the sun behind them giving them the benefit of having the sun at their backs.

They just stood there, silently; slightly leant forward. The towering figures were an impressive and harrowing sight, standing nine or so feet tall, with wide shoulders and long powerful arms that lay placid at their sides. There combined warm breaths creating tall plumes of steam, rising in to the frosty morning air.

On the city walls all waited, as they witnessed this inhuman army that was encroaching upon them. They fidgeted with their weapons. The tar pots in front of them now burning, ready for the arrows to be dipped in them. And those below the wall line waited with arms full of arrows and javelins, ready to be passed up and spent on the invaders.

All was still.

All was quite. The kind of silence you get when men contemplate the meaning of life; knowing full well that they might not live to see the day through.

In the distance a large Cramier bird silently flew through the valley pass. Its high pitched call echoing off the high valley walls, being the only noise heard through the stillness of the fresh morning air. It flew between the two groups. Then carried on towards its feeding grounds, oblivious to all that was about to transpire below it.

Suddenly in one swift movement all the standing silhouettes moved and began pouring down the side of the opposite mountain, taking tremendous leaps and bounds down the rock face, like vile flowing black water pouring fourth. They soon descended upon the small bridge, churning across it, filling it to its brim.

With matted manes of black hair flying behind them, clawed hands gripping the bridge walls pulling themselves along. But no noise came from the beasts; no bloodcurdling screams no howling - nothing. In a way those in the city would have preferred some kind of noise, compared to the silence issuing of these evil creatures.

The archers waited. Tendons on their bows pulled to there limits, with burning arrows nestled waiting to be released.

All stood poised.

Everyone was holding their breath.

Then as the beasts reached the middle of the bridge the archers released the built up tension, sending the arrows flying towards their intended targets. They rained down upon the churning army, who had now started to pass the halfway mark of the bridge. Burning arrows struck the first oncoming wave, sinking into heads, arms, through legs, and between ribcages. Blood rained down all around - countless fell forward twisting and reeling in pain.

Dozens toppled from the bridge, some taking sections of the wall with them. In the confusion and pushing many more fell from the now open gaps. Even as they fell no noise issued from their throats.

As falling burning bodies hit the bridge surface the tar became inflamed. What the arrows hadn't hit the flames now devoured. Black masses of burring creatures tumbling from the bridge. The flames were being fed by hair, skin and body fat. Flames flared backwards, leaping from body to thrashing body.

Soon the bridge was nothing but a burning mass of charred remains, with black stinking smoke blowing across the ravine towards the city and the archers, momentarily blinding them from their targets. As the valley wind blew it started to turn the black foul smoke towards another direction, away from the city walls. The archers could once again see the bridge and their targets.

But now coming across it was the second wave of hideous brutal beasts. These were using their clawed hands and feet to grip the rocky surface of the bridge, and pull themselves across underneath, hanging from the under surface, hauling themselves along. They were now using the bridge itself for protection from the flaming arrows, which were now simply bouncing off the hard stone surface.

As the dark figures came close to the cities outer wall, they started to fling themselves bodily against the rough surface, using brute force, to wedge their clawed fingers and clawed feet between the small cracks in the cliffs face. Now armies of dark creatures were surging up the fortified walls themselves.

The archers had to now lean over the wall and fire downwards, at an unnatural angle for releasing arrows. Some hit their mark, beasts dieing before they even released their grip, others were hit causing them to loosen their hold on the wall, plummeting to their death far below.

Some soldiers, having giving up with the bows, were now pouring the flaming tar down the walls, drenching the on coming wave with burring fire. Some were hit, being burned alive; others had to now navigate around the now blazing sections of rock.

There was just too many of them. Wave after black wave were just pouring off the opposite mountain, like ants from a towering ant net. Before the archers or javelin throwers had chance to rearm themselves; pull another arrow from their quiver; another two dark figures had already replaced the one they had just killed.

Some creatures climbing up the wall had many arrows sticking in them, if they didn't hit the head or important organs then they just carried on coming, with a long streak of blood behind them, trailing down the wall.

Then the first wave reached the top of the wall and jumped the lip onto the ramparts, next to the bowmen. The archers not expecting to have to fight hand-to-hand combat had only bow and arrows, the few that were lucky enough to have knives on them soon realized that they were as use full as toothpicks against these black creatures, that stood over two foot taller than them, and rippled with bulging muscles. The archers and javelin throwers were torn limb from limb. Some even jumped rather than die at the hands or serrated teeth of these creatures.

Now the dark army had access to the main cities outer ring.

Swordsmen clad in battle armor now ran forward slicing at the foul creatures, taking many down. Men with twelve-foot pikes came running and scouring through the beast, sometimes two at a time. Now the inner cities second wall of defense came in to play. Archers upon this smaller wall started to pick off the creatures one by one; aiding their companions on the ground below. The outer second inner city wall was just holding up under the onslaught.

King Sosamon sat at a wooden table in the northern tower writing, as the carnage outside unfolded. He finished the short letter, sealed it with red wax and pressed his rings into it, and placed it in a small wicker container; using a strip of leather he tied it to the carrier bird's leg.

These particular birds were specially raised. They were paired with another bird just after birth; these birds then join for life. After a number of years, once they grown to maturity together, they were then separated, with both birds being taking to separate kingdoms. When a message needed to be sent, the bird simple had the message tied to it then released. The bird had a gift of being able to search for its particular mate anywhere within large sections of land - or even in different kingdoms. How they done this was a mystery.

All the King had to do was pick a bird that had a mate in the particular kingdom he need to communicate with. He choose one what would head off in the Prackos Empires direction.

Walking to the open window, looking across the battle below, Sosamon released his grip on the bird, releasing it into the smoke filled air, where it then started to head towards its destination. He then turned, removed his sword from its scabbard, and headed for the open door.

Outside the archers, swordsmen and men holding long pikes were doing the best they could. All was starting to look like they might be getting the upper hand. It even seemed like they were managing to push the creatures back.

When suddenly an archer turned and fired behind him.

Confused the King turned facing the direction of the impassable cliff face.

Upon it thousands of dark figures could be seen descending its vertical face, using their claws to gain purchase, as they quickly descended into the very heart of the city itself.

Out numbered over a hundred to one, the battle was quickly over. Blood stained almost every surface. Dismembered limbs littered the stone ground. Weapons lay in cold hands.

The caves were quickly emptied of all living beings; their corpses thrown out on to the streets. Not one living soul was left breathing. Blood ran in small rivulets down the cities narrow avenues.

Once all were dead the creatures turned their attention to the city itself, starting with the false temples, which were torn apart with their bare hands. Idols were thrown from the city walls to smash on the valley floor, far down below in the ravine.

When the entire city was destroyed, they heaped the bodies up into huge piles inside their own temples and then set them a light. Piles of blood soaked bodies, men, woman and children, twisted beyond recognition; they became burring incense scarifies for Septon, their Great Goddess of War.

Zratous; High Commander of the fourth division of the holy army, stood on top the northern tower and surveyed all the carnage which lay around him. He gazed upon the many fires burning all round the city; thick dark smoke rising heavenwards, a pleasing gift for their Goddess.

He'd just finished writing a letter with the blood of one of the fallen heretics - the King himself, who he had only just killed with his own bare hands, after the last part of the city was finally taken. The letter was letting it be known that another pagan city had fallen.

He attached it to one of the six armored legs of the waiting hammerhorn, and sent the large flying insect on its way, back to the Kingdom of Carmour to deliver its message to their awaiting High Priestess - the ruling Queen - Salos.

The conquest had begun.

Printed in the United Kingdom
by Lightning Source UK Ltd.
105706UKS00001B/237

9 781413 775860